The Last Limerick

Jane Gillette

iUniverse, Inc.
New York Bloomington

The Last Limerick

This is a work of fiction. All of the characters, names, incidents, organizations, and dialogue in this novel are either the products of the author's imagination or are used fictitiously.

iUniverse books may be ordered through booksellers or by contacting:

iUniverse
1663 Liberty Drive
Bloomington, IN 47403
www.iuniverse.com
1-800-Authors (1-800-288-4677)

ISBN: 978-1-4502-2198-6 (sc)
ISBN: 978-1-4502-2199-3 (ebk)

Printed in the United States of America

iUniverse rev. date: 4/27/2010

AUTHOR'S NOTE

The story is set in the historic college town of Belmont on the Mississippi, as imaginary as the characters and their predicaments. New York remains New York with a few fictitious addresses and characters, all fully capable of disappearing when the tale ends.

I am indebted to my editorial platoon...David Bednarek, Roger Miller, Paul Salsini, Barbara Graham, and Paul Hayes...all wise, helpful, and generous. I thank you.

For my children,
Adam, Dave, and Ellen

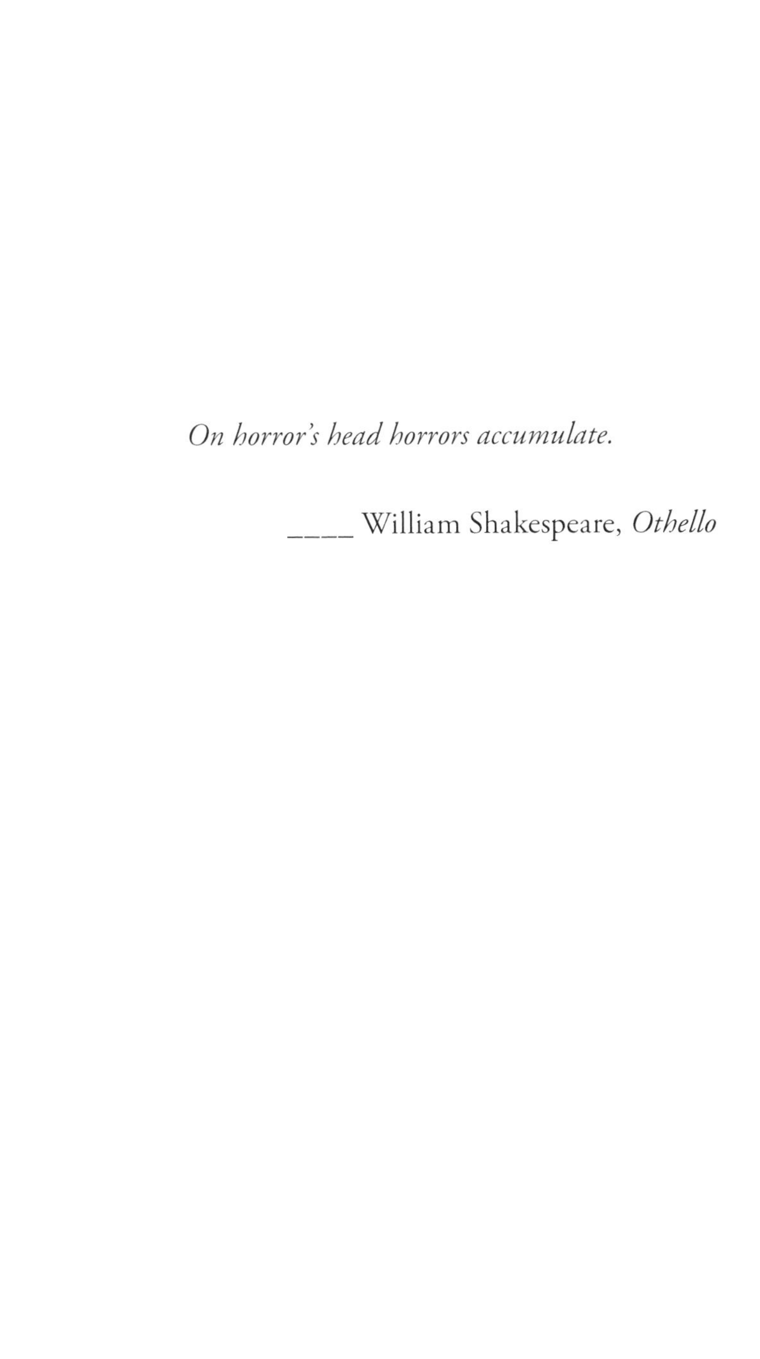

On horror's head horrors accumulate.

____ William Shakespeare, *Othello*

CAST OF CHARACTERS

OLIVER POOLE: Belmont police inspector

FREDDY DONOVAN: police detective

IRIS WOOLSEY: novelist and advice columnist

JASPER HOLMGREN: police chief

NATHAN BOMBAY: editor of the *Belmont Bee*

CHARLOTTE DOLBERE: wealthy widow

EVAN O'NEILL: Charlotte's son

ROGER FERRIS: popular television actor

INGRID AND REGINALD FERRIS: Roger's parents

GILBERT TWELMEYER: Ashbury College drama professor

VALERIE TWELMEYER: Gilbert's wife

JUSTIN FITZHUGH: theatre professor at Ashbury

ANNETTE WRENN: one of Roger's classmates

MEREDITH WRENN: Annette's cousin

ALFRED O'NEILL: Charlotte's deceased husband

FROGGY VERDUN: wealthy contractor

MARJORIE VERDUN: Froggy's wife

EDITH PECK: Roger's housekeeper

DOLLY BISHOP: Iris's best friend

BEATRICE WRENN: popular psychic

SIMEON DORSETT: Beatrice's reclusive uncle

LEONARD TROTTER: stable owner

ROSCOE THURSTON: Roger New York agent

VERONICA TROTTER: Leonard's alcoholic mother

FERNANDO: famous New York fashion photographer

DUCKY BLISS: New York private investigator

ADDITIONAL PLAYERS:

CHING: Donovan's red chow chow

MARYLOU LIPPENCOTT: drama department secretary

CATHERINE WOOLSEY: Iris's mother

RICKMEYER, SHIPSTEAD, AND MORENO: Belmont policemen

DOCTOR CROCKER SUTTER: county medical examiner

CHARLES MORGAN: Fitzhugh's friend

PROLOGUE

Belmont, on the Mississippi, twenty years ago.

It all began with a ride in the Lincoln. On Saturdays Uncle Simeon would drive her to the stables. The old gentleman was a timid, gray creature with a sweet mousiness that gave him a touch of color. She always thought of him as a mourning dove… in a French beret, a fragile innocent among sinners and thieves. The Wrenns were an old and powerful family, its rank and file populated with judges and doctors, eccentrics and scallywags, certainly respected but more often feared. She was finding the ancient tribe more fascinating as she grew older. And, she did not mind belonging to the clan.

On that particular Saturday morning, Simeon guided the vintage sedan at his usual twenty miles an hour, maneuvering the necessary corners with the deliberation of a surgeon, which he was until the war shattered his nerves. The familiar gravel road snaked up the bluff like one of the many rattlers hiding in the rocky ledges. She asked him to drop her at Clooneys' mailbox, halfway up the bluff.

"I would be happy to drive you to the barn, dear," Simeon said, almost apologetically. This harmless offer would be his only interference. He loved turning around in the big gravel parking lot. The soft crunching sound of the tires in the stones, he'd once told her, made him feel connected to the earth. She had pitied him, knowing he felt like an outsider.

"No, thanks, I'll walk the rest of the way," she answered politely. "Meet me right here at six." She jumped from the car and then leaned back inside to plant a quick kiss on Simeon's ghostly cheek. It felt like kissing feathers.

She turned and ran wildly up a narrow dirt path that tunneled the wood, swinging her sweater with a matador's flourish. It was her birthday; she was eighteen.

The riding academy consisted of four wood-sided buildings stained dull oxblood and a gray shingled cottage for the owners, Maybelle and Leonard Trotter. The academy lay scattered within the folds of Abner's Coulee, one of a dozen or more narrow valleys that creased the blunt-nosed hills that rose above the Mississippi. A large rectangular horse barn sat apart from the rest of the buildings with its back up against a hillock. That day, Maybelle and six young pupils were going through their paces in the paddock a good distance from the stable.

She entered the cool, shadowy barn much the same way her grandmother entered her damp, stone church. Both were tranquil sanctuaries, each with its own incense. The barn's was the earthy perfume of hay, oiled leather, and warm animals. Here, spikes of sun pierced cracks in the rough siding, and the low murmur of animals provided the only prayers. For as long as she would live, Saturday would conjure up these images and scents. For as long as she would live, she would remember this day more vividly than any other.

It was a love of horses that had drawn her to Roger Ferris and he to her. Otherwise, he would have ignored the tall, skinny girl who lived with her eccentric aunt and a crazy uncle. Roger was popular and handsome, a young man who looked a lot like his handsome father. Her adventurer father didn't understand a love of horses and riding; he loved flying. When he bought Colonel for her, a sturdy, gentle dapple-gray, he had said, "Pumpkin, horses aren't even as smart as pigs. But, I suppose you can't put a saddle on a hog, can you?" Her dear, capricious father. He had managed to kill himself and his young wife while landing his small plane in a field about a mile from here. The coroner said the pilot had been criminally intoxicated at the time.

Colonel was waiting and nuzzled for treats when she put her face against his soft neck. She held out an ear of dry field corn, which he chewed immediately, making that hollow crunching sound horses make with their big teeth. Four stalls stood empty. How irritating. Her friends had gone off without her, even Meredith, her cousin.

Still annoyed, she began to saddle up with the thoughtless snub pounding inside her head like a second heart. When she heard the side door slam open, she half expected to see Meredith or Roger, but it turned out to be Leonard Trotter, silhouetted against the noon light. He was a coarse young man in his late twenties with fat and muscle bound up in a clumsy, imposing body that reminded her of a raw roast. His comely face wore a perpetual sneer. He was dangerous, and she hated him.

Spotting her, he grinned in that nasty way he had and drawled, "Well, well, look who's here. Miss Fancy Pants." Steadying himself against the edge of the door, he swaggered over to her, pushing back a greasy cowboy hat as he walked. While he refocused his pink eyes, he swigged on a bottle of beer. Drunk already. A head start on his usual Saturday night entertainment. He would drink until he was blind and then come home to knock Maybelle around. The whole town knew about Leonard Trotter.

"How 'bout I give you a hand with that ol' nag," Trotter said in his Kentucky twang. Moving in close, he grabbed the bridle and jerked the horse's head. The stink of beer and sweat swallowed up the sweet, musky smell of hay and animal. Trotter sucked the last of his beer and tossed the bottle into a pile of straw bedding in the corner.

Looking him straight in the eyes, she snarled at him, "Get out of here." Turning back to the horse, she stroked the powerful neck and then settled a blanket across his broad back. She felt a need to hurry.

Sensing tension, the horse clopped backward and thrust his flank against the wall, shaking the boards, all the while keeping his big eyes on Leonard. Horses were like dogs; they could smell a mean, scared man up close. She watched Trotter take two steps back; he was a born coward. All bullies were.

"Just give me a li'l ol' chance, honey," Leonard whined, running his tongue over his mouth and his eyes over her body.

"Go shovel the shit, Lenny. Isn't that your job around here?" Rude as spit. "Get out of my way." Pushing past him, she lifted a heavy western saddle from the rail and heaved it with a practiced swing onto the animal's back. She was tall and strong, as tall as Leonard and in better shape. Trotter stood back and watched, not particularly brave but wary of anything bigger than a cat.

"Got a date with pretty-boy Roger? That li'l piss-ant." Leonard reached out and gave Colonel's harness another cruel yank. His snigger was crude. The horse snorted loudly and raised his big head.

She ignored Ferris and tightened the straps, concentrating on getting out of the stall.

"I bet your uppity grandma don't know what you and Roger do 'round here on Saturdays." This time Trotter placed a dirty hand on her cheek and let his fingers slide seductively toward her neck. She felt her face burn. She wanted to tear his eyes out.

She stood still for a minute and then lunged at Trotter without warning, slamming him against the stall wall. Trotter expelled a rancid cough and blinked with astonishment. But, before she could run out, he retrieved the reins and blocked the stall door with his body. Colonel chewed ferociously against the pressure of the bit and rocked nervously.

Leonard's face hardened and with a free hand he snatched the waistband of her jeans to jerk her close. Half-whispering, half-growling, he said, "You goddamned rich people make me wanna puke." He drew out the broad hill country vowels like a gardener uncoiling a hose. She felt herself go rigid. "Hell, half the time," he moaned, "you can't even stand each other." His unshaven cheeks were flushed and damp.

"Go to hell," she hissed. Her mind was racing.

"Maybe you should take a lesson from my mamma." Trotter's short, grubby fingers caught a strand of her shiny, tawny hair. "Would you like a lesson, cousin?" Giving her hair a stunning pull that drew her face close to his, he kissed her hard on the mouth.

The stale stink of Trotter mixed with her own sour fear and she felt sick. She spat at him and held her ground.

Trotter grinned like a fox and slowly wiped the spittle from his chin to his sleeve and then rubbed it into the horse's flank. "Kissin' cousin, you better be nice. You know what I can do to you and yours." He giggled and reached for her again, but in his haste the bridle slipped from his hand.

"In your dreams." With that, she kicked Trotter viciously in the shins with her hard-toed riding boot and watched him gasp. Hopping closer to her, he clamped a powerful hand on her arm. The skin burned and he increased the pressure. She rammed a free elbow into his soft belly and ground the heel of her boot into the toe of his sneaker. Leonard yelped and closed his eyes to the pain. This time she wiggled free and ran out of the stall and into the long corridor that bisected the barn. She screamed as she dashed between the stalls, but her cries brought no one. Only Maybelle's mare whinnied as she rushed past.

Glancing back over her shoulder, she could see Leonard stumbling behind, closing in. He was moving faster than she thought he could. Spotting a bridle left dangling over a stall door, she grabbed it, turned on her toes, and began swinging the leather harness like a lariat. When Leonard stepped into range, the metal bit struck his face with an abrupt snap and opened a long tear on his cheek. The blood oozed instantly.

Stunned a second time, Leonard sank to his knees on the concrete floor and cradled his jaw in a grimy palm. While he crouched and moaned, she scrambled back to Colonel's stable where she quickly mounted the animal, put a heel to his ribs, and trotted into the deserted, sun-soaked yard.

When she looked back this time, Leonard had reached the wide doorway, and for several seconds they stared each other down in complete silence. Then, he disappeared inside.

With a cluck of her tongue, she urged the horse toward safer ground, convinced that Leonard Trotter would never ride the high trail.

The path was steep and narrow in places, a wall of rock on one side, a sheer drop through underbrush on the other. Snakes lay coiled and hidden in the dark crevices.

Near the top, where the bluff stretched back, as level as a plateau, she headed for a small abandoned quarry sheltered on two sides by young trees. It was a secluded spot where she and Roger often met. No one was around; only the sound of bird calls broke the silence. Suddenly tired and nauseous, she dismounted and looped the reins over a bush rooted in stone. She sank gratefully to the edge of the crater and swung her legs over the side where a cool breeze ruffled her long, pale hair. She breathed slowly until her stomach settled down.

The excavation was deep and dry, its walls scarred with fissures left by the cutters, like a homely face pitted by acne. Here and there, a hearty sapling had sprouted from the rock and far below she could see circles of charred earth where picnickers had built campfires on the quarry floor.

A few minutes later, the sound of clopping hooves against the hard ground caused her to turn around. Had Roger finally come to find her? Her hopes were immediately dashed. All she could see was Leonard, bloodied and mean and so drunk he was clutching the saddle horn with both hands. He sat astride his wife's mare like a wounded warrior in a dirty plaid shirt. He was gripped by an anger and fear that would force paralysis or barbarity in almost any man. Without saying a word or moving a muscle, she watched the brute slip from the animal's back and land clumsily on the rough path.

With no time to remount and no place to run, she rose to meet him, wisely backing away from the edge of the pit. Keeping a safe distance at first, they circled each other like boxers, panting and clawing the air until Trotter stepped close enough to grab her arm. Once again she discovered a reserve of strength that surprised her. Wrenching free, she lunged and gave Trotter's heavy shoulders a tremendous push. The force knocked him back to the rim of the quarry where he dropped to his knees.

As Trotter knelt and struggled to get his bearings, she knew she had been given her only chance ...a few seconds to remount and ride off. But, she couldn't run. Instead, she moved in behind Leonard with three long strides. A delicious sensation of power was buzzing in her head. She planted her booted foot squarely against his rump and shoved.

Trotter released a groan and a low, beaten growl as he tipped over the side.

Across the broad quarry, shielded by trees, a lone witness hid from what he had just seen. Roger Ferris sat astride his mount in numb astonishment. The animal waited patiently for the touch of the rein on his neck, but his rider found it impossible to move. What had just happened? Ferris's breathing was quick and shallow; his hands, gripping the leather reins, were wet with sweat. Jesus! Had Annette Wrenn just kicked Leonard Trotter into the quarry?

Ferris ran a hand through his hair, as if trying to stir up an answer. Had this been an act of self-defense or something more? Had Annette lured the big jerk up to the cliffs to get rid of him? Certainly, her powerful leg had dumped him over the side. Ferris shook his head and tried to clear away the image of Trotter taking a high dive. Who was this girl? Ferris felt a chill run up his back.

One thing was clear; Trotter was no gem. He beat his wife, cheated his friends, drank too much and started brawls all over town. The police regularly locked him up. No one would seriously mourn his passing. Roger did know that Annette despised the man for some reason she kept to herself. But, more important, Leonard Trotter hated horses; he never rode! So, why was he riding today? It was Maybelle who ran the stables, who taught the classes and understood the business. Given that, why would this coward, who was terrified just to climb on a horse's back, pick his way up the narrow paths to the quarry? To collect something. Sex? Money? Knowing Leonard, it had to be one or the other.

Roger remained still, in no hurry to move from his safe spot on the other side of the deep hole, but he began to feel empowered. With the sweet twittering of birds and the gentle rustle of leaves surrounding him, he realized that he alone owned valuable information about a very serious situation.

A few minutes after watching Annette mount Colonel and disappear down the steep trail, Ferris slid from the saddle. He stepped cautiously to the edge of the pit where he peered over the side. None of his companions had turned up; they were still exploring a trail on the other side of the bluff. Far below, a body in a plaid shirt lay grotesquely sprawled and motionless on the stony ground.

Leonard Trotter was very dead.

Roger remounted and urged the horse along, cautiously at first, circling the perimeter of the pit to the south and then picking up a second trail that led to the bottom of the bluff. He wanted to see the body up close.

When Roger entered the quarry, he could see that Annette was already there. She had dismounted and tied her horse to a scrub birch. He did the same. She was not surprised to see him; perhaps she was in shock. When Roger joined her, they simply stood silently over Trotter's twisted remains, as if paying their respects. Roger saw no sign of life; neither of them touched the corpse. Roger knew then he never wanted to see another broken body. Annette appeared to be unmoved by the death or the circumstances, a reaction Roger found more disturbing than standing next to Trotter's lifeless bones.

Around them the abandoned three-sided excavation dozed in the early afternoon sun. Birds flitted overhead; an occasional snort from one of the animals broke the peace. The aged spot and its inhabitants were oblivious to the dead man lying on the rocky, barren ground. In spite of the fact that his heart was pounding in his chest, Roger found the old pit oddly peaceful and innocent.

Taking hold of Annette's arm, Roger gripped it firmly and said, "What happened?" Annette squirmed and yanked, but he held tight.

"Leave me alone, Roger." Annette pulled free and stepped back, defiant. "Poor Leonard must have had an accident." Her incredibly beautiful eyes went dark, and Roger watched this girl, a young woman he thought he knew, a girl he might have loved, disappear. It was scary as hell.

Annette stepped back from him and moved over to Colonel. She caressed the horse's neck and whispered to him. His big head bobbed up and down as if he understood her words. Her connection to the animal was uncanny.

Suddenly feeling an urgent need to be free of everything connected to this bizarre day, Roger said, "Look, you need an alibi more than you need anything else in this world. Do you read me?"

Annette's quicksilver expression told him that he had delivered a deadly blow. He plunged on. "When all the facts come to light, you might find yourself in big trouble."

"My knight in shining armor."

Roger ignored the jab and went on. Beyond that point, Annette never argued or explained. She listened to the fine print in Roger's contract and agreed to his terms. It was over in a matter of minutes. Their arrangement would last a lifetime.

Back at the stables, Roger telephoned the police.

A half hour later, Belmont police officers Freddy Donovan and Oliver Poole entered Abner's Quarry on orders to guard the body, as if this guy was going anywhere, Donovan thought to himself. Christ. He had never seen a dead body before, except Uncle Louie in his pine box with his hair combed in the wrong direction and too much rouge on his sunken cheeks. But, this dead body was not a corpse you wanted to look at for any length of time. The body parts were definitely out of alignment. Donovan shuddered and quickly reassessed his reasons for becoming a cop. He did have two uncles who were cops, burly, ginger-bearded Irishmen like himself, but there was no serious overriding reason for him to be working in law enforcement. In all honesty, he thought, he would have preferred building skyscrapers, impractical at this point, but a soothing thought in bad moments. He was entitled to fantasize. At any rate, here he was, next to his pal, Poole, a black-haired, film-star-handsome man who would never look like a cop. Poole, he noticed, was taking the horror in stride. Poole could do that. He would make a great detective one day, probably a better one than Belmont would ever need.

Behind them, the coroner's van was pulling into the patch of rough ground. Chief Jasper Holmgren, overheated with anxiety (and basic stupidity, Donovan quipped to himself), sat inside his hot car talking on the car phone, shouting out orders to the poor sap on the other end of the line.

Donovan looked over his shoulder and muttered to Poole, "Would you look at Hornby and Iversen over there, our darling rookies scouring the place for evidence like a couple of choir boys?"

Poole smiled and said, "Father O'Reilly would be proud."

Donovan grinned. "Looks like Trotter fell out of the sky and landed. Probably more evidence up on top than here at the bottom."

Poole nodded.

The coroner, an old G.P. with a black bag and an assistant who didn't look more than twelve, joined them and crouched next to Trotter's body. When the Doc began his examination of the corpse, Donovan turned away just as his stomach turned over. Poole stayed with it a couple more minutes and then stared at the scenery.

"What about those two kids over there, the ones who found the body?" Poole was saying.

"Nice looking pair of animals they have there." Their mounts waited as silently and patiently as two beautifully trained hunting dogs. The young man and woman stood just as still and silent. Nobody was talking much. "She's a Wrenn, you know, and he's Doc Ferris's kid. Jesus, the Chief'll tip-toe through this one like a new father." The Wrenns and the Ferrises were two of Belmont's oldest and most illustrious families, along with the Woolseys, Poole's in-laws. Poole understood all about tip-toeing.

"The Chief'll screw it up," Poole said, sounding certain, as always.

Eventually, the coroner concluded his examination. He figured the deceased had very likely died of a broken neck and internal injuries as a result of a great fall. When he said this, they all looked up to the rim of the quarry, as if to blame its bony edge for such a tragic accident.

Donovan and Poole took notes while the Chief questioned the two high school kids. Miss Wrenn, tall, lanky, pale-haired, with memorable blue-green eyes, eyes that somehow looked as if they could see more than they should, stated that she and Ferris had simply run across Trotter's body while riding. She said the red plaid shirt showed up against the stony ground and caught her eye. Fair-haired Ferris, almost as good-looking as Poole, readily agreed. He suggested Trotter might have slipped from the edge of the pit while riding or hiking. Ferris hinted that the victim might have had too much to drink. The stable owner had been swigging beer all morning.

Later that afternoon, back at the stationhouse where Donovan and Poole were making out their reports, Poole said, "A funny thing, Freddy, about those two kids. Considering the bizarre accident and the…the body." Poole paused. "They were quite calm and collected."

"Yeah, I noticed. No hysterics, no tears. Just the bare facts, like newspaper reporters who'd seen it all before."

Poole leaned back in his chair and closed his eyes, as if remembering the scene in the quarry. "Yeah, as cool as the other side of the pillow," he said, thoughtfully but without any admiration for their reserve.

Donovan would always remember that.

1

THE GAME IS AFOOT

Belmont, present day.

Spring was making its customary erratic debut in Belmont, trotting out a familiar bag of tricks, like crocus blooms and birdsong on warm afternoons. Professor Gilbert Twelmeyer reasoned that this kind of Midwestern magic fooled no one; the idyll rarely lasted. Sometimes it snowed in May.

On this particular afternoon, Gilbert found himself overcome with ennui and dozed off in an overstuffed chair in the Ashbury College faculty lounge. When the sound of wood striking metal jolted him back to earth, he swore softly, hoisted himself into a more dignified position, and glanced up to see Justin Fitzhugh standing poised in the doorway, certainly more agitated than usual and probably unaware that he'd just assaulted a steel wastepaper basket with an oak door. Justin was becoming too good at making entrances, Gilbert decided, an occupational hazard for drama professors.

"What's wrong this time?" Gilbert asked, trying to sound sympathetic, but his friend did tend to make mountains out of molehills.

"That bastard!" Justin thundered. The professor's fine features contorted into a peculiar expression of hopelessness and fury. With one hand he tossed his battered briefcase into the leather sofa, and with the other, he took a ferocious drag on a cigarette, as if nicotine might save him.

Gilbert watched with his usual fascination as Justin's stilt-thin body swallowed up the smoke. Had the man never learned to exhale?

"Calm yourself. You'll have a stroke."

"That second-class has-been!" Justin fumed. "That's his intention! To have me stroke out!"

As the flush in Justin's cheeks rose rapidly into his retreating hairline, Gilbert said, "Yes, yes, and I'll get stuck planning your funeral." What was Roger Ferris up to this time?

"And wouldn't our famous head of department just love that," Justin replied, allowing his melodious Richard Burtonesque voice to decrescendo with each syllable. "Ferris will be taking over the summer theatre workshop." Justin's long arms rose with his voice in a dramatic duet.

"Have you spoken with the Dean?" Futile advice, since the Dean was as crazy about Ferris as nearly everyone else at Ashbury, or in Belmont, for that matter.

"The Dean?" squeaked Justin. "Get real, Gilbert. The old fart hasn't touched ground since Ferris got here in January." He crushed his cigarette into a dirty ashtray and said, "Whitehead would insist Roger play the lead in the play as well."

Gilbert rattled off a few comforting phrases, more concerned about Justin's blood pressure than Ferris's latest example of arrogance. How many stunts would the man pull? Wasn't stealing Justin's promotion enough?

Justin obeyed like a good child and began circling the room with his arms flung behind his back.

Deciding that he had little more to add, Gilbert snuggled into a corner of his chair, but kept an eye on his friend. Professor Fitzhugh was a tall, spare drink of water (as Gilbert's mama would put it), five-hundred and twenty-eight months old (an amusing way of calculating the passage of time), and given to dramatic fits of theatrics. He possessed what Gilbert called an English cleric's face…hazel puppy eyes set between a long, pinched nose of considerable character and thinning brown hair. A tweedy, conservative wardrobe gave him the appearance of great sufferance. One almost expected him to quote the Psalms at any moment. The two of them had taught in the drama department for a long time. The unexpected arrival of Roger Ferris had caught their tails in the screen door, to repeat his southern mama again. Ferris was welcomed with open arms and immediately inserted into the drama department staff as its head honcho. It paid to have Broadway and television credentials these days.

Justin soon tired of pacing and poured himself a cup of coffee, doctored up with powdered creamer and sugar. "My God," he grumbled, shaking his spoon at a yellowing clipping pinned to the cork board over the refreshment table. "You'd think he was MacArthur returning to the Philippines." A spray of coffee splotched the notices. The offending newspaper headline read, "Roger Ferris, Famous Soap and Broadway Star, Returns Home." Justin yanked down the article and carried it over to Gilbert where he flapped it under the professor's nose.

Gilbert turned his head and said, "Why do you torture yourself with that?"

"I can't help myself. I walk in here every day and see that damned face smirking at me. Those perfect teeth! That hair! The son-of-a-bitch is killing me." Justin wadded up the article and threw it in the general direction of the dented wastebasket, lying on its side near the door like a wounded, overweight animal. Lifting his mug to Gilbert, Justin announced, "I'd rather have a whiskey, thank you very much," and ambled off to a comfortable chair next to the window.

Gilbert nodded. He understood. Palace politics created this kind of mental anguish, as it probably did at all colleges. "Do you have any part in the workshop at all?" he asked politely. He hoped this latest catastrophe had salvageable aspects. Ferris's brand of manipulation was unlike anything the Ashbury faculty had witnessed in its long history of prima donnas and elitists. And, now it sounded as if he was stealing Justin's pet project, the summer workshop.

"Dialogue coach. The nerve! This program is mine! Mine! Has been for eight years." Justin thumped the cracked leather arm of the chair and allowed a cramp of frustration to distort his face. "It isn't fair."

"I am sympathetic, Justin, but your life isn't over." Gilbert believed in getting tough when it came to Ferris. He'd had to.

Gilbert stretched out his legs and began filling a short stemmed pipe with Prince Albert, packing the mixture tight and igniting it with an old Zippo his father had given him years ago. As Gilbert puffed the tobacco to life, he tried again to console his old friend. "Roger will get sick of the paper work, Justin, if he ever figures out how to do it." Gilbert chuckled behind the smoke. "Besides, don't you think our star is a bit out of sorts lately? I do catch a whiff of gin in the morning."

"I've seen his hands shake," Justin allowed.

"Hah! Well, keeping our sense of humor about the man is our only defense. Perhaps he'll get himself fired without our help." Gilbert smiled. "Take a nap. You'll feel better."

Gilbert was right, of course. Justin smiled at his old colleague. Gilbert was always right, except when it came to his own life; then, he didn't know his ass from his elbow. Dear old Gilbert, such an innocent, such a babe in the academic wood. He could have been Freud sitting there, dispensing advice, transfixing his patient with those penetrating brown eyes, the light glinting off the ubiquitous horn-rims. Gilbert was superbly professorial with his sandy beard. But, the man's ordinary features were crazily balanced by a kind of pricey Long Island informality in his attire. Today, he was wearing well-tailored flannels and a hand-knit sweater, so casual and yet so sophisticated that he might have been on his way to a chic fish boil at the beach. Gilbert had style (nearly as precious as a head of hair) and an outrageous sense of humor, an absolute essential if you were married to Valerie. Incredible Valerie.

Justin turned to stare out the window at the landscape below Daly Hall. The broad south lawn lay in fresh green folds with neat concrete paths crisscrossing its gentle slopes. Two couples, their faces tipped to catch the warm sun, lay sprawled beneath an ancient beech, its trunk like an elephant's leg, all silvery in the strong light. He envied them their innocence.

"Just wait him out," Gilbert advised. "Ferris will get sick of Belmont and Midwestern academia. Life in the outback, as he calls it. He'll scurry back to New York, like the rat he is. What the hell is he doing here anyway? All that crap about a desire to teach." Gilbert scoffed behind his pipe. "The only great mystery about Ferris is his decision to abandon a rather lucrative career in television. No one is swallowing that old 'burn-out' excuse. I bet he was sacked."

Gilbert was sending up sweet aromatic clouds while Justin sipped coffee. Both were comforted by a companionable silence. Each found the genteel shabbiness of the old lounge well-suited to his moods. The Persian carpet was thin as a veil, the dark blue linen curtains sun-streaked and unevenly hemmed. An ancient calfskin sofa and half a dozen dark leather arm chairs ringed the room like wizened buffalo. Smelling of coffee and tobacco and a little egg salad, this sanctuary remained a haven for many of the heretics and monsters who made up the faculty. Ah, Academia, Justin reflected, so isolated and yet microcosmic. He and Gilbert weren't the only ones who had found demons in this cloister.

After finishing his pipe, Gilbert glanced over to see his friend nodding off, head resting on the back of the chair, one long, thin arm hanging limply over the side, the empty cup on the floor. Poor Justin. Once the bright star around Ashbury, he'd become as bitter and disillusioned as any middle-aged professor who has been passed over again and again. Of course, Gilbert had his own theories about Roger Ferris. One was that the actor was too clever for his own good; too much cleverness can be the same as cement slippers. But, Ferris had managed to charm and manipulate nearly everyone, especially the ladies. Ferris's cavalier treatment of men was shrewdly balanced by a consummate skill (such an appropriate term) with females. The opposite sex was Roger's forte. In a masterful, bravura performance, he seemed to bed women as handily as most men made dinner reservations. And, it was here that Gilbert had been made to suffer his own kind of humiliation, for Valerie seemed to find Ferris irresistible. His lovely Valerie (notorious for her indiscretions) was once again playing games. Gilbert wondered if she knew just how much she had offended him this time.

Running a hand over his owlish face, Gilbert decided that he was getting too old for the ordeals of marriage, infidelity, and over-sexed celebrities. As he gathered his books and papers and prepared to go, he could see that Justin continued to sleep, finding refuge in semi-consciousness.

As Gilbert strolled off to his three o'clock class, he thought again about Ferris. Slick or sick? Cunning or just tiresome? Ferris had invaded their relatively safe little patch, uninvited and untested. But, lately, the soap star's famous bravado wasn't ringing true. Too many women, too much booze, too many parties, too many hangovers. Too many days when Ferris had the haunted look of a man running for his life…or maybe running from something. Gilbert smiled and thought of Justin. To quote Sherlock Holmes (who had borrowed from Shakespeare), 'Come, Watson, come! The game is afoot.'

"He's coming back." Iris Woolsey tried not to sound apprehensive, even though she knew Dolly would understand if she was.

Iris switched the cell phone to her left ear and then dabbed her face with a towel. After taking a deep breath, she began a series of leg lifts, an amusing little game of torture designed for dancers by one Joseph Pilates, the dancing devil himself. A video whirred in the background. It was all so effortless for women who barely had thighs.

"Who's coming back?" Dolly Bishop asked suspiciously.

"A Fed Ex envelope was delivered early this morning. I thought I'd fallen into a '40s time-warp, you know, the door bell rings before breakfast and a guy in a uniform hands you something that has disaster written all over it. Anyway, the message reads: 'Old job a memory. Feeling and looking superb. Ha. Hot prospect in the old home town. Greetings to the sprouts. See you soon. Oliver.'

"Very touching. Oliver sounds perfectly normal. 'Looking superb!' Really, he's so modest." Dolly laughed.

Iris listened to Dolly's obvious delight; her best friend had always loved Poole, the good Poole and the bad Poole. That was the trouble with Oliver; you wanted to ring his neck and smother him with kisses at the same time.

"It's just like Poole." Iris tended to call her former spouse by his surname when she was suspicious of his motives. How quickly old habits took hold again. "The usual 'see you soon.' Does this mean today, this week, next week, in an hour?" Iris stopped and lowered her right leg to the mat. She was winded and sick of thinking about Poole, and sick of leg lifts. Besides, Poole had been gone too long to make a comeback.

And, God knows her body wasn't making a very good one either. All those damned Oreos.

"Listen, sweetie, we'll have lunch at Elmondo's. Oliver won't find you there; he's too cheap to spend that kind of money on pasta."

"I can't solve my problems with ravioli, Dolly. You know how it is with Oliver and me." Iris was referring to the days of years ago, after the divorce, when Oliver would come back every few weeks for what he called a 'reunion.' She must have been nuts.

"Hasn't he ever heard of long distance? Why Fed Ex?"

Iris laughed. "You've forgotten one of Oliver's best tricks. If he doesn't want to answer questions, he sends a one-way communication. It's like a bomb via Western Union, only we don't have Western Union anymore."

"Of course, and then acts surprised when nobody throws rose petals when he lands. I'd forgotten. The Return of the Prodigals, first Roger Ferris and now Oliver. What is so magnetic about Belmont?" Dolly paused. "Of course, Freddy Donovan will be sweeping off the front porch when he finds out. We did have some good times together."

"You're right, Dolly, but that is exactly what is driving me crazy. Maybe divorced people should hate each other; hate is so clearly defined and so easy to understand. What I feel for Poole is dangerously ambiguous." Iris didn't tell Dolly that just thinking about Oliver still brought a tug in her chest, an utterly absurd reaction after all these years, but there it was.

"Frankly, Iris, it'll be fun having him back. He's not hard on the eyes, you know."

"Agreed. But, what the hell is he up to? He could work anywhere in the country." Iris took a long swig of mineral water. "I bet you Freddy got him back on the force. You know, big shot detective, nice easy duty in a town like this. A lovely way to stick it to old Chief Holmgren, who'd sooner shoot himself in the foot than have to work with Poole again."

"The Police and Fire Commission would welcome Oliver back. Holmgren still doesn't know a felony from a misdemeanor. Frankly, I think Oliver's coming home just to win you back. A mid-life crisis move." Dolly sighed. "Don't get me wrong, Iris, Oliver can be a stinker…a very charming stinker…, but he's not twenty-five anymore and neither are you. Maybe he's ready to settle down, sit by the hearth with you and a dog." She laughed. "Besides, this historic little hamlet can always use another good looking guy at dinner parties. We can't rely on Roger Ferris to keep us all atwitter forever." Dolly took a deep breath. "By the way, poor Roger's beginning to fray around the edges, don't you think?"

Iris laughed. Her Poole Funk must be passing. "Maybe Marjorie Verdun's wearing him out."

"Can you imagine those two in the sack? I bet she has nighties with little red whales on them." Dolly crowed, her husky voice made rougher by too many cigarettes. "By the way, what does all of this Oliver stuff really mean?"

"Sounds like he's given the Bureau the boot and then badgered his doctor into letting him go back to work. Oliver will never be anything but a cop, in one disguise or another." With an eye on the TV screen, Iris attempted a torso strengthening move that made her back feel like she might be closing in on seventy-five. She clicked off the tape and leaned against the front of a chair.

"I thought he was supposed to give up police work? Too hard on the psyche after all he's been through."

"Oliver generally does what he wants, one way or the other. He's tough and stubborn and very persuasive." Iris put her head back on the seat cushion and looked at the ceiling. Dolly began a funny monologue about the futility of law enforcement, and Iris thought of how she'd always divided her life into neat little Oliver segments. Before Oliver. With Oliver. After Oliver. Now there would be an Oliver Redux compartment. Good grief.

Her ex-husband was a charming manipulator with magical powers and a keen appetite for crime and women, generally in that order. Through the years, the F.B.I. had struck the best deal with him, getting the bulk of his time and energy. A decade ago, his work and his hobbies had put an end to their marriage, a rather friendly end, Iris had to admit.

And so with great resolve and determination, Iris picked up Oliver's message, held it aloft like a symbol, and promised herself that Oliver Poole would be seeing a new Iris. Iris Woolsey (she had even retrieved her maiden name), was now a cool, self-reliant, successful novelist, impervious to charm.

Dolly was asking where Oliver might stay when he arrives.

Iris replied, "Who knows? Who cares? He's not boarding with me. I'm jumping with a working parachute this time."

Dolly laughed and asked, "What about Max? How will he fit into this new equation? Oliver isn't going to like Max Tarry."

"I thought about that while I was making the coffee and decided to do as I damned well please. If Oliver wants me back, he'll have to duel Max at daybreak…or pay him off." Iris smiled to herself. Playwright Max Tarry, her current love, wasn't a man who liked to lose. He was accustomed to bright lights, great reviews, and plenty of applause. "The admittedly aging Crown Prince of Broadway doesn't appreciate other men coveting his women. Oliver will learn that soon enough, if romance is what he's after. My, my, what a little Fed Ex will do."

The two friends laughed and said goodbye, forsaking the calories at Elmondo's…hip and thigh protection, Iris called it. Iris sat quietly a moment still clutching the note. Then, she carefully folded it into a tiny, neat rectangle and slipped it into the pocket of her T-shirt.

That night, Roger Ferris lay on his bed and thought about summer. The French doors stood open, and a warm breeze fluttered through the room, reminding him of other June nights filled with memories so bittersweet that his bones ached. A long time ago, he had rid himself of June and Belmont and a young woman best left in the past. But, ten months ago, June showed up on schedule and brought with it more than he had ever bargained for.

It had been a very grand party at a very grand house, the kind of party where young men were hired to park your car, and your car can't quite measure up to the treatment. The unmistakable scent of freshly cut grass mingled with the smell of old money. Strains of Mozart slipped from the long paned windows, and he knew he belonged.

He had conned an invitation from a friend, a guy who owed him a favor. He needed to see her in person. Just to make sure. The face on the cover of Vogue had caught his eye. Oddly, it was not exactly the same face, but he knew it just the same. It was the expression in the eyes, an expression which told him he was right.

His BMW was in the shop, so he borrowed a friend's battered Corvette, not nearly adequate for a neighborhood of vast estates hidden behind expensive landscaping. The whiff of privilege and big business hung in the air like ozone.

The driveway was long enough to make a big impression, and the stone manor house looked as if it had been shipped in crates from England. It rested on a modest rise, shielded on three sides by groves of elderly, well-pruned trees silhouetted against a pinkish sky. The park-like grounds had been shorn like the hide on a beaver coat, and a collar of dense shrubbery lay around the high foundation. On each side of the deep entrance were heroically proportioned brass lanterns that twinkled like jewels at its throat.

An unsmiling butler opened the door and admitted him to an entrance hall the size of a ballroom. Shimmering Rococo mirrors captured quicksilver reflections of beautiful people parading and preening. A carved staircase as broad as a highway wound past a collection of glum ancestors locked into gold frames. The string quartet had switched to Verdi.

At least a hundred guests drifted about, chatting and looking chic, sipping champagne. Uniformed waiters carrying heavy silver trays clinking with crystal glasses snaked smoothly around the room as if they were riding on ball-bearing roller skates. Someone had decreed elegance a long time ago and a lot of money had been spent carrying out the edict. This was the sort of solid elegance that brought good prices at Sotheby's when you needed the cash.

He plucked a glass of sparkle from a waiter who looked snootier than the company and wandered through the drawing room. It was paneled in walnut the color of high-priced caramels. The windows were open to the view, a simple landscape that subtly broke the monotony of the expensive possessions inside. He watched the women gowned by de la Renta and Blass, fingers and thin wrists ablaze with pretty stones. He was no fool; he paid attention to anything that cost big money.

He remembered loving it. All of it. The candlelight, the reserved laughter, the private, undisturbed world of serious wealth. He grazed unnoticed in the rustling crowd and hated that nobody recognized him… Roger Ferris, star of stage and television.

After ten minutes of roaming, he caught a glimpse of her at the far end of the room. She was wearing some frothy black dress, her ebony hair as plain as a ballerina's. Moving slowly in her direction, he stopped briefly to admire a small oil painting of spaniels. She was just as she appeared in the magazine photo, but as he inched closer, he experienced a twinge of doubt. Could he be mistaken? What if this gorgeous creature was exactly who she claimed to be? Then, as if cued, he heard her laugh, the throaty coo of a dove, a sound as unmistakable and as individual as a fingerprint.

Sensing his gaze, she looked over her shoulder and spotted him. The famous teal eyes grew wide with surprise and recognition. He grinned and stepped closer. She immediately stood back from her guests, excused herself, and then walked toward him, neither smiling nor acknowledging him further. As she glided past, she said quietly, "Follow me." Her long silk skirt brushed against his legs, and he caught the familiar sweet scent of gardenia.

She maneuvered smoothly through the crowd and disappeared into the empty entrance hall. He was close behind. She disappeared into what looked like a library on the opposite side. Following her felt more exciting and more dramatic than any part he'd played in years.

As he entered the book-lined room, he could see that she was posed like a mannequin next to a cold fireplace. "Close the door," she said, as if ordering a servant. He obliged.

"Roger." The pronunciation was matter-of-fact, like tossing off a brand name. "What are you doing here?" No sentimentality. No warm greeting for an old friend. He could have been an intruder. Of course, he was.

"I came to see you." He paused to get her reaction. There wasn't one. "Is it still Annette?" he asked boldly. "Or, do you have a new name?" He knew her new name, but he wanted to hear it from her. It didn't matter what she called herself; she would always be Annette Wrenn in his book. She remained silent, quite obviously still hurt and disappointed in him after all these years. He went on, "When I saw your face on the magazine cover, I knew it was you. But, you're not quite the same, are you?" He let that hang there in the air. What had happened? "Pure curiosity." He grinned. "I borrowed a friend's invitation." Still, she said nothing. "You don't seem very glad to see me." He laughed, hoping to give the atmosphere a positive charge.

"I'm not sure that I am," she said.

Annette leaned down to take a cigarette from a lacquered box on a mahogany table. She held it between long, well-cared-for fingers and waited for him to play the Cary Grant part. He reached into his pocket for matches and came up empty. Noticing a silver table lighter, he hurriedly flicked it afire and held it to the tip of her cigarette. She inhaled and kept her eyes on him every second before sitting down.

He tried to figure out how she'd changed. The jaw, the nose, the hair, the chin. She stared at him with the same absolute control she'd had when they were eighteen. Her long legs were crossed beneath the yards of silk. He wanted the whole story, but she was so cool. He would have to match it.

"Hey, I'm one of your oldest friends. I thought you'd be happy to see me." Nonchalant inquisitiveness.

"I have a new life. A different life and a new identity. And I like it that way." The tone was unemotional, the pitch of the voice a few notches deeper. After all, it had been almost twenty years and a lot of cigarettes. The gorgeous face revealed very little.

"I'm not trying to drag you back in time. My life is different too. I've been an actor for years. Have a terrific part on Yesterday's Children. The big soap on TV." He hated having to explain.

"I don't watch soap operas."

"I've been in two Broadway hits. Maybe you saw them." He was sounding like a high school kid and didn't elaborate on the shows. "The soap's a great part...at least until they decide to kill me off. A real possibility in daytime TV." He snickered. This time, she laughed lightly, as if in spite of herself. She was warming up. The old charm was working.

"I can't stay and talk, Roger, I have guests." As if he did not belong among them. She stood and put out the cigarette with some care. Her movements were liquid gold. She paused and added, "Perhaps we can meet another time."

"How about a drink some night, or lunch? We can catch up on two decades." He laughed. "My God, are we that old?" He took a step closer. "By the way, you look sensational." He spoke directly into eyes like the Mediterranean off the coast of Monaco. He'd forgotten how tall she was. "If you don't mind, I'll call you Annette, like old times," he said softly. "It still suits you."

"And, I'll call you Roger," she said, without emotion.

He could tell she didn't want to cause a scene, but she'd softened up. She said, "Why don't you call Tuesday, and we'll see." This time, she smiled, a sexy cover girl smile, as if throwing him a crumb.

"I don't have your number." He kept it easy and offered up a grin good enough to melt Queen Elizabeth.

She looked intently at him and then wrote a number on a piece of paper from a leather covered pad next to the phone. When she handed him the paper their fingers touched very lightly. The sensation was so visceral he knew they would be together again.

"I must be getting back to my guests. Are you staying long?" Meaning, you'd better be going. She hadn't lost control.

"I thought I'd circulate. Might run into a friend. I'm developing a second production company. You never know who could be useful." He made a casual gesture, as if he conducted business with billionaires every day. He wanted her to know he was more than a soap star. She nodded, but she wasn't terribly impressed. She was remembering the past and their old contract made within the rough, pitted walls of Abner's Quarry.

In the end, he left the party without making any contacts. He never met her rich husband until much later, under different circumstances.

Ferris slid beneath the sheet and willed himself to stop thinking.

Two months passed. It was the first of July, and ten days of tropical heat had parched lawns and tempers and sent flocks of cranky kids to pools and Pettigrew Beach. As Ferris made his way across Ashbury Commons, he recalled by some trick of memory that if it were August these would be the Dog Days, when the Dog Star rises and sets with the sun. These were the muggy, oppressive days when people prayed for rain and relief and wondered why they had ever looked forward to summer in the first place. His shirt stuck to his back; sweat trickled down the side of his face, and he was balancing an unforgiving hangover on four hours of sleep. Privately, he had slipped into a corner of Hell; but, he wisely told himself that getting overly dramatic would solve nothing. He switched his heavy briefcase to the other hand and kept walking.

After twenty years in New York, Ferris had run for home, to safer ground, or so he thought. His triumphant return during a January snow storm had drifted uneventfully through a bleak spring until April, when his peace of mind struck the bulkhead of that first grim message, a silly limerick composed of cut and paste letters, post-marked New York, and delivered to his office at Ashbury. Innocently enough, he believed his nemesis had written him off. Not exactly. Apparently, she had other plans for him. This first nasty bit of doggerel was followed a few weeks later by a second threat, similarly written and scented with gardenia. This one was post-marked Augusta. So, it was clear; she had boldly moved her enterprise from Manhattan to the home territory. Ferris hid the two envelopes in his library at the condo and vowed to take care of her if she came closer than the mailbox. Of course, the whole mess was his fault. He had played the part wrong from the start. Blackmail served up as revenge for rejection only worked in the movies. A year ago, when their affair began, he knew he wanted more; he got greedy, and she grew annoyed. When she eventually dumped him, he turned angry. When he blackmailed her, she got dangerous. Old story, new twist. Well, he had a little twist of his own, just in case.

Ferris climbed the three flights to his office in Daly Hall and cursed the cretins who'd vetoed air conditioning. He was tired and discouraged having just lived through yet another long play rehearsal best forgotten. He had spent three hours in the dim, Moorish recesses of the Beaumont Theatre, coaxing and cajoling performances from actors whose tongues seemed to be tied to their feet. The first summer workshop production was scheduled to open Saturday night and his stars, Oscar and Felix, were in a fog. They had muffed lines, tripped over one another, and in the end, Felix had actually wept after the last false start. Ferris, who rarely prayed, did so now. If his *Odd Couple* flopped, the insufferable Professor Fitzhugh would give him no peace. Ferris longed for a cold shower, a stiff drink, and the grueling schedule of daytime television. He longed to play Nick Halt again, week after week after week.

Making his way down the deserted corridor, he remembered that his housekeeper had promised to leave chicken salad and her homemade rolls for his supper. Lately, such simple things gave him so much pleasure. Ever since the arrival of the perfumed threats, he had indulged in a wild course of detours and diversions, swinging from classes and rehearsals during the day to rounds of parties and women at night. He craved distraction like a chocolate addict needs sweets. Of course, the diversions were only a temporary balm for the combination of fear and anger that lurked beneath the surface. Nights were bad, hours when her sing-song, taunting verses haunted him and created an uneasiness that vodka did little to wash away. The sweet, cloying stink of her favorite flower had drenched his brain's olfactory center, making it nearly impossible to distinguish any other fragrance.

Ferris stopped in the men's room for a pee. He took two aspirin for a headache. He needed a shave and his silk shirt had chili stains down the front. He was well aware that his recent dishevelment had become a ripe source of gossip around the drama department. His detractors were saying that Dean Whitehead had hired a lush. Could be. Just three nights ago, he had been forced to face his enemy at a party, right there in Belmont. He had nearly collapsed with panic. There they were, circling each other in a nice, tight orbit. She had been as brazen as a whore, playing the newcomer feigning admiration for a TV star. He had met her challenge and given the performance of his life. No one could have guessed they knew each other. Naturally, no one knew who she really was. Her own mother wouldn't have recognized her these days. The old face had disappeared long ago. She was a rich, famous model from New York now; she said she simply loved the quiet life of a small town. She had never met Roger Ferris until the night of Iris Woolsey's party. Who would ever suspect this woman of murder?

Drying his hands, Ferris tried to buck up...words of wisdom his father was fond of spouting. Dear old Dad. The son-of-a-bitch had nearly died at the hands of a jealous woman years ago. Was the danger inherited? God, if it weren't so awful, it would be funny.

Back in the office, Ferris fiddled with papers and put his desk in order. As he prepared to leave, his secretary, Marylou Lippencott, bustled in with the mail. "The painters are still on strike," she announced cheerily. "Mr. Dix says your office won't be finished until next month, but look on the bright side, the play opens Saturday and here's another one of those cute letters!" Marylou giggled girlishly and fluttered the familiar manila envelope under his nose. It reeked of gardenia. "Number three, by my count. Looks like a fan letter from a kindergartner." Marylou winked at Ferris and then stood there in her very short skirt, one hand on a generous hip, the other playing with a long earring. She was dying to know what was going on.

In spite of the rage churning inside him, Ferris managed a grin. "Righto, Marylou. My adoring public never forgets me. And they do seem to be getting younger. Are those department memos ready, darlin'," he added, hoping to get her out of there.

"Next on my agenda, sir." Marylou offered him a worried mother's smile and a mock salute. "I'll have them on your desk tomorrow morning." She teetered back to her desk.

Ferris waited until he heard the faint click of computer keys and then slit open the flap on the envelope. It was postmarked Belmont this time. He pulled out the contents, the same as the other two. Gluey, cut out words pasted on ordinary typing paper. Words and letters clipped from any slick magazine. This was *The Final Message.* Sweet Jesus! He was dealing with a deranged female. Weeks ago, in a fit of panic, he had bought a gun and learned how to use it. Part of the time he was scared to death, and part of the time he was ashamed and mortified that she had managed to trap him in a net of words. Would the two of them be eternally bound together?

Ferris took a deep breath and ordered himself to read the damned note. It said:

Remember a young man who thought
He was King of the World until caught.
Now you're a beast near the river,
In your cave you must shiver,
Knowing soon you'll be DEAD and not bought.

For a brief moment Ferris saw the bony elegance of an old man swim together with the beefy hulk of a second man in a plaid shirt. When the two fused, a third figure twirled in space like a baton flung up and left to fall to earth. This man bore his own likeness. At this point, the certainty of his own violent death was as real as the glue on the letter paper, as real as the obituaries in the *New York Times*. Ferris rummaged in a desk drawer for cigarettes, lighted one and inhaled as if it would be his last. Twelmeyer, his office partner, would raise hell about the stink of smoke. To hell with Twelmeyer. The poor guy was forced to look at his wife's latest lover every morning. Punishment enough. Ferris felt sorry for the professor on some ancient puritanical level he generally ignored. Twelmeyer did not deserve the humiliation, but Ferris wasn't strong enough to resist Valerie either.

Ferris found himself standing now, leaning against the desk, sweating like a race horse and shivering at the same time. Damn it! His mind raced to specifics. He could leave town, like he'd left after Leonard Trotter's death, like he'd fled New York last December. Or, he could kill her first. He couldn't go to the police; he had no proof about the identity of his stalker. The horrid limericks could have been written and sent by anybody. There was no proof that Ferris even knew his nemesis, in New York or anywhere else. They had been as discreet as spies. Besides, he couldn't accuse her of anything devious without involving himself. The private detective he had hired (his only professional ally) had come up with one or two well-hidden secrets that could be useful. A local attorney was taking care of his requests. Jesus, his mind was jumping and flitting, like bugs in a jar.

Then again, there was one solitary soul who might appreciate his circumstances, a sympathetic friend, who might be persuaded to help in a crunch. Ferris felt a prickle of hope.

But, friend or not, he needed a plan. His would-be assassin eliminated enemies as effortlessly as he memorized soap scripts. How many victims had there been over the years, he wondered? Could he reason with her? No. Her campaign of terror had little to do with blackmail and regrets. The catchy limericks were intended to drag him back through time. She wanted him to remember the old days. She was punishing him.

2

MYSTERY MAN

Edith Peck let herself into Roger Ferris's penthouse promptly at eight o'clock on Sunday morning. It was the fourth of July. Generally, she didn't work holidays, but Mr. Ferris was special, unlike a few other rich folks she could name, who didn't much care when they called or what they wanted her to do. And, they didn't pay double like Mr. Ferris.

Outside, the snap and bang of firecrackers and smoke bombs gave the day a poke of excitement, while St. Hyacinth's bells alerted the faithful to more serious matters. On her way over, Edith had spotted the high school marching band lining up for the parade. Wool uniforms on a hot day. "The poor things," Edith muttered to herself, "they'll be dead by noon." She liked chatting with herself...no back-talk and no bad jokes, she liked to say. Maybe she'd catch a glimpse of the parade from Mr. Ferris's terrace. He did have the grandest view of Belmont and the river.

Mrs. Peck set her vinyl tote next to the table in the front hall and tilted her face toward the cool air blowing in from the ventilating grills. The weatherman predicted another scorcher, and she was grateful to be in Mr. Ferris's lovely air-conditioned penthouse. From where she stood she could see a clutter of glasses and beer bottles in the living room, but the apartment was quiet. The early light shimmered through white gauzy draperies drawn across the terrace doors.

Her own cottage near the river on Pearl Street was a dim brick oven. And, she'd be another year older before her husband installed the new air conditioner, all cozy in its box after two weeks. The man was a curse, to be sure.

With the surge of domestic irritation to motivate her, Mrs. Peck rummaged through her bag for an apron, tied it around her thick waist and trotted off to the kitchen, noticing on the way that the master bedroom door was closed. "Sleepin' in again," she said. "Can't run the Hoover yet."

The up-to-the minute kitchen was cluttered with dirty plates and empty deli cartons, but she decided to start in the front room. She grabbed a tray, a plastic garbage bag and set to work after pulling back the curtains. From the look of the mess, the party must have been a good one. She had never heard of a cast party until Mr. Ferris told her about it. She tried now to imagine the actors in their costumes; unfortunately, she didn't know anything about the play and so visualizing details wasn't too successful. Rich people did find silly excuses for having a good time. She was content with her soaps, like watching Mr. Ferris playing Nick Halt, the bad guy on *Yesterday's Children*. She smiled. Nick Halt was a nasty, handsome villain; the show wasn't the same without him. But, she had to admit that dusting up for a big television star was just as good as cleaning for the president. When she was way up here on the top floor, she felt like she was wearing diamond earrings.

After filling the sack with debris and doing a bit of polishing and plumping, Mrs. Peck shuffled back to the kitchen and noticed for the first time a post-it-note stuck to a cabinet door. It read, `Mrs. P. An 8:30 wake-up, please. You're a doll.' She beamed. Only a big star would call her a 'doll.' Look at the time! It was nearly eight forty-five.

Puffing back down the corridor, wedgies slapping against the tiles, Mrs. Peck tapped on Ferris's door and waited. No response. She opened the door with care and peered inside. "Mr. Ferris. Oh, Mr. Ferris," she sang. "It's eight thirty, Mr. Ferris. Time to rise and shine." Still no answer. She tiptoed inside.

With the blinds closed, the large square room was nearly dark, except for a slender rectangle of light coming from the bathroom, where the light was still burning. The housekeeper switched on the dresser lamp and a splash of yellow light washed over the mirrored wall and onto the lacquered surface of the chest. Still, her employer didn't stir. As she tipped open one blind, she thought she smelled something odd. Must be the river, she thought. This heat brought out the worst in everything. She crossed the room and called softly, "Up, up, up, Mr. Ferris." Goodness, he was as hard to wake as her husband.

As she neared the side of the big bed, Mrs. Peck stopped short. "Jesus, Mary, and Joseph!" she cried; the words were like bones stuck in her throat. Roger Ferris lay on the bed as still as the pillows; his lean body wore dark blue pajama bottoms and his handsome face was hidden behind a wicked looking mask. The mask's wide red mouth grinned at her; its Pinnochio nose pointed at her like an accusing finger. The woman's eyes traveled further. The dull black handle of a large knife rose from the middle of the actor's chest. And there was blood everywhere.

Taking a huge breath, Mrs. Peck tried not to retch. All she could see now was blood...disgusting, dark red blood, the color of liver. The body lay in a rusty pool of it; the white skin was smeared with the clotted stuff. One hand rested in a sticky puddle where his fingers had clawed into the soaked sheet; the other arm lay outstretched to one side, as if reaching for help. Foolishly, her first thoughts were of the horrible mess. How would she ever get the stains out of the sheets? Then she prayed the actor was playing a prank. Surely, he'd sit up with a start, yank off the mask and pull out the knife...like an actor in a thriller. Then he'd start giggling like he did when he was feeling good.

But nothing like that happened. Mr. Ferris stayed where he was.

Dizzying stars began shooting past Mrs. Peck's eyes, and a soft buzzing filled her ears. She felt weak and ill and began to edge slowly backward along the side of the bed, desperate to get away and at the same time afraid to lose sight of the body, terrified of turning her back on it.

Just as she reached the end of the bed, something as soft as a caress touched her ankle. The woman shrieked so loudly that she stunned herself with the noise. Frightened again into silence, she began to trample the carpet, expecting a bloody hand to reach from under the bed to pull her down, to plunge a black-handled knife into her chest.

Whimpering now, she hysterically stomped the floor as if a huge insect were underfoot.

Tired and winded and nearly faint, Mrs. Peck soon realized from the stillness in the room that she was alone…with the dead body. There was no monster under the bed. Daring to look down, she was overjoyed to see nothing more menacing than Mr. Ferris's silver fox blanket lying in a heap at her feet.

"Ooohh, the awful thing!" the woman cried out. She shuddered and clasped her arms across her heavy breasts. Giving the fur a kick, she knew she couldn't stand the place another second. It was all too much… the mask, the blood, and poor Mr. Ferris lying there, just as dead as those animal skins. And the awful stink!

Feeling suffocated and almost dead of fright, Edith pulled the edge of her apron over her mouth and ran from the room.

When Mrs. Peck's call came into the station house, Lieutenant Freddy Donovan was in the process of digging himself out of a sand trap at the Curtis Park golf course. Inspector Oliver Poole (recently reinstated into the Belmont constabulary as an inspector after a long absence) was digging into a plate of room service scrambled eggs at the St. George Hotel in downtown Belmont. Three squads were immediately dispatched to the swanky Beacon Street Arms in the old warehouse wards...now called the Renaissance District, where condos with big price tags had been carved out of ancient storage buildings near the river. It was decided by Chief Jasper Holmgren to divert the high school marching band's parade route from Beacon Street to Copeland Avenue. Homicide demanded space, the Chief was insisting rather foolishly in this case. Donovan suggested that making changes wasn't necessary, but the Chief (still smarting over Poole's return to a high position in the department) was eager to let the world know who was still pulling the strings in Belmont law enforcement, even if it was only changing the parade route.

Since his homecoming in April, Oliver Poole had been residing in two rooms on the third floor of the restored St. George (owned by his former mother-in-law) with the idea that it was only temporary. Now, hurriedly gulping his breakfast, Poole wondered if the hotel's proximity to Iris on Two Tree Lane might have caused him to linger longer than necessary in his rented rooms. Obviously, this was no time to think about the past or the future, but he had made some progress. A real estate agent had called two days ago about a nice new condo in the capital. He bought it. A move and a murder; it was about time.

The inspector knotted an expensive silk tie around a softly starched collar, gathered up his essentials, and rode the elevator to the lobby. Donovan was parked out front with the engine running.

On their arrival at the crime scene, Donovan heaved himself from the car with dread in his bones. "We haven't handled a homicide in some time," he told Poole by way of making a preemptive excuse for the gaffs that were bound to happen. "Not since Desdemona Malloy shot her boyfriend at Hughie's Bar." The Irishman laughed. "She found out he'd killed her parrot and served it up for supper." Donovan grinned. "It's my favorite murder story."

Poole laughed and let himself out from the passenger side of Donovan's close-to-dead Buick.

Donovan couldn't believe his good fortune, to be working again with Poole. Oliver had risen quickly from rookie cop to the FBI training school and never turned back. Donovan wasn't so ambitious, and he liked small towns.

"Hey," Donovan said, "this case should put you right. Hair of the dog, so to speak." He waved a big freckled paw in the air as if he solved serious bugaboos every day. Poole nodded and kept moving ahead in his lopsided gait. Poole wasn't comfortable talking about what had happened back East...the injured leg, the breakdown, the early retirement from the Bureau. Donovan could wait; he'd pry it all loose in his own way and in his own time.

Beacon Street was bumper to bumper blue cruisers, press vehicles, and TV camera vans. In the distance the blare of trombones and trumpets sang sharply over the insistent tap and thud of the snare and bass drums. The parade folk were snaking their way toward Wrenn Park on the river. Kids in nearby neighborhoods were setting off firecrackers and cherry bombs. The pops and whistles gave the morning a whacky sense of normalcy. When Donovan spotted the Chief's vintage Cadillac parked next to a fire hydrant, he was tempted to write the old fart a ticket, but didn't. The red and blue flashes of squad car lights winked back and forth; the crowd behind the barrier tapes stood by, quiet and orderly, unaccustomed to mysterious turmoil.

He and Poole threaded their way through a crowd of capital reporters shoving for space and shouting for details. Cameras clicked constantly. Photographers with Cyclopean video camera eyes followed their path and swept over the building like military sharpshooters. Poole lagged behind a bit.

Spying the elephantine editor of the *Belmont Bee* hustling down the walk, Donovan declared, "Bombay's closing in. He'll probably put you on the front page, Poole." Instantly recognizable in his ubiquitous white suit and fine Panama hat, Nathan Bombay didn't miss much. "This little event will be covered properly now," Donovan added quietly. The Irishman's respect for Bombay approached his reverence for his own mother. Each always knew what was going on, and each demanded the truth.

"I hear Bombay's weekly is damned near as popular as my wife's novels these days." Poole sounded grumpy.

"You might say that," the Irishman replied, smiling to himself. Poole and his ego. "Ex-wife."

Poole grunted. "Not a bad turnout, for a holiday on a Sunday. All we need are tightrope walkers and tigers."

Donovan figured the great detective needed another cup of coffee and stuck two sticks of Juicy Fruit in his mouth while he gave a few last minute instructions to some of his men near the entrance of the building. After today, the Beacon Street Arms would become the stuff of local legend…the apartment house where New York actor Roger Ferris got himself stabbed to death on the fourth of July. Nothing like a celebrity to put a little sparkle in a homicide. Donovan couldn't help but grin a little.

Donovan and Poole ducked under the yellow police tape. A rookie cop assigned to guard the entrance pulled open one of the heavy glass doors. Donovan prayed for guidance; the serious business of death lay upstairs. He figured Poole could take care of himself.

"The Chief's on eight, Lieutenant. Lewis is at the back." This came from Sergeant Rickmeyer, standing just inside.

"Righto, Sergeant. Get Shipstead to help string up the rest of that yellow tape, but first call Willy Steele; we'll need some back-up."

Winking at Rickmeyer, Donovan added, "The sheriff will pout if he's not invited."

Poole found the large square lobby as austere as the building itself, a pleasing combination of thirties moderne and present day contemporary. An impressive curved wall of glass brick rose eight stories behind a gentle coil of cantilevered stairs and a shiny steel railing. The sun sparkling through the thick glass made Poole feel as if they were under water. One patrolman stood at the foot of the steps and another next to twin elevators; the metal doors were enameled with black streamlines, as if pointing to the horror upstairs.

"Nobody's allowed on eight without I.D. No press," Donovan was saying. "Doc Sutter, the medical examiner, and his crew from the state lab are on their way."

Donovan's orders came naturally, which surprised Poole a little. Donovan was a homicide amateur, but so far, Poole was impressed and let him set the pace. Donovan told the officers what to do about the residents who lived in the building, and then, they stepped into the elevator. The bleached mahogany cubicle was a shoe box of silence.

"This building reminds me of going to the dentist when I was a kid," Donovan said quietly. "Same architecture. Long corridors with blond wood doors and frosted windows, the names of doctors and dentists in black letters. Smelled like peppermint and alcohol. Boy, I hated that place." He snickered and cracked his gum a couple times. The story got them to the top floor.

A young, freckle-faced officer guarding the penthouse door looked anxious, but Poole figured he was just as relieved to be stationed far away from the dead body. The kid flung open the door with the panache of a good butler.

Once inside Donovan managed a whistle around the gum and said, "Well, well. Roger's little tree house."

The foyer was as big as a modest bedroom. One wall was paneled in what looked like slate and the other in clay colored linen. A contemporary painting with more white space than color hung opposite the door. An ebony and burled wood console placed against the interior wall was surmounted by a round mirror framed in polished steel.

"Our Mr. Ferris had good taste, Freddy," Poole remarked. He preferred simplicity in his surroundings and good art on his walls. He could have moved right in.

Donovan would have preferred a big TV and a corduroy recliner. The cop shuffled ahead into a spacious high-ceilinged living room with a view of the river. A balcony terrace lay beyond a wall of French doors.

"The Ferris Art Gallery, from the look of it," said Poole, taking in details like a hungry man. Hugging the white walls were imposing canvases executed in primary colors, like extraterrestrial maps. Placed among the sparely designed furnishings were plinths supporting sculpture of polished stone and metal. Precisely positioned ceiling spots were directed at the artwork leaving the rest of the room in shadow and natural light. Ferris had made sure that nothing would interfere with the impact of his collection.

"Belmont Trump Towers," Donovan offered. "This is what the slick magazines call 'urban serenity,' Oliver."

Poole chuckled. Urban serenity. What the hell did this oversized Irishman, who more closely resembled a sheep farmer from County Cork, know about urban serenity? His old colleague was a character out of O'Casey. Broad-shouldered, well over six feet with red amber hair, the cop's dense, curly beard could have been an animal hide. When Freddy smiled, his brilliant green eyes nearly disappeared, as if they'd just swallowed up something delicious. He had never been any different.

"Very expensive serenity." Poole took a closer look at a bronze figure of an old man. "And, more than a trifle grand by Belmont standards. He had to be the richest man in town."

"According to my wife, who keeps track of local details, Mr. Ferris combined two apartments to make this one. Took a couple months to do it. Fast work. It took longer to put up my new garage." Donovan laughed. "I don't pay extra for speed."

"A spot of glamour, to be sure." Poole continued to be impressed.

A chunky, gray-haired woman of some seventy years sat perched on a black leather sofa with her short, stout legs sticking out like pegs. She was dabbing her nose with a handful of tissues.

"Mrs. Peck," Donovan whispered to Poole, "the housekeeper who found the body." The Irishman had been briefed at the station house. Donovan asked the woman to wait. They would question her later. One uniformed officer secured the corridor leading to the kitchen with its rear exit, another blocked the entrance to the master bedroom.

Jasper Holmgren strolled out to greet them. The chief's beefy face was tinged with green, Poole noticed. "It's about time! Jesus, you two," he growled, "did you stop off at Billy's Bar?" This was a jab at Donovan, known for his love of drink, and the chief's feeble attempt at letting Poole know that top dogs get to cut down the pups...even inspector pups... whenever they want.

Donovan didn't respond; neither did Poole, who figured Holmgren was just another fool to be tolerated and avoided, as often as possible.

"Moreno says nothin's been moved or touched. All accordin' to the book." Holmgren addressed his remarks to Poole as sarcastically as he dared. Poole had told him weeks ago that he was a stickler for detail.

"The medical examiner will be delighted," Donovan replied with a small smile. Poole nodded. "It's really the Doc's show until the body is carted out of here."

Holmgren grunted and hitched up his pants, a pair of tight western cut jeans that a paunchy middle-aged man should have given to Good Will years ago. He said, "I'll leave you two in charge. I'm going back to my office. Police business." He sounded officious and eager to escape the horror inside.

"Keep that machinery oiled, Chief," Donovan said. "We'll be along a little later."

Holmgren snorted. He was an ignorant man, eager to play detective but unsure of the procedure. Poole knew from the old days that Jasper Holmgren didn't have an ounce of instinct about good police work. The old fat-head would play the wounded general for the duration of the investigation. Poole was still surprised to find Jasper still on the job after all these years. Small town politics. What the hell was he doing back here?

"Try to get this right, boys," Holmgren declared. And, with that, he slammed a gray Stetson on his head and marched out of the room with as much dignity as any man can with diminished authority and trousers binding his crotch.

"Our first big break," Donovan hissed, as Holmgren disappeared around the corner. "Jasper's one of the all-time great gas-bags. We just have to divert his attention. Keep him busy with traffic violations and stray dogs."

Poole nodded. "The world's full of Holmgrens," he said, "some in tight pants, some in Armani suits." He paused and added, "I have to tell Moreno something. Be right back."

Donovan stayed where he was and waited, in no hurry to see the vivid remains of Roger Ferris. He leaned against a sturdy steel sculpture that resembled a wacky space ship. Art. He supposed it was art. Frankly, he preferred Mona Lisa's smirk or the Virgin Mary's kind eyes. And then there was Poole, expert on dead bodies and how they got that way, still dapper as hell, his black hair graying in the approved manner for gentlemen of distinction. Still smart as an old nun. The bad leg could only bring him good luck with the ladies. And, in spite of rumors to the contrary, Poole was looking fit, no outward signs of the reported breakdown. The leg might be creaky, but Poole's psyche seemed fine to Donovan. The man's narrow face remained nicely drawn with a shadow of beard creating good angles. He never sweated. Who would in those clothes? Donovan always had trouble reconciling Poole's wardrobe with the dirty business of hunting bad guys. Homicide and haberdashery, strange bedfellows, and two elements of life Donovan could live without.

Poole interrupted Donovan's musings with an invitation to look at the good stuff. And with that, the two detectives pulled on plastic gloves and entered the scene of the crime.

Ferris's bedroom turned out to be the antithesis of his lofty parlor. Mysterious and dramatic, the bed chamber was a midnight blue sanctuary with mirrors and soft lighting. A king-sized bed rested like a bier against one wall, its padded headboard and trappings in a dark quilted fabric, the linens in white. The intended glamour had soured considerably with the stench of death and the body of the actor sprawled against blood soaked sheets.

Apart from the disruption of death, Poole found the room neat and undisturbed. Drawers and closet doors were closed; there were no signs of ransacking. Ferris's wallet, keys, loose change and a comb lay on the dresser. The victim, or perhaps the killer, had apparently put away his clothes; there were no garments thrown over chairs or shoes tossed in a corner. Ferris had been a tidy man; Poole could appreciate his personal habits. Silvery slat blinds on the wide windows and terrace doors were closed except one which was tilted to illuminate a small slice of space. If there were smears and splashes of blood on the walls or floor, the deep colors made it difficult to see without floodlights. The lab crew would be taking care of that.

From a prudent but still thorough look at the body, Poole figured the actor had been stabbed in the chest and throat four times. A crime of modest enthusiasm, he thought. An amateur might call it rage, but he wasn't so sure. Through the years, he had seen worse. And, even the best detectives had been fooled from time to time; a clever killer could just as easily calculate four stabs as well as one or thirty-five. Sometimes it was a sadistic game to throw investigators off the path. The weapon, which appeared to be a kitchen knife, protruded from the final wound in the victim's chest. A garish theatre mask with a leering mouth and a long nose rested on the victim's face; it seemed to watch them in a mocking fashion. Poole wondered what they might find beneath it and what the hell it meant. Freddy was following along, willing to keep his distance, probably wishing he were back on the golf course. The formal examination would begin with the medical examiner, but Poole figured the actor had been dead at least six to eight hours.

"Looks like the killer tried to clean up in here," Donovan called out from an oversized dressing room and bath adjoining the bedroom.

Poole carefully entered what looked like a luxurious spa in a fancy health club, the walls of smoky glass and mirror, the floor and fixtures in flesh-colored marble. The lighting was low-key and unrevealing. A hotel-sized porcelain basin and lacquered cabinet were smeared with blood; a thick white monogrammed towel discolored with smudges lay abandoned on the rim. A second soiled towel had been tossed on the floor next to a Jacuzzi tub. Once again, both he and Donovan touched nothing and took care to avoid the faint stains on the floor.

"The tub's filled with water," said Donovan. He sniffed appreciatively. "Scented, clean water. Ferris must have planned a nice relaxing dip before retiring."

"Maybe Ferris was expecting company. A bottle of good wine, a pretty girl and a chummy soak. The latest entertainment, Freddy. Could be the date turned nasty toward the end."

"Jesus, Poole! That'll put me off bathing for weeks." The big man shuddered.

Poole grinned. "If he was entertaining a lady, she didn't leave anything behind." He was surveying the room with a good housekeeper's eye. "No stray lingerie or cosmetics."

The sound of voices signaled the arrival of the forensic team; the detectives stepped back into the bedroom to greet Doctor Sutter and his assistant, a bland young woman with a long, sad face and a reluctance to speak. Sutter reminded Poole of a country doctor. The M.E. was a tall, skinny Kentuckian, pushing fifty and still partial to blue seersucker suits and white bucks. He might fit the part of country bumpkin, but Poole knew better; Crocker Sutter possessed excellent credentials.

Donovan and Poole automatically moved back and took places on the sidelines. When Sutter presided, he liked to tell his colleagues, he needed plenty of air and preferred the local boys cool their heels in the cheap seats until he was ready. Nobody ever complained.

A few minutes into the examination, Sutter casually announced that he'd found an interesting trinket. "We might have a calling card, gentlemen." He pointed to a small gold object lying next to the actor's foot, tucked close to the bare heel.

Poole stuck on his glasses again and bent closer. It was a gold ornament, the replica of an old house, like a pendant from a charm bracelet. The powerful flood lamps had picked it up like a diamond in the grass.

Donovan leaned over for a look. "Maybe the killer's a woman."

"Righto," said Sutter. "A crime passionale. Or, maybe it was just meant to look like that." The coroner began singing snatches from 'My Funny Valentine' in a reedy drawl. His young assistant looked pained and closed her eyes for a moment.

"A planted clue? Another touch of theatre, like that damned mask?" Donovan seemed to be on a roll. Sutter admitted that it was possible.

Poole said, "This whole scene has more than enough drama to suit me. An actor is stabbed to death in his bed with a knife that could be a prop in a corny play. He's left to die with that damned mask on his face. It's either meant to be very symbolic of something important or the killer had an odd sense of comedy and a flair for staging."

"You said it, Oliver. We're getting hit over the head with clues right out of Hollywood and the comic books."

"Exactly," Poole replied. "When do you figure he died, Doc?" He suddenly thought again about the unfortunate Desdemona Malloy, still locked up in prison. A life wasted on a dead bird and a vicious, unfeeling lover. Talk about Hollywood.

"I'd say somewhere between midnight and three this morning. The room is fairly cool. We'll know more later, of course." Doctor Sutter carefully removed the mask and cheerfully announced that the victim's handsome face remained unscathed.

"His fans will be grateful," Donovan said solemnly.

The doctor continued the gruesome business in silence, except to say that there was nothing to indicate that the deceased had been knocked unconscious before the stabbing. He may have been dozing or taken by surprise; they couldn't discount drugs. A plastic vial of Valium on the bedside table was obvious for all to see; the booze bottles in the other rooms indicated a large party.

Without picking up the pill bottle, Poole could see that it was half full, and the prescription date a month old. The pharmacy was in Belmont; the physician a local doc he knew. If Ferris had been drinking and in the habit of taking tranquilizers, he would have been quite sleepy.

Very little was said after that. Each officer and technician attended to his special assignment quietly and efficiently, as if violent death were like any other job. Donovan excused himself to speak with the press. Ten minutes later he was back. Poole paid attention without getting in the way. During the following hours, the gold charm was added to the collection of physical evidence. Everything was boxed, bagged, tagged and sealed. The photographer and fingerprint man covered every angle and inch. A few obvious clues would push the investigation in one direction at first, but Poole knew the case would really begin with the victim himself. Something about Roger Ferris would lead them to his killer, just as something about Roger Ferris had caused his death.

"Did you see him?" Mrs. Peck asked the detectives. "Agghh! Such a sight! The poor darling boy all soaked in blood. And that horrid thing on his face. Did you take it off?" The old woman snuffled loudly into a handful of tissues.

Donovan slipped his arm around the housekeeper's shoulders and tried to comfort her. Her pie dough face softened a bit, and she gave in noticeably to his hug. "It's all taken care of," he told, as if she might be one of his daughters.

"He looks so foolish," Mrs. Peck said sadly. "But, that's nonsense, isn't it? He surely doesn't know how silly he looks, does he?" The woman's pronounced Irish brogue offered another element of theatre to the proceedings. Poole wasn't a superstitious man, but the stagy overtones of this case had put him on the alert for more.

"I suppose not," Donovan answered her. "Tell me, now, when did you last see Mr. Ferris? Alive, that is."

Poole noticed that Freddy was using his kindly Irish priest's voice, an interviewing trick good enough to pull family secrets from a Mafia princess. He had perfected this charming persona during their rookie days.

"Yesterday mornin' about eight thirty. Sippin' coffee, he was, in his own kitchen. We was discussin' the party for Saturday night. The actors would be stoppin' by after the play over at Ashbury." Mrs. Peck sighed loudly.

"How did he seem?" asked Poole, who decided to take turns with Father Donovan.

"Roarin' to go. A bit better, if anything."

"Had he been ill?" Poole asked.

"Had the jitters. For weeks and weeks. Drinkin' and smokin' like the gin and the fags might be seized by the sheriff." Mrs. Peck's tightly permed gray head shook from side to side. "Had me worried, he did."

"What was bothering him?" Donovan prodded gently.

"Wouldn't say. Liked to play the mystery man, like he did on his old soap opera, you know. Not a morsel of gossip ever fell from his lips."

A bit of good news, Poole mused. A victim with jitters. The reason might prove interesting.

"Any odd phone calls or messages on his machine?" asked Donovan.

"The southern lady rang Saturday mornin.' He took the call in the library."

"Do you know her name?" Poole wanted to know.

"No, Inspector. But she called one or two times when I was here last week."

"Did the calls bother him?" Poole asked. Mrs. Peck didn't think so.

The detectives inquired about Ferris's friends, his social life, maybe visiting guests from New York. The housekeeper said he'd given one or two parties for his old high school chums, but none recently. And he didn't entertain ladies overnight either. Mr. Ferris wasn't that kind, she assured them. Poole and Donovan exchanged looks of mild amusement. The Mayor himself was aware of the actor's social life; Ferris had cut a wild path through Belmont in a short time.

"Did he date anyone in particular?" asked Poole.

"I don't think so. He got invited to just about every party in town, he did. He was a big star, you know."

Donovan gave Mrs. Peck a wink. "Any love letters?"

"Ooh, Lieutenant, probably a bag full, but I never read any." The motherly old woman seemed a bit embarrassed. "He did get mail from Eagle Eye in New York and from Mr. Thurston, his agent. Notes from his friends, I suppose. The usual e-mails on his computer. His papers are all filed away in his desk, like teeth in a mouth. He was a fussy man. Hated a mess."

Then, he would have hated his own end, Poole thought. It was abundantly evident that dust never had a chance to settle in Ferris's perfect world; Mrs. Peck was a formidable housekeeper.

"Were you here at the cast party?" asked Donovan.

"No, I only got things ready during the day on Saturday."

"Did he leave a guest list?" Donovan inquired.

"In the kitchen. But, his secretary, Mrs. Lippencott, at the college would know more about that."

Donovan dispatched an officer to fetch the list.

"Was the penthouse locked when you got here?" Poole went on.

"Yes, sir. I used my key. The rear service door was locked too." Her answer was firm.

"How many keys are there?"

"Two that I know about. Mr. Ferris's and mine. There's no spare under the mat." Again, Mrs. Peck was positive.

"Have you seen the mask before?" asked Donovan, as his officer handed over a sheet of paper with a neatly typed list of names on it.

"Heavens, yes. Ugly things, like the devil himself would wear. Terrible faces starin' from the wall in the library." The housekeeper gestured to a room off the dining room.

"And the knife?" asked Poole.

"Looks like one of them French ones from the block in the kitchen. One's missin.' She dissolved into tears, and Donovan sent the officer off again, this time for a glass of water for the housekeeper.

"We're nearly done, Mrs. Peck," Donovan said soothingly. "You're doing very well." He patted her dry, fleshy hand.

Poole leaned forward and showed the housekeeper the gold charm safely tagged and tucked into a plastic bag. "Do you recognize this?"

The housekeeper peered closely and said no.

"Thank you," said Poole. "Now, we'd like a look around. Take your time. Just tell us if anything's out of place or missing."

The officer returned with a paper cup of water, which Mrs. Peck drank down. She seemed composed again.

The three of them, amateur and professional, toured Ferris's rooms, side by side, in what Poole could only imagine was a thrill of sorts for the housekeeper.

Poole continued to be impressed; Ferris had been a man of considerable sophistication. The art was expensive and appealing, the furnishings first-class, probably German and Italian, and the accessories few and carefully chosen. Ferris had transported his chunk of high-priced culture from New York to Belmont. It looked as though he had intended to stay. But, why? Why had this highly successful actor abandoned a prime role on television for a small college in his home town? It didn't make sense. And, where did the man get his money? Did daytime TV pay this well? What the devil was Eagle Eye? When it did all add up, they would have their killer, of this Poole was almost positive.

"None of his treasures is missin,'" Mrs. Peck soon announced. "Your common burglar wouldn't try stealin' these."

The detectives laughed and agreed.

"These sculptures was special to him. He let me know the first day, bless his heart. Said he didn't want me spraying polish all over his good fortune." Mrs. Peck snickered and stood respectfully in front of a massive bronze sphere mounted on a black marble cube. "He never criticized me in all these months. As sweet and generous as a prince, he was." She wept softly into her apron. Donovan and Poole allowed her a few minutes of private grief.

Collected again, Mrs. Peck directed them to the library where it was easy to see where the mask had hung. Twenty antique and contemporary theatre masks were mounted on the fabric-covered wall opposite fitted bookcases. Interesting collection, observed Poole, but why had the killer placed one over the victim's face?

The library, like the rest of the apartment, was expensively furnished. A small leather couch sat beneath the mask collection; the teak desk was positioned in front of the large windows. An impressive number of volumes in the bookcases were arranged according to subject, Poole noticed. He could see a decent selection of popular fiction, volumes on the history of theatre, bound plays and scripts, and a substantial number on contemporary art and sculpture.

After Mrs. Peck declared the apartment in order, Poole asked the young officer who brought the water to drive her home. He didn't want the woman to witness the removal of the body. The sight of the still form wrapped in black plastic, like a modern mummy on a gurney, might be too much for her. After years of corpses and coroners, Poole still found the image of the bagged dead body the most disturbing.

3

HAIR OF THE DOG

"Did you talk to Ferris at Iris's fancy buffet last week?" Donovan asked Poole, as they pulled away from the condominiums. Donovan lurched to a stop at the intersection. Poole mumbled something under his breath. He'd forgotten Freddy's gift for driving. By now, it was early afternoon, and they were on their way to question Ferris's parents, Reginald and Ingrid Ferris.

Donovan waited patiently at the stop sign while half a dozen parents carrying collapsed lawn chairs and coolers crossed the street. A string of sweaty kids straggled along behind. Two fathers pulling four whining youngsters in red coaster wagons festooned with streamers and flags chatted amicably as they rattled along the pavement. The parade was over, time to get home, put the tiny folk down for naps, and then regroup for fireworks that night at Wrenn Park. Donovan was reliving the early years with his three daughters. He gave the revelers a friendly wave and then continued on, absentmindedly leaving the transmission in second gear.

"I talked to him for three minutes. Tops," said Poole. "Just to see what the ladies were fainting about. Frankly, Roger wasn't my type."

"I noticed who your type was," remarked Donovan with a wide grin spreading among the whiskers. He raised a caterpillar eyebrow.

"That tall brunette, Iris's new neighbor, the one with the legs." If Poole had come home to woo his ex-wife, then he was certainly taking his sweet time. But, in all fairness to Poole, Iris had been out-of-town a lot promoting her new book.

Poole's homecoming was creating sparks, and Iris was none too thrilled about Poole looking over her tony circle of pals as possible date material. Donovan was lapping up the sparks; Belmont needed fireworks more than once a year.

Poole grinned. "Ah, yes, the lady with the legs. Mind you, she called me first….a very modern woman. We've been to dinner, but don't get your hopes up." Poole smiled. "And, for God's sake, shift into third."

"Our Mr. Ferris was tight as a tick that night," Donovan replied as he changed gears. "Could be he had a wee problem with the sauce. Could be that was the reason for his departure from daytime television."

"A good possibility. We'll know more in a few days." Poole lighted a cigarette.

Donovan turned at Avon Avenue. A half dozen teens wearing bright blue band uniforms and lugging beat-up instrument cases were trudging up the street with their plumed hats pushed back. They looked hot and tired.

"There's something damned familiar about the guy, Freddy, but my memory is stuck in neutral." Poole frowned and blew smoke out the window.

"Middle age, Oliver; it does a number on your head and a few other body parts." Donovan managed to light a cigar of modest pedigree while maneuvering around badly parked cars and pedestrians eager to get home.

"Did you ever catch him on the soaps? I called my bride on my way to your hotel this morning and asked her if she knew much about Ferris. She said most ladies thought he was a cross between a young Robert Redford and a character out of mythology. Too bad we didn't pay closer attention." Donovan turned down Charles Street, one of a few still canopied with elms. The house where Roger Ferris grew up was in the next block.

Poole said he didn't watch daytime TV and pointed out that a rolling stop at an arterial was still illegal.

"You can always walk, your royal highness."

The senior Ferrises resided in a twin-turreted Queen Anne in a quiet, expensively landscaped neighborhood where wide boulevards, terraced lawns, and three-storied houses clearly separated the rich from the rest of society. Most of the mansions, architectural monuments to the success and presumptions of upper class Victorians, had been snatched up during the hungry eighties by wealthy doctors, lawyers, and professional types. They made their money in the capital up the road but preferred to sleep in Belmont. The ancient river town was loaded with history and charm and a lot of people just like themselves.

Decorated in the popular Painted Lady style, the Ferris house wore a frosting of lavender, rose, and cream on its elaborate spindle-work, arches and pillars. To Donovan, the house looked as demure as a bridesmaid. He and Poole tossed their smokes in the bushes and Donovan cranked the old door bell.

A middle-aged housekeeper in a gray cotton uniform opened the doors and showed them into a large library on the west side of the house. The high-ceilinged room was cheered by lemon flowered chintz curtains and comfortable sofas and chairs covered in the same fabric. The long curtains stirred gently in a breeze at the bay windows. An ornate cast iron fireplace and fitted bookcases were painted pale yellow like the walls. Donovan felt immediately at home.

Reginald and Ingrid Ferris joined them almost immediately. Ingrid was red-eyed from crying but composed. Her husband was remarkably calm and resigned. Oddly enough, they seated themselves like strangers at a party, he at one end of the sofa and she at the other. Donovan found this distracting and sad. Why wouldn't they seek each other's physical comfort at such a terrible time? The mysteries of marriage slid another foot deeper into the black hole of conventions he found imponderable. Poole had spoken with Doctor Ferris at the morgue just an hour ago. Reginald was a well-known surgeon and professor at the medical college in Augusta. He had insisted that he and his wife should be interviewed that day.

The doctor was a handsome man standing no more than five eight and close to sixty-five, Donovan figured. With his athletic build, he appeared robust and energetic. His charcoal hair, worn slightly longer than fashionable, lay in graying feathers along his ears. In an expensive yellow knit shirt and white trousers, he appeared natty and untouched by tragedy. Was he more annoyed than grieved, Donovan wondered? Perhaps he was missing a golf game at the country club.

Ingrid Ferris was clearly shaken; she held tightly to a lace edged handkerchief. Roger had favored his pretty, statuesque mother. With her thick straw colored hair coiled on top of her head, Ingrid brought to mind the Swedish countryside.

They had last seen their son three days ago, Doctor Ferris informed the detectives. "Roger was acquainted with a great many people, here and in New York. Generally, I think he was quite popular and well-liked. Of course, there is always the odd-ball character who despises a successful man. Maybe a jealous old friend killed him."

Ingrid Ferris said nothing. Was she submissive, Donovan wondered, or, simply numb with grief?

When asked if Roger might have had trouble with a woman or money or a colleague at Ashbury College, Reginald insisted that their son had been royally accepted at the college and had plenty of money. Poole, Donovan noticed, was scowling, as if annoyed by the surgeon's monologue.

"Weren't you shocked when he gave up his TV career for a position at Ashury?" Poole asked.

"Yes, we were shocked," Ingrid replied strongly. "He was such a success." She paused, her voice shaky. "Perhaps he made an enemy in New York. A professional jealousy?" Her look of helplessness was stinging.

"His housekeeper, Mrs. Peck, says he was out of sorts for several weeks. Too much booze. Bad nerves. Did he seem troubled to you?" Poole respectfully continued.

"Nonsense," the doctor replied. "Roger said he needed a change. Said he was tired of the TV rat race. His nerves were fine."

"He may have had a touch of early mid-life boredom," Ingrid put in with a hesitant smile. "As if coming home ever cures anything." She smiled again.

Donovan liked her a good deal more than her husband.

"Damned silly notion," Reginald muttered. He rose from the couch and took a stack of leatherette covered books from a nearby library table.

"Here," he said, thrusting four Belmont High School yearbooks into Donovan's big paws. "These might give you some clues. I've marked photos of his friends in red." The surgeon resumed his seat and crossed his legs. "One of them," he added almost offhandedly, "might have held a grudge. Maybe one of them is a maniac!"

Astounding, Donovan thought. The doctor's self-possession was remarkable. Hours after his son's murder, he had managed to dig out old school annuals. Did the study of medicine instill this sort of cool-handed steadiness in the face of death? The Irishman thought it probably did. Poole was eyeing the good doctor with controlled distaste. Maybe he'd experienced enough of doctors in the last year to last him a life-time. Doctor Ferris seemed eager as hell to put the finger on his son's old pals. What happened to the notion that everybody loved Roger?

"What were the provisions of his will?" Poole asked.

"His attorney is in New York, but we do know that he left his estate to his mother." Reginald reported this as matter-of-factly as a TV anchorman. Ingrid's beautiful, sad eyes filled with fresh tears.

"Your son never married?"

"No," the doctor replied bluntly.

Donovan wondered if old Reggie might have envied his son's freedom. And, why was the father excluded from the will?

"What about the mask and the gold charm?" asked Poole. "The items we told you about earlier."

"They mean nothing. Right, Ingrid?"

This time Ingrid spoke up. "We're dealing with a very sick person, Inspector. An insane actress. A mad director." Her eyes fixed a frantic, nearly hysterical bead first on Poole and then on Donovan, as if willing them to find the killer within the hour. "I doubt it was one of his old friends." She looked over at her husband when she said this, but he didn't respond.

Was she putting her husband in his place? Donovan found her statement curious. Few people want to believe a friend could kill another friend. Ingrid Ferris might really think that this peaceful, well-heeled village could never harbor a jealous, angry, unstable soul bent on homicide. Surely, most folks believed that Belmont was a safe haven, where you could leave your doors unlocked and trust the neighbors to water the plants if you took off for a long weekend. Donovan decided that he and Poole needed to speak with Ingrid Ferris when her husband wasn't around.

"It's too early to know what we'll find, Mrs. Ferris," Donovan answered calmly. Then, he stood to conclude the interview.

The Ferrises rose from the sofa together but remained apart. "Keep us informed, Lieutenant," the surgeon said, leading the way to the grand foyer. "I'd like to read the autopsy report, Inspector Poole."

Poole agreed to the request, and Donovan figured it was a courtesy to a physician.

A wall of muggy heat greeted them as they stepped outside and onto the porch. As they walked to the car, Donovan speculated on the possibility of Reginald caving in and letting go in private. Would he eventually sob into his wife's arms? Or, was he not really shocked by his son's violent death?

"Jesus, I could use a beer," Donovan said, as he settled in behind the wheel. He turned the key and the old car shuddered to life."

"Nice idea, Freddy, but there'll be no time for Pfeiffers today. I'd like to get back to the Beacon Street Arms and talk to a few more of Ferris's neighbors."

Donovan sighed softly and slowly pulled away from the curb. His routine was going to be ruthlessly altered, he knew that now. His hours at Billy's were about to be cut dangerously short. And, his rounds of golf. Homicide, he thought crazily, had far too many drawbacks to be as popular as it was.

The street was mercifully deserted by now, only infrequent firecracker pops in the distance brought the holiday to mind. The Irishman said, "What do you make of them? I sure hope that pretty lady fixes herself a tall gin and tonic…it'll be the only comfort she'll get in that household. The Doc's a real horse's hinder, isn't he?" Donovan shook his head sadly. People in his sprawling family didn't act like Reggie Ferris.

"A bit lofty. Obstructive. Obviously hiding something."

"What's he hiding, besides the fact he didn't much care for his son?"

"Exactly, Freddy. We'll be peeking under a lot of beds on this one."

As they drove Poole flipped through the pages of Roger Ferris's annual. Donovan glanced to his right from time to time to catch the soft ripple of pages with their small black and white photographs, scribbled with brief messages. A few pages were lacy with long tributes in stylish, girlish handwriting. Roger must have been a popular lad twenty years ago. There were red ink check marks beside several photos. Dear old Dad's rogues' gallery of suspects.

"Peeking under beds. Jesus, Oliver."

"Don't get soft on me now," Poole said bluntly. He paused to light a cigarette. Then, he sat up straighter and said, "Freddy, did we meet a young Ferris on a case years ago? Here in Belmont." Poole dropped the yearbook into his lap and looked over at Donovan.

Donovan slowed a bit and thought seriously. He glanced again at the youthful photographs on the pages in the annual and at Ferris's in particular. Poole was pointing to it with a finger. Scrubbed and innocent faces. Then, it dawned on him. "Yes, you're right; we did!" He thumped the steering wheel with the flats of his hands. "Some drunk fell to his death in the bluffs. Remember that? It was summer. Didn't Ferris and a girl find the body?" He turned the corner carefully, still in thought.

Poole squinted into the light and fumbled for sunglasses in his inside jacket pocket. He slipped them on. "Abner's Quarry. A broken neck, as I recall. Our first mysterious death."

"Mysterious?"

"Well, I think I called it that for some crazy reason I can't remember. Too many years ago, Freddy. Too many broken necks. There was a hitch, a tiny knot that needed undoing." Poole shook his head and then laughed. "I can't get the details straight right now."

"It'll come back to you when you're sleeping." Donovan smiled. He did remember a pair of beautiful horses. But, that was all that came to mind. "Well," he said cheerfully, "if I can't have a beer, then we'll both have chili dogs and custards. I'll be damned if I'll give up all the necessities of life for this Ferris guy."

And, Donovan turned sharply into Kipper's Custard Stand and ordered everything to go.

The dinner hour had rolled past by the time Poole and Donovan stepped from the elevator at the Beacon Street Arms a second time that day. Officers Shipstead and Moreno interviewed tenants that morning, but

Poole had a few questions of his own. The interviews turned up one or two clues, nothing dramatic. More than likely, the murder had been a quiet affair with no one within range to hear any disturbance, if indeed there had been any.

"I half expect to see Fred Astaire dance down those stairs," Poole remarked, still pleasantly distracted by the lobby of the building. Cocoa leather banquettes were positioned against peachy tinted walls. A nougat marble planter near the glassed entrance was planted with exotic greenery. "It's a '30s movie set." Early evening light filtered eerily through a glass block wall; a half dozen fluted wall sconces, reminiscent of holy water fonts too high to reach, provided indirect lighting.

"Don't forget Ginger Rogers," Donovan quipped. "I know you like modern, Oliver, but, hell, what's the architect trying to hide here? All this stark steel and streamlining. Seems to me, he's keeping the precious stuff to himself." Freddy unwrapped a stick of Juicy Fruit, folded it in half and pushed it into his mouth.

Poole smiled. "There's nothing to hide. It's a clean, unadorned example of form and function coming together."

"I'd like to see this case come together." Donovan shoved open the heavy glass entrance door; a wall of heat sat like a bulldog on the other side. "How about a couple of bacon burgers and a whiff of the river?"

"Lead on, Father Donovan."

The two had always teased each other about ancestry. Donovan kidded Poole about King Henry's defiance of the Pope. Poole's great-grandfather had been a Church of England archbishop. Donovan could claim two Catholic priest uncles back in Dublin. As boys, Poole and Donovan had endured years of parochial school ruled by nuns wielding large, hard blackboard erasers and very good arms. A good sense of humor had given it all balance.

Poole's vintage Porsche sat baking in the long rays of a setting sun. The car's original red paint was streaked and faded from years of salt and bad weather. It was Death Valley inside. Poole rolled down the windows and took off at a fast clip toward Main. He turned sharply on Second, bumped along the ancient cobblestones, cussing, rattled over a double ribbon of Milwaukee Road track, and finally swung into Deedee's Burgerland across from Wrenn Park, a strip of green that hugged the waterfront above the levee. A few families had spread their blankets in the grass, eager for the fireworks celebration. The streets were filling with cars and people.

"A very refreshing ride, Your Highness. Worth at least four traffic tickets."

After getting their order, Poole found a small space to park a block away. The two stepped from the little car, hoping for any cool breeze the river could offer, and began to walk the promenade.

Poole stopped toward the middle, leaned his long arms against the iron railing and devoured the first bacon burger without saying a word. Directly across lay the lush green oval of Pettigrew Island, a mid-channel dollop of real estate that always reminded Poole of French Island, a more secluded dollop down river. When he was a boy, he splashed in the shallows on hot days like this one. He had spent his youth on this river, fishing and swimming, hiding from grown-ups. So had Roger Ferris. Each had escaped only to return twenty years later. Was it the pull of the land? The charm of the river? The people? The urgency to return to one's birthplace was a powerful one and not something Poole clearly understood. Who did? He did hope his homecoming would have a nicer outcome than Mr. Ferris's unfortunate end.

While Poole day-dreamed, Donovan stood nearby happily gobbling up a second burger and dribbling sauce down his shirt front. Freddy was the same old Freddy. Time had done nothing to dull his wit or sour his disposition or improve his wardrobe. And, Poole felt strangely gratified for this continuum. The two men silently watched a flotilla of decorated pleasure boats chugging up river for the evening's fireworks show at the other end of the park. Poole would not have minded spending the evening on the water.

"What did you think of Ferris's neighbors, Freddy?"

"Pleasant, polite. Well-off. Most of them childless, judging from the relative peace and tidiness of their apartments," Donovan wisely replied. "Too bad nobody heard anything." The tenants had not offered any motive for the Ferris homicide. "To them, he was a good neighbor, a charming man, and a bit of a thrill, when they wanted to admit it."

"We have one interesting vanity plate." Poole wiped his fingers on his handkerchief.

The Beacon Street Arms building manager spotted two automobiles parked out front around one in the morning. A late model Toyota that he knew belonged to a tenant's visiting parent and a new Mercedes Benz convertible with a plate that read LDYBUG.

"I'll run the plate when we get back," Donovan said. He polished off the fries and tossed the wrappers in a nearby basket. "Sounds familiar. I've probably seen it around town."

"Don't get your hopes up."

"Yeah, a killer with vanity plates; not likely if he's smart."

"Paintings the size of trucks; sculpture that weighs as much as my car. That kind of art takes big bucks, Freddy."

Donovan puffed on a dollar cigar. A pleasant breeze was rustling its way through a grove of cottonwoods.

"TV stars make major money, Oliver."

The pair strolled the promenade again, along with several young couples with small children. The Spanish-style stucco bathhouse on Pettigrew Beach rose on the horizon like a Castilian villa. Lacy iron grates protected its arched windows and doorways. The broad ribbon of sand was crowded with fireworks fans huddled on blankets, their glowing bonfires putting romance in the air. Stork-legged lifeguard chairs gleamed white in the dusk.

"We'll have a look at his financial records, bank account," Poole said matter-of-factly.

"If we're on the right track, Ferris used to be just another good looking guy from Belmont…like the rest of us. After high school he ditched it all for the big city and eventually landed a part in a soap called *Yesterday's Children*. He played the popular villain. Joanna said he was abruptly written out last December. Next thing we know, he's here at Ashbury College teaching our young how to play Othello." Donovan scratched at his beard.

"And, when did you dig up this information?"

"Cell phone. I called my bride again. Very handy. Brides and cell phones." Donovan smiled smartly.

"Don't get smart. I have a phone. I don't need a bride. Let's eat that Hershey bar that's half-melted in your pocket." Poole pointed to the limp candy.

Donovan obliged, and they ate the chocolate quickly.

Families and couples carrying blankets, hampers, and six packs were filling up Front Street. The Big Bang fireworks display would erupt as night fell, around nine.

Poole produced a fairly immaculate handkerchief again and wiped his chocolate-coated fingers. "I'll call his agent tomorrow. Find out if Ferris was fired or planned to go back to the TV show. We need to know the works on this guy, Freddy. From the movies he saw to where he bought his shirts. And, most definitely, where he got his money. Soap stars don't all live *that* well. An educated guess."

Donovan nodded. It was getting dark. "Shouldn't be too hard. Our Roger was this town's only celebrity, except for Iris, of course, and Beatrice Wrenn, if you count psychics."

"Could be somebody around here doesn't like rich celebrities."

They had reached the end of the promenade and stopped to admire the River Queen as it eased away from the pier, all dressed up in fresh white paint. Her ebony smoke stacks pierced the sky like clarinets. The decks were lined with people eager for supper and a cruise up river to watch the pyrotechnics. Rows of tiny lights winked along the pilot house roof; bunting hung from the rails, and dozens of miniature flags sprouted from the bow and stern. The old boat's giant paddles churned the vessel into the main channel.

Poole began humming along with the jazz combo playing on board. In his mind's eye he could see Teddy Wilson's fingers dancing elegantly over the ivory keys. Poole played piano, owned a nice rebuilt Steinway still sitting in storage. He'd just recently joined a nice jazz combo in Augusta. The guys noodled the classics on week ends. Freddy always told him he was nothing more than a Renaissance snob with a WASP veneer and a great collection of jazz records. Homicide detectives, he said, don't play piano and paint watercolors and go off to work in thousand dollar suits. Poole always told him to buzz off.

Donovan yawned loudly. "Nice night for beer and rockets." He licked his chocolate smeared fingers and stuffed the candy wrapper into a jacket pocket bulging with debris.

The two detectives walked back to the car, not very eager for more work. Sweet notes from the steamboat's calliope sprinkled the warm air with reminders of carnivals and merry-go-rounds. And nights when there wasn't a dead man in sight.

The next morning Poole pulled into the Village Hall parking lot at seven. Heat rose from the asphalt like primordial vapor. Had it always been this damned hot in Belmont? Poole automatically locked the Porsche, an unnecessary procedure given the car's condition and age, but habits died hard. The inspector felt as attached to the car as he was to his legs, even the bad one. He was still waiting for the old heap to draw its last breath on its own. If he traded too soon, he reasoned, it would be akin to shooting the family dog.

Sometime in the last century the city fathers had erected a massive five-storied pile of limestone in the center of town, a heap tweaked with Gotham City arches and a deep gloomy entrance. The structure housed the Belmont water and tax departments on the first floor and the constabulary on the second. The jail sat in the basement, while the mayor occupied the top floor. Even a hundred years ago, the town fathers knew how to keep their priorities straight.

Poole hauled himself up the long, broad steps, pale maple treads worn smooth as a baby's bottom by years of shoe leather. He stopped by the squad room to drop off a box of doughnuts and to pick up a coffee from the drip machine. Looking tired and overwhelmed, Officers Shipstead and Moreno greeted him cordially and said they were thumbing their way through Ferris's papers and files.

"Keep at it, gentlemen," Poole said, warmly. "Is Freddy in yet?" He selected a jelly-filled before it was too late.

"In his office," replied Shipstead, a young cop with a crew-cut and an almost frightening earnestness about him. His uncle had worked for the Belmont P.D. years ago.

"The Chief's out. Out cold, we hope," Moreno smarted off with a snicker. Poole guessed that the dark-haired, energetic Moreno didn't take life as seriously as Shipstead.

"Keep your fingers crossed," Poole quipped. "Find anything interesting?" They'd been briefed the day before on what to look for.

"I put his personal papers and his date book on your desk, Inspector," Shipstead told him. "It's all Greek to me."

Poole thanked the men, wrapped up three more pastries in a napkin and tucked the lot under his arm, leaving him free to negotiate his cane and carry the coffee. He strolled carefully down the crooked hallway to Freddy's 'laboratory of crime,' a line from the Irishman's Boris Karloff shtick.

"The computers are still down at the DMV," Donovan announced when he looked up to see Poole.

"Don't worry. It's early days, Freddy. Have a doughnut."

Poole took a chair near the west window, hoping to catch a breeze and to savor the morning's first cup with a fried cake. He could just make out the line of the river through a grove of trees in Wrenn Park, far below. Just knowing it was out there, that close, made him feel more at ease with the old surroundings. But, he wasn't home yet. It was taking a long time for some reason. Perhaps if he could see Iris more often. But, she was out on a book promotion tour half the time. When she was home, she was banging out her columns and seeing that damned Max Tarry. It definitely was not the old days.

"Give me your impression of Ferris's party guests," Poole asked Freddy. The students and professors interviewed the night before had thrown a beam of light here and there.

"Ferris clearly made an enemy of Justin Fitzhugh over at Ashbury." Donovan's voice was hoarse from talk and cigars. He broke off a bit of doughnut for Ching, the red chow chow who shared the office and owned a space under the desk. "This Fitzhugh seems to have had motive and opportunity. I asked him to stop by for another chat at his earliest convenience."

"Good idea, Freddy. I like the midnight phone call. We'll check the local phone company, just as soon as they wake up." Nothing worked terribly fast in a small town.

Donovan leaned back in his not very top-of-the line executive chair and looked fairly comfortable with the investigation, so far. He lit a cigar with an Ohio Blue tip.

"No signs of forced entry, no struggle, nothing stolen. The killer either had a key or maybe hid in a closet until the rest of the guests left. Or, maybe Ferris let him in."

"Or her," Donovan added quickly. "The gold charm and the perfumed bath water say female to me." He raised his eyebrows in a man-to-man expression and gobbled up the rest of his doughnut. He could smoke and eat at the same time, a feat that somehow annoyed Poole.

"Sounds like our Roger's modus operandi. My guess is that either Ferris knew the killer well or he was expecting to know the killer a lot better." Poole narrowed his eyes with some appreciation for the scenario Roger had anticipated. Freddy, never of man of dalliance, winced, and Poole was happy to see that his friend's romantic standards were still higher than his own.

"Ah, sex and violence in an American hamlet." Donovan sighed. "According to the lab, no prints on the knife or the mask or the charm. The autopsy report isn't ready yet. The coroner's got three stiffs lined up down there. It would seem that two of Belmont's dimmer bozos engaged in a deadly disagreement about fireworks last night." He puffed out a great cloud of blue smoke. "One lost."

Poole nodded. He had heard about it on the car radio. "Have your smartest lads check the guests' alibis for the hours after the party. Our Roger was last seen standing alone at his penthouse door at twelve forty-five a.m." The rest of the guests would be interviewed later that day.

"I still favor the esteemed surgeon," said Donovan, expansive and daring for Freddy. He was rocking gently in his squeaky chair.

"What's his motive? I can relate to the doctor's perverse personality. My old dad's just as warm and fuzzy." Years ago, Poole's arrogant father abandoned his family and a successful engineering business to live in a trailer in the California desert where he executed bad oil paintings of minor Hollywood celebrities. Poole refused to talk to the man.

"Ferris left his worldly goods to Mom. That tells you something. Jesus, my poor Irish family, vast as the Atlantic, possesses little and shares everything."

"The great surgeon might be too fastidious to stab his victim."

Donovan agreed. "After you left last night, I called Ferris's agent, a man named Roscoe Thurston. Ingrid Ferris found his name and number. Got him out of bed, but he was polite enough. Said he'd be in town later this week. The funeral's scheduled for Saturday, according to our efficient Doctor Ferris, who phoned me at home this morning. Saturday, that is, if the coroner or the D.A. does not delay it." Donovan took a deep breath.

Poole swallowed the rest of his coffee and said, "Was Ferris fired from his day job?"

"Absolutely not, according to Mr. Thurston. The producer of the soap, in Thurston's words, was 'absolutely devastated' when Ferris flew the coop."

Poole processed this news quietly and then said, "Be on guard for the press today, Freddy. Celebrity murders smoke out anybody with a Bic pen or a cell phone. My guess is the swarm will hit Belmont by mid-morning."

They were interrupted by Officer Moreno, who tapped on the door and then waltzed in looking pretty pleased.

"The Ladybug plates belong to a Marjorie Verdun, Lieutenant. Nice address." Moreno grinned, as if he liked homicides. Ching wandered over to sniff Moreno's black shoes and then sat at attention hoping for a treat.

"Marjorie Verdun?" Donovan groaned. "Keep a sock on this, Moreno. Nobody but us knows. And, you and Shipstead get over to the college this morning and go through Ferris's office."

Moreno hustled out before he could pat Ching on the head. The dog, bored with police business, settled down for his first nap of the day in front of a south window.

"Marjorie Verdun and Roger Ferris," Donovan said quietly, by way of explanation, "were an 'item,' as they say. A 'closet item,' if you know what I mean."

Poole nodded and smiled a little at the terminology. "Isn't Froggy Verdun putting up most of the buildings in this part of the world. I see Verdun Construction signs every few blocks." Poole began circling the office, an old habit that helped his brain work. Every few feet he tapped the furniture with his stick.

"The construction czar of the Upper Mississippi Valley. I am acquainted with the Verduns. This will be a trifle awkward." Donovan shifted uneasily in his chair.

"Ahh, hanky-panky," replied Poole. "One of the oldest motives for murder and often the most entertaining." Poole grinned and sat down again with his stiff leg up on a chair seat, the cane across the desk top. The case was developing character, meaning the plot was getting complicated and muddy. Freddy was right. The hair of the dog was just what he needed to complete his recovery. And, the bonus was going to be watching Freddy Donovan hack his way through the underbrush.

Oliver liked to keep a part of himself hidden. It was one of the things that made him intoxicating and one of the things that drove Iris crazy. He had just called to say he would be stopping by. True to form. No reason was offered and she refused to ask. At least it wasn't another Fed Ex message. Besides, it was too hot to pursue the point or to move too many muscles. Iris stayed on the couch.

Glancing around the living room, stretched by old beams and anchored by an imposing fireplace, Iris imagined how she must look, settled among pillows exuberant with pink camellias. She thought immediately of the famous Impressionist painting of a young woman in white, reclined on a chaise longue with a parasol to shade her pale face. Such tranquility. Such gentility. Was there such a thing anymore? Iris sat up straighter and didn't think so. Her afternoons of leisure were so rare she couldn't remember the last one. Her life flip-flopped between turmoil and peace, book tours and writing, squabbles with the kids and discussions with Bombay and the occasional day like this.

In the past, she could blame Oliver for unrest in the hive. Now that he was back, she could only hope life remained only minimally complicated. The children were grown; she was independent; Oliver was alive and well. That was good enough, wasn't it? She had given up worrying about him. He refused to discuss his abrupt departure from Washington and the Bureau. It was rumored the mysterious mob had done a number on him. Iris wasn't sure she believed that. It sounded so Hollywood. Be that as it may, Oliver had simply transferred his talents to a new game board, and the Belmont Police and Fire Commission was delighted to let him play in the village toy store. She and Oliver had seen little of each other since April; so, why did she feel as if a long, long frayed cord was tied from her ankle to Oliver's?

The slam of a car door brought Iris to the front hall where she squinted through the screen to see Oliver cross the lawn, placing his cane with care in the soft grass. She felt the familiar sensation in her chest. Hell's bells. She gave herself a stern warning. They were divorced. End of story.

"You look wonderful," Poole said, and he leaned down to kiss her cheek. "You've been working in the garden; the flowers are terrific."

"Thanks. I have the dirty fingernails to prove it." He was still irresistible. She wanted to immediately pack and move to Paris. "Let's sit on the porch."

Iris led the way to the back of the elderly establishment, an historic Federal relic, an old inn that she and Oliver had once shared with their children. One of Iris's ancestors had won the place in a card game (always a lucky bunch), and now it was her turn to occupy it. The place lay snoozing in the heat like a library reading room; it was an aged silence that only a doddering, liver-spotted dwelling such as this one could impart to its keeper. Iris never felt as if she owned Woolsey House; she was simply its provisional caretaker.

Poole tagged along behind. He loved the place as much as she did. Maybe he was just stopping by to absorb the spirit of the house. A tall case clock ticked the time away in the foyer, as it had for two centuries in an assortment of halls and parlors. Iris lived well, thanks to her books and her grandmother's money. So be it. Poole understood the power of money; he'd just never appreciated or admired the people who had it. For him, big money meant dirty money. Iris wasn't sure she liked that side of Poole. They stopped in the kitchen for a cool drink.

"I put my money down on a condo in Augusta. Nice and close to the university where I can keep an eye on Charlie and Lydia. Just what they want, their old man sniffing around." Poole grinned and leaned against the counter while Iris poured tea over the ice.

"Good heavens, I thought you'd be living at the St. George until you needed a hearing aid and drooled while you read the paper in the lobby." Iris laughed. "When's moving day?"

"Very funny. Three days. Somebody else is in charge. I haven't the time."

"You can get your beloved Steinway out of storage." Iris handed Poole a glass and proceeded to the porch at the rear of the house.

"Yes. It should be played or it'll croak on me. Know any good piano tuners?"

"Red Pipkorn. Excellent. He's tuned mine for years. He will be easy to find in the capital. Even the governor uses him. He's proud of that."

Iris retreated to a wicker chair with sun-faded rose cushions. Potted pink begonias swung gently overhead. "So, what else is up?"

"The Ferris case, of course. Tell me about the boy." Poole rested his stiff leg on an ottoman and drank thirstily. "Freddy's over at the college questioning Ferris's secretary. I'm off to visit with Nathan Bombay when I leave here. Freddy says between you and Bombay, I'll get the scoop on our dead TV star."

"My impression is probably the same as everybody else's. Handsome, charming, a bit bold, more than a little naughty." Iris grinned slyly. "He reminded me of a cougar. Or a sunrise. Or maybe melted butter over waffles." Iris still enjoyed teasing Oliver.

"Enough!" Poole laughed.

"I'm hardly alone in my assessment. Did you notice Marjorie Verdun at my little buffet last week? Had her eyes glued to Roger all night." Iris recalled the soap star's near perfect features, the famous smile. "Marjorie was in deep trouble with that one." Iris knew all about trouble with a handsome man.

"A real heartbreaker, I take it. How many hearts did he break around here? We've heard rumors."

Iris thought Poole was looking at her with more interest than was necessary. Should she squash any notions he might have brewing?

"You've missed so much." Iris sighed. "But, how would you know? You're the new kid on the block again." She left a longer than necessary pause and went on. "It seems Roger and Marjorie renewed their old high school romance when he got back. Froggy found out and got into a helluva row with Roger a few weeks ago at the Currents Cafe, a restaurant up river. Bloody noses, black eyes. And plenty of spectators." Iris laughed. Romantic entanglements these days were more amusing than heartbreaking.

"When Froggy caught them again at the party," Iris went on, "he tore after Roger and punched his lights out. The male animal so rarely disappoints." Iris clinked the ice cubes through the tea and watched Poole shudder at her cynicism.

"Where was I when all this happened?"

"The fight was after the party. From what Dolly tells me, Marjorie went upstairs to have a cigarette and Roger followed. Froggy got suspicious and caught them....in the big lounge chair in my study." Iris found herself raising an eyebrow. "This is where I'm supposed to use a French phrase that clearly describes the action." She wisely kept her sights on a bed of snapdragons edging the patio. This territory was too familiar.

Poole cleared his throat and said, "Pretty daring. For Verdun and for Ferris. Where was the fight?"

"Froggy followed Roger to Hubble's Alley where Ferris had parked his car. They argued and Froggy beat him up. Threatened to kill him."

"How did you find out?"

"Gail Liebermann. You remember the Liebermanns who live on the corner. Blew up their kitchen a few years ago." Iris played with the slice of lemon in her glass. "A good way to get a new one, I'm told. Fortunately, cooking doesn't interest me enough to bomb my appliances." She grinned. Oliver understood. He was familiar with her cooking. "Anyway, Doc Liebermann heard garbage cans crashing and raced out to see what was going on." Iris rested her head on the back of the chair and listened to the delicious mix of birdsong and insects buzzing. Should she be talking to Poole about infidelities and homicide? She sat up and said, "You don't think Froggy killed Roger?"

Poole frowned. "Marjorie's a lot like your mother, Iris. Selfish, humorless, very rich, willful. She isn't the type men kill for."

"Women like Marjorie have their attractions, Oliver. She has pots of money and likes to do charity work. Dolly and I are taking her to lunch tomorrow. Might be informative."

"Just how serious was Marjorie about Ferris?" Poole asked. "Suspects are lining up like ducks in my brain." He smiled.

"It was rumored that Marjorie would have sold her children to keep Roger Ferris."

Poole scowled again. "And, was Roger just as smitten with Mrs. Verdun?"

"I doubt it. Roger was only smitten with Roger." Iris paused. "You know the type." That was cruel, but Iris couldn't resist. Poole and Ferris did run on parallel tracks in some respects. She rose from the sofa and busied herself with a large potted fern.

Poole ignored her jab. He said, "Marjorie and Froggy are out of town today, but we'll get to them." Poole drained his glass and set it on a wicker table. "Anything else? This is like working the web."

"Roger was a busy boy. Kept a string of willing ladies." Iris stood still for a minute.

"Just how well did you know this guy?"

"Well enough." Iris watched Oliver's neck go red.

"What the hell does that mean?" Poole grabbed his walking stick, stood, and took a step closer. "Better get your alibi in order, my darling, we'll be talking to all of his girlfriends."

"Ah, a long suspect list." Iris gave him an inscrutable smile.

"This isn't one of your novels, Iris."

Then, without another word, Poole dropped his stick onto the ottoman and took hold of her shoulders. Before she could protest or wriggle, he kissed her…a trifle too passionately and far too long for a man who was no longer her husband. Then, he let her go.

Iris heard herself gasp, and by the time she could think of a comeback, Oliver was making his exit out the porch door.

4

YESTERDAY'S CHILD

On the other side of town, Freddy Donovan was driving along River road to Ashbury College. He loved the old campus more than any other spot in Belmont. To him, the little college sparkled in the middle of the town like a fancy pin on a lady's hat. Pretty poetic stuff for a cop, he supposed, but he couldn't help it.

At one time the school was a Methodist teaching academy. It had grown over the past hundred years into a respected fine arts college, known chiefly for its remarkably fine drama department. A bit of academic irony, Donovan thought, considering its restrictive religious roots. He had a Methodist aunt who didn't believe in dancing, smoking, drinking, or card playing. Poor soul. He doubted she believed in fun in any shape or form. She would not have appreciated Ashbury's transformation.

Freddy and Joanne Donovan took in plays, guest lectures, and concerts at Music Hall. But, over and above the 'culture,' Donovan admired the buildings. He nibbled at police work; he saved his real appetite for architecture in its various postures, and Ashbury offered up a sumptuous buffet. Right now, he could just make out the Hall's white cupola winking through the thick trees, a sight that always released a ping of pleasure and a stab of regret to his nervous system. He still dreamed about studying architecture, but knew damned well he was too old and too busy to even think about it. He motored on.

A prim row of iron spikes mounted on a low brick wall enclosed the college grounds. Marking the main entrance were a pair of slender stone pillars topped by granite spheres. Donovan carefully guided the car into a narrow lane, just missing the iron gates standing open at the sides. He was reminded of St. Michael's Grade school, secluded and proud, ruled by nuns who didn't know the meaning of the word failure. Elms, miraculously spared, bowed over the road. Dead ahead rose the original hall, a Greek Revival masterpiece, left largely untouched since it was built in 1845. It was his favorite building with its grand wings of rosy brick.

Ashbury's potpourri of structures went from the sublime to the ridiculous, even to Donovan's self-educated eye. On his way to the parking lot he cruised past the Chancellor's Italianate house done up in apricot and cream and then glanced over at Grace Chapel, planted like a small Greek temple in a grove of maples. He'd been there once for a small wedding. Just through the trees and over a slight rise sat the Beaumont Theatre, a gaudy Moorish picture palace built in the twenties, an homage to Hollywood. Not far from the parking lot and protected by a juniper hedge rose a romantic Gothic farmhouse where the head caretaker resided with his family. The hodgepodge went on over the gentle landscape of the grounds.

Donovan found a visitor's stall, pulled it, and then strolled leisurely toward Daly Hall, a massive stone pile closely resembling Village Hall, its thick pachyderm hide tickled by a row of arched windows along the upper floor that mimicked raised eyebrows. He particularly liked the narrow tower on the south end with its conical roof and slot windows. He never failed to imagine bow-men hiding there, shooting arrows at the enemy. He playfully ducked when he approached the entrance.

Inside, the main corridor was cool, dim, and quiet; summer school classes were still in session. The walls were lined with photographs of stage productions going back forty years.

His meeting with Dean Whitehead lasted ten minutes. Donovan found the old dean extraordinarily obtuse or bewitched or both on the subject of Roger Ferris. Whitehead seemed to regard the actor as a golden, amusing child star who had suddenly gone missing. Donovan concluded that if Ferris had been in any kind of trouble or caused any, the Dean never would have noticed. It was rumored that the aged Dean was on his way out.

Hoping Ferris's secretary might prove useful, Donovan slowly climbed three flights to the spacious corner office Ferris had shared with Professor Gilbert Twelmeyer. According to Whitehead, Ferris's new quarters were being redecorated. While waiting for Mrs. Lippencott, the secretary, Donovan roamed the room with a paper cup of water from the dispenser. Hot muggy air was creeping through four stone faced windows, carrying with it the buzz of cicadas and an invitation to nap in a hammock. Not today. And no time soon, Donovan reminded himself.

Ferris's regulation steel desk was parked in front of the windows and faced the door. The top was orderly with papers neatly stacked or filed in plastic bins. Donovan picked through a few notes and discovered that the methodical Ferris had possessed penmanship almost as bad as his own. An oversized ceramic coffee mug sat to one side, its pale blue glaze stenciled 'Yesterday's Children - Roger Ferris.' Donovan felt sad just looking at it.

The late actor's half of the office was as tidy as his apartment. Ferris had been a genuine fusspot. The wall near his desk was decorated with four framed theatre posters, two for summer stock productions featuring Ferris, and two successful Broadway plays, 'Money, Money,' and 'Mixed Reviews,' in which he'd held supporting roles.

Professor Twelmeyer's territory was quite the contrary, an amusing melange of academic and personal rubble. Towers of yellowing newspapers and dog-eared books fought for space with piles of wrinkled magazines and stacks of file folders. A silk tie hung abandoned on a chair arm; a sweater blanketed the old typewriter. A fortress of opened and unopened mail teetered on one corner of the desk. The wall behind the desk held a collage of autographed photos of famous stage and screen actors. Donovan could relate to this man and looked forward to meeting him.

The quiet was eventually broken by the click of high heels, and Donovan soon found himself face to face with Nancy Lippencott, close to a stage production herself. A woman of plain features, Mrs. Lippencott had turned herself into a middle-aged Barbie Doll with a head of savagely bleached hair curled into a remarkable replica of a Johann Sebastian Bach wig. Great smudges of electric blue eye shadow blinked at him. After closing the office door, Mrs. Lippencott introduced herself and took an arm chair. Her grass green skirt rode dangerously high on her plump thighs, but she didn't seem to mind or to notice. Donovan retreated to safety behind Ferris's desk and sat down.

"How did Mr. Ferris appear the last few days before his death?" Donovan decided to leap right in and prayed the secretary wouldn't be too eager. She looked like an embroiderer.

"Worried, but a little calmer. He hadn't been himself for weeks. He was jittery and preoccupied." Mrs. Lippencott's painted face creased with concern.

"Why was that, Mrs. Lippencott?"

"Please, call me Nancy." The secretary smiled nicely. She was trying to be helpful. "When he first arrived last winter, Roger Ferris was a breath of spring around here." Nancy smiled at the memory. "Quick, witty, charming. Everybody just loved him! A big star right here on the faculty. He took charge and learned fast. Sent a few feathers flying, let me tell you." The feathers precipitated girlish giggles.

"When did the jitters hit?" Donovan tried to steer her back on track.

"Before the term ended, late March, I think." Nancy's voice dropped to a confidential tone. "He smoked more. Didn't dress as carefully… sometimes he'd wear the same shirt two or three days in a row. I could smell gin in the mornings." She paused, genuinely pained, and added, "I think he was ill."

"Did he confide in you?"

"Not a word. And I would have heard if he told anyone."

Donovan was pretty sure Nancy's fingers rarely left the pulse of the department.

"How about the tiff with Professor Fitzhugh?"

Taking a deep breath, Nancy said, "They didn't get along. Professor Ferris got the job Professor Fitzhugh was supposed to get. And they had a big row over the summer theatre project, which has been Professor Fitzhugh's pet for about eight years." A brace of silver bracelets clinked in a melodious accompaniment to the woman's story.

"Did they quarrel openly?"

The woman tugged at her skirt and said, "When Professor Ferris told Professor Fitzhugh he was taking over the summer workshop, Fitzhugh accused Ferris of piracy! Called him Captain Hook and offered to wring his neck on stage if he had to."

As Donovan listened, he was transfixed by Mrs. Lippencott's bouncing curls. His wife's hair didn't seem to move like that. He moved his chair back another few inches.

"Did Fitzhugh ever threaten Ferris again?" The Irishman sipped the tepid water and longed for a cold beer.

"Every so often. But people say things when they're mad. It doesn't mean Professor Fitzhugh killed Professor Ferris." Nancy would be loyal to both sides.

Donovan thought Fitzhugh's wish had come true rather conveniently. "How about a soda, Nancy? I noticed a machine in the lounge down the hall." The secretary said that would be lovely and watched Donovan amble off. He soon returned with two sweating cans of Coke.

"Now," Donovan was grinning like an old chum, "tell me what you know about Mr. Ferris's social life. We have heard he was quite the lady's man."

Mrs. Lippencott immediately warmed to the subject. "He was such a flirt! But I'm not sure who he dated...exactly." Like hell, Donovan thought. She was waiting to be coaxed.

"Nobody special? No real hot romance?"

Nancy weakened. "Well, there was Mrs. Twelmeyer, the Professor's wife." The secretary revealed this in a lovely stage whisper. "Quite a scandal here at the drama department. Miss Valerie does have a reputation of sorts." That information included an arched eyebrow. "And Professor Twelmeyer is such a dear." And, a shake of the head.

"What did Twelmeyer do about it?"

"He never threatened to kill anybody, if that's what you mean." The secretary was fierce on this point.

Donovan made a notation in his book. "Any calls from a lady with a southern accent?"

Nancy thought not, but offered that Miss Valerie spoke with a southern accent but rarely called the office.

The Irishman made a note of this too. "Why do you think Ferris left New York for Ashbury?" he asked.

"Nobody could understand it. He said he was burned out." Nancy remained unconvinced on that point.

"Was he a happy man?"

"I would say he was having a good time until his nerves gave out."

"Anything seem out of the ordinary?"

Nancy closed her fluorescent lids for deeper concentration and when they popped open she said, "He did get three funny envelopes in the mail, Lieutenant Donovan. With cut-out words pasted on the outside. He said they were crank letters from a fan."

Donovan's considerable stomach lurched in response. He asked if the letters might still be in the office.

"No, but I'm sure he kept them. I looked in his waste basket for them, but they weren't there." Nancy raised both penciled eyebrows. "They looked like those ransom notes you see in the movies." She smiled, as if her interpretation of evidence might get her a job at the police station. Then, just as suddenly, the chilly expression of fear washed over the secretary's round face. Donovan wondered if she had never thought about the dark significance of the strange fan letters. Ransom notes? Crank mail? Jesus, Mary and Joseph. Poole was going to dance a jig when he heard this.

Before leaving the cop asked for an updated list of party guests. While he waited for Nancy to fetch the names from her desk, Donovan quickly poked through Ferris's files but found nothing interesting. Earlier that morning, Moreno's search had uncovered an inscribed gold cigarette case in a jacket Ferris left in his closet. The trail of crumbs was as short and obscure as the inscription on the case. It read 'For all the yesterdays. Love, A.' No crank letters had turned up.

Nancy soon returned with the list, dabbing her eyes with a tissue as she teetered on her heels. "I hope you find the killer, Lieutenant. Professor Ferris didn't deserve to get murdered. Everybody loved him." She sniffed.

Donovan offered her a sympathetic smile and said, "Well, maybe just one person didn't, ma'am. I do appreciate your help." He presented his card and suggested she call if she remembered anything else. As he clasped her hands to say goodbye, he marveled at how the woman typed with fingernails as lethal as hawk claws.

After leaving Iris's house, where he had to admit he had surprised himself, Poole drove immediately to the newspaper offices on Half Moon Street. He had forgotten how jealous he could be about Iris. And, he realized, perhaps more realistically than before, just how much he wanted her back. How well had she known Ferris, or was she just pulling his leg? The good one. Wasn't Max Tarry enough, the arrogant bastard? Poole had met the playwright. Tarry had made damned sure Poole knew about his relationship with Iris. Goddamned tom cat. Why was this Broadway luminary writing and directing plays in Augusta, the boondocks from a New Yorker's point of view?

Enough, Poole told himself, and he parked in back of the newspaper. On entering the rear of the old house, he asked to see the editor and publisher. The office manager said she would let Mr. Bombay know immediately; he was on the phone.

The little weekly would never claim a roster of famous reporters or a corporate dining room, but it did boast an impressive number of plaques and framed certificates on its walls for achievements and awards over the years. The *Bee* comfortably occupied the first floor of the restored Victorian. Nathan Bombay lodged upstairs in his private bachelor quarters. A dedicated staff of five managed to fill forty pages once a week. Bombay was satisfied that his newspaper's impact in this part of the state was significant and quite respectable. Poole couldn't argue with that; the weekly was an admirable publication.

The prodigiously built editor soon bustled out of his office to greet Poole, apologizing for the delay and mopping his brow with a handkerchief. They retreated to Bombay's roomy, sunny office at the rear and far removed from the office manager's acute hearing, as Bombay put it later. A window air conditioner rattled in the background.

"Tea?" Bombay asked. "It will be hot, even on a day like today." His many chins wobbled with enthusiasm. The editor loved his food and drink.

Poole said he needed it; he felt Bombay looking him over. After all, Poole had once belonged to Iris and the FBI, a kind of rare coupling that begged scrutiny from a journalist interested in his fellow humans. Besides, Iris was Bombay's favorite female; she had stayed on to write the Aunty Em advice column long after her novels became best sellers.

Nathan Bombay admired loyalty as much as he admired talent. He was a highly decorated Chicago journalist, now content to inform the river folk, as he sometimes put it. Poole had stopped to see him his first week back home, believing it wise to stay on good terms with one of the best newsmen in the business and certainly the largest. Bombay seemed to be weighing in around three-hundred these days.

After pouring two cups of pekoe from a china pot, Bombay suggested Poole take a seat in the editor's prized 'stolen-from-the-National-Press-Club' lounge chair. The big man said, "I'm delighted to see you again, Inspector. Even more pleased that you're here on this nasty Ferris case. We'll need your expertise. The closest thing to high crime around here is generally a hold-up at the Shell station out on Cold Spring road." His booming laugh filled the room.

Poole smiled and carefully removed a teetering stack of yellowing newspapers from the purloined chair before settling in with his tea. He said, "I understand you interviewed Roger Ferris when he first arrived in January. Any thoughts on our subject, now that he's dead?" Certainly, Bombay's love of a good, complex story was as fierce as the man's love of good food.

Bombay eased himself into an oversized leather chair and leaned back, after first giving his green eye shade a twist to the west. He was attired, as always, in white flannel trousers, a crisp blue shirt and red braces. "I like you Poole. You're a man who comes straight to the point, and you dress like a civilized human being. Fine attributes. And, to answer your question, I can only say this, Roger Ferris was a man possessed." After saying this, the editor pursed his tiny mouth and gave Poole a hard look, as if challenging him to ask the right questions.

"How so?" Poole was curious but remained controlled. It rarely paid to get too eager about deeply instinctive observations.

"Ferris was building his homecoming upon a lie, Inspector Poole. He claimed he was professionally burned out; but, frankly, I didn't believe a word of it and neither did anyone else who listens and observes carefully. Ferris spoke at great length about the TV show he'd abandoned, his work on it, and how much he loved his acting career and his fascination for New York." Bombay shook his head and his wattle of chins jiggled in response. "He was in hiding is my guess." The editor snapped his red braces as if to punctuate the remark.

Poole could accept this conclusion to a point. "Hiding from what?"

"That, my friend, is your task. Find Ferris's demon, and you will find his killer." Bombay grinned and sipped his pekoe. His sharp blue eyes twinkled, and Poole was reminded of a gossip columnist he once knew in Washington, who dearly loved her job and food as much as Bombay. She was the finest story-teller on the East coast.

"Did he say anything revealing or puzzling?"

Bombay rocked gently in his chair. "Ferris asked if I ever wrote obituaries. I said I did, when the deceased had made a name for himself. I told Ferris that I would have his obituary ready for the files within the week. This is standard practice in newspaper offices for citizens in the community who are well-known or important. I asked why he wanted to know. He laughed, a bit nervously, I thought, and said that he would never read another obituary as long as he lived."

Poole was clearly perplexed by this. "Odd, wouldn't you say?"

"My reaction, as well, Inspector. Ferris could be mysterious, mind you. He did say, maybe in fun and maybe not, that his analyst forbid it."

Poole rubbed his chin. He and Bombay exchanged looks of bewilderment. "Artistic temperament? A Woody Allen complex?" put in Poole.

Bombay chuckled and refreshed their cups. "Or, the biggest clue you've had so far."

"We'll have to go over the condo again, Freddy. Cut and paste mail is rarely amusing to the people who get it." Poole was splashing cold water on his face in the police station washroom, a room he found about as charming as the rest of the place. Donovan had just briefed him on the interview with Nancy Lippencott. "Let's hope Ferris filed them away with his old love letters," Poole said. "He's the kind of man who would save a thing like that." He ran the icy water over his wrists.

"And, there is Valerie Twelmeyer," Donovan added. "Maybe she's the jealous type. Or, maybe she and Marjorie Verdun teamed up to get Ferris." The Irishman raised both furry eyebrows, liking this idea.

Poole smiled. "You sniff out Froggy Verdun tomorrow and make sure Justin Fitzhugh makes an appearance. I'll locate the Twelmeyers. One of the party guests said the professor is quite the practical joker." Poole managed a wink through the water on his lashes. "Maybe our witty professor likes to send funny letters, too."

"Maybe Twelmeyer got rid of his rival." Donovan lit a cigar.

"Send Freelander and Shipstead over to the condo; they're the brightest of the bunch. Tell them to tear apart those bookcases in the library. We'll be over later. I want to go over Ferris's personal papers myself, and we should call his agent again." Poole dried his face on brown paper towels, smoothed back his hair with his hands, and rolled down his shirt sleeves.

"The Chief wants Shipstead on that gas station holdup." Donovan puffed extravagantly.

Poole watched his friend's reflection disappear behind smoke clouding the streaky mirror. He said, "I'll take responsibility for stealing a few hours of Shipstead's valuable time."

Poole was still grouchy, and he was preoccupied with Iris. She could always light a fire in him. "The chief must learn to share," Poole reminded Freddy. The chief had made one too many cracks about the FBI. Poole would get his due. He plucked his jacket from a hook loosely mounted into the old tile wall and opened the washroom door.

"It's your fight, my man," said Donovan. "Use your stick on him if he gets ornery." The Irishman flicked a bit of ash into the sink and tagged along. Blue smoke followed them out like a specter.

Several hours later, after a second search of the victim's penthouse, Poole and Donovan stood in front of Chief Holmgren's big oak desk with 'the goods,' as Donovan put it.

"What I can't understand, gentlemen, is how you missed these damned poems the first time?" Holmgren pronounced it 'pomes' and still looked pretty pleased with himself.

Holmgren was enjoying the blunders. A second search, red faces. It was all just peachy, as far as he was concerned. Holmgren was the kind of man who thought the homicide game was fun if somebody else got caught doing something stupid.

"We've uncovered evidence that might show motive," Poole explained calmly. "Blackmail, for starters." Poole pulled up a chair and sat down. His leg was aching.

"These damned letters could be meaningless crank mail," Holmgren retorted. "This so-called blackmailer could be some fat cat TV producer in New York who likes sixth grade jokes. Or, our killer could be a gangster who wanted Ferris to pay up a gambling debt."

Holmgren's modest brain was whirling faster than usual, and Poole wouldn't have admitted it under torture, but the man could be right. These were all possibilities. "One envelope is postmarked New York; two are local," Poole said. "A nice twist." He smiled indulgently at the chief.

"The Mafia has wheels, Poole. The Mafia flies in airplanes. Those creeps'll do anything to scare the shit out of people."

The chief had seen all the *Godfather* movies. Unfortuately, Poole understood all too well how the Mafia worked. Was the chief giving him a nasty dig about the old days?

Donovan said, "You got to give Shipstead and Freelander credit for finding those letters, chief. A superior bit of sleuthing." The Irishman jabbed at the air with his finger. "They were hidden in a hollowed out book. Talk about a scene out of an old detective novel." Donovan and Poole laughed. Holmgren didn't find it funny.

"Sounds like somebody slipped up the first time. We can't afford mistakes, gentlemen. The national press is on our tails. I've had calls from the governor and that new attorney general who likes to play cop in everybody's yard but his own. And damned if I don't have *People* magazine camped out on my front lawn!" The Chief was skillfully rolling his cigar from one corner of his mouth to other as he spoke. "Mrs. Holmgren doesn't like it, not one little bit."

Holmgren was trying to act indignant, but he wasn't fooling Poole. The man loved each snap of the cameras and every inch of video tape showing his ugly puss on TV. And, Poole was pretty sure Mrs. Holmgren was smiling for the photographers.

"Too bad about the publicity, Jasper," Poole quipped.

"I don't have time for all those damned reporters. You two handle the wolves. Just let me know when you've got some big news. And, keep quiet about these damned poems." Answering questions for the press had proved trickier than Holmgren realized. Having his picture taken from a distance was the easy part.

Jasper Holmgren stood and hitched up his trousers, a habit, Poole was learning, almost as routine as watching Donovan stuff his pockets with chocolate bar wrappers. Holmgren wasn't a pretty cop. His nose had begun the raspberry glow of a hard drinker, and he'd lost most of his hair, a process begun twenty years ago when Poole first joined the department. Their dislike for one another went back just as far.

Holmgren reach for his Stetson, perched on the edge of his desk for quick get-aways. He apparently fancied himself a western hero, now that he owned a horse. Hell, Poole thought, he'd give Donovan's dog a hundred bucks worth of doughnuts just to watch old Jasper crawl up the side of a horse to land in the saddle. Freddy liked to say he'd pay big just to watch the Chief slip on something in the stable yard.

The chief rested his cigar butt in the ashtray, the disgusting chewed end facing his detectives. The dressing-down was over. "Full reports on my desk, gentlemen, tomorrow morning. Full reports."

And with that the big man marched out of the office…with the posse at his heels.

A bit later that evening, at dusk, when the light and the dark play tricks on the eyes, young Evan O'Neill stood at the kitchen window and thought he saw someone moving through the back yard near the garage. It couldn't be his mother; she was out. Friends had picked her up an hour ago. Maybe the neighbor kids were playing after-dark games again. This block was perfect for hide-and-seek with its rows of dense yew hedges, tall cedars, stands of mature oaks, and big shadowy houses set well back from the street. He watched as the figure disappeared into the fading light.

A detached garage sat at the rear of the property and was often left open to the alley. It would make a great place to hide, Evan decided. He finished making a bologna and pickle sandwich and switched off the kitchen light. As he did so, he glanced out the window just in time to see a dark sedan pull away from the garage and speed off down the alley. It was impossible to recognize the model of the car or the driver. The whole scene had a Hollywood thriller quality to it.

Evan put down the sandwich and hurried out to the garage. Inside, his mother's sedan occupied its usual space; his convertible was parked alongside it. The garage was warm and stuffy, quiet and orderly. It smelled faintly of gasoline fumes from the lawn mower. He paced the perimeter and noticed nothing unusual. Down on his hands and knees, he peeked beneath both cars. There were no bombs taped to the axles. He didn't see any suspicious packages or containers on the shelves or in the corners. He had grown up understanding danger... kidnapping, murder, extortion, and blackmail. His stepfather had been a cautious, obsessive rich man who trusted no one completely and suspected everybody of deviousness. Without wanting to, Evan had caught the fever of this kind of thinking.

After closing and locking the garage door, Evan walked back to the house and went inside. It was probably nothing, just kids fooling around, having fun, kids turning a July night into something scary and mysterious. And, for that moment, he was envious of their fun.

So, he was gone. Murdered in his bed. Annette experienced a strangely ambiguous sensation…like burning a finger on an ice cube. What was it about Roger that always evoked this profound emotion? A longing for that first love? She quickly and expertly brushed on black mascara. It was Monday. The day after a holiday was always too normal.

Of course, dear Roger had provoked his own untimely death….a shame really. He did have a talent for entertaining an audience. And, here she was. Her greatest enemy lay dead, and she was mourning the man almost as much as she had loved him and then loathed him. The paradox that was Roger Ferris. They had always stirred tortuous feelings in each other. This time the feelings had grown deadly. It all began last fall on a rainy afternoon in downtown Manhattan. It played over and over in her mind like a film she had seen too many times.

"I need to talk to you." Roger's deep, sensuous voice tickled her ear. The call came on a raw autumn morning in New York, only two weeks after she had given him walking papers. "I promise, no nasty scenes," Roger said. "I need your advice. Strictly business." He sounded sincere and a trifle desperate.

He needed one last favor.

They agreed to meet at Alfie's, a small bar usually crowded with nobody they knew. She explained that she could spare only a few minutes.

Roger was waiting at the bar, a martini half gone. They picked a booth in back and ordered another martini for him and white wine for her.

"You look terrific," he said, touching her hand across the narrow table. A thatch of expensively cut wheat hair fell in wisps over his broad forehead; it matched his linen jacket perfectly, as if the flax and the locks had grown together in the same field. He knew how good he looked.

Annette pulled her hand away and said, "Thanks, but no thanks." She smiled but didn't mean it and prayed she didn't look nervous. "Now, what is this great problem you have?" She assumed he was having difficulties with Eagle Eye, one of his television production companies.

"Nothing too serious. A small kink. You could be a big help, darling. It's a simple deal, really. Nobody will know about it." Roger spoke earnestly, calmly, with a tiny smile on his lips, but none, she noticed, in his seductive gray eyes.

A twinge of apprehension pinched her chest. Roger went on talking, using the evenly modulated voice of a man explaining something very complicated to someone who wasn't very bright. She thought he understood their break-up; she had ended their brief affair, an arrangement never meant to be permanent. There would be no divorce and no wedding.

The waitress, dressed as an 18th century barmaid, hurriedly set down the drinks and bustled off.

Roger took a large swallow and said, "I need additional working capital. The company is solid, I swear, better than we dreamed, but we could use more funds." He made it sound as if he were running UNICEF, his expression needy and persuasive.

She didn't hesitate long before answering. "I don't think so, Roger. My money is tied up." Money, again. He was always begging for favors. She began pulling on her coat, eager to get away, knowing now that it had been a mistake to come.

"Wait," Roger said, laughing, reaching for her arm. "Hear me out. This is an offer you can't refuse." He mimicked the old salesman's pitch. He was buzzed and getting trite.

"Old joke."

"Look," he took hold of her wrist and held it tightly, "this is a great opportunity for you. An up-and-coming company, talented people. You helped out before. What's the problem now?"

"Drop the pitch, Roger, and let go of my hand." Annette jerked free.

"OK. Forget the personal side to this. That's just a few gorgeous memories. I understand." His tone turned sympathetic, but it sounded phony. "You like your life the way it is." He was all charm and grinning like a fool. "But life can be full of surprises. Life doesn't always stay the same." His lips twisted almost cruelly.

"I'm not interested in making any changes." Her voice sounded surprisingly strong. "And my life is no longer any of your business."

Her words barely touched him. He brushed them off like lint from an expensive suit. He was loving the whole scene... the setting, the power plays, the parrying and exercise of wits. Master of the angelic monster, beautiful Roger had spent years on daytime television, honing this diabolical character. He was obviously infatuated with his own creation.

"I think you should reconsider." Roger paused dramatically and swallowed the gin like water. "I'm afraid that my way is going to be the only way." He threw in his trump and signaled the waitress for another round.

Annette watched him lean back in the padded leather booth, pleased with his punch line, the low-key lighting painting shadows on his fair face. The laughter and loud music began fading in and out in her ears and alarm rose in her throat. She wasn't sure she could sip the wine or speak. What was he saying?

Roger waited, all patience and benevolence.

She had to answer. She was sitting in his trap, as if lashed to the old oak booth by a chain of smart remarks. A hurried gulp of wine melted some of the fear, and she decided to ignore the threat. "I think you should find another investor. Perhaps one of your partner's little friends." His business partner wasn't one of her favorites. "You don't need me or my money. I'm going." She began to slide to the side of the booth.

"I suppose I could call Alfred."

The words stopped her.

"He's in the chips. Has banks full of money for new investments. Billions, I'm told." Roger's speech had gone sloppy, but he was full of self-assurance.

"My husband isn't interested in television production." She could feel the pull of the conversation going Roger's way.

"Perhaps he would be more interested in how much his wife has already invested in my company, with my expert guidance. Or he might like to know about your personal encouragement these past few months." Another cocky grin.

The smugness disgusted her. He sat there in the security of the dark booth, sipping gin, full of himself, as always. Hate welled inside her, mixing with dread, like a tropical fever. She knew what he was up to and had never suspected it of him.

"You wouldn't dare." She spat the words at him. "You haven't the nerve." And, for the first time, she leaned toward him. Their heads were close enough to catch the other's scent, like two beasts snorting and pawing before a fight. The indignity of the scene crawled up her spine.

Roger went on. "Your spouse is a very clever fellow. Smart, cautious, proud. And very jealous. He demands perfection and loyalty from everyone around him. Wasn't that his reason for marrying you, my darling? Alfred wanted the perfect, beautiful wife." Roger let the words sink in and then went on, "What if dear old Alfred were to find out that his prized possession was screwing a soap opera star?" Roger clipped off the last phrase, making his occupation sound bourgeois.

She couldn't look at him. Instead, she pinned her gaze on the dark green wall behind him and kept her face expressionless.

"And," he droned on, "what if he were to find out that she had lied to him? About certain things?"

She refused to touch the bait.

A devilish smirk crept across Roger's face, and he said in a hoarse whisper, "What if he were to find out about... Leonard?" Roger had been holding two trump cards.

Leonard. Leonard. Leonard. The name bounced around the booth like a fly trying to escape a small room. She thought they had left Leonard at the bottom of Abner's Quarry years ago. Trotter's death had been ruled an accident.

"You bastard."

They watched each other, neither one moving or speaking.

"What do you want?" she asked. She wanted to kill him. He took another swallow; the clear liquid looked so pure disappearing into Roger's sexy, wicked mouth.

"That's obvious. Money. How about $100,000. To start. I'll work out a mutually acceptable schedule of payments for the future." Roger ticked off his demands as if ordering groceries over the phone.

"Are you crazy? I can't write a check for $100,000."

"Let me help you out. I'll wait until tomorrow. That gives you a whole day to make arrangements. Make it easy on yourself, hand over those diamonds Alfred's hiding in his safe. I have a pal in the sparkle business, who will hand over cold cash for stones like that." Roger's tone was condescending, the smile shrewd. "This is goin' to be the best investment of your life, darlin'."

The Texas tycoon accent was the booze talking. Corny son-of-a-bitch, she thought. Her growing uneasiness about Roger a month ago had been dead on correct. The diamonds were real enough too.

"I'll drop by the apartment tomorrow about four." Roger looked like he was enjoying himself enormously.

Annette didn't respond but rose to her feet. She calmly draped her coat over her shoulders and walked quickly into the crowd. Spilled popcorn crunched underfoot. Patrons were laughing and flirting, celebrating the end of the work day. She wished she were one of them.

A young man held the door, and she slipped out into the chilly night. A cold drizzle was varnishing the pavement. The curbs were lined with pedestrians hailing taxis and holding umbrellas and papers over their heads.

Leaning against the pub window, she thought she could feel heat from the red neon sign on the other side of the glass. She pressed one hand against her stomach and felt sick.

5

A FAST UNDERTOW

At seven Tuesday morning, Poole was sitting in his tiny office at the police station. He had slept badly after a repeat of the usual nightmare. The shrinks had warned him about dreams. The searing images might diminish, but they might not disappear altogether either. His brain recalled only portions of the past. The last psychiatrist he saw told him to consider himself lucky. And, Poole did.

The inspector got on his feet and fastened all three limericks, enclosed in plastic sleeves, to the free-standing bulletin board set up in a corner. Neatly cut letters and words were pasted in straight lines on plain paper; the verse was properly rhymed for the limerick form and had a nice meter. It wasn't Ogden Nash, but it was a pleasant change for a detective who had read worse. And it wasn't composed by a crackpot. Poole read aloud the first:

Number One

There once was a guy so surprising
For his amateur try at sky diving.
Now, a star shakes in his bed,
Out of fear he'll be DEAD.

'Tis fatal to blackmail, my darling.

Ah, the power of the written word. Was it this power that had made Ferris so afraid of obituaries? The first tricky part came in the first limerick. The second tricky part came in the third. Poole stood back from the board and looked at all three messages. It was all a matter of interpretation, like figuring out an imitation T.S. Eliot. He and Freddy had stayed up until midnight the night before, loosening the brain cells with Pfeiffers, listening to jazz, and making a stab at doggerel dissection. Poole moved to the window. Nice morning, evolving toward miserably hot. His high-ceilinged monk's cell didn't offer much, but he could see the park and the river. The buzz of bluish fluorescent lighting was casting a pall and a drone over the square room. The periodic appearance of Killer, a calico cat aptly named for his facility with mice (he belonged to the desk sergeant) and his domination of Donovan's dog, added a spark to the place. However simple and mundane the changes were in his life, Poole keenly understood the importance of them.

He tapped out a mindless cadence with a number one Ticonderoga, while personal sticky wickets stirred things up with the limericks. His thoughts often wandered to Iris and how he might get her back.

Examining the blackboard set up next to the cork board, he read again the rows of names, clues, and possible links neatly listed and cross-matched wherever possible. He was grateful for the one reliable staple of life...homicide. This he understood.

Think, man, think! The star of this first limerick was probably Roger Ferris, and he'd apparently blackmailed someone over something *that* person did or perhaps another person did. But, sky diving? No doubt a bit of poetic symbolism for a feat other than actual sky diving. An adventurer? An imaginative actor? A Chinese trapeze artist? A nasty opportunist trying to land a plum role that Ferris wanted? But, why would this necessarily result in blackmail? Did Ferris have dirt on this guy? So far, Belmont and New York offered no light on the subject. He and Freddy had called a long list of Ferris's show business pals and come up dry. Buses, planes, trains had been checked. Nobody particularly suspicious had arrived and departed Belmont or Augusta.

There was a female in the second limerick. Ferris may have witnessed an evil deed and offered to keep his mouth shut for a fat stipend.

Blackmail and revenge. Poole limped over to the cork board and read it aloud:

Number Two

There once was a man with gold hair
Who captured a maiden so fair.
He tricked the poor lass,
Then stole all her cash,
And now he is trapped in her lair.

The man with gold hair was Roger. He'd taken money from a blonde bent on revenge. This poem was fairly simple, but what did it have to do with the first poem? Just another reference to blackmail… large sums of money he had spent on expensive art. Ferris had warned his housekeeper about spraying polish on 'his good fortune.' That could be interpreted in more than one way, Poole supposed, but he liked the obvious one. The blonde had apparently done a decent job of scaring the wits out of Ferris before she killed him. If she killed him. There were others standing in that line-up.

While he was up, Poole recited the last limerick:

The Final Message

Remember a young man who thought
He was King of the World until caught.
Now you're the beast near the river,
In your cave you must shiver,
Knowing soon you'll be DEAD and not bought.

Damned silly stuff. Very high school. Why stalk the victim with poetry? Unless the limerick form meant something? King of the World sounded like a corny reference to the blockbuster film *Titanic,* yet another theatre connection. Had Ferris believed he was a Big Apple soap opera King? Caught doing what, besides blackmailing the blonde? Was Ferris guilty of a more serious crime? Either way, he had paid with his life. The female was one tough broad...either the full measure of revenge or nothing. Poole didn't want to run into her. Not yet.

Poole swallowed two aspirin with his coffee. It was still too early in the game; they didn't have enough information to make sense of it. And his head hurt worse than his leg.

If Ferris had been so damned terrorized, why not hire a body guard? Where was his gun? Or, were the limericks nothing more than a college hazing prank, sent by Twelmeyer to keep Ferris off guard and away from his wandering wife.

The poems were not likely to cough up any new secrets this morning. He needed breakfast. Ah, waffles at the Half Moon. Freddy would be up by now; he'd call and meet him at the café. He locked the limericks in his desk. As he headed for the door, he recalled a friend's wise counsel years ago: 'Be patient! Homicide investigations are like good sex; it always pays to take your time.'

Poole laughed out loud and gave the waste basket a swat with his cane.

Several obvious adjectives sprang to mind when Poole first saw Valerie Twelmeyer, most had to do with dessert, like luscious, delectable, delicious. More specifically, cupcake, angel food, and strawberry milk shake. The whole thing made him feel as if he'd put too much syrup on his pancakes an hour ago.

The professor's wife stood in the doorway of a newish Colonial style house, a heavenly proportioned female in a pink halter top and shorts. She brought to mind erotic soft sculpture dolls. Once Poole pushed his mind past the body, he concentrated on her enviable English complexion, skin that begged to be touched. He resisted. Valerie Twelmeyer, as his old dad used to say, was a real dish.

Valerie greeted Poole cordially and gave him an appraising glance. She showed him into a Williamsburg living room, heavy on cabriole legs but pleasant. Frank Sinatra was singing 'The Most Beautiful Girl in the World' on the stereo. Before she seated herself, Valerie turned off the music and brought them each a glass of iced tea. Poole took a chair near the fireplace, while Valerie slipped out of her gold sandals and curled up on the sofa, bare feet tucked beneath her.

Without wanting to, Poole found himself comparing this woman's confectionery prettiness to Iris's feverish beauty. Iris comparisons were an old habit. Mrs. Twelmeyer's allure might be too sweet, he decided, like rich food that didn't sit well after the first few bites.

With that out of the way, Poole dove into the deep end. "Just how well did you know Roger Ferris?" he asked.

Unaffected by the inspector's blunt implication, Valerie replied, "Roger was one of my husband's colleagues." The smile was Valentine candy. Questions from a cop were not turning a hair. Poole detected a soft drawl.

"It's my understanding that you and Roger liked to go out, have a few drinks." Poole directed his eyes into hers, a game he played well.

Valerie met his gaze and matched it. "Roger and I were just friends, Inspector." She was admonishing him. "We shared a common interest in the theatre and films. I studied drama before my marriage to Gilbert. Of course, I'm devastated that Roger is dead. Like everyone else." Her full pink lips pouted while she gently stroked a wing of vanilla hair that swung against her cheek like silk embroidery floss. She was flirting.

Poole thought Mrs. Twelmeyer looked something less than devastated, but perhaps this was the best she could do on short notice. "Did you grow up in the South?"

"Virginia. But, I attended college in Georgia. Young girls are so impressionable, and I'm afraid I've never lost the accent." She offered him a Miss Georgia Peach grin. Her teeth were small and white and perfect.

"Did you call Ferris Saturday night about midnight?"

"Midnight? Heavens, no. I would never call a gentleman at that hour."

Stock indignation in the face of bad manners. This woman was very good. Poole found himself smiling. "Did you call him at home Saturday morning?"

"No, I did not." Valerie turned her attention to the tea and fussed with the soggy napkin coaster.

Mrs. Twelmeyer's phone records would be checked, even though they knew that the midnight call to Ferris's apartment came from a public phone box in Augusta. "You and your husband had a noisy row about Roger a few weeks ago. Tell me about that."

This bold statement of fact caught Valerie off guard. She demanded icily, "Who told you such nonsense?" Then, perhaps thinking better of it, she responded. "Married couples have little misunderstandings, Inspector. My Gilbert tends to be a little jealous." She tilted her face coquettishly. "I don't flatter myself that Roger took any interest in me."

Like hell you didn't, Poole thought. "Your little misunderstanding sent your husband to a room at the YMCA." Poole grinned, chiding her. "A neighbor heard Gilbert threaten to throw Ferris off the bridge and one or two alternative measures." He smiled again to let her know that he understood these matters.

"Our domestic problems are private. You shouldn't be askin' such personal questions." Another admonishment delivered in a tone so girlish that Poole felt oddly disadvantaged. Arguing with this woman was like reasoning with a spoiled child on her birthday.

"I'm investigating a homicide, Mrs. Twelmeyer. Lots of people will be asked sensitive questions. "When did you last see Ferris?"

Valerie switched positions on the couch before answering. She reminded him of Vivien Leigh in *Streetcar*; perhaps she had adopted the character as her own. Was she stalling or thinking; he couldn't tell. She replied, "About three weeks ago. I happened to run into him at a cafe downtown. He was with a tall, dark-haired woman in a big hat. Very glamorous." Valerie seemed to be offering Poole a delectable clue. "And large sunglasses. She looked like a New York actress to me."

"Did you recognize her?"

"Afraid not. I certainly didn't wish to pry."

Poole had never known a woman who wasn't curious about the competition. He said, "Did you see Ferris the night of the murder? At the play or the cast party? Your name was on the guest list."

"I attended the play with friends and afterward we had a drink at the Sand Bar. Then I came home and went to bed. I didn't accept Roger's invitation to the cast party." She offered this as either proof of her self-control or of her good judgment, Poole couldn't be sure which.

"You didn't go backstage to congratulate him?" Poole made notations in a small notebook. "It was his big night." He pretended surprise at her apparent lapse of good manners.

Valerie shook her head, as if she'd won another point in a Ping-Pong match.

"Can you give me the names and phone numbers of your theatre friends?"

Valerie frowned and put down her glass. "I am shocked. Are you suggestin' I need an alibi? That I may have spent the evening elsewhere? I was in my bed by half past one." She did finally take the notebook and wrote down the information.

Taking umbrage at perceived insults was one of Mrs. Twelmeyer's specialties. This woman had a real talent for demanding complete trust. Was her husband naïve or very modern? Poole had to wonder. Probably just crazy about her. Poole took back his notebook and thanked her.

Before he could continue Valerie added, "If you think I killed poor Roger, you are way out of line, Inspector. You might check on his other lady friends." She pointed a dainty finger at Poole. A feline had emerged, licking her whiskers with a tiny pink tongue.

"What other ladies do you have in mind?" The earlier delicious adjectives for Miss Valerie were no longer as mouth-watering.

"I could name two young ladies at Ashbury. And, let's include Marjorie Verdun on that list." The kitty had claws.

Poole would play dumb about Marjorie. "What about Mrs. Verdun?"

"Ask her about Roger. And, while you're at it, inquire about Doctor Reginald Ferris, too." Valerie's clear blue eyes twinkled with malice. "Roger's daddy. A trifle kinky for my taste." The kitten had turned into an old cat.

"What are you saying?" Poole was justifiably mystified.

Valerie leaned toward him, a well-practiced pose that put her decolletage to clear advantage. "A good friend of mine saw Marjorie and the illustrious surgeon in the cloak room of the Rowley Hotel at a Heart Association Benefit, just two weeks ago. And they were definitely not discussin' charities, if you know what I mean." Mrs. Twelmeyer sat back and looked very satisfied with herself.

"What did your friend see?"

"Let us say that you would think the insufferable Doctor Ferris and the very borin' Mrs. Verdun would have been more discreet in a public place."

"Can I have your friend's name and number?"

Valerie obliged without hesitation this time. "You know, Inspector, I've heard stories about those two before. And the best part is that Roger and his father hated each other!" She giggled, obviously appreciating the sexual tension the three must have generated. "Makes that naughty trio all the more fun, wouldn't you say?"

The professor's well-informed wife winked at Poole, and he hoped his mouth wasn't open.

With Mrs. Twelmeyer's wisdom thickening the atmosphere, Poole took a moment to review his notes and drink his tea. He found it interesting that she expressed no jealousy or outrage at her lover's romantic adventures. Either she possessed a highly developed sense of noblesse oblige or she was a better actress than he'd imagined.

"Do you think Roger knew of this alleged liaison between his father and Mrs. Verdun?"

"He never said anything to me about it, but then Roger was a real free spirit when it came to women. Roger did love to goad his father."

"How so?"

"He did things to irritate him. Frankly, I think he came back to Belmont just to bug Reggie. Maybe he was sleepin'with Marjorie for the same reason." Mrs. Twelmeyer seemed to admire Roger's mischievous side.

"Did Roger ever say he had been threatened in the past few months?"

"Heavens, no!" Mrs. Twelmeyer's attention was corralled again. Good. Poole wanted to leave her with something to chew on. She looked genuinely horrified, more disturbed than by any discussion of the actor's murder. She said, "He must have kept that awful secret to himself."

Poole guessed she might be suspecting her husband, and he rather hoped the woman did have some affection for the professor. Marriages were seldom black and white. The same held true of divorces. Poole stood and slipped his notebook into a pocket.

As Poole headed for the door, he turned and said, "Mrs. Twelmeyer, did Roger ever say why he never read obituaries in the paper?"

Mrs. Twelmeyer laughed, obviously finding the question as peculiar as the subject. Poole could understand that. "Good heavens, Inspector, how very strange. I have no idea. Maybe Roger had a little fixation about death." She smiled sweetly, as if she might manage to skirt the issue altogether.

"Could be, Mrs. Twelmeyer. Could be."

Leaving the delectable female with enough information to tantalize and worry her, Poole thanked her again and walked out to the street. As he settled gingerly into the hot leather seat, he had to admit she had won as many rounds as he. She was manipulative, poised, and very coy. But, was she jealous enough to murder her lover? Poole turned the ignition key. Somehow, he doubted Valerie had ever suffered a twinge of jealousy. Gilbert, on the other hand, probably lived with it like a nagging allergy. Jack Sprat and his wife.

A Ferris-Verdun-Ferris triangle had emerged. Or, was it more of a rectangle? Surely, Froggy created a side, too. Four equal sides? Poole doubted it. Nice twists and turns in this case. Poole shifted into gear and headed toward the Ashbury campus for a chat with Gilbert Twelmeyer. Who would have thought Belmont had such a fast undertow?

Poole caught up with Gilbert Twelmeyer around noon, just as the professor was leaving for lunch. Poole suggested they go for hot dogs and a stroll around Ashbury commons. Twelmeyer was agreeable.

A busy vendor with an umbrella cart set up in front of the student union prepared frankfurters with the works. Lunch in hand, the two men headed down the path toward Science Hall, a century-old red granite structure that could have doubled as an armory. Poole remembered a geology course he'd taken in that building, and the charismatic professor who had taught them to appreciate Earth. Shortly after that, Poole had gone off to join the FBI.

The sidewalks were congested with summer school students, most burdened by single-strap book bags slung over a shoulder. The uniform of the moment seemed to be baggy chino shorts and message T-shirts that relayed a philosophy of life or pushed a product for nothing. Poole's opinion of clothing with a point of view stamped on it was about the same as bumper stickers that revealed one's religious persuasion or political preference.

"That's quite a building," Poole remarked. He gestured with an elbow toward the old red heap that housed chemistry and geology.

Ashbury was an architectural hodgepodge. He preferred a more homogeneous architectural plan but understood the demands of funding and benefactors that seem to produce hodgepodges.

"I can remember chemistry experiments in that dreadful hall, Inspector." Twelmeyer sounded very congenial, for a suspect. "A friend of mine went out for coffee one afternoon, leaving some concoction cooking over a Bunsen burner, and when he returned learned that it had blown up the entire laboratory. He's doing high-brow brain research now in Germany." Twelmeyer smiled, and the two walked on, munching on their hot dogs.

Twelmeyer seemed to be neither nervous nor inconvenienced by a visit from a homicide inspector. Poole knew from drama students and others that Twelmeyer was well-liked and intelligent. Given the professor's fairly serene and sophisticated nature, the students found it particularly funny that Twelmeyer was such a prankster. He loved to play practical jokes. For Poole, this combination of traits was a curious one. He couldn't appreciate the sophomoric humor of Limburger cheese on radiators and mooning strangers and friends through car windows… not that these were Twelmeyer's kind of joke...but, Poole wasn't fond of death threats by mail either.

"As Ferris's office partner and colleague, we are hoping you might shed light on this nasty business," Poole began, stopping to wipe mustard from his chin. It was hard to manipulate his cane and lunch at the same time.

As they strolled along the walkway, Poole was struck again by the monastic atmosphere of a small college. It was hard to imagine harm coming to anyone who worked here. Was it possible that any teacher or pupil could cultivate the very singular capacity for murder? Poole's training and experience warned him against sentimentality. Homicide knew no special environment or boundaries and certainly didn't play favorites.

"I'll try, Inspector. It's a terrible tragedy, of course. And, Roger's students will miss him." Twelmeyer's voice was low-pitched and remarkably soothing. Of just average height and in his mid-forties, Twelmeyer looked every inch the college professor. He watched Poole with intense brown eyes. Poole found the man to be comfortably urbane in his wrinkled khakis, blue gingham shirt, and leather boat shoes worn without socks. Poole sensed many contradictions in this self-assured gentleman.

"Who might have wanted to kill Ferris?"

"That's getting down to business quickly," Twelmeyer chuckled and finished off his hot dog. "I have no clear opinions. Roger and I were quite different men. I didn't know him well." The professor spoke with poise, without hesitation, and he politely adjusted his usual fast pace to accommodate Poole's lame gait.

"How did you and Ferris get along?" Poole stepped aside to let a group of female students pass. One of the young ladies smiled at him, and he automatically returned it. Very pretty girl. Poole would never tire of pretty girls.

"Fairly well. I'm not as tidy as Roger and my side of the office annoyed him." Twelmeyer smiled as if annoying Ferris had been a nice entertainment. "But, he did sneak a smoke now and again."

Having seen Twelmeyer's den in Daly Hall Poole could sympathize with Ferris. "We've heard that Ferris may have paid rather too much attention to your wife, sir." Touchy territory.

Twelmeyer crumpled his paper napkin and stopped to discard it in a wire waste bin. Poole thought the drama professor appeared uncomfortable for the first time. "My wife and many other women found Roger fascinating. A big star in a small constellation." The answer was politely evasive.

"You haven't answered the question."

"I merely asked him to confine his attentions to single women. I thought it in poor taste for him to flirt with the wife of a faculty member." At this point Twelmeyer headed across the lawn toward a bench under a stand of silver maples. He must have sensed a greater need for privacy. Poole noticed, too, that the man would not be baited into hot-headed remarks.

Poole willingly followed, wishing he'd bought a Coke to go along with the dog. "Did your wife continue to see Ferris?" He made a direct assumption here, suggesting that Ferris and Valerie were having an affair, hoping to get a reaction from Twelmeyer.

"I don't know, Inspector. It's possible." Twelmeyer apparently agreed with the assumption and reacted by simply looking very unhappy. Again, there was no flare of temper, no indignation. The professor took a seat at one end of the wood bench and stretched his legs in front of him, a relaxed pose perhaps, but Poole felt it revealed great resignation, as if any discussion of his wife's infidelity would simply produce a submissive response. Had he reacted the same way to her indiscretions? Had she continued to torment him in hopes of getting him to show some emotion? Complex psychology. Or, was Twelmeyer pretending not to care just to keep Poole at arm's length?

Finding the shade a relief, Poole shed his jacket and sat down on the other end. "Are you and your wife living together at this time, sir?"

"We've been separated since June. I'm living at the YMCA in Augusta. Until things get sorted out."

A tentative address. Poole knew about the move. Was Twelmeyer counting on a quick reconciliation, now that Ferris was out of the way? Poole said he was sorry to hear that, and then asked if Twelmeyer attended the play and the cast party Saturday night.

"I went to the play alone and planned to go to the party, but I wasn't feeling well and went back to my room." Twelmeyer changed his position on the bench and turned to watch some students throwing a Frisbee on the commons.

"Can anyone substantiate that?"

"The deskman in the lobby may have seen me come in, but I have a single room and didn't speak to anyone." Poole noticed that Twelmeyer nervously swung his leg. What was he lying about? He'd been fairly straightforward until this last point.

"Do you remember Ferris getting some peculiar cut and paste envelopes at the office?"

Twelmeyer twitched a fraction. "Yes, Inspector, he did. Odd. Childish. Envelopes with colored words pasted on them." The professor appeared slightly agitated.

"How did he react?"

"He was very distressed. Said it was crank mail."

"How many of these letters did he get?"

"Three, I believe. Our secretary would know. She thought they were funny."

"What did you think?"

"Roger did not act as if he'd been invited to a party. He actually looked quite ill when he opened the second one. I happened to be there when he did."

A flock of gray birds swooped into the branches overhead and rustled among the leaves. Poole hoped he and Twelmeyer wouldn't be targets. "Did Ferris talk to you about the letters?"

"No, and I never saw the contents." Twelmeyer dabbed at his forehead with a handkerchief. The day had grown extremely humid.

"Did you send the letters? A small joke to give him a jolt or two?" Poole smiled to sweeten the question.

Twelmeyer laughed and turned to look at Poole directly. "I see my reputation for pranks has preceded me. No, I did not send the letters." He sounded wistful, as if he wished he had. Poole wasn't sure if this was good acting or merely an honest reaction.

"Take a look. I have made copies of them." Poole took three pages from his briefcase.

Twelmeyer reluctantly accepted the pages, read the limericks and shook his head. "Looks like Roger was up to his neck in muck." He handed them back. Again, Poole wasn't quite sure how to read the man.

"Any ideas on the identity of the woman, the mountain king, or the sky diver?"

Twelmeyer caught Poole's train of thought and said with some vigor, "No, sir, I do not." Twelmeyer was skilled at keeping his distance.

"When did the first one arrive?"

"April, I'd say. About the time he decided to revamp the summer workshop. What a fuss!" The professor laughed as he glanced into the branches overhead and wisely checked his shoulders. Poole did the same. "Poor place for a bench."

Had the crank mail caused Ferris's drinking and his bad nerves? Poole asked. Twelmeyer said it was possible. Celebrities must take the good with the bad, he added without much sympathy.

"Roger acted unhinged occasionally. Said he wasn't sleeping well. I suppose he took the threats seriously." Twelmeyer didn't sound as if he'd cared then or now. "Odd, he got through the play without crumbling. Must have doubled his Valium intake." The professor offered this as a physician might explain a peculiar cure.

Poole found this interesting. Had Ferris experienced the peace the fatally ill often experience shortly before death takes them?

"One of your neighbors tells us that the day you moved out, you and your wife had a loud argument on the back porch, about you throwing Ferris off the bridge?" Poole couldn't help smiling. He couldn't see this man tossing a dead fish from a bridge. Perhaps he'd saved his fury for the night he murdered Roger.

"Valerie and I have had our share of fights, and I cannot say that I recall the exact wording of any of them. We're not living Noel Coward's 'Private Lives,' but on a good day we come close." He managed a grin. "I did not kill Roger Ferris, Inspector Poole." Twelmeyer sat tall and straight, his posture revealing directness and honesty, something that could be real or merely posed, not a complicated reaction for a teacher of theatre.

"How serious was the rift between Fitzhugh and Ferris?" Poole disliked asking a man to tattle on a friend.

"Justin disliked Roger. That was obvious to everyone. Roger stole Fitzhugh's prize job. But, Justin could never kill another human being anymore than I could." The stern, pedantic tone came close to putting Poole in his place, and Poole was pleased to see the man hang on to his dignity under pressure. He'd endured long years of practice, no doubt, holding his head up while his wife was busy turning him into a damned fool.

Poole rose from the bench stiffly, collected his belongings and leaned on his cane. "You've been very cooperative. Thank you, sir." He handed Twelmeyer his card and shook his hand. The professor's manner had not changed appreciably during the interview. Either he had little to hide or he was as good an actor as he was a coach. There was the alibi to consider. Had he gone home to bed? "Stop by the station. We'll need a formal statement."

"I'd be happy to, Inspector."

The two men crossed the lawn together and bid each other a good afternoon. Twelmeyer headed off toward Daly Hall and Poole to the parking lot.

Back in his office Twelmeyer settled into his chair and surveyed the large airy room, his own again. He sighed contentedly. The blinds were tipped against the strong midday sun; the room arrangement was back the way he liked it with his desk in front of the windows to catch the breeze. Ferris's things had been removed. This moment of satisfaction was dulled slightly by Poole's request to sign a statement, an order that was dangerously official. Could he be in serious trouble? No more than Fitzhugh. Suddenly, the professor felt nervous and alone and wished he and Valerie had stayed together, if for no other reason than to give each other an alibi.

Poole's car occupied a handicapped space in back of Ashbury Hall. He started the engine, popped in a CD of vintage Benny Goodman and listened awhile, the music nearly perfect in its execution, like the effortless idling of the car's old, well-tuned engine. He backed out of his spot and cruised slowly toward the main gates. Gilbert Twelmeyer, another good man, another good suspect, who was lying about something.

Iris,Dolly, and Marjorie had been swimming in the same social pond since birth, a circumstance which counted as friendship in a small town like Belmont. Iris wasn't sure she approved of pre-planned friendships based on family position and generous inheritances, but this was life as they all knew it. She and Dolly were a few years older than Marjorie, but the pond held fishes of many ages and species. Oliver liked to say that Marjorie was part shark….if she ever stopped moving, she would die. Maybe they were all sharks. The three were lunching at Birch Hill Country Club for the sole purpose of prying information out of Marjorie.

"Roger was insane to leave New York," Marjorie said softly, as the three of them settled around a window table. "He was a big TV star. He'd been on Broadway." Marjorie touched her sprayed hair, as if to test whether or not she was something special. Her hair didn't move.

Marjorie Verdun was a mass of contradictions. Fond of preppy outfits in primary colors, the woman looked every inch the perfect, morally prissy society matron, until you found out she was secretly having it off with Roger Ferris in his penthouse while her three kiddies were at school. Iris had to admire that brand of maneuverability.

Today, with that damned ladybug pin perched on her collar like an insect watchdog, dear Marjorie still looked the part she was doomed to play, new money with an aerobics class veneer, the ideal twenty-first century hybrid, a woman who lived to swing a racket, gossip at the health club, and host political coffees for conservative candidates. Her affair with Roger had given her a dash of spunk, Iris decided, at the expense of making her husband, Froggy, look foolish. That was the sad part. Twenty years ago Froggy Verdun would have done anything for Roger. It wasn't the same anymore.

"We thought poor Roger was burned out," Iris commented politely after Marjorie insisted Roger had chosen academia over television, because it was time to give something back to Belmont.

Dolly looked a trifle stunned at this and ordered a large gin and tonic. She quickly said, "Frankly, sweetie, I thought he was quite out of sorts these past few months. Academia must have been too much for him." She winked at Iris when Marjorie looked down to fuss with her napkin.

The waitress took more drink orders and left menus.

"Roger might have been slightly burned out. But, a really good actor can conceal his worst personal problems, can't he?" Marjorie sounded unnaturally coy and then neatly laced manicured fingers at the edge of the table.

What in the world did she mean by that? Iris wondered. She frowned and so did Dolly. Was Marjorie as ignorant about Roger's personal life as everyone else? Had she simply accepted the actor for what he was, an over-sexed male who willingly satisfied her raging hormonal appetites? Fortyish baby boomers did tend to go bonkers. Who didn't know that?

The drinks arrived, and the ladies ordered lunch.

"How did you get to know Roger so well?" Dolly asked, as innocently as she could. "Did he confide in you about his problems?"

Marjorie shrugged her neat shoulders. "We've been friends since childhood. You know that. He and Froggy were buddies in high school. Roger simply found moving back home tougher than he'd imagined. Adjustments. A new job, seeing his parents again on a regular basis."

Not very convincing, Iris decided.

"What happened between Roger and Froggy after Iris's party?" Dolly asked. "The Liebermanns are telling the story all over town."

Dolly and Iris were laughing now.

Marjorie looked pained this time. "It was nothing! A teeny weeny misunderstanding between the boys."

"Come on, Marjorie, a misunderstanding?" Iris laughed again. "Sam Liebermann swears he heard Froggy threaten to kill Roger." She took a fortifying swallow of her drink. And, teeny weeny? Good grief, this might turn into a three G&T lunch. "Didn't they have a fist fight at the Currents Café a month ago?"

"Froggy got very jealous over my friendship with Roger." Marjorie's thin lips hardened. "Absolute nonsense. Why shouldn't old friends have supper together?" She concentrated for a moment on her wine and then dabbed her mouth daintily with the napkin.

Iris hissed across the table, "Some of us thought you and Roger were planning to run off to New York." She followed the salvo with an 'I'll-never-tell' grin.

"Really, Iris! That's preposterous!" Marjorie's blush quickly tinted her perfect tennis court tan, and she quickly fingered the bug pin on her collar. A small comfort token, perhaps.

Iris remembered how the actor looked that night, a fair-haired god, surrounded by adoring females, and never without a drink. Marjorie would throw him a possessive glance at every opportunity. Iris had watched him blow her a sexy kiss when he thought no one was looking. Dreams of running away with Roger must have filled Marjorie's days and nights. Iris doubted Roger ever dreamed the same dream. An eternity had passed since that pretty June night.

"Didn't you and Roger get together in New York last year?" Dolly asked. "When you and Froggy were separated."

Marjorie had spent several months in New York, after abandoning her children and Froggy for a trial separation.

"Occasionally…for a drink or lunch." Marjorie sounded evasive. "I was staying with Bunny and Leo. You remember the Drummonds, my aunt and uncle who retired to Long Island? He passed away while I was there, sweet old darling."

Iris remembered the Drummonds, a peculiar couple who were first cousins and looked like twins. It was rumored they were actually brother and sister. Leo inherited a railroad fortune when he was twenty and rarely spent any of it. Luckily, there were no children.

Dolly said, "Did Uncle Leo remember you in his will?"

"I was his only niece, and Uncle Leo absolutely adored Froggy and me."

Dolly looked over at Iris. Enough said. Marjorie now had enough money to start her own country.

Dolly said, "Lucky you. I've heard that Roger ran a couple of TV production companies. Did he offer to make you a business partner?"

"He did. Even though he was doing quite well." Marjorie eyed Dolly with suspicion now.

"You have always had a good nose for a smart investment," Dolly replied simply.

Iris would have bet her own bank account that Marjorie had counted on Roger to rescue her from boring Belmont, if she handed over enough cash. Marjorie's discontent with small town life was almost as old as she was.

"Roger had a business partner. A rich society woman, I think. Those New York blue bloods have a thing for good-looking celebrities, you know. They swarm like vultures out there. You should see them." Marjorie grinned, maliciously. The wine has loosed her tongue.

Their salads arrived. Iris sighed internally and looked around her. Here they were, eating a predictable lunch at the country club, a predictable choice. Why did they always order salads? Why not just dessert and to hell with the calories and cholesterol? The elegant dining room overlooked the back nine with its immaculate expanse of perfectly tended green, shaded here and there by oaks. The room buzzed with polite conversation, the only kind allowed at Birch Hills. Few guests ever laughed out loud. Iris had grown up eating lunch at snooty clubs like this. Her family founded this one a hundred years ago. One of her great, great uncles had a passion for golf and money. She would have preferred Elsa's downtown where customers didn't look like they might fall asleep or die before coffee was served. But, Marjorie had insisted on the country club.

"Have the police called on you?" Iris asked as she attacked the salad. "I'm sure we'll all be questioned."

"Actually, I'm more worried for Froggy," Marjorie told them in a hushed voice. "He left the house the night Roger died… after midnight. And, he took my car."

Dolly dropped her salad fork. The utensil landed on the carpet with a dull thud, which made Iris realize that hers was mid-air, dripping oil and vinegar. What did Marjorie say?

"Do you think Froggy went to see Roger?" Dolly asked, barely breathing and trying to retrieve her fork at the same time.

"My car was seen in front of the building. The building manager called to tell me. It could have been Froggy. He....he hated Roger." Marjorie picked at her greens, perhaps uncomfortable about telling too much.

"What did Froggy say about this?" asked Iris.

Marjorie shook her head. "Nothing. I keep thinking he'll tell me."

Iris was stunned. Dear Froggy. Did he love Marjorie so much that he risked another show-down with Roger? Was the man crazy enough to kill the actor in his bed? Suddenly, the salad and the G &T didn't look very appetizing.

Dolly said, "I hope Froggy has a good lawyer." She put down her fork, her hand heavy on the table, her pretty, expressive face revealing her distress.

Iris prayed that what they were all thinking was not true. Froggy was such a nice man.

"Freddy, it's Iris. Dolly and I just had lunch with Lady Marjorie."

"Ah, missed my chance again." Donovan was in his car on the cell phone. He was meeting his wife for BLTs. "Her car was parked in front of Ferris's building that night. Keep that under your curls, Babe." Ching was sitting up front like a hairy old man, keeping an eye on anything that moved and a nose tuned for entrancing smells.

"In the vault," Iris promised. "Marjorie actually pointed her finger at the Frog! Hard to believe. She thinks Froggy drove over to see Roger and used her car. The woman makes my blood run cold."

"Definitely reptilian," Donovan agreed. "Is she sure it was Froggy? Does she have teenagers who drive?"

"No. Too young. It was the Frog. Or, she'd like everybody to think so. Do you think she might be the driver?"

"A possibility. What else did you find out, my girl?"

"Roger had a rich business partner. No name. A well-to-do female… blue-blood, what else? And, she admitted she saw Roger last summer in New York, when she and the Frog were separated."

"Nice work, Babe. Want to join the force?" Donovan pulled up in front of the Half Moon Luncheonette, directly across from Iris's office at the weekly. "I can practically see you from here."

"I am trying out my new ergonomically designed chair which promises to save my posterior from either atrophy or the dreaded spread." Iris laughed.

Donovan could see Iris waving from the front bay window. He tooted the horn. Iris always made him feel like a teenager.

"I have two jobs already. Besides, you have Oliver. Dead bodies are his business. He's lived through this stuff."

"For a price. I'm not fond of guys who break knee caps for a living."

Donovan soon rang off, climbed out of his car and tied Ching to an awning pole outside the restaurant. After promising the dog extra bacon, Donovan followed his nose inside.

6

THRILL OF THE HUNT

Later that afternoon in the police station waiting room, Professor Justin Fitzhugh seated himself in a molded plastic chair the color of swimming pool water and immediately found he could slide down and forward every few seconds without any effort at all. The chair's idiotic design was so annoying he began to dream of ways he might toss the chair out a window, without notice. His mood was black and not helped by the fear building in his bones. What could Lieutenant Donovan want? Questions Sunday night and now more? Should he have an attorney? Or, should he have told Gilbert? No, poor Gilbert had his own rows to hoe. There was Valerie. Drama school never prepared either one of them for the role of murder suspect; Justin felt cheated and took a deep breath.

The small waiting room was a drab square that smelled of old varnish and cleaning compounds. Two arched windows stood open to air so pregnant it was nearly liquid. Outside, the Mississippi was providing its neighbors with a distinctive redolence that brought to mind rotting boats and bait pails. Summer wasn't Justin's favorite season; he preferred the purity of snow, the diamond clarity of icicles. With the morning brilliance gone, he smelled a storm brewing and felt the sinister hand of trouble on his thin shoulders.

Who had chosen those awful curtains, limp panels of oatmeal cotton splashed with orange and yellow leaves, a dismal reminder of fifties decorating? Or, was it the awful seventies? Hell, nobody had any taste in either decade. And who was that young woman behind the desk, staring at him as if he were either naked or terribly famous? Fitzhugh screwed up his face at her and then picked up his book, *Brat Farrar* by Josephine Tey.

As the minutes passed, Justin found himself racing through a ridiculous medley of tics and coughs, enough to make the desk sergeant snicker into her hand. After clearing his throat and polishing his glasses a third time, Justin popped a breath mint and returned to his mystery novel. When he looked up and saw the young woman staring at him again, he crossed his eyes at her and stuck out his tongue. This time she covered her mouth with her hand and giggled out loud. Horrid little female.

Not a minute later, a large red chow chow appeared at the top of the stairs, followed by Lieutenant Donovan and Inspector Poole. The detectives greeted him cordially while the dog sniffed his trouser cuffs. The four of them proceeded down an oddly crooked corridor to Donovan's office.

Inside Freddy's office, Poole suggested they get started and he took a chair by the window. Fitzhugh seated himself uncertainly in a visitor's chair; Donovan assumed his position of authority behind the desk. Ching hunkered beneath it for a nap. Donovan explained the interview procedure again and turned on a small tape machine. The machine triggered a fresh batch of squirms and coughs from Fitzhugh, clear indications to Poole that Mr. Fitzhugh was terror-stricken. He offered the professor a cigarette, which Fitzhugh managed to light it without too much embarrassment.

"Professor," Donovan began, "run through that cast party again, will you?" He flipped open a brown notebook and touched a stubby pencil to his tongue. Donovan smiled at Fitzhugh, a genuine smile, an expression of compassion rarely seen in this line of work. Poole admired Donovan for it.

Fitzhugh repeated his story, the same information he had recited Sunday night. About fifteen or twenty students and faculty sat around Ferris's condo for drinks and a late deli supper. It was all very friendly.

The play had been a big success. Fitzhugh inhaled deeply and then politely blew the smoke to the side. While Fitzhugh described the celebration, Poole listened and took stock of the man…fortyish, tall, thin, with a British handsomeness to his long face. His clothes were conservative and expensive. Poole guessed the man was gay.

"Any arguments, uninvited guests?" Poole asked.

"No. The party was unusual only in that it was held at Ferris's apartment. Most cast parties are held on stage or at a local student hang-out." Fitzhugh's voice had lost some of its quaver.

Poole tried to imagine Fitzhugh conquering stage fright. He asked why Ferris chose to have the party at his residence?

"He obviously wanted to show it off. There was considerable curiosity about the place. Most of us can't afford penthouses outfitted like art galleries." Fitzhugh's tone was snotty.

Poole surmised that apart from professional resentment, there may have lurked within the professor a strong sexual jealousy. "Was your friend Twelmeyer there?"

"No, he went home. Said he didn't feel well." Fitzhugh was settling down. He ground out his cigarette and helped himself to M&Ms from Donovan's ashtray candy dish.

Donovan asked, "How was Ferris?"

"Fine. Played the gracious host, a bit grand, I thought. He was pleased with the production. He did have a few vodka tonics."

"Did he spend time alone with anyone? A young woman perhaps?" Donovan wanted to know.

Fitzhugh said he had not noticed.

"When did you leave?" Donovan put his weight on his elbows.

"About twelve-thirty." Fitzhugh named the colleagues who left with him and those who stayed behind.

Donovan got up and sat on the corner of the desk. "What do you suppose made Ferris so nervous the past few weeks of his life?"

Fitzhugh said he had no idea.

Figuring the professor could withstand a major offensive at this juncture, Poole said, "Ferris got your plum job in January, didn't he?"

Fitzhugh's newfound control crumbled immediately. "Roger had Broadway and television credentials," he sputtered. "I could never compete with that kind of experience and notoriety. On the other hand,

Roger had no teaching qualifications whatever. He was hired for his celebrity." Fitzhugh was still angry and was making no bones about it.

"You and Ferris battled, right?" Donovan kept going.

"We didn't see eye to eye on departmental matters. He was ignorant of certain academic policies and procedures." The snotty tone had crept back.

"You were heard to threaten Ferris, especially when he took over your summer program." The students had mentioned Fitzhugh's moods and fights with Ferris.

"Explosions of temper." Fitzhugh allowed himself a weak smile. "Roger loved power plays."

"But, Ferris wound up dead, Professor, and you are still walking around." Donovan kept his voice civil.

"I did not kill Roger. We didn't like each other, but I wasn't the only one at Ashbury who'd had a belly full of him." Fitzhugh stomped his foot on the floor, probably without thinking, Poole decided.

The noise woke the dog, who crawled out from beneath the desk to sniff Fitzhugh's polished loafers. When Fitzhugh brushed the dog away, the animal retreated to Donovan's side, unaccustomed to rebuff. Once again, Poole found the whole thing very theatrical, like a scene out of Agatha Christie seventy-five years ago.

"Go on," said Poole. He was still trying to link Fitzhugh with the limericks. He didn't see the nervous professor in any of them. Of course, the killer didn't necessarily have to be the author of the threatening letters. Ferris had accumulated an admirable number of enemies in his few months in Belmont.

"Ferris didn't deserve the job, and the Dean was gaga over him. Big TV star, the legitimate theatre, a feather in the Dean's cap. The prestige and publicity for the school was tremendous. The old geezer loves lots of show. And, big contributions."

Fitzhugh got up and began pacing. "The ninny doesn't know that Ferris called him a goat, a pathetic back-lander. Used to imitate him in the lounge." And in a rush of confidence, Fitzhugh pointed his finger at the detectives and yelled, "How dare you accuse me? There are plenty of others who had motives." Then, the professor let his long arms fall to his sides in a gesture of surrender.

"Don't get your drawers in a twist," Donovan advised the man kindly. "We ask everybody hard questions. Who else had motive?"

"Heavens, check into his love life. There must be a dozen husbands lined up and waiting to kill him. And you can't tell me he didn't make enemies in New York after twenty years?" Fitzhugh couldn't offer anybody specific.

"Where did you go after the party?" the Irishman asked.

"I met a friend at Elsa's about twelve-forty-five."

Elsa's was a popular downtown hangout, haunted by the well-dressed and the well-heeled, an upper class meat market. Donovan asked for specifics.

Fitzhugh hesitated, thought better of it, and then gave out Charles Morgan's name and number. "He's in the English department. We went back to my place."

Outside, the sky was darkening, much like Fitzhugh's mood and situation.

"Did you see the threatening letters sent to Ferris?" Poole asked. He slipped the plastic covered poems over to Fitzhugh.

Fitzhugh read the limericks carefully and then gushed, "You have got to be kidding!" His astonishment was real enough. "Was our Roger leading a double life? These could make anybody act crazy." Fitzhugh looked somewhat elated after reading the threats.

Out of the mouths of babes and murder suspects, Poole thought. "Did Twelmeyer mention these?" This would be the kind of thing two old friends would find very funny.

"No, he didn't." Fitzhugh's mood had risen to cheerful.

"Any idea about the poet's identity?" Poole asked. He found it odd that Twelmeyer had never shared his scant information about the odd letters with Fitzhugh, his best friend. Was Twelmeyer suspicious of Fitzhugh?

"There are plenty of clever people at the college who would find this hilarious."

"Did Ferris ever tell you why he never reads obituaries?" Poole asked. He was still trying to find somebody who might know the answer to this one.

"Obituaries? No, Inspector. But, I would imagine he'd be stunned to see his own, don't you think?" Fitzhugh managed a tight smile. "I'm sure he never dreamed of murder."

Standing again, Donovan said, "Well, Professor, we appreciate your cooperation. You'll have to sign a statement, of course, but you can go now."

With this abrupt dismissal, Fitzhugh fairly flew out of the room. Poole closed the door behind him.

"Scared rabbit," Poole observed quietly. "Nice motive. We'll see what Mr. Morgan has to say. What do you think, Father Donovan?" Poole thought his brogue was improving.

"I feel sorry for the guy. He got a rotten deal at Ashbury. He could have gone back to the penthouse on some pretense that night. Ferris might have let him in. Fitzhugh's pal, Morgan, might back him up." Donovan threw a handful of M&Ms into his mouth. "Why are we in this racket?" The Irishman mopped his face with a handkerchief. "I'd sooner haul in window peepers."

"The thrill of the hunt, Freddy. Look who is in our lair… Lady Marjorie and her quick-tempered husband, Froggy; the mysterious villains in the limericks, including our wildly unbalanced poet; a pair of eccentric professors, and the always lovely, Miss Valerie. It's like the cast of Bat Man." Poole wiped dust from his shoes with a tissue and tossed it into the basket. "We're lining up the ducks."

"It's your swamp, Oliver."

Poole understood. And, Freddy would never feel at home in it.

Fitzhugh left the police station in a state of alarm, bedeviled with shallow breathing, dizziness, and a strong desire to flee, even though his legs felt incapable of flight. He recognized the symptoms of panic attack; he'd read about it in the 'Ask the Doctor' column just last week. As he wobbled to his car, Fitzhugh prayed for his own survival.

Before getting into the Saab, Fitzhugh glanced up at the Hall's second story windows where Donovan's office overlooked the parking lot. Were they spying on him? Would a cop in a bad suit tail him for days? His phone would be tapped. They knew so much so soon; their efficiency shocked him. The detectives had dubbed him their number one suspect in just three days.

Settling behind the wheel, Fitzhugh ordered himself to calm down again or things could get worse. Once cops smelled fear, you were as good as behind bars, he told himself smartly. He buzzed down the window. The muggy air was holding its breath; the storm was only minutes away. God, he needed a drink. But, first, he must call Charles, one of his old pals, someone who might help him.

Fitzhugh drove almost wildly the short way to the Wrenn Park public phone box. He was afraid to use his cell. He and Charles could work out a story, that is, if Charles was a true friend. He would soon find out.

Beyond a row of weather-worn brick warehouses, a coil of black thunderheads was rolling in from the plains like a band of Indians ready to attack a wagon train. Two blocks south, the steel river bridge rose to face it, a single skeletal arm poised to fight off the siege. Did the world have to be so damned dramatic? Fitzhugh continued to mutter as he pulled in near the pier.

As he alighted from the car, a gust of wind tore across the pavement sending a spiral of grit into the air to powder his face. Spitting in disgust, Fitzhugh ran for the phone box next to the River Queen Cruise Company ticket office. Its tiny window was shuttered against the storm. Rain the size of silver dollars began to pelt his head and shoulders as he dove into the phone box.

Charles answered on the second ring and sounded happy to hear from him, happy until he understood what Fitzhugh was asking him to do.

"Justin, I don't know," Charles whined without troubling to cover up his contempt. "I'd rather not get involved. A homicide investigation? Alibis? Not exactly my kind of thing."

Morgan's glibness infuriated Fitzhugh more than his refusal to help.

"Damn it, Charles! You must tell them we were together!" Fitzhugh leaned against the side of the booth which rocked and trembled with each new blast of wind. Rain curtained the small glass windows causing Fitzhugh to go slightly claustrophobic. "I can't believe this. We're friends, for Christ's sake."

Lightning flashed at the far end of the park and cracked a tree, splitting off a limb and dropping it to the ground with a crash. Fitzhugh wondered if phone booths were as safe as cars during a storm.

"Can't you see my side?" Charles was trying to sound reasonable. "We'll have to testify in court. Think of the publicity, the gossip, our jobs." He stalled. "I don't want my name and reputation dragged through a murder trial."

Coward. "In other words, you think I'm guilty!" Fitzhugh wanted to tear the little hair he had right out of his head. "You don't want people to know what they've already figured out. Charles, you're out of the closet, whether you know it or not."

"Not exactly, Justin."

"What the hell does that mean?" A stab of hate whizzed through Fitzhugh's heart. Up in the heavens a pair of wood paddles smacked out another clatter of thunder, like punishment. "And, you don't mind seeing me wrung through the wringer," Fitzhugh exploded. "I am a suspect, whether I like it or not. And whether you like it or not, you are my alibi. The police have your name." Hah! One small triumph.

"That's a goddamned threat." Morgan was fighting back. "You don't have to get so damned nasty about this. Give me time!" Morgan moaned as if injured. "I'd hate to think I'm your only salvation." And he slammed down the phone.

"I wish you weren't," Fitzhugh screamed into the dead receiver.

Salvation? What did Charles Morgan know of salvation? Fitzhugh was fuming as he drove home. Old Charlie's back wasn't up against the jailhouse wall. Forcing Morgan to step into the light was a minor inconvenience by comparison.

Once back in his apartment on Caledonia Circle, Fitzhugh lay on a damask camel-back sofa with his shoes off and a cold cloth on his forehead.

"Games. More goddamned games!" Fitzhugh groaned aloud. The sour taste of fear had coated his tongue. His pulse was fluttering rapidly. His hands were clammy. What was he supposed to do? His fingerprints were all over Ferris's penthouse. There were witnesses who'd heard him threaten to kill the bastard, more than once. If Charles didn't come through, he'd have to hire a lawyer, a very good, very expensive lawyer.

He thought immediately of Burton Dance, who some said could have persuaded a jury to free Charles Manson.

Fitzhugh got up and began circling the room, feeling the smooth wood floor through his socks. He nervously ran his hands through his hair and began a litany of profanity aimed at Ferris, Morgan and anybody else who'd ever disappointed him. On his last turn around the living room, he altered the orbit and headed for the kitchen where he switched on the lights. A drink would help him think more clearly. But before he could take another step, lightning ripped the sky and punched out the power, leaving him in the unconditional dark of a closed wardrobe.

Fitzhugh cursed the darkness again; the profanity was insignificant but comforting in the windowless space lined with cupboards and appliances. Fumbling his way along the cabinet doors, he opened the last one, knocking over something that crashed to the tile floor and broke. When he finally felt the familiar shape of the vodka bottle, he quickly unscrewed the cap and gulped, dribbling liquor down his chin and shirt. Treachery surrounded him. The storm, the dark, booby-trapped cupboards, and broken glass. He could feel a sharp splinter puncture the bottom of his foot. He swallowed more alcohol, faint fumes wafted up his nose. He loved the subtlety of vodka, the purity of it.

Leaning backward against the counter Fitzhugh drank until his mind began to fuzz over. The vodka was working its usual magic. Cunning vodka. He knew this would solve nothing; he was in serious trouble. The police knew he had motive and opportunity. Of course, any damned fool could have stabbed the son-of-a-bitch with a kitchen knife. It had taken little skill or preparation. Fitzhugh's panic began to smooth itself into a nice straight line.

Holding tight to the bottle, he slid down the slick cabinets to the floor, somehow missing the broken glass scattered around him. Tucking the bottle beneath his arm, he pulled off his sock and carefully plucked the offending glass from his toe. Then, he sat for a long time, darkness wrapped around him like a shawl, rain pelting the windows, the grumbling thunder moving off to the east. He decided to get drunk as long as he was close anyway, and soon the quiet closed in until all he could hear was the hum of the refrigerator and his own breathing.

"I wonder if Gilbert will help me. Jeesuz." Fitzhugh spoke aloud, his slurred words bouncing crookedly off the stove. The darkness was almost as scary as the thought of going to prison. He could have wept but instead fell into a fitful sleep filled with bloody knives and uniformed guards carrying billy clubs.

Fitzhugh's nap turned out to be as brief as the storm, and not ten minutes later he woke to find the overhead light shining on him. His scavenger's nest was feathered with broken glass, a lone tan sock, and an empty vodka bottle cuddled next to his hip. He made no effort to move, knowing he had drunk far too much. One thing was perfectly clear; Ferris's death had solved nothing. While he was still alive, Roger managed to make life miserable for him and a good many others. It would seem the man was doing an even better job of it now that he was dead.

A minute after Fitzhugh disappeared down the corridor Poole took a call from Ingrid Ferris. She suggested he wait for the storm to pass and then stop by before dinner, before Reggie returned from the hospital. Poole said he would be there in about an hour. Ingrid Ferris had been Roger's favorite parent, and Poole was counting on her to tell him why.

"This was Roger's playroom when he was little," Ingrid said, as she and Poole entered a large third floor room. The storm had passed fairly quickly, leaving the world renewed and sunny again. "When Roger was older, we converted it to his sanctum sanctorum." Ingrid laughed a little at the pet name. She seemed comforted by the rooms.

As they toured Roger's private quarters, Poole felt a great sadness for the woman. Her only son had been murdered, and the press had been hounding the family since Sunday, waiting like vultures for the funeral and the burial, waiting to learn who had butchered a handsome local boy known to millions who watched afternoon television. No aspect of Roger's life or his parent's life would be too trivial. Overnight, a minor celebrity's existence had become fresh fodder for the kind of tabloid sleaze that made Poole's teeth itch. Media junkies fed on misery and frailty and didn't mind turning a homicide into ten minutes of thrill and chill entertainment.

The inspector's impression of Ferris remained unclear; the penthouse more closely resembled a place of business or a gallery. Here, in this boyhood sanctum with its comfortable old furniture, a collection of beer cans, and posters of rock stars and athletes, Roger had revealed more of himself than he had as an adult. His love of art and austerity had obviously come later.

The small bedroom that faced the back yard held a double bed, desk, and chest of drawers. Shelves and bookcases were cluttered with sports trophies, magazines, framed photographs. It appeared that Ferris had been an excellent tennis player and swimmer, and he'd loved to ride horses. The Ferrises had left the rooms as they were twenty years ago, clean and orderly for his return.

Situated at each end of the roomy third floor were identical tower rooms, windowed all around like tiny lighthouses, miniature hideaways that must have been magical places for a child and a young, imaginative boy. The view stretched across Belmont to the Mississippi on west and to the ridge of bluffs rising in the east.

"Very nice. Spectacular views," Poole commented to Ingrid, as they took in the magnificent valley panorama.

"Roger loved it up here. He called it his dream tower."

Poole asked if he might look through Roger's things and Ingrid agreed, leaving him to search. After fifteen minutes Poole realized that there was little to be found except a photo album on a shelf crammed with sports magazines. A quick glance showed snapshots of Roger and his friends taken during high school, clowning at the beach, riding horses, posing foolishly at parties, sitting on the hoods of cars. They were the usual goofy pictures people take when they're young. Most were annotated and dated on the back. Ferris's penchant for organization had begun early.

"Tell me who these kids are," Poole said, sitting down on a lumpy sofa with a blue slipcover. "I feel I should know some of them."

Ingrid bent over the photo album and recited names, "Marjorie and Froggy Verdun, Diane and Peter Sorensen, the Morton twins and their girl friends. I'm using married names now. Most still live around here." She pointed out familiar faces. Froggy Verdun had amassed a fortune in the construction business after getting an engineering degree. Ingrid offered thumbnail sketches of the others. Poole was vaguely familiar with a few of the names and faces but not well acquainted. He was a few years older than this crowd.

"How about the blonde?" Poole pointed to a tall, slender girl who appeared with Roger in several pictures. In this one she was dressed in western hat and jeans and big sunglasses standing next to a dapple gray horse.

"That's Annette Wrenn. She was Roger's girlfriend for a short time. Of course, he dated Marjorie too. They all loved riding and boarded their horses at a stable in Abner's Coulee."

"Annette Wrenn? Is she Beatrice's niece?"

"Yes. Her parents died in a plane crash. She lived with Beatrice and the grandmother. Quiet girl, but nice enough. Took the death of her parents very hard."

"Does she still live in town?"

"Last winter I tried to get Roger's friends together for a party and called Beatrice about her, but she had no current address for Annette." Ingrid sounded annoyed. "Why can't children keep in touch with their families?"

"Perhaps she married," Poole replied. "By the way, I seem to recall a case I worked on about twenty years ago….a young man fell to his death in the bluffs. The body was found by your son, I believe, and a girl. Am I right about that?" Poole had planned to look up the old case hadn't found the time.

"Why yes, Inspector. He and Annette found the body. I don't recall the details."

Poole made a mental note to dig further." He pointed to another girl in the pictures who looked like Annette's sister.

"That's Meredith, Annette's cousin. They were inseparable. I never knew her well. A rather odd girl, as I recall. Barely spoke."

"The Wrenns are an eccentric tribe, aren't they?" Poole said with an appreciative smile. He liked people with an edge, with peculiarities.

"Frankly, Inspector, Beatrice is just what we need in this town. She is known affectionately as our 'kick in the pants.' I can't remember who stuck that moniker on her." Ingrid laughed."You know, Inspector Poole, my husband was once married to Beatrice. A long time ago. She tried to strangle him one night," Ingrid said, laughing and with genuine appreciation for what had happened. "After catching him in bed with his nurse." Ingrid Ferris apparently bore no grudges. "I would have done the same thing. He knew he deserved it and never pressed charges. They were divorced soon after and Beatrice never married again."

Poole found the story funny; he'd never heard it before. "I trust Beatrice isn't still after him."

"No, but they still annoy each other, no end. It's part of the old feud. The Wrenns and the Ferrises have no love for each other. To make matters worse, Beatrice and I are very good friends." She laughed heartily at this and then grew somber. "I want you to know that Roger was not himself this spring. I couldn't tell you with Reggie around. He doesn't want me to say anything about Roger's drinking or his bad nerves."

"I understand," Poole said. "What was bothering your son?"

"I don't know. But, I think he was afraid." Ingrid frowned and dabbed at her eyes with a handkerchief. "I think he was very, very afraid."

"Did he say he'd been threatened?" The limericks, tucked away at the station, came to mind. Poole needed time to examine them further before he showed them to the Ferrises.

"No, but he did say that he owned a gun."

Ingrid Ferris was obviously tired and distressed. Poole said by way of some small comfort, "We'll find the killer, Mrs. Ferris. Count on it."

Ingrid seemed relieved and suggested he take the photo album. Poole was bothered by the fact that no gun had been recovered among Ferris's belongings. Where in the hell was it?

Outside on the street, an almost lethal humidity robbed Poole of breath and instantly suggested the restorative powers of a cold beer at Billy's. He knew Freddy would be there.

"Oliver," Donovan said with rare authority, "before we go leaping off a cliff that's not nearly high enough to do the job, we need to know *exactly* where Fitzhugh and the Twelmeyers really were that night. And the Verduns." Alibis needed more checking. Donovan hitched his chair closer to the table and tucked a large white napkin into his collar.

Hog Heaven. That was the name of the restaurant, a rib joint on the south side of town, the finger-licking version of the higher-toned Depot establishment near the brewery. They'd had a beer at Billy's and moved on to supper.

"Shipstead's checking everybody again, but I get the feeling a few of our suspects weren't sleeping in their own beds that night."

Poole gave Donovan the standard guy look. Freddy figured Oliver ought to know. He picked up the menu card and looked it over…..pork ribs, short ribs, eye-watering sauce, lip-burning sauce, and sauce for chickens. Very catchy. Oliver had just given him the gist of the meeting with Ingrid Ferris, and Freddy relayed Iris's latest gossip about Marjorie. They would catch up with the Verduns tomorrow.

"There is Marjorie's car," Poole pointed out again. "And, the old feud between the Wrenns and the Ferrises, which has an intriguing ring to it; and Annette Wrenn, one of Roger's old flames, mysteriously missing." Poole rubbed his hands together. "Lady Marjorie is not our only suspect, Freddy. We have been blessed."

Donovan watched his old friend. The bits and pieces that made up a homicide had energized him. Oliver. Work always rehabilitated any man who loves his job.

The two detectives gave their dinner order to a college kid, who would never be a waiter for life, and drank Pfeiffers with appreciation. The heat of July wasn't giving up without a fight, storm or no storm. A half dozen standing rotary fans, relics from the forties, were cooling the eatery with intermittent gusts of air that lifted the edges of the tablecloths and ruffled hairdos. No air conditioning had been installed in this old hole-in-the-wall.

Donovan would have liked to talk baseball for an hour, or get Oliver rhapsodizing about an obscure jazz combo, but he figured it would never happen. Hell, he'd even listen to Oliver play a few tunes. He was sick of homicide.

"Marjorie's rich, spoiled, and wouldn't tolerate getting dumped."

Oliver was going on, a born terrier with a new sock. Donovan refilled their glasses from the sweating pitcher.

"Let's say Marjorie and Ferris rekindle the fires in New York. She gives the guy a heap of cash for his art collection or his enterprises…. she thinks she's investing in her own future. On some pretense, each one returns to Belmont. True to his genetic code, Ferris starts fooling around with Valerie Twelmeyer and a half dozen willing coeds and bored housewives. Mrs. Verdun gets mightily pissed off. Eventually, they fight; Ferris says get lost. Lady Marjorie decides on a course of revenge…..a few nasty poems to scare the hell of out of him, and then a knife to his black heart."

"Sounds OK to me. You're the expert." Donovan munched on a large pretzel dipped in hot mustard. "What about the postmarks on the limerick envelopes? One from New York, two from Belmont. Marjorie came back home long before April."

"She probably hired an unsuspecting pal in New York to mail it for her. Got her old auntie to do it."

Donovan thought this might be stretching it.

Poole tried the fat pretzels while taking stock of two pretty women at a nearby table. One looked vaguely familiar to Donovan. Where had he seen her?

"Now, Oliver, the blonde's half your age and twice as cute." The Irish priest scolding the sinner. "Isn't it time to start looking for older ladies." He giggled like a kid.

Poole ignored the advice and gave the blonde a well-practiced smile. "I might be closing in on fifty, Freddy, but I'm not dead."

"Getting back to your theories, Oliver. Remember, the theories should come close to fitting those damned limericks. Who's this 'King of the World' character? What about the reference to sky-diving? This all sounds like the New York crowd to me. Nobody around here sky dives."

Poole frowned. "Notations in Ferris's appointment book shows what looks like an 'M.V.' a half dozen times in the three weeks before his death, including the night he died. Marjorie Verdun? And, our boy noted appointments with 'A' between June and December of the previous year. A pet name for Marjorie, no doubt. Angel cakes, maybe?"

Donovan told Poole he was full of it. "We can't trust his handwriting; it's worse than mine. They could be dates with his masseuse or a bookmaker." Donovan wanted his supper.

"Don't forget 'A' for Annette, if you like long shots. Think I'll have Beatrice Wrenn read the tarot cards for me."

Donovan grinned. "There's a blonde in your future. So young she's never heard of Brubeck." The young women at the next table were enjoying Poole's scattered attention.

The ribs arrived, glistening with red sauce and sharing the plate with crispy cottage fries and coleslaw speckled with red and green peppers. With its chrome and Formica accoutrements, Hog Heaven might be short on atmosphere, but no one could deny the mouthwatering food and the delectable old photos of Marilyn Monroe that spruced up the walls.

"Autopsy report came in when you were out." Donovan's famous appetite waned at the recollection of vivid police photos of the victim. He managed a few healthy swallows of Pfeiffers to push aside the spasms. "No good prints. Blood type in the bathroom was Ferris's. Same for the knife. Death from deep wounds in the chest and throat. Alcohol and Valium in his blood, not enough to kill him, not enough to knock him out. A mellow fellow." Donovan rattled off the rest. "Ferris was a normal, healthy male for his age. No serious diseases."

"Could have guessed as much. Too bad about the prints." Poole poured ketchup on his cottage fries. "And the mask?"

"Had nothing to do with his death, according to Sutter. Cute touch, he called it." Donovan licked his fingers and pulled another rib from the rack.

"We might get lucky on the charm and the cigarette case. It's still early days, Freddy. And, the murder costume might turn up."

"Maybe our killer works in the buff, Oliver." The Irishman leered over a forkful of coleslaw. "The boys went through every dumpster and trash barrel for blocks. Must have taken his wardrobe with him, if he had one. Or, she."

Poole stole another peek at the blonde. "Ah, she's an actress at the Repertory, Freddy." Poole nodded subtly toward the blonde. "Very sharp. Terrific legs. Probably knows Max Tarry like the back of her hand."

"Why don't you pass her a note, you old hound. Offer to buy a pint of sauce to take home." Donovan smirked. He loved watching Poole operate. And, he noticed, Poole was still stewing about Iris's current beau, the illustrious playwright, known for his work and a splendid collection of beautiful ex-wives....all of them actresses.

"And you would know all about it, I suppose."

"Go for it, you randy devil," the very married Donovan hissed back. "Ooops, almost forgot. A bartender at the OK Lounge in Augusta called while you were with Mrs. Ferris. He said Ferris and a tall, dark-haired woman came in two weeks ago. The woman had an ankle wrapped in an Ace bandage. Miss Sprain, he called her. They had a few drinks."

"Did Miss Sprain have a southern accent?"

"He didn't hear her speak. Ferris did the ordering."

"We'd better double check. The delicious Mrs. Twelmeyer has a Georgia drawl and she studied dramatics." Poole shifted in his chair. "She could be our phone caller; she could be Miss Sprain."

"Mrs. Twelmeyer?" Donovan giggled and wiped his whiskers with a napkin. "A weak ankle to go with her other weaknesses. I like that."

Poole smiled. "Valerie might be a dish, but she also has a disposition for theatrics. She might think it's a hoot to put on a wig, fake a twisted ankle, and pretend to be somebody else. Her story about seeing Roger with a lady in a big hat could have been a description of herself." Poole sounded comfortable with the rationale. "Or, Ferris had another lady friend. The man's appetites were impressive."

Donovan grinned. A nice observation about appetites from a man who was currently dating two women, flirting with a third and still longing to get his wife back.

Poole's cell phone sang out. He listened, clicked off, and said, "That was Moreno. I sent him back to the condo to have another look around. When I checked Ferris's papers, I never found any references, invoices, or bills on the artwork. Not in character for Ferris, who was obsessively orderly about paperwork. Moreno says he found a manila envelope of receipts hidden in a kitchen cabinet, inside a bag marked 'Bags.' Clever." Poole grinned. "The art was paid for with …cash. *Cash*, Freddy."

"I like that. A nice twist. We need more twists. Cash, huh? Thank you, Mr. Ferris. But, for now, how's about we drop the murder and concentrate on getting you a date with that pretty lady over there?" Donovan was sick of theories.

"OK, OK. Let's have your best advice, Father Donovan."

Poole stood on the curb in a big city and watched a dozen black sedans drive slowly down the road. They all had dark tinted windows, but he knew who was inside. The cars were following a gleaming black hearse with a thick blanket of white roses on its long roof. He thought it a strange place to put flowers.

The cemetery was gray, damp, and deserted, except for the twelve occupants of the twelve cars, the hearse and its driver, and a priest in white vestments who stood bowed and respectful over a freshly dug grave. A huge beech tree shaded the deep grave.

By the time Poole arrived, the only place left for him to sit was in the beech tree. The long horizontal branch was quite comfortable, and he could hear every word the priest was saying. Actually, he could hear every word that was spoken by the twelve mourners in their black cashmere topcoats, homburg hats, and black leather gloves. They were congratulating themselves on a job well-done.

The prayers were brief, and soon the twelve mourners drove away in their shiny cars. Poole was left to watch the gravediggers lower the casket, fill the hole with earth, and push the gray granite stone into place. The stone was unmarked.

Poole awakened from the all too familiar nightmare with a sharp pain in his leg. He sat up and rubbed the calf and smoothed the skin as if to calm it. The peculiar dream would be forgotten in seconds, but, it would be back another night. He was always left with a single disjointed image of a metal object of undetermined form and covered in blood flying through the sky like a rocket, and the sound of a dirge rung by church bells. There would be nothing else.

7

UNDER SUSPICION

The Verduns owned one of a half-dozen private swimming pools in Belmont, and Marjorie led Poole through the house and out to the patio without saying a word. Umbrella tables, padded lounges, giant pots of purple petunias, and soft, atmospheric music provided the pool and its flagged terrace with enough charm to satisfy the fussiest homeowner. Not much was missing. Poole made his way to a lacey iron chair beneath a striped umbrella. It was a hot afternoon. He would have preferred poolside at the country club where pretty young things in bikinis and big smiles might be diving or sunbathing. Marjorie in a beach robe didn't make the cut.

The shade allowed Mrs. Verdun to remove her dark glasses. Her faded eyes were tired and wary, but she pretended to be cool, an act that might fool her children but not a policeman. She had to know she was a prime suspect. Vanity plates were hard to hide.

Marjorie was a member of Belmont's highly conspicuous upper crust. It would take drop-dead accurate evidence to nail her, because she would hire the best criminal defense in the country. Poole had dealt with the Marjorie Verduns of the world before. Actually, he'd been married to one for several years. He would be cordial, and he would push his prejudices about socialites under the mat. But, he would make her squirm.

The two proceded to cover familiar territory, Roger's return, the fist fights, and Marjorie's months in New York, when she claimed she simply saw Roger casually one or two times. Her more recent rendezvous with Ferris were strictly platonic, she insisted with great seriousness. Two old chums having a few laughs. The woman, Poole soon realized, expressed no genuine sadness over Roger's death. Was she glad he was gone? Had she assisted his departure?

"Were you and Ferris planning to run off together?"

"That's horridly rude, Oliver!" Marjorie slid to the edge of the patio chair and looked ready to bolt.

"Calm down. This is murder, Marjorie, not dinner table chit-chat. Somebody stabbed Roger four times for a reason." He wanted to remind her that her lover's death had been a grisly affair.

Marjorie set her face in a grim mask of phony grief and belligerence, as if plotting how to make Poole pay for his intrusions and bad manners.

Poole would let his insinuation sink in. "Where were you the night Ferris was killed?"

"Froggy and I were at a private party at the club and then we came home." Her tone implied that country club affairs were off-limits to cops and detectives like Poole.

"Do you and Froggy share a bedroom?" Poole continued to dig a big hole.

This time Marjorie's eyes smoldered. "Because of Froggy's early schedule, we have separate rooms. What are you driving at?"

Had she studied acting with Mrs. Twelmeyer? Both had shock and indignation down pat. "Which one of you slipped out around one to see Ferris? Was it Froggy?"

"I don't know. I was asleep, wasn't I?"

"Were you? Your Mercedes was parked outside Ferris's building at one."

Marjorie fiddled with the buttons on her terry-cloth jacket.

"Are you saying it was Froggy?" Poole lit a cigarette and slipped the lighter back into his trouser pocket. He would quit another day.

"Why don't you ask Froggy?"

Poole knew Donovan would be asking Froggy that very question the following afternoon. They would know soon enough. "Do you own a gold charm bracelet?"

"Absolutely not!" Marjorie answered sharply, as if he had just asked her to take off her clothes.

"Know anybody who does?"

Marjorie shook her head and scowled. Why did these pampered women always look alike? Tanned, aerobically fit, and so very ordinary. Marjorie looked incapable of seduction. Unaffected, unmussed, and unamused. How tedious. Better move on to dicier matters.

"How well do you know Reginald Ferris?"

"Our families have been close for years." Marjorie made it sound as if the Poole family might have sprouted in a laboratory petri dish.

Belmont's old money clique. Over a hundred years of in-breeding dollars. Their off-spring probably suffered from cash flow disorders. Poole admitted to himself that he was getting pretty corny on the subject. But, he couldn't help it. "Are you and Reggie lovers?"

"I don't have to answer that."

"It's never a good idea to lie or to cover up the truth in a homicide case." Poole sighed as if very weary. He turned to eye the cool, blue-green water of the pool, more tempting than Mrs. Verdun.

"Is nothing private?" The flush in Marjorie's face told Poole what he wanted to know.

"Very little when someone's been stabbed to death. Did Reggie and Roger know about the two arrangements? Or was one kept in the dark?"

Marjorie sat stone-faced and barely breathing.

"Did Roger tell you about the threatening poetry?"

"Threats? Poetry? How silly. And for your information, Froggy's threats were certainly idle ones. He couldn't kill anything!" Marjorie made it sound like a major character flaw.

"When did you last see Roger?"

"At Iris's party."

Poole doubted it, since Ferris's appointment book showed her initials on dates up until the day he died.

"Is Annette Wrenn around here anymore?"

"Annette Wrenn?" Marjorie regarded Poole with stronger suspicion. "I don't think anybody's heard from her since high school."

It was obvious that Marjorie didn't like the woman. What did she know about Annette Wrenn? Had she seen Roger and Annette together just recently? Maybe the mysterious Annette had been the last straw. More nooks and crannies in a case loaded with them.

He'd let Marjorie stew a little longer. Standing, he said, "That should do it. For today." The emphasis fell on today. He wanted to keep Mrs. Verdun uneasy, an emotion he doubted she had experienced in a long, long time.

Hospitals intimidated Donovan, almost as much as most doctors, and so he tried to keep his distance from both. University Hospitals in the capital was like any other, not for the fainthearted even with the redecoration job and softer chairs in the waiting rooms. The main lobby reminded Donovan of a medium class hotel with pink ladies instead of bell boys.

After following what seemed like miles of colored stripes glued to the polished vinyl corridors, the lieutenant located Reginald Ferris's office in the new wing. A pretty secretary named Cindy asked him to wait and offered coffee as a bribe.

The surgeon's private office was a handsome, expensively furnished room. The usual cold tile and eerie fluorescent lights had been replaced by subtle wall-coverings and table lamps. The rug was an old Chinese silk; the desk early New England; and the botanical prints authentic English. Donovan knew his antiques. He'd been hunting treasure with Joanna, his wife, and Iris for over twenty years. Missing were the usual diplomas and certificates. Donovan wisely concluded that they were displayed in the examining rooms where patients needed reassuring reading material.

After fifteen minutes and a cup of good Columbian coffee, Donovan was treated to the entrance of Doctor Ferris, all self-important and preoccupied. The secretary followed with a tray neatly set with a china teapot, one cup, a cloth napkin, and a plate of granola cookies. Ferris thanked her, poured his tea, and let Donovan know that he didn't like interruptions.

“The maintenance man at the Beacon Street Arms says he overheard an argument about a month ago between your son and another gentleman concerning a lady named Marjorie.” The doctor didn’t blink. “Could that gentleman have been you, sir?”

“I don’t recall, Lieutenant. Roger and I have had our disagreements, like any father and son.” The surgeon reacted as if asked about a traffic violation.

“The janitor said he recognized your voice because he talked to you just a half hour later about finding your car in the fire lane. Does that ring a bell?”

Ferris carefully shifted positions in his genuine Windsor arm chair and drank his tea. “I recall some nonsense about where I could and could not park.”

“How about the spat? The janitor heard you shout about leaving Marjorie alone.” Donovan was a patient man.

“Any discussion with Roger was a private matter. It has nothing to do with your investigation.” Ferris made this sound like the last word.

“Unfortunately, Doctor, lots of personal business comes under our scrutiny in a homicide case. We need your cooperation.” Donovan’s tone was stern this time.

Ferris sat back, obviously resigned. “Very well. Marjorie Verdun and I have been...ah, intimate friends...ah,… for about three years.” He coughed. “These things happen. Our friendship has been discreet. When Roger returned, he tried to see her again. The situation became ludicrous, shall we say?” The great surgeon was trying to be candid.

“Did your son continue to see Mrs. Verdun, or did you?”

“I don’t know what Roger did. Marjorie and I have not talked for some time.”

Donovan found the doctor remarkably composed, sitting there drinking his Earl Grey and calmly discussing a mistress he might have shared with his now murdered son, a woman he now ignored. “Did Mrs. Verdun know about your disagreement?”

“I certainly didn’t tell her. And I don’t want her dragged into this mess.” Ferris’s caution was sharp and, oddly enough, revealed some genuine emotion for the lady, rather more than the doctor displayed toward his wife or exposed over his son’s death.

Suddenly annoyed with the doctor's attitude, Donovan asked abruptly, "Where were you the night of your son's death?"

"I beg your pardon." The perfectly tanned face in front of Donovan turned scarlet, and Reginald Ferris leaned forward in his chair. "Just what do you mean, sir?" With elbows bent, his torso nearly touching the desk top, his fists clenched in front of him, Doctor Ferris looked like a giant lizard guarding his territory. Donovan half expected a long spiked tongue beaded with poison to dart from his thin lips.

"You need an alibi, Doctor."

"This is outrageous!" Ferris rose abruptly and marched to the office door; his rigid stance told Donovan that he was now prepared to bounce the policeman into the corridor. Donovan was shocked to witness such impulsive behavior from a man who generally held a scalpel.

"Just tell me where you were Saturday night between midnight and three on Sunday."

Strangely enough, the doctor's temper cooled as quickly as it had flared. "Very well," he said, "Make a note in that damned book of yours that I find these questions offensive and unnecessary," and he returned to his chair. "My wife and I attended a dinner party at the home of Doctor Hugo Busby. We left about midnight, drove home and went to bed. Ingrid will confirm this."

"Were you called out during the night, sir?"

Ferris acted surprised at Donovan's grasp of a surgeon's routine. "As a matter of fact I was. Car accident. Left for the hospital about two. Returned home about five."

"When did you get the call?"

"About one-thirty." Ferris didn't seem quite as officious or robust as he had earlier.

"And your wife will confirm all of this?"

"We have separate rooms. The hospital can."

"Did you or your wife invest in your son's television production companies, Vista and Eagle Eye?"

Without hesitation Ferris replied, "Certainly not. I would never put money into television." He made television sound like a string of seedy massage parlors.

"Did your son show you the threatening letters he received?"

"Threatening letters? Heavens, no. What did they say?"

Donovan was pleased to see a fresh burst of emotion. "They spoke of blackmail, a wronged woman, death threats."

"He said nothing to me. Are they genuine or just celebrity crank mail?"

"We're treating them as the real thing, sir. We believe your son was seriously frightened by the letters."

The surgeon ran a long fingered hand across his face. He looked more stunned by this than the murder.

"Do you or your wife have a key to Roger's apartment?"

"No. Roger was a grown man. Why would we have a key?" The response was plausible, the tone condescending.

"Why indeed, sir?" Donovan rose and thanked the surgeon.

On his way out, Donovan noticed the secretary watering a row of potted azaleas on the window sill, busy ministering to the great physician and his environment. The Irishman wondered where she washed up the tea things and who had baked the cookies.

"There are no coincidences, Ingrid. It's my business to believe that, and I've had queer feelings about your Roger since he rode into town." Beatrice Wrenn turned off the gas beneath the copper kettle, warmed the teapot with hot water, poured it out, and proceeded to make a fresh pot.

Ingrid Ferris sat at the pine table in Beatrice's kitchen, a bit stoic, Beatrice thought, but receptive. Ingrid could be so damned Swedish at times, keeping things locked up. But, that was who she was, and Ingrid was one of her oldest friends. After all, they had shared Reggie, the randy old bastard.

"So, Beatrice, do you think she's lurking about? Back here in the neighborhood?" Ingrid allowed her shoulders a meek shudder. "You know you're the only person I can talk to about this."

"I haven't heard from her, if that's what you mean." Beatrice poured two cups of tea from a English china pot her mother had always used, pink roses on white porcelain…it brought to mind the long-suffering woman and the judge, and the terrible plane crash.

Ingrid helped herself to cream and sugar. "She's the one with motive. It's an old one, but it's powerful, Beatrice. And, it would be the reason why he was killed here in Belmont."

It couldn't be easy speculating about who killed your son, Beatrice concluded, sitting down at the table. Ingrid was stumbling through it all and doing well enough. She had already reached the point where you have to go back as far as you can to find the answer, and that was about twenty years.

Ingrid went on, "I can't imagine that nice Professor Twelmeyer doing it. And, Justin Fitzhugh would sooner jump off a building than stab anybody."

Beatrice had heard the same rumors; the town was electric with speculation and gossip. She said, "The police have a long list of suspects."

"Marjorie Verdun may not have the nerve for murder, even though she has plenty of nerve for other things." Ingrid tipped her nose slightly skyward, as if to show Beatrice that she had risen above the petty machinations of infidelity.

"Funny how things come around to where they all started. Life runs on cycles." Beatrice grinned. "People have to get used to it. It is part of the 'Misfortune Telling' advice that I hand out when I read the cards." Beatrice laughed lightly and then grew serious again. "The girl could be skulking about in the shadows, I suppose. No girl anymore though. She'd make sure nobody knew her or saw her." Beatrice sipped her tea and took a bite of cinnamon cake. "One thing's sure. She was never like other children…complicated, secretive, unnerving at times."

Ingrid listened intently with her hands embracing the big china cup, the steam of fresh tea wafting across her pale skin. Ingrid came over regularly for advice, comfort, friendship…or a good laugh about something going on in the village. Beatrice had no wish to fail her old friend.

Ingrid said, "I remember her fairly well. Pleasant enough, stubborn, well-mannered but not lovable. She always reminded me of a terribly expensive and absolutely accurate camera. Those eyes." Ingrid closed hers, as if to hide from the picture in her head.

"Yes. Those eyes. Try the coffee cake," Beatrice said. She pushed the cake plate closer.

"Reggie disliked the girl on sight. Too gawky, too stern. And, then he'd go into his familiar tirade on the Wrenns. Horse thieves and drunkards!" Ingrid laughed at the silliness of it. "My God, his great Aunt Lil kept a brothel in Iowa City for decades. But, I must not go too far afield. We're talking about the girl with the strange eyes." Ingrid smiled and took a bite of cake.

"Frankly, I haven't seen or heard from our Annette in years. I do know she isn't dead. Her attorneys occasionally send papers about the property. She owns this house, you know. I have no idea where she lives. The lawyers are from New York, but that doesn't mean she's from New York. She's a woman of great financial substance, of that I'm certain. And, she's a woman of determination. She has never come back whining and begging for help."

Beatrice was suddenly reminded of young Suzannah Porter…seized by convulsions in her back yard, poor thing. Accidental poisoning was the coroner's conclusion at the inquest. The girl, no more than twelve, had been a friend of the family. At the time, Beatrice had been plagued with questions and doubts. Even now, her recollection of faces at the funeral was frighteningly vivid and as precisely drawn as the roses on the teapot. She recalled Annette's narrow face very well.

"Could be she never recovered from her parents' death," Ingrid said solemnly, still musing. "After all, she was only twelve when the plane crashed, wasn't she?"

Beatrice nodded. "A child can suffer betrayal and abandonment forever. I don't believe she ever forgave her father." Beatrice said nothing about Suzannah. It was the kind of secret Wrenns guarded with their lives.

"Do you think we're nutty old broads to even think about her...as a killer, I mean?" Ingrid poked at the coffee cake with her fork and took another bite. "Delicious, Beatrice."

"Absolutely not. I might not work for the cops, but I've been called in on a case or two in my time." Beatrice laughed. "Psychics are respected by a detective here and there. Freddy Donovan's wife comes regularly to my séances."

"Do you think Kenny could have done it?" Ingrid suddenly asked. "As revenge for his humiliation in court. He swore he'd get Reggie if he lived to be a hundred."

"Ah, Kenny, the little viper. Not much more than an ambulance-chasing shyster, and my brother to boot. I try to stay clear of him." On occasion, Beatrice could be brutally honest about her kin. "Wrenns hate to lose, Ingrid. But, in all fairness to Kenny, I think the little putz would have strangled Reggie with his bare hands, as opposed to stabbing your son to death. Kenny's brand of retribution would be more basic and simple-minded. His case against Reggie should have been thrown out of court the first day."

"You're right. Killing Roger would be too complex for Kenny."

Beatrice smiled. The Wrenns were a mixed bag of nuts to be sure, but her thoughts did stray again to the orphaned girl who grew up in the old Wrenn environment, all inclusive, a fascinating world of esteemed jurists, revered doctors and lofty scholars, nicely balanced by a raft of miscreants forever bent on revenge and extortion, pay-backs, and dark secrets, all well-understood by most but rarely by an unsuspecting child and the rest of polite society.

"How do you suppose she looks now?" Ingrid asked moodily. She hadn't much wanted her as a daughter-in-law, she told Beatrice, quite honestly.

"Wrenns tend to grow into their beauty. Lordy, Ingrid, I don't look a day over thirty, do I?" The two giggled over this. "What is Reggie's theory on the murder?"

"Thinks the Mafia did it or one of Roger's old school pals, suddenly gone unbalanced and jealous. He actually suggested names to the police. Can you imagine? He pointed a finger at Froggy Verdun."

"Hardly a failure, but certainly compromised." Beatrice raised an eyebrow, thankful again that Reggie's temperament was under Ingrid's supervision and not hers. She'd never regretted the divorce. She did regret not breaking the man's neck when she had the chance.

"I do drift back to Marjorie. I'm not fond of her. So cozy with Reggie at the moment." Ingrid frowned. "Hard to believe she could be interested in both father and son."

Beatrice admired Ingrid for her worldliness and her self-control. They both knew about the rumors. "Marjorie would not get her pretty hands dirty. She would hire a thug to kill an errant lover," Beatrice said, and polished off her tea.

Ingrid smiled and said, "Perhaps that is exactly what she did."

"Mr. Verdun prefers a hands-on approach, Lieutenant Donovan. He's rarely in the office during the day." This came from an efficient looking Mrs. Coyne, Verdun's secretary.

Mrs. Coyne straightened the silk bow at her throat, already painfully perfect, to Freddy's way of thinking. Her dark blue suit was about as spiffy as a nun's nightgown. Her haughty manner suggested that cops didn't belong on corporate carpets, and she swiftly directed Donovan to a construction site on Capitol Square, where Verdun was supervising a job.

Donovan drove downtown and parked on one of the side streets that radiated like wheel spokes from the square's hub. He strolled a block to the future home of Midwest Home-Life Insurance. A sure-to-be-seen white sign posted at the corner told the passersby that the project architects were Freeman and Spriers, Augusta; general contractor, Verdun Enterprises of Belmont.

A high plywood fence with peep holes for 'amateur engineers' barricaded the site from the sidewalks on two sides. Donovan considered Augusta to be the most confusing town on the planet. All major streets were anchored by the great granite statehouse. And, to make matters worse, there were no numbered streets anywhere. The cop liked to say that the only reason the city grew was the fact that nobody could find their way out.

The cop followed the wood wall to a truck entrance on Jefferson. Once inside the gate he could see that the superstructure was half completed, and by quick count, ten of the twenty levels were up. Its steel skeleton grew as he watched, with monstrous cranes lifting and swinging beams like pencils. Sun-browned, well-muscled men in yellow hard-hats and blue jeans tended to business, at home in the heat. The site was bone dry and dusty from lack of rain. By some miracle of nature, the capital had escaped the recent storm. Donovan figured it was a hell of a way to make a living in the middle of summer, or in the dead of winter, for that matter.

Verdun's field office turned out to be a yellow mobile trailer with Verdun Enterprises painted on the side in green letters, a logo in these parts as familiar as Pfeiffer Lager. The child-sized door stood open to any breeze. Donovan found Froggy Verdun standing over a work table strewn with blue prints. Attired in a yellow T-shirt and jeans, he could have been a member of the crew. He didn't look like the CEO of an empire. Two oscillating fans moved the air but weren't very good at it. Donovan and Verdun had met socially but didn't know each other well. Donovan guessed this interview would be less awkward if they were strangers.

Verdun grunted a kind of recognition, probably thinking the same thing, and waved the cop to a high stool in the corner. He didn't act like a man who suffered interruptions with good humor, but he did offer Donovan a cup of coffee from a big steel thermos. Verdun leaned against the table, eyes squinted, the corners well marked with crow's feet, a belligerent face fastened on Donovan's own. He was a handsome, rugged man with graying curly brown hair, a man approaching middle age, if you planned to live to one hundred, just like the rest of them.

"Sorry to bother you at work, but we have a few questions about Roger Ferris." Donovan fished a notebook from his pocket. "He was an old friend, right?"

"You might say that." Verdun crossed one oversized foot over the other, heavy boots that could have walked into combat. He resembled a young John Wayne in a Victorian parlor.

Donovan tried to warm him up. "Why do you think Ferris chucked a good career in New York to come back here?"

"Said he was sick of the rat race." Verdun's low voice owned a gravelly quality, like the construction site.

"Had you kept in touch over the years?"

"Not really." Verdun folded his arms across his broad chest, staring first at the wall behind Donovan and then directly at him. "What the hell's going on? Am I a suspect or are you just wasting my time?" Finesse wasn't Froggy's strong suit, but he did get to the point. The Irishman could appreciate this.

"Hold on, man." Donovan raised a hand and waved it gently like the enemy fluttering a white flag. He didn't know if he should address Verdun as sir, Froggy, or Mr. Verdun. "This is routine. We need to know when you last saw Ferris?"

"My wife keeps track of that sort of thing."

An odd response, Donovan thought, under the circumstances. Was he being facetious or did he mean that Marjorie took care of all the social engagements, like most wives? He'd keep it light. "Does your wife keep track of your fights too?" He grinned in a friendly way over the rim of his paper cup. "Like the one you and Ferris had in Hubble's Alley and the squabble at the Currents Cafe?"

Verdun swore. "That was between Ferris and me, Freddy." Verdun would set the tone after all. First names. A man-to-man talk. Donovan watched him pour coffee with steady hands and decided he'd reciprocate to ease the tension.

"Look, Froggy, Sam Liebermann swears you threatened to kill Ferris if he didn't stop seeing your wife."

"My quarrel with Romeo had absolutely nothing to do with the bastard's murder. Hell, I couldn't kill anybody. I was just trying to scare the son-of-bitch." Verdun uncrossed his feet and tucked in his T-shirt, an extra-large, Donovan figured. "Somebody did me a big favor. And a lot of other guys." Verdun looked directly into Donovan's eyes and let him know that he didn't mind that Ferris was out of the picture.

Donovan mumbled a word of sympathy for Verdun's dilemma. "Where were you the night Ferris was killed?" He deliberately left out the part about Marjorie's car.

"Marjorie and I were at a country club party for friends who are going to get married."

It was difficult to tell by his tone if Verdun disapproved of the party, the friends or marriage in general. "Did you go right home afterward?"

"Yes. About midnight."

"Can your wife substantiate this?"

"I suppose so." Verdun scratched his scalp ran a big brown hand over his face. The original Marlboro Man, Donovan was thinking, virile and charged with energy. He would have been a tremendous adversary for Ferris.

"Are you aware that your wife's Mercedes was seen parked near Ferris's building about one Sunday morning?" Donovan held his Bic pen in his teeth and watched Froggy with care.

"Jesus!" Verdun was a pot ready to boil over. He slammed his empty mug on the desk.

"Did your wife pay a visit to Ferris or did you?"

"I know this sounds bad, but that bastard was fooling around with my wife. He was making a mess of our lives. I drove over there to talk to him. I'd had a few days to cool off...after the fight. Marjorie's unpredictable and unhappy. I was trying to get her back." Sweat glistened on the man's forehead. His backward grip on the edge of the work table was so tight that his knuckles were white.

"What happened?" Donovan was hoping this wasn't going to be a murder confession. He liked the guy.

"Once Marjorie was asleep, I drove to the Beacon Street Arms." Verdun was pacing back and forth in the cramped quarters, turning the trailer into a tiger cage. "I took her car because mine's got a bum muffler. I rang Ferris's buzzer but nobody answered. It's a locked lobby; so, I left and came home." Verdun's brown eyes were as plaintive as a kid's and Donovan wanted to believe him.

"Wasn't it a bit late to go calling?"

"Not to a party animal like Ferris."

"Anybody see you ring the buzzer and then take off?"

"I don't think so. But, I wasn't looking for an alibi."

"Stop by Village Hall. Make a statement and get your prints on file." Donovan used his Irish priest's voice to keep things calm. "And, we'll take a look at the car."

"Marjorie's driving it today. You won't find any blood stains."

Donovan was watching a man who was sliding beneath the surface, trying to tread boggy water. The infidelity of his wife, the betrayal of an old friend, and now the homicide of the man he'd grown to hate. The crisis with his wife wasn't over yet. Donovan could see the wave of humiliation and despair washing over Verdun. Donovan could only sympathize. When Ferris was yanking him around, the Frog had tried to beat some sense into the guy. Most men would have.

Donovan wondered if Verdun loved his wife enough to lie for her. Maybe it was Marjorie who made the late night visit. "Did you see Ferris after the fight in the alley?"

"No. We no longer had anything in common." Verdun kept his eyes on the floor.

Nothing, Donovan thought soberly, except your wife.

Donovan decided to bypass for now Marjorie's long holiday in New York and her friendship with Reginald Ferris. He suspected Verdun didn't know about the doc. "Just out of curiosity, do you know where Annette Wrenn is these days?"

"Annette Wrenn?" Verdun smiled in spite of himself. "A name out of the past." He sounded almost normal again, happy to have the heat lowered. "I don't know where she is. Haven't heard about her in twenty years."

"Were Roger and Annette a serious item those days?"

"Sure, we were all buddies. But, right after graduation, Roger headed for New York. Wanted to be a big stage star." Verdun grunted. "Guess he didn't do too bad." He shook his head. "Annette cleared out too. Marjorie and I got married after college." The man's eyes were sad.

Donovan dropped his empty cup in the wastebasket and reminded Verdun to stop by the station to make a statement. Verdun agreed and stood at the small trailer door as Donovan walked away.

On the way back to Belmont, Donovan pulled into an A&W for a root beer and a pair of chili dogs. Verdun was a powerful man, in every respect. Ferris would have had his hands full with him. Donovan considered the cause of all this grief, Lady Marjorie. Recalling the woman's prudish face, Donovan decided it wasn't the face that would make his heart race, but, to each his own. He gobbled up his spicy dogs and drank the root beer.

Donovan drove off, reminding himself to check the Verduns' neighbors. Somebody may have seen one of them coming and going that night. Verdun was a jealous, angry man with a solid motive and all the right impulses. And, he wouldn't mind getting his hands dirty either.

Chin in hand, Marjorie Verdun half listened to the usual luncheon chatter. The Ashbury College Scholarship Advisory Board was wrapping up another meeting, this one up river at the Currents Café, a popular bistro perched like a bird on the wooded river embankment. She hated the place. A dusty moosehead over the fireplace stared at her with hideously real glass eyes. Roger had called the place quaint. And, it was here in the parking lot, just a few weeks ago, that Froggy had punched

Roger's lights out. Her life had turned upside down that afternoon, sliding from giddy and optimistic to a headlong dive into bitterness and now fear.

Feeling more peevish than usual, Marjorie turned to look out the windows at the river rushing far below the embankment. It looked like a whip of silt. She could never appreciate the Mississippi's indiscriminate power to rip saplings from the banks and at the same time dredge up ancient logs as white as old bones. To her, the river and its high bluffs were as sinister as walls surrounding a medieval city, and she had wanted out since childhood. Her resentment over her choices in life ran so deep that she was willing to do almost anything to get away. Roger had promised that the price for abandoning the Frog was ridiculously cheap, that he'd spring the trap and New York would be theirs. Another lie. His life had been full of them.

Sipping iced tea, Marjorie thought again about her lunch with Iris and Dolly, two silly middle-aged hens, snooping for gossip. Who did they think they were fooling? About as subtle as a rock through a window. Marjorie smiled to herself. They could all worry about Froggy now. Did he or didn't he? She was a suspect too, but she wasn't going to be a small town fool. Belmont was crammed with suspects. Maybe those silly cops would never figure it all out. Wouldn't that just cook Oliver Poole's goose?

"So, we're all under suspicion." Twelmeyer slumped in a chair in the Ashbury lounge. "An elite group, I must say. The Verduns, Doctor Ferris, my dear wife, and even you, Justin." He smiled wanly at Fitzhugh. "I never thought hating Roger would get me into such fancy company."

"I'm not sure it's all that fancy, Gilbert. Not with me in the ensemble." Fitzhugh laughed almost gaily. "Actually, I've been cut from the list. Charles bailed me out."

Twelmeyer thought Fitzhugh was acting remarkably relaxed and carefree. He'd gone a hundred-eighty degrees in a few hours. Amazing what an alibi could do for a man. Twelmeyer hated what he was thinking, but he did wonder if the alibi was legitimate. Charles Morgan was a man who could be bought fairly cheaply. And, Fitzhugh could afford it.

"The Verduns are filthy new money," Justin was saying. "Nothing terribly grand there. And who knows what the police will dig up in that soap opera crowd due to prance through here on Saturday. Which reminds me, I need to get my blue suit cleaned for the funeral." Justin stirred a large carton of strawberry yogurt while he talked. It was lunchtime. "My money's on a jilted actress who flew in from New York, stabbed the little weasel, and then flew out again."

"Sounds good to me, Justin. Of course, there's no use hiding the fact that Valerie and Roger were taking a spin around the dance floor, so to speak, and that I knew about it."

Twelmeyer closed his eyes and rested his head on the back of the leather chair, his face gray with fatigue and worry. An untasted egg salad sandwich lay in its wax paper wrapper in his lap. He'd forgotten to eat breakfast.

"Valerie wouldn't kill anything, Gilbert. She may have a weakness or two," Fitzhugh tiptoed through the words, "but she wouldn't murder a man."

"Especially in bed," Twelmeyer quipped without missing a beat. He might be compromised but he wasn't stupid. He watched Fitzhugh spoon in the yogurt.

"My car and apartment are clean, according to the cops. No blood stains to worry about." Fitzhugh smiled and pulled a thick ham sandwich from a brown sack and took a big bite.

Twelmeyer watched this ravenous consumption with a touch of nausea fluttering in his throat. "Your alibi is in the bag, I take it…from the look of all this food."

"Rock solid. If I never have to go back to that dreadful police station, I will have lived a charmed life. My God, I had no idea this town still closeted its cops in the last century." Fitzhugh rolled his eyes dramatically.

"The jail is worse, I'm told."

"What do you think about Froggy Verdun? Frankly, I think he would have throttled Roger with his bare hands. And that snooty wife of his certainly has depth, wouldn't you say? Rumor has it she was sleeping with Roger and his father. Positively old Greek tragedy, right?"

Fitzhugh drank his soda in long, thirsty swallows. Twelmeyer envied his friend's renewed lease on life.

"No theories, Justin, and no alibi either. The detectives have found out that I did not go back to my room after the play but waited in my car for Valerie to come home until four in the morning. Mrs. Mackie, the old bat next door, reported me to the police. Gaps in the alibi story, I'm afraid." Twelmeyer closed his eyes. "You are eating lunch with a condemned man." He rewrapped his sandwich and tossed it into a nearby wastebasket.

Fitzhugh muttered soothing sounds and said, "Will you be going to the funeral?" He made it sound as if they'd been invited to an inaugural ball. "It should be fun... mingling with the New York crowd, don't you agree? We're so out of touch here."

Twelmeyer hoped Fitzhugh wouldn't go around collecting autographs. "Funerals are funerals," he said wearily. "Like weddings. Usually more fun, for some ghoulish reason. Of course, if I don't go, I'll look guiltier than I do already." Twelmeyer snapped shut his briefcase and stood. "The crime lab has searched everything we own." He suddenly saw himself in church, on his knees praying, with the police van outside waiting to cart him off to prison.

"Stop worrying." Fitzhugh rose and patted his friend on the shoulder. "You need a few laughs. Let's hit Elsa's after classes. We'll play detective. Ask strangers probing questions, like Holmes and Watson. My God, Gilbert, you already have the pipe." And, Fitzhugh laughed heartily at the whole scheme.

Twelmeyer smiled but felt more like a convicted man. "Very well, I'll meet you here at five." As he headed for the door, he turned and said, "You, my dear Watson, can wear the damned cape." And, he slipped out into the corridor.

Fitzhugh laughed and decided to stay a bit longer. He'd noticed that Gilbert was wearing one blue sock and one green. It reminded him of Roger's chili-stained shirts in the weeks before his death. The coincidence was spooky. As he pulled an apple turnover from the deli sack, Fitzhugh realized that he was genuinely concerned about Gilbert. The man was suffering too much. Fitzhugh bit into the flaky pastry and thought again about the limericks. Were they a silly gag out of Gilbert's bag of tricks? Give nasty Roger a few jolts for banging his wife. He could hear Twelmeyer giggle as he cut out the words and pasted them on the paper. What the hell, a few Manhattans would bring him out of his funk.

After two more bites, Fitzhugh shoved the last half of the turnover into the sack. Maybe he and Gilbert could put suspicion on somebody else. Cook up a story to make the police look in other corners. Ferris was loved and hated all over town. Nobody would catch on and fooling the cops might be fun. The investigation seemed enormously entertaining… now that he was in the clear.

Noticing the hour, Fitzhugh tossed his leftovers into the basket and grabbed his jacket. Could be the crime would never be solved. He left the lounge humming.

The following day Poole walked into Billy's Bar and Grille on Main, ordered a tap beer, and slid onto a bar stool near the door. A faint breeze was trying to stir the languid air, and the sun was making an attempt at burning off the damp, no simple geophysical feat along the Mississippi. Freddy said he'd drop by around noon.

Little had changed at Billy's, an archetypal all-male saloon that was an institution in Belmont as infamous as the river front and just as cherished. Out of curiosity a female or two might stop by from time to time, but few came back. The old watering hole upheld the division of the sexes, like a seventh century tyrant. Actually, Billy and his old father and grandfather were simply scared to death of women. That was the scuttlebutt.

The establishment was as roomy as a boxcar and about as charming, with a long, oak bar running the length of the narrow space on one side and a dozen mismatched tables and chairs with uneven legs on the other. Aged grooved paneling the color of tobacco spit covered the walls and four paddle fans churned the blue air. The gloom was punctuated here and there by globe lights suspended on metal rods from an embossed tin ceiling. Most of the patrons tended to squint.

Poole swigged on his beer and contemplated the painting over the back of the bar, a much loved raven-haired beauty with sleepy eyes, a charmer who had been reclining on those red satin pillows for nearly a century. She wore lots of bracelets and little else and that was why she stayed up there. Some time during the twenties, a band of overzealous temperance ladies had dared to remove her to the curb out front, but her exile was short. It was said that Billy's grandfather carried her back as the teetotalers batted him with umbrellas. Through the years every brush stroke and curve had been memorized several times over by the art lovers securing the bar stools. Poole was immediately reminded of the voluptuous Valerie Twelmeyer, perhaps a modern, fair version of the lovely Miss Raven. Miss Valerie would be flattered.

Billy was about sixty and not quite as sophisticated as his saloon. His patrons said he'd inherited the place and that included the dirty apron. He only cooked two things, burgers and split brats, with or without onions; he was suspicious of anybody who turned down onions, and he pushed Pfeiffer lager, the local brew. If a customer asked for a Budweiser, he was invited to cross the street to O'Reilly's.

While Reba McEntire launched into something sad, Poole leaned contentedly against the bar and listened to Billy and the regulars reexamine the toning-up of Belmont. Since his return home, Poole had learned that when Billy's soothsayers spoke, few ever doubted the Holy Word. Freddy called Billy's string of regulars blackbirds singing on a wire. Damned poetic for a cop.

"It's those snooty professionals from the capital," observed a rustic gentleman who preferred brandy to beer. "Think their Volvos won't run if they can't rest them up in the suburbs overnight." He coughed and kept a tight grip on his glass.

"We call 'em the crusty uppers," offered Billy with a smile missing a few teeth. The regulars applauded his droll wit with cackles. "They're scooping up all the good houses and seem hell-bent on remodeling everything else." He scowled his disapproval with a slap on the bar with a grimy towel.

"It's getting pretty trendy around here," Poole commented. "Boutiques, designer pizzas, California cuisine. Cafes with plants and pink napkins."

"Where you're likely to get spiders in your soup," commented another old patron, who didn't look as if he ate much soup and rarely used a napkin.

"You should see what they did to the country club," said another wizened fellow, a very unlikely guest at a country club, fixed up or otherwise, Poole imagined.

The blackbirds took time for swallows and generalized grumbling.

"We've been taken over by the Chamber of Commerce, Inspector Poole," explained Billy. "And the Ladies for the Preservation for Damned Near Everything Old!" He grinned at his joke and wiped his damp face with the bar towel. The faithful accompanied him in a low rumble that sounded like 'rutabaga, rutabaga.' "Damned if they won't keep us old farts alive, too. Just out of spite!" More laughter.

"We're a real estate broker's paradise, Sonny," said an unlikely property owner with ketchup on his tie. "Buy quick if you're rich or drive over to Stone Bank."

Poole nodded his appreciation and cracked a few more peanuts. The floor was littered with shells and a dusting of cigarette ash.

The regulars' observations were cut short by a phlegmy orator's baritone from the other end of the bar. "Gentlemen, gentlemen, we're in a time of economic flux. It's a new age. Money, money, and mountainous poverty." A hacking cough broke the flow for a moment and soon a body that somehow matched the voice materialized through the dinge and made its way toward Poole. "My friends, our struggle to honor the past may be lost," the voice said. "Those of us who love the old Belmont might be forced to lie down before a few young generals who have all the bucks." A din of grumbling rose from Billy's board of directors; they agreed with the gentleman's assessment of the times and didn't like it.

"Ambrose Feather!" Poole called out, as if no one in the place knew the speaker. He held out a hand and Feather honored him with a firm greeting. "Belmont's renowned sage, raconteur and sauce fancier," Poole added lightheartedly. Feather possessed a name and a face with a reputation. The gentleman had spent the better part of his career writing an advice column under the unlikely name of Aunty Em. Was it any wonder the man drank? Iris had succeeded Feather in the job when he lost his battle with the scotch bottle. He was a legend, who devoted most of his time these days to a residency at Billy's and other more sophisticated watering holes.

"Inspector Poole, it is a pleasure to have you among us. You will be ridding us of the undesirables, I take it."

Feather was still the most genteel drunk Poole had ever met, nattily attired in white duck pants and a Hawaiian shirt, wholly appropriate for Belmont on a hot day. He was barefoot. His handsome face was remarkably unlined, and his shock of pure white Mark Twain hair was gathered into a short pony-tail.

"We will be doing our best, sir. Were you acquainted with the deceased?" Poole liked playing along with Feather's aristocratic way with speech.

"Absolutely, sir. I am still uncommonly well-connected." He cast a glance at his audience; they were enjoying the performance. "I dined with the man at a sumptuous party only days before his unfortunate demise. At the time, he seemed intent upon drinking me under the table, which we all know is a futile endeavor. An utterly charming lush, nonetheless. However, I must tell you, Inspector, he was a frightened animal, a beaten dog. His eyes, sir, were brimming with alarm. For himself." Feather wobbled slightly on his pegs but still held himself erect. "Your ears will be the first to hear my story, Inspector." Feather turned to the regulars and added, "And, your ears, as well, my good fellows." He smiled at the boys at the bar.

Poole nodded, more than willing to listen to Feather's story. Feather began his soliloquy while swaying and gesturing with a half-empty glass of scotch.

"You believe he was in danger, sir?" Poole prodded him along a bit.

"Without a doubt, Inspector Poole. My instincts about people are infallible." Feather leaned closer to Poole and whispered, "You do recall my occupation for more than a decade." And he raised both generous white eyebrows.

Poole smiled. "Indeed, I do. Did Ferris say who might be hounding him?"

"He was well into his cups near midnight, it was, and the young man confided that a woman was after him. His very turn of phrase. 'After him.' An evil woman, he said, and she meant to do him great harm." Feather polished off his whiskey and glided to the bar for a refill. The blackbirds were hanging on every word. Speculation about the Ferris murder had kept them in conversation for hours. Now, this was fresh material.

Poole moved closer to Feather and asked quietly if Ferris had identified the woman. Feather said he had not. "But, I did have the feeling that she was one of us. Do you know what I mean, Inspector?"

He didn't wait for a serious reply. "A native, sir. Someone Ferris had known all his life." Feather picked up his refill and tested its contents.

"Why do you say that?"

Feather leaned against the smoky air, nearly falling backward, and stared intently at the old tin ceiling. "I cannot say, sir. I just know that I'm correct on this point. I will not waver in my conclusion."

And with that, the old columnist excused himself with a gentlemanly bow and wandered off in the direction of the men's room.

A rumble of commentary started up immediately among the regulars, and Poole was left to contemplate Feather's tale. The man's instincts about people were superb. It was indeed possible that Ferris had been killed by an old acquaintance. Could Doctor Ferris have been right, after all? He recalled the marked pages of Ferris's high school year books. But, which old friend was the bugaboo. They'd talked to a good many in the last two days.

Reba McEntire finished her sad song; the old juke box dropped in something sassy by The Judds. It wasn't Brubeck or Beethoven, but Poole had to admit that these old river towns ran more smoothly on country tunes. He was feeling more at home with every strum of the guitar.

8

PEERING INTO THE DARKNESS

Reginald Ferris left the hospital at 4:30 that afternoon, earlier than usual, after a particularly grueling day in surgery, the kind of day he loved to brag about. Lieutenant Donovan had spoiled the essence of it with his intrusiveness, and Reggie worried that he might have revealed too much. The cop had cornered him. If Ingrid ever found out about Marjorie, a messy divorce would erupt and there would be hell to pay as well as a small fortune.

As he drove down Avon with the sun beating through the windshield, Reggie wiped perspiration from his face and swore mightily at the BMW Corporation. He was unaccustomed to inconvenience and air conditioners that broke down on a ninety-degree day. His mood was made no less disagreeable by the fact that the magnificent canopy of ancient elms that had once shaded this particular street were now gone, hit by elm disease and carried off like carcasses. He swore at the Dutch too.

At the intersection of Avon and Sixth, a woman in purple wearing a large hat festooned with orchids swerved her bicycle into his path. Reggie hit the brakes and screeched to a halt in the middle of the street. The bike rider skidded into the curbstone but remained on her feet.

Reggie stuck his head out the window and bellowed, "Who taught you to ride that thing, you old bat!"

"Old farts like you shouldn't be driving cars!" was the old bat's reply, and she gave him the finger before pedaling off.

"Witch! Spook!" the doctor bellowed before pulling his head back inside the car. "Beatrice! Jesus, she'll put me in the hospital yet!" Reggie pulled away and watched as his first wife rode on home, just up the street. "She would have the only house in town I ever wanted," he grumbled. "And, she's turned it into a sorcerer's cave!" He swore again and drove on. Actually, he had not entered Wrenn House since he and Beatrice parted way many years ago. Ingrid insisted that it was the picture of good taste. Females. They all stuck together.

Reggie took a deep breath and pulled into his drive. His huge capricious Queen Anne with its towers and gables was a masterpiece of carpentry, but Reggie had always preferred the old houses with more discipline, like Wrenn House, an Italianate beauty positively redolent with restraint. And, he reminded himself that his longing for the old mansion had nothing to do with any lingering desire for its owner.

After parking in the carriage house at the rear of his property, Reggie made his way across the lawn to the back entrance, stopping first to admire three new rose bushes he'd planted two weeks ago. Inside, he found Ingrid washing salad greens and listening to an opera.

"I damned near ran over Beatrice just now. Riding around on that old Schwinn. Why can't she drive a car like everybody else?" Reggie kissed his wife's cheek, threw his suit coat on a chair and headed for the pantry to make their usual martinis. He'd called Ingrid earlier to request an early supper.

Ingrid laughed and said, "Why do you let Beatrice bother you? She's been riding that bike since childhood." She began preparing a salad dressing.

"Does it on purpose, just to humiliate me. Stir in some sour cream, darling." Reggie took down a bottle of Beefeaters and selected two glasses.

"You're not supposed to have sour cream."

"I don't give a damn about what I'm not supposed to have." Reggie poured out the gin and added a drop or two of Vermouth to each glass, two olives a piece, and a dash of olive juice for Ingrid, the way she liked it.

"That's not what you tell your patients. Did you talk to Beatrice?"

"She talks to herself, damn it. I yelled at her, of course. Dressed like a gypsy, the crazy old witch. She should be locked up." Reggie set Ingrid's drink on the counter and took his to the sofa at the far end of the spacious remodeled kitchen.

Ingrid took a sip and joined her husband. She stroked his arm and said, "Beatrice is harmless and unique. She'll outlive all of us with her bike riding!" Ingrid laughed again. "And, I bet she never eats sour cream."

His wife's Swedish lilt always reminded Reggie of Ingrid Bergman. Cornflower eyes, hair like young willow. He did love Ingrid, but she was statuesque (taller than he), something he found mildly irritating. The world seemed to be built around tall people, and he didn't like that either. They'd grown a bit closer since Roger's death, and in response to his feelings, he put his arm around Ingrid's shoulders. For an instant he wondered why he had bothered with silly Marjorie. Glands. He would blame it on glands.

"Don't make jokes. Beatrice is a constant reminder of a scandal I'd rather forget." Reggie squeezed her gently and then concentrated on his drink.

"I'm not making fun, but you should put the feud to rest. Just because some old Wrenn fur trader put one over on your great, great, great grandfather." Ingrid sighed. "Beatrice is one of my oldest friends... even though you don't like knowing that...and she's just as smart and high-minded as any of your old aunties. Beatrice just directs her own little marching band; it parades quite nicely back and forth between this world and the other. I find her Friday night séances quite amusing." Ingrid rose and pulled place-mats and napkins from a drawer.

Reggie had heard it all before. His only reply was a soft grumble. His first wife and his second wife... good friends. Damnation! Why did these things happen?

Her piece said Ingrid set out the plates and silver. Reggie had put his feet up on the coffee table and picked up a newspaper. He'd be quiet now. She suddenly remembered a time a few months ago, when Roger was still with them. Roger and Reggie had quarreled, because Reggie insisted on bringing up the business about Annette, how Roger had nearly married the girl, and how Reggie had convinced him otherwise. Roger was outraged that the girl's name was even mentioned. Reggie refused to apologize, and Roger had stormed out.

The family feud was ridiculous. No one knew which act of treason had started the war. Speculation that Wrenns had co-habitated with Indians in the 1700s was apparently too much for the prudish, self-righteous Ferrises. When Beatrice and Reggie married, the clan members on each side were outraged. The couple's well-publicized divorce after six months created more disgrace for both families.

"You don't suppose your famous feud had anything to do with Roger's death, do you?" Ingrid asked carefully. She placed a bowl of daisies in the center of the table.

Her husband sat up straighter. "I'd never thought about that. Kenny's the worst of them. Bad-tempered Irish bastard. Not as great a barrister as he thinks." Reggie smiled to himself, still smug over his legal victory. A patient's suit against him had been soundly put down. "Kenny hates losing."

"Maybe Kenny hired a goon to kill Roger. Retribution for his courtroom embarrassment." She recalled Beatrice's cross words about her brother.

"He's capable of it."

Ingrid said nothing more and checked on dinner. Twenty years ago there were losses on both sides. And, more now. Had Roger pretended to love Annette just to get Reggie's goat? Their son had a perverse streak. And, where was Annette?

Humming along with Kiri Te Kanawa, lightly tossing the Puccini with the greens, Ingrid wondered if Annette might be living close by, keeping a safe and private distance from the old home town. She could be married with a new name and living in Augusta. It was easy to remain lost in a large city. After high school, Annette had fewer reasons to stay in Belmont than Roger. But, what if the scenario was more complicated? Given their history, Ingrid knew that if anybody had a motive to kill Roger, it would be Annette. No matter how many years had gone by.

"Professor Twelmeyer!" Donovan shouted. Twelmeyer walked on and disappeared into the entrance of the Beaumont Theatre. Donovan was forced to run or miss the man altogether. It was after six, and the campus was nearly deserted.

The audacious Beaumont always reminded Donovan of Aunt Hedy, his father's only sister. She was named for Hedy Lamar, the famous actress. Hedy O'Hara (she'd taken her first husband's name) was a free-spirit who wrote poetry and wore turbans and false eyelashes. When the war ended in Europe, she ran off to Paris, where she lived for years with a succession of sculptors and novelists. She eventually claimed four husbands and twice as many lovers, a scandalous roster for an Irish Catholic family, and ended up with a modestly talented painter with a family fortune in nuts and bolts. Last time Donovan heard, Aunt Hedy was living in Hollywood with Uncle Felix where they enjoyed a kind of minor celebrity status. As much as Donovan would hate seeing his daughters follow Hedy's example, he had to admit that he adored the lady and her nerve.

Today, Aunty Hedy would be just as out of place in Belmont as the Beaumont Theatre, an outrageous Moorish creation, greatly resembling a sultan's palace, with a pagoda dome that hovered among the treetops like a spaceship about to touch earth. Majestic Palladian windows flanked a canopied entrance crested with iron filigree. A sense of humor helped anybody looking at the Beaumont. Inside, the cavernous lobby sat as dim and cool as an Egyptian tomb, a fitting climate for a hall guarded by gilded serpents and sphinxes with glowing red eyes. Nobody built picture palaces like this anymore.

Twelmeyer was nowhere to be seen. Donovan crossed the lobby, opened a second set of brass bound doors, and entered the main auditorium, where a rehearsal was in progress on the enormous bare stage. Amateurish voices drifted over the deep blue velvet seats. Donovan could see Twelmeyer seated about half-way, center section.

The Irishman strolled down the aisle and took a seat next to the professor. He whispered that he had a few more questions. A woman, who appeared to be the director of the play, sat about fifteen rows back. Twelmeyer suggested they listen to the run-through for a few minutes; he was interested in the performance of one of the students. Donovan said that was fine.

How seductive it all was, the yawning mouth of an bare stage, rows of bodiless seats, the faintly stuffy smell of velvet and varnished wood, the players, tiny and vulnerable, suspended like marionettes within the great space of the hall. Donovan breathed it in. Phrases of dialogue swept over them and bounced off a half dozen stone goddesses sitting cross-legged in niches around the perimeter of the house, the walls awash in blue and yellow lights. A dazzling gilded sunburst supported by dragons swept seductively across the proscenium, calling to mind The Arabian Nights, or at the very least, an old Valentino movie set.

Donovan felt oddly vulnerable. The bleak stage was bringing back memories of his disastrous theatrical debut when he was sixteen. Shaking with terror, he'd made his entrance in a silly high school operetta and had gone blank. Standing there, unable to speak or sing, he could see his fellow actors fidget; one began coughing. When he finally recognized the loud hissing of the prompter off-stage, calling out lines of dialogue, he grabbed hold of each word and recited the lines like an automaton. The audience began to squirm and snicker and finally guffaw in a great crescendo. With his face burning, Donovan realized that the lines were incorrect. This was a serious scene…no one was supposed to laugh. The prompter was feeding him the wrong lines! Somehow, he'd turned it around and made a graceful exit, but the incident ended his career as an actor.

Slouching low to get a better look at the fancifully painted ceiling, Donovan heard Twelmeyer say, "It's good to feel the pulse of an empty theatre, don't you think, Lieutenant?"

Donovan straightened up and agreed. "A blind stage. If I were a playwright or an actor I'd have to sit alone in a nearly darkened hall. It might be here that the right words and inflections would come into my head." Donovan suddenly felt self-conscious about what he had said.

"Nicely put, Lieutenant. I take it you are a fan of the theatre." Donovan said he was.

Twelmeyer rose and suggested they sit further back for privacy. As they shifted, the lady director, who sounded British, gave instructions for the scene to play again. The actors regrouped, and the voices swam across the seats.

Once settled, Donovan asked in a half whisper, "Where did you go after the play on Saturday night?" In checking Valerie's alibi, they had inadvertently stumbled onto a discrepancy in Gilbert's story. An alert neighbor with insomnia called with a tip.

Twelmeyer rearranged himself in the seat and cleared his throat."I know I should have told you before," he whispered, "but, I was afraid. My relationship with Ferris wasn't good. I was trying to protect myself." He glanced around to make sure no one was eavesdropping, but they were alone in the back row and the rehearsal was moving along.

"After the play, I followed Valerie and her friends. When I lost them, I decided to wait at the house. I parked across the street and sat there in the car until quite late."

"Your neighbor saw you from eleven until shortly after 12:30. Then, she said you left and returned about 1:30 in the morning. Where did you go?"

"I was getting sleepy. I drove to an all-night truck stop on Highway AA. Bought a coffee and came back to the house. Valerie's car was still gone. I stayed until three or four and then drove back to the Y." Twelmeyer sounded more embarrassed than frightened.

"Alma's Truck Stop on the corner of AA and Lime Kiln Road?" Donovan made a notation in his book.

"Yes, that's the one. Ask the night waitress; Vera's her name. I stayed fifteen minutes or so, used the men's room, ordered coffee and a sweet roll and left."

"Will do, Professor." Donovan liked Twelmeyer and sensed his helplessness and humiliation.

Twelmeyer leaned closer to Donovan and hissed in his ear, "I didn't kill him. My problems with Valerie are hardly the stuff of homicide."

"My friend, men fighting over women on Saturday night causes more trouble than anything else." Donovan grinned a little.

Twelmeyer clasped his hands together as if to comfort himself. "There are plenty of creative souls at Ashbury capable of executing those limericks and more than one man in Belmont capable of stabbing Roger." Twelmeyer had regained some of his composure.

"Got anybody specific in mind?"

Twelmeyer didn't say but added that Ferris's own father didn't even like him.

Donovan said they'd have to check Twelmeyer's room, car, house, the office; it was routine. Twelmeyer agreed. The two shook hands.

As Donovan strolled up the gentle incline of the carpeted aisle, he hoped Professor Twelmeyer was telling the truth.

“Marjorie, Roger, and Dr. Warmth,” observed Donovan as he took a swing and then watched the golf ball sail off. “A new dimension in sexual perversity.”

The Irishman’s smile was crooked with embarrassment. Bedroom high jinx made Freddy about as comfortable as starched collars and silk ties, which made Poole smile with a certain experienced detachment. He and Freddy were keeping in shape at Burt’s Hole Nineteen Driving Range. Poole tried a shot or two, but it had been too long.

“It’s your knee, Oliver. Blame those slices on the knee. Best excuse you’ll ever have.” Donovan slammed another one. Better. And, they had the place to themselves. It was getting late.

“Ferris is coming across as a nasty game player, Freddy. Liked to push people to the edge.”

“Yeah, what kind of man publicly humiliates his oldest friend and beds his father’s mistress? It’s not so farfetched to see him blackmailing a woman.” Donovan lobbed another ball.

Poole tried another swing and vowed to give up golf.

“Time for a beer, Oliver. Neither one of us is going to qualify for the Open.”

Poole agreed, and they retreated to Burt’s bar and took their drinks to a table in back that was private.

“So, with paintings and sculpture weighing in at several hundred thousand…I’m betting...he must have blackmailed a very rich lady. And, for cash! Hell, I think it’s hard to get $20 extra at the grocery store.” Poole started in on the popcorn.

“Did he buy any big items after December?” Donovan lit a cigar.

“Nothing. The well ran dry in New York.”

“Maybe the blackmail victim dug up some dirt on Ferris. Counter blackmail. Counter threats. Put a stop to the whole thing.”

Poole was trying to figure the cash angles. “And, we still can’t find his stock market files. Nobody with his kind of income stays out of the market.”

"Maybe he hid his paperwork at Mommy's house. She's going to get everything." Donovan grinned, liking his theory. "How about a safe deposit box at the bank?"

"Good point. So far, we haven't found the key or the location of the box. It's not in any bank in Belmont."

Donovan reviewed his conversation with Twelmeyer at the Beaumont. "You think Twelmeyer might have set up this whole scheme, like a tiny play with a cast of red herrings?"

"You mean he confuses the issue with the story that Valerie didn't come home that night. Puts the focus on himself because he thinks his wife killed Roger?" Poole took another handful of popcorn.

"Is Twelmeyer that diabolical?" The Irishman looked doubtful.

"A man hopelessly in love with a woman is capable of anything."

"I feel like a real outsider on this damned case, Poole."

"It takes years to get accustomed to homicide."

"It's like peering into the darkness, Poole, scary as hell and twice as confusing."

"How does it feel to be a murder suspect?"

Froggy Verdun was sitting on the edge of the bed in his wife's bedroom. This wasn't their first discussion about Roger, but it was the first since his murder. Froggy had managed to avoid Marjorie most days.

"Don't act so damned smug," Marjorie replied. "As I see it, the police have you at the top of their list." She didn't turn around but continued to scrutinize her reflection in the dressing table mirror, her fair hair bound back with a pink ribbon. "You're the genius who threatened to kill him in front of an audience. You're the brain surgeon who drove my car over there that night." Marjorie smoothed cold cream over her skin, taking care not to dip the sleeves of her silk kimono into the open jar.

"Threats were nothing new to an S.O.B. like Ferris. Even the short list of suspects is long in this murder." Froggy leaned back on one elbow, dressed for bed in striped pajama bottoms and a white T-shirt. He felt like a stranger in this room, lying on this bed. "You must love all the excitement. A nice diversion from the boredom you're usually bitching about."

"If I didn't bitch, you'd never come home."

Froggy caught her reflection in the mirror; she was watching him, baiting him. They'd sparred over this a million times. Froggy knew the dialogue by heart.

Marjorie massaged cream around her eyes. "We should alibi each other," she said calmly. "No matter what. We can do that much for each other."

"What the hell does that mean?" Froggy thumped the thick quilt with his fist; his head was whirling with possibilities. Had Ferris told her to get lost? Conceivable, knowing both of them. "I want to know where you were that night?" He pushed himself off the bed and stood a few steps behind her, feeling suddenly larger than life in her fussy lace bower.

"I told you; I was driving around." Marjorie turned her white creamed face to him, a kabuki actress ready to step on stage. "Let's not get coy." She began swabbing away the dark mascara and eye shadow with tissues.

They had driven two cars to the party, returned to the house and started to quarrel again. Marjorie had stormed out, taking Froggy's car which was in the drive. Later, she confessed to driving around to cool off until three in the morning. Froggy knew it was a lie. But, in Marjorie's favor, the cops had found nothing incriminating in either car or at the house. Either way, the two of them were still on the list of suspects.

"We're in up to our necks." Marjorie spoke quietly.

Froggy roamed the room, picking up and putting down framed photographs, tiny porcelain boxes, magazines. "Agreed," replied."We cover for each other, if it comes to that."

"It's the smartest thing to do."

Marjorie sounded uninvolved. Froggy wasn't sure he knew her anymore. And he couldn't be certain of anything she said or did. The trust was gone. All they had now was a manufactured loyalty to save each other from prosecution.

Froggy stood by the door that connected the two bedrooms. "God, I hate what's happened to us, Marjorie. Don't you ever want to start over?" His big hand held the edge of the door as if he needed its support. As he watched his wife expertly wipe away her makeup, her eyes grew smaller and older. Her tanned skin without its artificial contours of color looked undistinguished. His wife was an ordinary looking woman bearing down on fifty. Had Ferris really been serious about her? Would she have run off with him? Freddy wasn't sure of any answers. Weren't trysts and affairs meant for the young and the beautiful?

The pain he felt over Marjorie's infidelity was mixed with confusion and anger. His best friend had turned him into a goddamned cuckold. He couldn't forgive Roger that insult even in death. But, for a reason Froggy didn't quite understand, he knew that one day he would pardon his wife.

"It's agreed then." Marjorie sounded abrupt. "We'll be steadfast in the face of the law. I refuse to give Donovan or Poole an ounce of ammunition."

Froggy believed she might be more concerned about putting one over on the detectives than in salvation. Jesus, she was selfish. A spoiled child turned into a spoiled, rich woman. Why did he still care so much? She continued to fuss with her bottles and jars, no longer paying any attention to him. The summit meeting was over.

Froggy crossed the threshold into his own room and closed the door, nearly overcome with a dragging, heavy desire to sleep and to never wake up.

Meredith Wrenn staggered off to the kitchen. It was time for some serious drinking now that Queenie had flown off. "Ooops," she sang out, "mustn't use the royal name. Our queen doesn't approve." Meredith giggled. "Dear cuz, do you ever have any fun in this tiresome life? Better still, does anybody?" She poured a large gin.

Glass in hand, Meredith wandered back into the living room, and once safely tucked into a corner of the couch, she let her mind wander backward to the days when she and Annette were better friends. They'd been close as twins out of necessity. Each one suffered fast-living parents and a clan of eccentric relatives, all too busy for two little girls. Annette's mother and father had managed to kill themselves in a plane crash. Crazy darlings. Her own parents still lived and played in Augusta, her father as an attorney, her mother a society matron, of sorts. Meredith had no interest in seeing either one of them. She drank deeply and prayed she could wash away her frightening dependence on Annette.

She and Annette had always kept each other's secrets. They had spied on their negligent parents and pulled brutal pranks on people who didn't like them. As children, they'd killed a cat or two to make a child or a mother weep. And, there was the incident involving Suzannah. They did not talk about that. As the years wore on, confidences, veiled truths, and life in general bound them together as neatly as skin wraps the body. Meredith had been sworn to eternal silence and loyalty long ago, a dangerous position. One of the benefits of booze was an acquired capacity to shrug off the bad things, for a time. It had grown to be her most trusted companion.

Tragedy and blessings, too, had drawn the two cousins close. Meredith had learned to accept the fact that Annette's glamorous life would always take precedence over her own. What a peculiar leap of conceit that had been. Meredith smiled and rested her head on the back of the sofa, savoring the warm glow swallowing her up, that heavenly release from fear and pain. Coming back home might have been a good idea after all. Lately, the notion of independence had started to bloom in her head. Up until recently, Annette's words were the only words to live by or suffer the consequences, words that made gin more important than daily bread. But, Meredith was toying with autonomy more and more, and she had actually accomplished one or two solo 'missions,' as she called her attempts at breaking away. She was proud of herself.

Of course, it had always been safer to be with Annette than against her. Her demanding and yet generous friendship seemed to override losses and disappointment. The death of Meredith's young husband almost twenty years ago had evaporated into dreamy obscurity. Meredith could barely describe the young man's face without a photograph. Ironically, the automobile accident that devastated Meredith turned out to be Annette's good fortune, and Meredith had learned to be content with her new assignment in life. She rolled the half empty glass back and forth between her palms.

Unfortunately, Annette was on the warpath again. This time it was Marjorie Verdun who had earned the traitor's label. Annette did not tolerate disloyalty. Therefore, the past and present were about to suffer an eclipse of permanent proportions. Annette's remedies for sedition were swift and final. Meredith closed her eyes; her skull ached. She had been doing a lot of thinking lately, and her head didn't know what was going on.

"Maybe a wee whack at the throne is what we need," she blurted out. "I wouldn't mind wearing a crown." Meredith frowned. But, reigning alone could be scary, like moving into a third world country. On the other hand, look at Auntie Beatrice and her séance enterprise. A single woman beholden to no one. Meredith sat up, as if ready to move on. She could change her life without anyone noticing. Nobody ever knew who she was, then or now. Hell, she was a kind of ghost child. And, if Annette had taught her anything, it was the value of anonymity.

Feeling energized, Meredith stood with some effort and smiled with quivering lips. "To hell with you, Queenie!" she cried with unexpected boldness. "A wee whack at the throne it is!" And, holding her glass aloft, Meredith wobbled a bit and then with a shaking hand toasted herself in a solitary ceremony.

Central Casting must have sent him. Short, stout, and fiftyish, Roscoe Thurston was Hollywood's version of the theatrical agent, the powerful, natty little guy who got all the grief and most of the snappy lines in all the old movies. Poole figured Thurston must have approved. The man had bought the image down to his pointed Italian shoes.

Thurston strolled into the Belmont police station Thursday morning at eight o'clock sharp, like a symphony conductor taking center stage. He swung a gold-headed walking stick and smelled of expensive cologne and Cuban cigars. His smooth moon face was tanned the color of creamed coffee and becomingly framed by a cap of steely Persian lamb curls. His ivory linen suit was custom-tailored and a blue silk tie matched his eyes. Poole was immediately impressed.

Tucking his stick beneath his left arm, the agent extended a small, manicured hand and said, "How do you do. I am Roscoe Thurston."

Who else? Poole quipped to himself. "Inspector Oliver Poole," he replied. Thurston's handshake was surprisingly firm. His dazzling smile revealed square, white teeth, most likely capped. "We'll talk in Lieutenant Donovan's office," Poole said and led the way to Freddy's big corner sanctum. "Please, have a seat, Mr. Thurston. We have a good many questions about your client, Roger Ferris. The lieutenant will join us in a minute." Poole took a position near the windows. He liked his back to the light.

"Certainly, Inspector. Anything I can do. Anything at all." Mindful of his light suit, Thurston gave the worn visitor's chair a quick once-over with a white handkerchief. Poole appreciated the fastidiousness. He might have done the same, if he owned a suit like that.

When Donovan lumbered in a minute later, Poole smiled at the obvious contrast between the two men…a kindergartner, learning to dress himself, up against the king of Italian haberdashery.

Introductions completed, Donovan pulled out a battered notebook and the business of homicide took precedence over fashion.

"Tell us about Roger Ferris and your relationship with him?" Donovan started out. He eased himself into his faux leather executive chair, which let out its usual squawk of protest.

With that homely sound Poole eased himself a little deeper into his new life in familiar territory. He felt immersed once again in the warm, seductive waters of the home town pond…splashing around with old friends and nibbling on a nice, complicated murder. Iris was close by; a great rib joint sat right down the street, and he'd found a Chinese laundry in Stone Bank for his shirts. Life was growing more tolerable.

"Roger Ferris was my client for fifteen years. We worked together to build a very decent career for him. The man survived summer stock, Broadway, the soaps and some wild women. What I cannot understand, gentlemen, is how he got himself executed in this little crack in the sidewalk." Thurston waved his arm expansively; the crack was intended to include the heartland of the country as well as Belmont. His accent was a stagy mix of upper class New England and British movie star, his own creation, Poole imagined.

"Mr. Ferris was born and raised right here." Poole pointed out quickly. "Maybe our victim came back home with bad habits acquired elsewhere, habits our killer took great exception to." Poole was oddly aware of ending his sentence with a preposition and almost expected to be corrected by Thurston, who did not look like a gentleman who tolerated imperfections.

Thurston, however, was outwardly untouched by bad grammar or Poole's insinuations. He carefully laid his stick across the desk and proceeded to light a cigar with great ceremony. He began by shooting immaculate cuffs fastened with heavy gold links; he proceeded to clip the tip of the cigar with a small scissors designed for that purpose, and finally lit the cigar with a gold lighter. He puffed expertly, gracefully balancing the cheroot between thumb and fingertips while showing to advantage a well-cut sapphire ring which rode his pinky like a saddle.

Donovan was utterly captivated by the procedure, as if he'd just witnessed an intricate bit of surgery. He asked, "Why did Ferris come back home? Was his career in New York fading?"

Thurston sighed. "Roger said he was burned out. Awful term, don't you agree? I much prefer bored or uninspired. At any rate, he said he needed a change, a rejuvenation, a return to his roots. So plebeian, but you can't always argue with someone in personal conflict." The agent shook his head in disbelief and continued to smoke. "It was madness, Lieutenant Donovan." He wobbled his head dramatically. "I tried my best to dissuade him. Fought with him, begged and pleaded. Threatened."

The agent stopped at this point and flashed a coy smile. "Now, now, gentlemen, don't misinterpret. I did not fly here Saturday night, quarrel with Roger, and stick a knife into his pretty chest. We parted friends last December. We were business associates; it would have been very foolish of me to kill off a good client." Thurston crossed one short leg over the other, taking care not to rub his pale leather shoe against the light wool fabric.

"The producer of *Yesterday's Children* says Ferris was in no danger of losing his job. Is this correct?" Donovan asked. The cop helped himself to M&Ms from his ashtray candy dish and then offered some to Thurston. The agent recoiled.

Thurston said, "Heavens, Roger was a well-loved villain; the audience adored Nick Halt. And, as his agent, I was willing to wait for him to tire of this nonsense here in Belmont. Teaching the young. Such foolishness! I was his best friend, gentlemen. I knew Roger better than anyone." He carefully traced the curve of his upper lip with the knuckle of his index finger, as if encouraging an invisible moustache.

Poole turned a few degrees to look outside. Below, two boys were looping around parked cars on skate-boards. It was a perfect morning. He asked if Ferris had problems with booze, women, money, drugs or anything else.

"Roger was well liked, had scores of friends, male and female. He was vain, charming, arrogant, and most of all determined. He went after what he wanted, and I've been around to help him. The man was no Larry Olivier, but he did have enormous sex appeal and more than average ability. Drank a bit of gin, didn't like to gamble, adored expensive things. Wanted to get rich, but that doesn't usually get us murdered, does it?" Poole noticed that Thurston readily included himself in Ferris's class. Poole figured Thurston saw to it that his vanities were generally satisfied.

"What about Vista and Eagle Eye Productions. What do you know about these companies?" asked Donovan. He pulled a cigar from his shirt pocket and lighted it with a kitchen match. The procedure was short and to the point, and he smiled a little after completing his task. Thurston took it in and seemed a trifle diminished by it. Poole wanted to laugh but did not.

"Eagle Eye was formed a year ago, Vista about five years ago. Both are quite profitable. Roger's business partner is an old actor friend, Barry Winsome, who is working on a movie in France this summer. He is Roger's age and has wealthy connections. The corporations are TV production companies, relatively modest and legitimate and in no serious trouble that I know of." The agent spoke in a straightforward manner.

"We'll need Winsome's phone number and address," said Donovan, and he handed Thurston a pad of paper and a short pencil. "Who put money into these ventures?"

"Roger assured me that Barry raised a good portion, but, strangely enough, Roger's father invested as well. A well-fixed surgeon, I understand." Thurston sounded surprised that the medical professional had thrived in this remote part of the world.

Poole looked over at Donovan; something wasn't right. Thurston's statement was contrary to what Reginald Ferris had told Donovan...that he had never put a dime into his son's companies.

"Why was it strange that Ferris's father invest?" Poole asked. He'd decided to keep Reginald's story in the vault, so to speak.

"I had the distinct impression that Roger and his father disliked one another intensely. Roger was given to audacious satires of him at parties, imitating a haughty gentleman with a tremendous ego." Thurston smiled, as if recalling the performances.

Poole smiled too, thinking Ferris had probably given equally outrageous parodies of Roscoe Thurston. Both men had the exaggerated personalities that invite satire.

"His art collection cost a small fortune," Poole said. "Are soap stars paid that well?"

"Some are, Inspector, and Roger was. But, he had other investments; I wasn't his accountant, only his agent."

"He paid cash for an art collection worth well over a million. Cash. Over a three month period." Poole raised both eyebrows at Thurston and then squinted.

Thurson readjusted his position in his chair and leaned forward. "Cash? Are you certain, Inspector? I am deeply disturbed to hear this."

"We have his marked receipts. Think about this and let us know if something comes to mind." Poole cleared his throat and went on. "What about women? Had Ferris ever married? Have any serious relationships go sour?"

Thurston chuckled and said, "Roger loved women and women loved Roger; he was never without companionship. Strictly a lady's man, mind you. Nothing funny about him." The agent winked. "Never married, that I was told. He was seeing a woman quite seriously last summer and fall, a well-to-do married lady." Thurston disapproved.

"Marjorie Verdun?" Donovan asked, puffing smoke rings toward the ceiling. Freddy might not shoot his cuffs or employ a gold cigar scissors, but, by God, Freddy did have a few smoking tricks up his sleeve. Poole nearly laughed out loud this time.

"Roger never said. He was very discreet. He might have been a cocky guy on his worst days, but he didn't gossip about his love life. Roger never wanted any trouble, just a good time. I liked that about him." Thurston laughed affectionately, like a father telling stories about a favorite son. Poole felt the man had been genuinely fond of Ferris, unlike his real father, who seemed judgmental and critical, even jealous. Odd, too, that Ferris had been so indiscreet about his affair with Marjorie here in Belmont.

"Did he know a woman with an obvious southern accent?" Donovan jumped back in.

The agent shifted his compact body in the chair and thought before he responded. "Nobody close. Of course, in the theatre one has actor friends who can easily speak with any number of accents. Why do you ask?"

Donovan explained about the phone calls and the notations in his diary of appointments with someone initialed 'A' and 'M' from June to December of last year. Thurston could offer nothing new.

Poole brought out the inscribed gold cigarette case and handed it to Thurston. The smooth gold rectangle glinted a little through the plastic bag, and Thurston ran his fingers over it, as if to feel the incised pattern on the case. "I'm sorry, Inspector," he said, "but, I've never seen this." And he handed it back with some reluctance; the trinket obviously appealed to him.

"While we're touching on physical evidence, we'd like your opinion on this too?" Poole offered up the gold charm in its plastic bag.

"Very charming, Inspector, but certainly not a man's bauble."

Poole went on to the three limerick messages and watched closely as Thurston read them.

The agent's brilliant blue eyes widened, and his poised manner stiffened. "Blackmail? Death?" He touched the pages with great care, as if they might soil his skin through their protective cover. His small nose wrinkled in distaste. "My dear fellow, these are extraordinary, but most assuredly just vicious crank mail. All actors get their share." He replaced the pages on the desk and rubbed his fingertips together, like an insect cleaning itself. "What do you make of them, gentlemen? This sort of thing is your department."

"All evidence is taken seriously," Donovan replied. "Did Ferris hint at this? A scheme that backfired?"

Head lowered and jowls resting on his pale yellow shirt collar, Thurston looked concerned for the first time, as if the reality of the crime were finally hitting him. His favorite client wasn't playing a nasty part on Broadway or on TV. He was dead, murdered under very disagreeable circumstances. Poole could see that Thurston was suffering.

"I am completely in the dark on this. Roger never confided anything sinister to me. Threats, a wronged woman wishing him dead, a mysterious King of the World...my God, a clear reference to the movies and that silly director!" Thurston rolled his eyes. He gestured and spoke dramatically. "I spoke with Roger once a week. He seemed to be himself. Naturally, I was trying to persuade him to return to civilization. We corresponded on business matters. We were very close, but, as I have told you, his private life was often closed to me. Perhaps he had to handle this situation alone." Thurston leaned forward and placed his dead cigar in Freddy's dirty ashtray.

"You have no candidates for the worldly king?" Poole pressed.

"Again, I must disappoint you. The only worldly king I can think of right now is my analyst!" He laughed. "I think he wears a crown to bed."

"It couldn't have been an arrogant director, a producer, another actor he'd worked with through the years?" Poole insisted.

Thurston shook his head and looked disturbed.

"What about the mask found on his face?" Donovan asked.

Thurston curled his lips and covered his eyes with his tiny hand. "That fact is so macabre, I can barely digest it. Roger collected those masks like he collected books on theatre and costuming. Who is to say? What goes through the mind of a killer?" The man sighed. "Perhaps it's pointing to someone hiding his identity or assuming another."

Poole tended to believe the same thing. He said, "Ferris was suffering from a bad case of nerves during the weeks before his death. He was afraid to read obituaries. Did he sound stressed or ill to you?"

"This is my first and only trip to Belmont." The agent's tone implied it would also be his last. "Roger sounded normal to me, but of course one can hide a good deal over the phone." Worry was beginning to cloud Thurston's earlier brilliance. "Roger did seem quite out-of-sorts when he abruptly left New York last winter. I assumed he'd broken up with his lady friend." Thurston frowned. "Afraid of obits? Very bizarre. Perhaps his ladyfriend died, or perhaps he had an unreasonable fear of death."

"Did he know a woman named Annette Wrenn?" Poole asked.

"Ah, the mysterious initials in the diary. You did have someone in mind, didn't you?" Thurston grinned, appreciating a policeman's attempt at drama. "Annette Wrenn." He closed his eyes and lifted his chin to the ceiling. "No, never. Who is she?"

"An old girlfriend who seems to have vanished."

Thurston raised an eyebrow. "Vanished? Perhaps on purpose, gentlemen. Perhaps on purpose." He winked, suggesting that the relationship between Roger and his women might be more complex than the murder itself. "You must know, gentlemen, that losing Roger is like losing a son. His friends and associates might be helpful… scores will be flying in this weekend for the funeral." Thurston had tired during the interview, leaving his smile and manner dulled. As he glanced around Freddy's well-worn office, he showed an eagerness to escape. Poole could understand. Thurston was a man unaccustomed to shabbiness and violence.

But, Donovan wasn't finished. "Mr. Thurston, where were you Saturday night between midnight and three a.m.?" His eyes twinkled, as if the question might be too over the top.

Thurston released a genuinely hearty laugh, enough to cause his inquisitors to grin. The preposterous question had turned around the man's mood. "Lieutenant," Thurston replied very evenly, "you cannot seriously think that I murdered my own client ...with a kitchen knife." He made it sound so absurd that the three of them managed a chuckle together. "I attended a dinner party Saturday evening in The Hamptons at the home of Mr. and Mrs. Howard Cohen. I spent the night in the guest cottage of an old friend who lives nearby. I can substantiate everything with names and numbers, which I will give to that pretty blonde secretary in the outer office wearing the world's most unattractive uniform." Thurston was making a rapid recovery.

"Where can we reach you here?" asked Poole, standing to conclude the interview.

"You don't give a man many choices. At the St. George. I'll be flying out after the funeral on Saturday evening." Rising, Thurston collected his ebony cane and smoothed his jacket, only slightly wrinkled. "I'm counting on you both," he warned them with a school master's eye. "My Roger died in your little village. Let us hope you catch the killer... tout de suite!" And with that, he hustled out of the office.

"Well," Donovan said, "that was a little like interviewing Cecil B. DeMille." He scooped up a handful of M&Ms.

"Yes, and I liked his response about Annette Wrenn...a woman gone missing on purpose. He might have a good point there." Poole began humming a few bars of 'Take Five.' Was this mystery woman the key to the case? He had no good reason to believe it. "I do like the long history between the two. Roger and Annette did discover a dead body twenty years ago."

"Jesus, Poole, that's stretching it, don't you think? As far as we know, they haven't seen each other since."

Poole didn't answer. He picked up his own walking stick and caressed the polished brass head, not nearly as grand as Thurston's ebony and gold number. Gold. Big money. Annette Wrenn and the enigmatic king. Poole thought a while without moving and then stroked the knob of the cane three times...for luck.

9

SHOW BUSINESS

Donovan showed up at Billy's around twelve-thirty, overheated and in need of refreshment after an hour with the dentist. One cheek was noticeably swollen. He and Poole moved to a table by the window where the sun was trying to penetrate a tawny skin of aged nicotine on the glass. Donovan gave Billy the high sign for a pitcher and launched into a brief summary of his dental expedition and what he'd accomplished after that.

"I've been talking to the folkssth at Asthhbury again." The Irishman's speech was suffering the residual effects of painless dentistry and was drooling. "Peething together our Roger'sth lassth daysth." He wiped his mouth. "Damned sstthuff!"

Poole was laughing. "Your eses are spilling over, Freddy."

"Pisstthh off, Poole." Donovan motioned the barkeeper to hurry up.

Donovan lisped on with his story, saying that the last funny envelope was delivered on the Tuesday before Roger Ferris was killed, according to the secretary. She said he looked upset by it and went home and was much improved the following day.

"Queer, huh?" Donovan rubbed his jaw vigorously and wiggled his tongue around in his mouth.

Poole agreed, still snickering, while Billy plunked down the pitcher and a complimentary bowl of pretzels. While Billy always treated the police with respect, he liked Donovan the best. The barkeep hurried back to his post without a word.

"So, Ferris suddenly gets his nerves under control. Pills, I suppose." Poole nibbled on a pretzel.

"Looksth like the minute he letsth down the guard, he getsth himssthelf killed." Donovan took a long pull with his eyes squeezed tight in pleasure. A tiny dribble of beer escaped his numb lip and disappeared into his whiskers.

A kid in skin-tight trousers, cowboy hat, and a rhinestone in one ear took their food order. He was getting a fair amount of attention from the noon crowd. Obviously a newcomer.

"Billy's nephew," Poole explained. "Trying to keep the lad out of our lovely jail by giving him a job."

Donovan rolled his eyes and suggested the kid try Broadway or Las Vegas.

Poole filled Freddy in on his interview with Ingrid Ferris, detailing the feud between the Wrenns and the Ferrises and the fact that Roger's girlfriend had been Annette Wrenn, Beatrice's niece, when he wasn't chasing after Marjorie. "Nobody knows where this Annette has gone. Odd, I would say, for the famous Wrenn family."

"What else did you dig up?" Donovan massaged his jaw.

"Sid at the Deli called. Said he noticed a tall woman in a big hat and sunglasses hobbling into the Beacon Street Arms with Ferris a couple days before the murder."

"One of his many admirers, no doubt." Donovan fired up a cheroot for comfort. "Valerie in disguisth?"

Poole smiled. Freddy's frozen mouth was hanging tight.

The midnight cowboy returned with split brats on chewy buns and lots of fried onions. He acted as if he was doing them a favor by putting the plates on the table. Donovan pushed him to the limit by asking for ketchup.

"I prefer ssthSally at the Depot," said Donovan, examining his lunch. "Do you think the kid would ssthabotage our brats?"

"Billy's got his eye on him."

As they dug in, Donovan chewing on the left with his head tilted, a trio of familiar voices sang out behind them. A Lauren Bacall baritone boomed, "Hard at work, I see." Poole didn't turn around; it was Catherine, his former mother-in-law. Trouble adorned with precious gems.

Iris, Dolly, and Catherine approached the table like a pack of cats. "I didn't know policemen were allowed to drink alcohol on duty," observed Mrs. Woolsey in her usual friendly manner.

Still stirring the pot, Poole observed silently.

"No law against it, Catherine," Donovan explained cheerfully. He asked the ladies to join them. The women pulled up chairs and crowded around the table. Mrs. Woolsey brushed off the seat with a napkin before sitting.

"Slumming?" asked Poole.

"We were on our way to Elmondo's when we saw your handsome faces through the dirty windows," Dolly replied brightly. She ordered a white wine from the rhinestone cowboy, who looked bewildered by the females and the order. Iris and Catherine would have the same. The big world was getting tougher and tougher for the cowboy.

"Make sure the glasses are clean," came Catherine's directive.

Poole looked up from his food; the kid looked as if he'd been hit by a rock.

"Our cowboy's like a rapper forced into the Methodist choir," Donovan remarked shrewdly. Appreciative laughter all around, including a few patrons at the next table.

"Where's the chief?" Iris asked, not meeting Poole's eyes. He figured she was still bothered by the kiss. So was he.

"Conferring with the D.A." replied Poole.

"Good. Make the silly man suffer an hour with Jasper Holmgren," remarked Catherine, who disapproved of nearly every elected official in the county and the D.A. in particular because he was a Democrat. An hour of Holmgren and Catherine would be something to see, Poole was thinking.

The wine arrived along with five bags of corn chips. Billy was going to kill the females with kindness, and pray to his old grandfather that they never come back.

"What's safe to order?" Dolly asked.

"Beer in a bottle," Iris replied. "I do love this place…absolutely free of pretense, wouldn't you say, Oliver?"

Poole looked over at Iris, narrowed his eyes and answered, "I'm particularly fond of the cigar smoke."

"What time is the funeral on Saturday?" asked Dolly, as if she didn't know.

"Three. First Presbyterian," replied Poole.

"The Reverend Brightbill must be peeing his pants by now," said Catherine.

"Mother, really!" Iris replied with some surprise.

"And, Oliver and Freddy will be there, skulking around tombstones, just in case the killer shows up," commented Dolly, examining her glass for lipstick or worse.

"The press will do the skulking, Dolly. By Friday, show business will be landing. It'll be wild around here." Poole tore open two more bags of chips.

"Half of them are here already," Iris said. "Main Street is swarming with reporters and photographers and magazine and tabloid columnists. Bombay's going nuts. There's a TV reporter practically living under his desk." Everyone liked that.

"I wouldn't miss this funeral for anything," cooed Dolly. "People will be fighting to get into the church."

"I'm only going because of Ingrid," Catherine said. "Otherwise, I wouldn't be caught dead at that circus."

"Right, Catherine," they all chimed in, not believing a word of it.

The cowboy politely took lunch orders and disappeared. He'd apparently learned from Uncle Billy that no good would ever come from antagonizing the police or Mrs. Woolsey.

"What's the latest on Marjorie Verdun?" Iris asked. "I thought you would have arrested her by now. Her car was parked in front of Roger's condo that night."

"It's too early," Donovan replied. "She's not the only suspect, as you well know."

"Did Roger ever pay Beatrice Wrenn a call?" Iris asked. "Actors are notoriously superstitious. And, we've heard that someone was stalking him."

"Beatrice?" Donovan looked quizzical and cast an inquiring glance at Poole.

"Lots of famous people go to fortune tellers when they're in trouble," Dolly pointed out.

"Roger didn't seem the sort," said Catherine. "You could ask Ingrid, but I doubt if Beatrice would divulge private information. Confidentiality. Like a priest or a doctor."

"Actors are drawn to magic and myths, lucky charms and omens," Iris went on. "Break a leg. Never say 'Hamlet' in the theatre, that sort of thing. Roger might have gone to Beatrice for a psychic reading. Lots of celebrities rely on psychics."

"Besides, Roger was practically related to Beatrice," said Dolly.

More guffaws. They all knew that Reginald was once married to Beatrice.

"Very resourceful, I always thought," said Catherine, "…Beatrice wrapping his bathrobe cord around his neck." Even Catherine appreciated the humor in that attempted murder. "Reggie deserved a nasty scare. Hasn't done him much good though."

Poole gave Donovan a look and then said they were checking all angles.

"Are you close to catching the killer?" Catherine asked, while peering into her glass as if something might crawl out.

"Would you like to be added to the suspect list?" countered Poole. He and Catherine had been enemies since the day he and Iris married. Poole had not emerged from the right social circles. This time both Iris and Catherine threw him withering glances that placed him with other lower forms of life, like dictators and kidnappers.

"Who else could have done it, besides Froggy and Gilbert Twelmeyer and his pal, Fitzhugh." Dolly said all of this sympathetically. "Frankly, I thought Roger was a stunning man. Fairly skittish, but so many artists are. Do you think he did drugs?"

Lunch with the girls, Poole mused and stuck his paper napkin on the empty plate. A fine diversion on a hot summer day, if you liked torture. He said, with rather more authority than usual, "Time to move on, Freddy," and pushed back his chair. He picked up his walking stick and prepared to leave.

"How about dessert?" mewed Dolly. "Chocolate mousse?" She lifted her forearm slightly as if the table was sticky.

"You can have mine, Dolly," replied Donovan. "Good seeing you gals."

As Donovan hurried to catch up, Poole looked back to catch the last of the ladies' conversation.

"Edgar will never believe we had lunch at Billy's," Dolly was saying.

"Gin Joint doesn't begin to describe this place," Catherine put in, as she surveyed the dingy tavern. Her diamonds winked in the one spot of sun that made it through the haze.

Iris mused, "I wonder how long it will take Oliver to call on Beatrice?"

"Do you think," Dolly said softly, "that cute little waiter would put lemon slices in the water glasses, if we ask nicely?"

Was he looking down the wrong alley? Was Freddy right? Poole supposed his curiosity about Annette Wrenn might be straining patience and logic. Then again.

Poole proceeded haltingly down Main, stopping for three relatively unnecessary traffic lights, and took a right into Pointer Heights, the posh quarter of Belmont, as Iris called it. Here, gentle, shaded and manicured knolls protected dozens of Victorian era homes, newly restored to their former majesty by the robber barons of the present day. Nothing much had changed in Belmont, except fashion and hair styles. The place had always reeked of money. Two blocks up on the corner and not far from the Reginald Ferris house, Poole stopped in front of a buttery yellow Italianate set behind a low painted fence. He cussed the heat as he parked beneath dense maples lining the boulevard. It was Washington, D.C., without the public buildings. If he'd been a crazier man, Poole would have thrown a rock at the sun. Instead, he climbed out of the car, mindful of his leg, good these days for holding him up and predicting the weather and very little else. Right now, it was telling him that rain was on its way. During the past few months his desire to recover his lost memory had gone from an obsession to a frequent itch. He still wanted to remember the circumstances of his injuries, but for the present, he was content to simply find out who had stabbed Roger Ferris. Compensations.

Wrenn House could have made the cover of *House & Garden*. A wicker basket filled with yellow daisies hung from one of the double-leaved doors, certainly not a front porch designed by a sorcerer. There were those in Belmont who called Beatrice a witch and worse. Shouldn't the door be black with a devil's mask doorknocker? Poole figured that psychics were often mistaken for ladies who dabbled in witchcraft. He didn't believe they all belonged to the same club.

Poole rang the bell and was soon greeted by a tall bird-like woman in baggy black trousers and a violet smock, its large collar turned up around her throat like an Elizabethan ruff. She resembled a tinted flamingo in brilliant evening clothes.

"Miss Wrenn, I'm Inspector Poole. We spoke earlier on the phone." She had agreed to see him on short notice...no psychic reading necessary. Poole was happy to hear that the popular seeress had a sense of humor about her work.

Beatrice ran her eyes from his head to his feet and silently waved him through to a spacious hall. An elaborately carved clothes tree bristling with an assortment of hats stood across from a graceful staircase fitted with a Turkey carpet. The house was cool. Miss Wrenn had figured out how to install air conditioning, an invention Poole considered more important than air flight, especially since the airline had lost his luggage yet again on his last flight.

Standing by the stairs, her long bony fingers wrapped around the newel post like a parrot clutching its perch, Miss Wrenn presented a picture of some cachet. All the same, Poole prayed she wasn't as eccentric as she looked. She was handsome with an aristocratic, sun-browned face and clear green eyes. He guessed she was a bit over fifty. It was hard to tell. An abundance of curly brownish hair was piled atop her head and secured by a Dutch Boy cap speckled in blue and yellow paint. Perhaps this was the way psychics dressed these days. Poole knew she normally dressed only in purple.

Eyeing the cap, Poole said, "I hope I'm not interrupting a big decorating project, Miss Wrenn."

"Don't be ridiculous. Haven't painted a thing in years." The woman's alto was clipped and husky and distinctly Midwestern. She seized his arm and propelled him into the parlor.

The sitting room was exceptionally pretty, arranged with good antiques, Persian rugs, and vases of fresh flowers. Tables bore huge stacks of books and magazines, and the stereo was playing Beethoven's Third. It was not the kind of room that beckoned the supernatural on its own. In the adjoining dining room, Poole could see an old gentleman seated at the windows. He'd parted the curtains to peer outside and took no notice of Poole. Must be Simeon Dorsett, the old uncle, his nerves hopelessly frayed in the last war.

"Sit down," Beatrice commanded, and Poole selected a velvet arm chair near the marble fireplace.

Hoping to win the woman's confidence, Poole smiled engagingly and said, "We know that your niece, Annette, was Roger Ferris's girlfriend years ago. Unfortunately, we can't seem to locate her. We're hoping that you might know where we can find her."

Miss Wrenn pulled up a small needlepointed bench and fluttered down to it. Poole noticed for the first time that the woman was wearing black high top tennis shoes with yellow laces, another trademark. She leaned toward him and said very solemnly, "Annette isn't with us anymore, Inspector."

My God, the girl's dead? Poole felt immediately deflated. But, before he could respond, Beatrice added quite cheerfully, "She moved away, right after high school. Didn't like living with weirdos; that's what she said when she left. Her parents were dead, of course." Beatrice squinted closely at Poole and waited for a reaction to her little joke.

Poole grinned. "You had me there, Miss Wrenn," he said. "But, we still need to know where she is."

"Don't know. She never writes." The hard dialect was tart and economical. Poole wondered if he sounded like her. "My mother willed this house to her when she died, with the provision that she let Simeon and me live here. Annette's lawyers handle everything."

"Do you have the name of the law firm?"

"I might. Won't do you any good. Annette didn't kill Roger Ferris, if that's what you're driving at."

Poole looked up from his notes, surprised by her assumption. "Why do you say that?"

"She escaped the Ferrises years ago. Smart girl. Too savvy to bother killing one." The psychic spat out the words like cherry pits, making it sound as if a Ferris was poisoned fruit.

"You were once married to Roger's father, isn't that right?"

"Hah!" Miss Wrenn was amused that he knew. "For a short time, sir, a very long time ago. Odious little man. Roger took after his father in some ways." She rose and turned on a lamp. The sky had suddenly darkened.

"How do you mean?"

"Arrogant. Untrustworthy. Selfish." Miss Wrenn's eyes held to something just over Poole's shoulder, as if she were conjuring up an evil Ferris on the wall behind him. Not surprising, Poole thought, she did deal regularly with the spirits. Freddy said she conducted séances in the parlor on Friday nights. What did Uncle Simeon do while Beatrice was summoning voices of the dead? Poole noticed that the old gentleman seemed disconnected from what was going on just a few feet from where he sat at the window.

"Isn't there a feud between the Wrenns and the Ferrises?"

"The Wrenns have hated the Ferrises for close to two hundred years, Inspector." The woman's regal carriage stiffened, revealing pride in this particular family legacy.

"What started it?"

"Goes back to the days of Indians and fur traders." Beatrice flapped a full sleeve toward the river and flashed her jewel eyes as if Poole should be familiar with the scandalous deeds of the region's first settlers. She didn't reveal any details.

"Who do you think killed Roger?"

"Could have been his father, but I doubt it. They never did get along." Miss Wrenn adjusted a huge gold hoop earring that swung against her collar. "Reggie isn't that mean."

"Did Roger ever drop in at your Friday séances? Theatre people are often superstitious." Poole was thinking about Iris's suggestions that day at lunch. She could be right.

Miss Wrenn squinted slightly, as if considering her answer, and then said, "No, he never did."

Poole felt as if he'd been put off. Perhaps fortune tellers didn't reveal their client list, as a matter of privacy. He put this to her. She simply repeated her earlier response, that Ferris had never attended a séance. For now, he would let the matter drop.

Before he could go on, a soft, almost otherworldly voice drifted in from the dining room. "I know who killed Percy," it said. Both Beatrice and Poole turned sharply to see Uncle Simeon looking in their direction. He'd been listening after all.

"Quiet, Simeon." Miss Wrenn stood quickly and hurried to her uncle. She wrapped her wing around his narrow shoulders.

Poole followed and quickly asked, "Who's Percy?" He was afraid he'd walked into a remake of *Arsenic and Old Lace* with a dozen bodies buried in the cellar. A rumble of thunder shook the house.

"My father, Judge Percy Wrenn, has been gone for years. Died in a fall. Simeon is my mother's youngest brother and a bit confused." She gave Simeon a hug. "The Judge wasn't a bad man, just couldn't hold all the liquor he liked to drink." Miss Wrenn laughed and Uncle Simeon smiled shyly, like a boy might react to an older sister's joke.

Simeon listened attentively. He was a cherubic looking man , perhaps not much older than his niece. His face was unlined. He seemed to have the easily frightened disposition of a rabbit.

"What do you know about the Judge's death, Mr. Dorsett?"

"He knows nothing, Inspector." Miss Wrenn tugged at Poole's sleeve to draw him away.

Poole carefully removed her hand and said firmly, "Please, Miss Wrenn, let's hear what your uncle has to say." The woman's handsome face turned sullen, but she stopped fussing.

Simeon squeezed his hands between his knees and refused to look at Beatrice. He said, "We gave them money to move away. It was better that way, wasn't it, Beatrice?" He glanced up for her approval and she appeared exasperated.

"Who got the money? And for what?" asked Poole.

"Nothing. Absolutely nothing. It's all in his imagination." Beatrice patted Simeon's head absentmindedly, as if she were consoling him with other matters on her mind. Simeon looked away, neither disturbed by her brush-off nor interested in anything else.

Poole was sure Beatrice had just muzzled the old boy. He said, "If either of you knows something about a homicide, you should tell me."

"There isn't a murder to worry about, Inspector. Except Roger's." The psychic marched toward the hall; her rubber soles squeaked on the polished wood floor. Her stride clearly indicated that Poole was to follow and make his exit.

Miss Wrenn would have made a helluva reporter, the inspector decided, with all those succcinct sentences and terse phrases. But, he would drop the matter for now. "How long has Mr. Dorsett lived with you?" Another roll of thunder rattled the teacups on the sideboard.

"Simeon came back from the war in Vietnam with his nerves all shot. Never left home again." Beatrice explained this with sympathy and understanding, and Poole liked her for it.

"A nice gentleman," Poole said. As they stood in the dim hall, Poole said, "I spoke with your brother, Kenny. He has no love for the Ferrises either. Especially Reggie; some trouble over a law suit."

"Kenny's always been too big for his britches. Thinks he's the hottest lawyer around. If Kenny had wanted to kill a Ferris, he would have strangled him with his bare hands." And with that, Miss Wrenn opened the front doors. A rush of cool, fresh air swept over them; rain had begun its dance on the porch roof. "His daughter, Meredith, doesn't much care for him either. She and Annette suffered from neglect. And, silly, dead parents."

"Where is Meredith these days?" Poole asked with renewed interest in the Wrenns.

"I wouldn't know, Inspector. But, she and Annette were two peas in a pod when they were young. Perhaps they are still together. I wouldn't be surprised."

Poole touched the edge of the door. "Try to find the name of that law firm, will you?"

Miss Wrenn nodded half-heartedly and shook Poole's hand. He thanked her and hobbled off toward the car with the downpour soaking his suit and puddling inside his shoes. It was like getting caught in the rain on the way home from school.

Once behind the wheel Poole glanced back at the house; Miss Wrenn remained on the graceful veranda, perhaps enjoying the delicious ozone as much as he. He guessed that behind the gruff exterior and the exotic wardrobe, the famous medium was a very smart and a very sentimental lady. And, she knew more than she was telling.

The *Belmont Bee Dining Guide* was a column personally researched and written by Nathan Bombay, all Donovan ever needed to know. Bombay published his latest hits and misses once a month. Four forks indicated food as good as home cooking (provided the cook was exceptional), reasonable prices, and a pleasant atmosphere where the lighting allowed customers the opportunity to read the menu, and music that did not forbid conversation. Bombay readily admitted that he served a population unaccustomed to continental cuisine, but the region did offer a number of fine eating establishments. One was the Half Moon Luncheonette across the street from the newspaper offices.

Donovan and Poole stopped by for an early supper Thursday night. The special was roast beef, mashed potatoes and gravy. Poole told Donovan slid into the back booth by the front window. Poole was smiling. Donovan could tell he was just about home again.

The Half Moon's fifties' time warp decorating… teapots and ivy wallpaper, counter stools and booths dressed in turquoise Naugahyde…. never failed to make the Irishman feel good. Plus, the juke box played Patti Page and lots of doo-ahh tunes.

"How can you eat here twenty times a week and stay so trim?" Poole teased. They had just ordered from Angie, their favorite waitress, who had returned with coffee in crockery mugs pearly with age. The Half Moon didn't have a liquor license, since it occupied valuable space just a half block from the Praise Our Savior Evangelical Lutheran Church. The town fathers favored the clergy when it came to demon alcohol and its ability to turn saints into sinners. Donovan wasn't sure he liked the Lutherans or the city fathers on this point. But, he wasn't willing to run for mayor either.

"I have the body and soul of a dancer," Donovan responded with a pat to his paunch.

Angie laughed. "How's the murder case going? My mom's a wreck. Makes me check the closets and under the beds every night." Angie rolled her big brown eyes and groaned, "Mothers."

"Making progress, honey. Tell your mom to buy a big dog."

Angie winked and said, "Gottcha. Hey, we're thinking you guys'll arrest some wacky actress at the funeral on Saturday." She pushed her pencil up under the rim of her pink checked headband.

"You never know, Angie," Donovan said. The village was starting to crawl with show business types and more press, all dolled up in oversized sunglasses and funky clothes. He recognized three TV guys gobbling mashed potatoes two booths away. "Anybody offer you a part on daytime television?" The Irishman winked at her.

"Got a few offers…but, they weren't for acting." Angie arched a reddish penciled eyebrow. "Geez, Lieutenant, some of those guys!" She whistled and headed for the kitchen, her neat little shape all dressed up in gingham and moving very attractively. He and Poole watched her disappear behind the swinging door.

No hour in a restaurant was complete without a wrap-up of police business. On Wednesday afternoon Poole had met with Kenneth Wrenn, Beatrice's lawyer brother. Poole was still toying with the notion that Roger's murder was tied to the old Wrenn-Ferris feud. Kenneth turned out to be a man of few words and even fewer answers. He claimed to know nothing current about the Ferris family and did not like hearing the Ferris name in his office. He had lost a big malpractice case against Reginald Ferris a few weeks ago and was still feeling the sting. So, the ancient rivalry was alive and well. When asked about his daughter, the attorney replied without much misgiving that he and Meredith were estranged, and he hadn't heard from Annette in twenty years. He added that Annette had been a pain in the ass when she was a kid and probably still was. End of interview.

"The Wrenns prefer to live by Wrenn rules," Donovan reminded Poole while expertly rolling a toothpick from one side of his mouth to the other.

"Marching to your own drummer doesn't work well for most people, even though I admire the concept." Poole looked out the window, hoping to see Iris waving from the newspaper office across the street. Wishful thinking was generally a waste of energy. And, Poole proved it again.

"Solo marching works fine if you have lots of money." Seeing Angie approach with a tray, Donovan tucked a napkin into his collar and switched his focus.

"Here you go, boys. Don't make pigs of yourselves now." And Angie was off to another table. The Half Moon was humming; customers were standing in line outside. Most of them looked like the Ferris crowd from New York, a little too glitzy casual to be real, and a lot of the folks far too slick to be local.

The gravy was running into the carrots; Donovan quickly dug in. "I spent another hour talking to jewelers around the state who might have made that gold charm. No luck."

Poole said, "I checked the Augusta phone directory and found a Meredith Wrenn on Flint Street and stopped by to see her. Turns out Miss Meredith was slightly indisposed…in the alcoholic sense. The tendency to drink seems to be a strong family characteristic. A housekeeper let me in, and Meredith tried her best to be cooperative. Unfortunately, she had trouble sitting up on the couch. I don't think she's seen or heard from Annette in years."

"Hell, who does know where all the cousins are hiding or buried in a big family?" Donovan shook his head in bewilderment. "I couldn't tell you a thing about my cousin, Stewart."

Poole sprinkled Sweet `n Low into the coffee and avoided the cream. "Frankly, Beatrice left me with the impression that Annette was in complete control of her assets, one of which is Wrenn House, and everything else. Somewhere. And, Uncle Simeon seems to think he knows about an old murder and a pay-off. Jesus." Poole concentrated on his dinner.

"We're not exactly short on suspects, Oliver. Most are capable of wielding a knife. Reggie does it on a daily basis." Donovan buttered a hot roll. "My money's on a lover's quarrel with Marjorie. Evidence or no evidence."

"The lab reports Marjorie's car is clean; she left no fingerprints in the penthouse, which makes me think they never met there. Looks like we're stuck with Froggy's story and his prints don't match any in the apartment. No hair and fiber match-ups either. The D.A. prefers a sliver or two of physical evidence."

"Marjorie had motive and opportunity and probably plastic gloves, booties and pure dumb luck."

Poole grunted and asked, "What's new on Twelmeyer?"

"The waitress at the truck stop confirms his story, and the deskman at the Y saw him come in about four. He was dressed pretty much as always, the man said. Wasn't toting a bloody trenchcoat or a plastic bag. His clothes looked clean, no stains."

"He had plenty of time to kill Ferris, change clothes, get rid of the murder outfit, go for coffee and return. As much as I like the professor, we can't rule him out, Freddy. He hated Ferris. Ferris made him look a fool."

Donovan agreed and said, "Roscoe Thurston wasn't much help."

"No, but he might think of something later." Poole put catsup on his roast beef. "Like Ferris's millions in cash." Poole ate a few more bites. "Miss Valerie, on the other hand, spent the night with her dentist, a chap named Douglas Heinzel, at his apartment. Returned home about eight Sunday morning. The lady likes to make up stories."

Donovan scowled. He dipped a corner of his napkin in the water glass and attempted to clean a large spot of gravy from the front of his yellow golf shirt. Poole shook his head and wondered if he wasn't more offended by the stain removal operation than he was by Mrs. Twelmeyer.

"Does Heinzel confirm this?"

"Absolutely. He's divorced. Wants no trouble with the police. Or publicity."

"Who spilled the beans?"

"One of Valerie's girlfriends, Mitzy Wilcox. Owns Mitzy's Fine Apparel on Third. They were all together at the bar after the play. She called us."

"You've been busy."

They spent the next few minutes finishing their supper.

As the two were about to leave, Donovan's cell phone sang its tune. He listened and then said, "We're on our way."

"What's so important?" Poole asked.

"The dispatcher just received a call. Marjorie Verdun was admitted to St. Luke's Hospital ten minutes ago. She's in critical condition but has managed to tell the paramedics that a black SUV forced her off the Grand Peak road late this afternoon on her way home from playing golf at the Country Club in Augusta. After crawling from her convertible, she was assisted by two hikers who carried her several hundred feet before the car exploded in a ball of fire."

"And, the SUV?"

"No witnesses, so far."

Nathan Bombay had taken a freedom of the press stance in the I.C.U. waiting room at St. Luke's. He wanted the Marjorie Verdun story. The great attempted murder caper. How a pretty society matron survives a harrowing accident and a nothing-short-of-miraculous rescue. Page one. He couldn't beat the six o'clock news, but he could whip the pants off Hammacher at the Augusta *Post-Gazette.* Hammacher was a bitter rival, another old Chicago newsman who routinely got his goat.

Froggy Verdun was explaining why his wife could not be interviewed. Bombay was countering with his own argument, that an accurate account in the town weekly with Mrs. Verdun's nearly fatal experience on the front page could very well lend great assistance to the police in apprehending the driver of the SUV who had forced her off the road.

Verdun was frazzled; his wife was in terrible shape. Bombay understood this, but he understood getting the story more. "I'll check with her doctors, Bombay, but I doubt they'll let you talk to her. She has a skull fracture, serious internal injuries, and a broken shoulder. I'm amazed she's still alive. Perhaps in a few days."

"Absolutely," Bombay replied. "But, my friend, a good news account often jogs the public's memory. We need to job memories quickly." Bombay nibbled on the end of his ballpoint. "Did she recognize the driver?"

Verdun shook his head.

As Bombay and Verdun negotiated, Bombay could see Donovan and Poole approaching at a fast clip down the corridor.

"We'd like a word with your wife, if that's possible," Poole said immediately.

Verdun nodded. "So would Mr. Bombay here and several other reporters."

Just then, a white coated doctor came up to them and asked Verdun to come with him. The doc's expression was grim.

Several minutes later, the doctor returned to the waiting room. He looked at Bombay and Donovan and Poole and the assembled reporters and said, "Mrs. Verdun did not make it, gentlemen. Mr.Verdun wants you to know that his wife has died."

"So, it's over. Why so soon?"

"And, you think I did it?"

"I'm an experienced bystander."

"So you are. Details annoy me."

"But, there is no delight without the detail. Somebody famous wrote that." Meredith was amazed at her nerve so early in the day.

"My, aren't we literary today."

Annette was avoiding the question.

"The accident was nicely done," Annette was saying. "I've always preferred the accident. Clean, spontaneous, fewer risks."

"Where does all this secrecy leave me?"

"Where it always leaves you."

"You're a cruel woman."

"Don't ever try to be me, Meredith."

"Why not?"

"You'll never pull it off."

Meredith hung up the phone and poured herself a drink.

Nathan Bombay rather enjoyed funerals. Not that he liked to see people die. It had more to do with the ritual itself. Wedding ceremonies had grown into hideous extravagances with sorry attempts by the bridal couple to rewrite classic liturgy and to substitute modern song lyrics where the congregation once heard hymns. The average wedding turned out to be a flimsy theatre piece with bad costumes. The deceased, on the other hand, rarely wrote his own material.

Funerals, in the main, offered better music...Bach over Billy Joel, no discourtesy to Mr. Joel, but Bach still had the upper hand. And, mourners generally dressed with more dignity than wedding guests, who often failed to take a look at their wardrobe before leaving the house. He recalled a female guest wearing a baseball jacket. Funerals were more dignified and honest. If you hated the one who passed over, you passed on the ceremony. No invitations, no obligations, no reply cards, no gifts. And, the ritual was irrevocable. No one ever contested a funeral.

Down at Billy's, where Bombay routinely took the pulse of the town, he found that the 'regulars' had decided that the fuss over Roger Ferris's death was about equal to the fuss over President Reagan's speech at the VFW Hall in 1984. They had a kind of Richter scale for measuring this sort of thing. Both gentlemen were celebrities, both had spent very little time in town, and both had captured for a brief time the intense interest of the press and the villagers.

Billy's Blackbirds (the barstool wags) agreed that once Reagan's motorcade passed down Main Street (appropriately swathed in patriotic bunting), and the press gobbled up the stop-over for a few newspaper column inches and two minutes on the evening news, the candidate's visit to Belmont was as quickly forgotten by the national press as a grain of sand might be removed from its great eye. The inhabitants were left to wallow and bask in the after-glow.

And, the Blackbirds believed the same thing would happen with the Ferris funeral. Belmont, through no fault or effort of its own, had found itself back in the spotlight after more than a decade, and from the town's peculiarly naïve vantage point, the citizens had easily concluded that high profile violence and big-time politics were not exactly strange bedfellows. Both were circumstances fraught with character assassination, hatchet-jobs, back-stabbings, dragon-slayings, morbid public interest, and media overkill. The public's fascination was as limited and easily satisfied as the media's attention. Both drew cameras and reporters like flies at an Elks Club picnic.

This time around, Bombay was observing, Belmont seemed to be accepting media invasion with sophistication, praiseworthy for a small town trying hard to rise to a new level. It exuded a charming noblesse oblige, so rarely found these days (even in big cities) that it was leaving reporters nonplused. A lot of the town folk said they felt sorry for this generally hard-boiled lot of journalists, assigned to cover scandal and forced to nibble on scraps and turn them into a banquet every day. Billy, for one, remarked that it was a pitiful way to make a living. The mayor, mainly concerned with how the image his city was 'impacting' (his latest new word) the state and the country (his eye on the governor's mansion), was urging his lieutenants, the chamber of commerce, assorted civic and religious leaders to exhibit cooperation and good humor in the face of celebrity tragedy. He might be the mayor of Belmont, but the man did understand the cornerstones of smart public relations. If they were wise, Belmont could turn this free publicity into something worthwhile… like money. Bombay couldn't help admire a man with this kind of flair for modern government.

By early afternoon on Saturday, the town knew about Marjorie Verdun's unfortunate death. Some believed she was forced off the road with the intent to do harm and others insisted that she was simply a bad driver. Bombay tended to believe the dying woman's final statement… that the SUV driver had attempted to kill her. It was in the hands of the already befuddled Donovan and Poole. Bombay could feel only sympathy for the detectives.

The editor strolled down Main Street with a bag of Esther's Fudge for company; he was gathering color for his editorial. It was clear that the funeral was drawing a distinctly different crowd. Show business had come to town. The press was slipping into the second banana slot. Mamie Spryer's Bed and Breakfast was filled; the St.George was booked solid; the Blink `n Nod and Sleepy Hollow motels, that anchored the town on each end, were sold out; and the hotel business in the capital ten minutes away was brisk. Cynics were saying that Roger Ferris might end up more famous dead than alive, once the media finished with him. Bombay agreed.

By two o'clock beautiful theatre and television people of every description (underweight, overdressed, strangely coiffed, all wearing designer sun-glasses) were roaming the streets licking Bitterman's ice cream cones and proclaiming the town 'cute' and 'quaint.' They consumed homemade pies, bought rag rugs and quilts, wrote hundreds of checks, and signed autographs. Glamour and increased receipts were cutting a wide path through the ordinary.

George Foote, who ran the only taxi in Belmont, overheated his old Bonneville driving back and forth from the Augusta airport and was forced to borrow his brother-in-law's new Toyota to finish out the afternoon. He stuck a hand-lettered 'Taxi for Hire' sign in the window and kept going. He confessed later that his favorite passengers had been the female stars of Ferris's soap opera, three young ladies with lots of luggage and what George called 'pretty daring costumes' for a funeral. And, they tipped 'real good.'

The Reverend Harvey Brightbill, pastor of the First Presbyterian Church on Tower Street and funeral cleric, woke early that morning with an exceptionally colorful case of hives and had to call Dr. Liebermann at home for a prescription. The doctor suggested a large brandy until the drugstore opened. Bombay learned this from the pharmacist.

Local folk rationalized a need to attend the services at the church and at Wanderer's Rest as a kind of civic duty. They felt an irresistible desire to touch the hem of a celebrity spectacle. Certainly Ferris never knew he had so many close friends. By four o'clock, Bombay had taken up a position near the Wrenn Family mausoleum on a slight rise near the center of the cemetery. Lieutenant Donovan and his chow-chow stood back from the crowd. Inspector Poole was taking the shenanigans in stride. Bombay knew that during the past twenty-four hours the investigators had questioned about two dozen of Ferris's out-of-town friends and colleagues. Donovan informed Bombay outside the church that if Ferris had an enemy in New York, nobody was naming names.

By four fifteen a silver hearse and a string of black limousines, transporting the deceased, his immediate family, and a chosen few, entered the small graveyard. The day was shirt sleeve warm and cloudless. Donovan and Poole were scouring the crowd for anyone suspicious. Bombay noticed that Beatrice Wrenn and Uncle Simeon entered at the last minute and stood back near the narrow road. Apparently the ancient Wrenn-Ferris feud did not forbid funerals. Froggy Verdun was not there. The several hundred mourners were remarkably quiet.

In the hush and peace of the graveyard, Bombay found that the ceremony had been nicely orchestrated. A somber prayer from the Reverend Brightbill (ever so slightly pink with hives) was accompanied by soft weeping and nose-blowing. A flock of mourning doves cooed in the tall pines, as if paid for their performance. At the end of the short service, an employee from Antoine's Funeral Home released a dozen white doves which willingly flapped their way to freedom. And it was over.

Bombay knew that once the casket was lowered into the earth, the insanity of the past few days would lift like early morning mist. Life would return to normal… that is, if the vicious murder of a television star in a small Midwestern town is ever normal.

10

THE FAIRIES

It was midnight, the day after Roger's funeral, and Annette was thinking about the old warrior. How odd that certain childhood images could drift in and out of memory for years and years. Would there be others? Who could be certain? One thing did remain constant. It was her ability to recall detail. She could remember with perfect clarity certain scenes and words and emotions, some going back to childhood. Her gift of memory was almost as impressive as her gift for survival.

She recalled now, in an instant, that December evening in New York…

She and Meredith had been Christmas shopping in the city all afternoon. Around five o'clock, a cab dropped her at Manor House; Meredith continued on to her own flat a few blocks away. She rode the elevator to the twentieth floor and let herself into an elaborately designed three-storied apartment where she placed her packages on a round mahogany table of great pedigree centered on the foyer's black and white marble floor. After slipping out of her fox coat, she tossed the fur onto a settee near the staircase and entered the library to fix herself a drink. She was surprised to find her husband at the fireplace, jabbing the burning logs with a poker. He was dressed in evening clothes. A noble fir, its sprawling branches spiked with white lights and silver ornaments, glittered from its place by the window at the far end of the room.

"Alfred, darling, you're home," she said. "I thought you were going to a banquet tonight." She kissed Alfred's cheek lightly, but he abruptly turned away.

"What in the world is the matter? Are you ill?" She reached out to touch his face, but he thrust her hand aside, nearly upsetting his drink. He acted as if he wanted to say something but couldn't and walked stiffly to the other end of the book-lined room.

She could only wait for an explanation.

Finally, Alfred said, "I have met a friend of yours." He paused. "A Roger Ferris. He came to see me with a most interesting story. Do you have any idea what he told me?"

Alfred stood with his back to her, choosing to address the periwinkle sky tenting Central Park far below. She remembered the distinct color of it, gray-violet streaked with spiraling snow, like the blueberry marble cake her grandmother used to bake. Recalling this comforting childhood image was better than thinking about where this conversation was leading.

Roger's name lingered in the warm, smoke-scented air longer than the other words. On hearing it, she experienced a modest palpitation and a flutter of nerves. The reaction didn't last long. She could always draw strength and a fierce kind of control from a place deep inside. She believed an old warrior lived behind her heart.

"No, Alfred," she replied evenly, "I don't know what you're talking about." She began making a scotch and soda by dropping ice cubes into a crystal glass. No longer nervous, she felt as tranquil as a priest saying Mass.

"You deny knowing this Ferris?" Alfred turned at the end of the long room and walked toward her.

Her drink made, she kept her eyes on the hearth where she warmed her hands, as if they might be discussing the guest list for a party.

"Roger Ferris." She repeated the name casually. "Isn't he an actor? I may have met him...at a charity cocktail party or an opening somewhere." She sounded unconcerned. "What story could he possibly have to tell you?"

Alfred came up behind her and leaned against the mantle-piece to catch her face in the firelight. She knew what he was doing; he could be so transparent. He was watching for signs of fear and deception, emotions she had learned to conceal long ago. Reserve and discipline were her strengths, qualities that Alfred admired.

"Ferris told me that you lied about your past. He said that your family is composed of drunkards and lunatics; that you changed your name. He said you were mixed up in a murder years ago." She remained impassive. "Mr. Ferris maintains that you and he were lovers twenty years ago and still are." Alfred stopped here and waited, his bony fingers clenched into a claw on the mantle-shelf. "Don't you have anything to say?" His breath smelled of brandy and came in labored pants.

"He's lying," she replied. Then, she laughed lightly and sat down in a velvet fauteuil, loving the heavenly down cushions. She automatically arranged the folds of her skirt; posing came naturally to her. She said, "He is obviously trying to get money from you. It's a con game. How could you be foolish enough to believe a story like that?" This time she looked Alfred directly in the eyes when she spoke. Alfred liked directness.

"I don't think I've been foolish at all, my dear." This time it was Alfred who used the passage of seconds to his advantage. He downed the remainder of his brandy and poured another. He said quite matter-of-factly, "I've had you investigated. I received the report this afternoon."

"Investigated?" She sniffed and re-crossed her long legs, swinging a narrow foot in a slow tempo, suppressing a growing impatience. "By whom? One of your sorry little background detectives? Someone as delusional as your Mr. Ferris?"

"The investigation was conducted by a well-respected agency right here in New York. The gentleman in charge took his time and uncovered some fascinating information." Alfred seemed to be warming to the subject and kept going in a hurried tone. "One notable tidbit that Ferris did not know, or I'm sure he would have brought it up, was the heartwarming fact that your son is illegitimate. If Ferris had known that fact, his price would have been higher." Alfred managed a meager chuckle, as if pleased to have saved the family fortune.

"I'm afraid your detective needs a refresher course in detecting, Alfred. This is a set-up. You are an extremely wealthy man; you have a well-known wife. These men have devised the perfect scam." She held her husband's gaze with complete confidence.

"I found the records to be quite convincing. How convenient for you that changing your name can be so simple. Which name does your lover use? Or, does he have a pet name for you?" The alcohol had numbed Alfred enough to allow this modest sparring. Normally, he was simply an old man who possessed a huge inheritance, a patronizing attitude, and a rather dull wit.

"Don't be absurd. You know my name. You're drunk."

She rose from the chair and walked out to the hall where she crossed the stark black and white squares of marble. She gathered up the Christmas packages from the table and started up the steep spiraled stairs to the second floor. At the first landing, she placed a few boxes on a small table and then continued up the steps to her third floor bedroom. When she reached the top, she could see Alfred following, moving uncertainly up the graceful curve, clinging to the handrail and his brandy glass. She wished he would leave for his dinner.

It would appear that Roger had called her bluff; he had squealed to Alfred about her secrets. He had threatened to do this if she refused him more money. During the past six weeks she had paid Roger a small fortune for his silence. But, true to character, he wanted more. When she told him she was sick of paying and suggested he find another rich plaything to dupe, she never imagined he would reveal the past or their affair. Unfortunately, her husband was a man who hated scandal more than he feared death. Roger had made a serious error.

A minute later, Alfred stumbled into her room and leaned against the door frame, winded from the climb and still agitated. "How much do you think it will cost me to keep Mr. Ferris quiet?" The words were slurred, and Alfred's pale, slightly bulging eyes made her cringe.

"I have no idea, and I don't care. If you paid him one penny, you were stupid. Now, leave." She immediately took hold of her husband's arm and tried to turn him around, but he grabbed her wrist and held tight. "Stop acting like a bully!" she shouted as she yanked free of him. Alfred's use of force was uncharacteristic; he usually employed other methods for getting what he wanted.

"Mr. Ferris appears to be fairly well-fixed and quite resourceful. For an actor." Alfred was sneering again. "Perhaps you should run to him. You are obviously as common as he is." Alfred waved an arm at her and began moving backward into the hallway, sniggering hollowly. He never let her

forget that his ancestors had stepped onto the land from the Mayflower, that they had remained infinitely more powerful and prosperous than a good many others.

"If I were you, I would keep my mouth shut."

"You, my dear, are in no position to tell me anything. When I divorce you, you'll end up with nothing! And that includes Evan. The boy will be mine. Mine!" Alfred's reedy voice had risen sharply with each segment of the threat. "You're unfit! Unfit to be anyone's mother." The final damnation was delivered in a low growl while he shook his glass at her like a tent preacher brandishing a Bible at the sinners.

She watched droplets of liquor erupt from the crystal rim and spill onto the carpet. Alfred had coveted Evan from the start. He was an old man who needed an heir, genetically pure or otherwise; it no longer mattered to Alfred at his age. He had to possess a son, and he had made Evan his own.

"Murderer!" Alfred shrieked. "Traitor!" The man's small shrewd eyes popped with the sting of betrayal and the kind of ugly disbelief peculiar to men who win and then lose wives who are ornaments.

God, Annette thought, he had exhibited that same expression on his long, pinched face the night she met him. He had been quarreling with another man at a party. She focused on him now, a cat eyeing a rodent. She listened to the terms of her future with a silent composure learned long ago. What could she say to this smug, self-righteous prig who would dare take away her son? He was a bigger fool than any of the others. No one would ever take away the boy. No one.

Without giving Alfred a moment's preparation, she lunged at him and slammed his face with her closed fist. The blow was so hard that he stumbled backward and bumped against the scrolled iron balustrade that stretched across the landing. The rail caught him in the curve of the spine. As Alfred struggled to regain his balance, she watched his lean frame teeter across the bar, seesawing on the pivot like a trapeze performer executing a trick.

She knew exactly what to do. Alfred's long thin legs were no match for his heavier torso, and she grabbed his ankle. In one deft move, she tipped the elegantly trousered leg toward the ceiling and let go. She could feel his silky sock in the palm of her hand. Alfred's black clad body plunged into the deep well of the staircase. It passed the intricate balusters and the coil of the polished brass rail, silhouetted to perfection against the squares of black and white marble below. The sharp contrasting images would have pleased an artist's eye. Smiling at the beauty of the composition, she held her breath as the body fell through space.

The old man made a horrid sound as he fell, not really a scream but something worse. Next, the tinkle of broken glass and the thud of the body as it all hit the stone floor. The exquisite mahogany table was spared.

By the time she reached him, she could see that Alfred was dead. The distorted position of the head, the unblinking, prominent eyes, thin mouth agape, a trickle of blood seeping from a portion of the cracked skull and the ears. She had seen that expression of horror before, many years before. Crouching, she placed two fingers over the artery in the thin neck and felt nothing but warm skin. Alfred was gone.

Rising again, she stood next to the body and regarded the form as dispassionately as she might have scanned a bill of sale. She felt amazingly light-headed, free and utterly triumphant. But, the sheer exhilaration of killing didn't last very long. For her, it never did. There were things to do.

Returning to her room, she picked up the packages and bags and turned out the light. Descending again to the second landing, she retrieved the few boxes she'd left there and returned to the entrance hall where she dropped the bags to the floor, just inside the door. It was then she noticed the broken glass scattered over the marble squares. She side-stepped the pieces and moved quickly into the library where she found her own glass. She took it to the kitchen where she washed it and put it in the cupboard.

Before calling the police, she telephoned Meredith and asked her to come immediately. There had been a terrible accident, she said. A kind of accident. Meredith would understand. With that completed, she stood near the door and waited.

Ten minutes later Meredith arrived by cab. The cousins looked down at the body in what could have been seen as a brief and unemotional memorial. Neither one spoke.

Finally turning away, she called the police, and Meredith retreated to the library to make them each a strong whiskey.

Meredith did most of the talking when the police arrived while she sat on the settee with the fox coat draped over her shoulders, a widow in shock. Meredith explained to the investigating detectives that she had received a call from her cousin a half hour ago, about finding Alfred dead on the foyer floor. She said her cousin had sounded hysterical.

The police were surprisingly polite and considerate. Apparently, very, very rich people were sometimes treated with kindness by New York City cops. The detective in charge asked a few obvious questions. Had Mr. O'Neill been drinking? Had he been alone in the apartment before Mrs. O'Neill's return? The officers assumed after a look around that O'Neill had somehow fallen from the third floor balcony. The proceedings were almost as cut and dried as the investigation into Leonard's death years ago. From behind her fur, she watched Meredith conceal a tiny smile.

After the body was removed and the officers departed, the cousins had another drink and savored the bewitching serenity that follows the extinction of a demon. Evan would have to be told. Meredith offered to call his boarding school and reached for the phone.

"All done with the car, Simeon?" Beatrice called out when she heard the screen door slam.

Looking up from a sink of dishes, Beatrice watched her uncle shuffle into the kitchen; his Wellingtons squished against wood floor. From his pained expression, she knew something was bothering him, and he'd tucked his fists behind the bib of his overalls.

"What's the matter, does the Lincoln have a scratch?" He loved Eleanor's old car more than just about anything else.

Simeon squirmed into a slat back chair and pursed his lips in silence. His pale gray eyes fixed themselves on the tabletop.

"You can tell me. If you broke something, we'll fix it straight away." Beatrice pulled out a chair for herself and pushed a plate of cookies in his direction.

"Have one; you'll feel better. Peanut butter with criss-cross marks on the top, just the way you like them." She smiled, encouraging him to respond. It had taken a long time to win his trust after Eleanor's death, but niece and uncle now shared a solid kinship, more like mother and son, even though Simeon was a mere ten years older. Thank God, her nerves were in better shape than his. She had inherited her father's tough constitution and Eleanor's intolerance of naughty behavior.

Simeon picked out a cookie and said, "I heard them talking at the funeral, in the back of the church. I couldn't help it." His voice was apologetic, his boyish face nearly unmarked by the years, as if his internal stress had protected him from aging.

What had prompted Simeon to think of the funeral, Beatrice wondered. He had remained silent since the burial.

"Who said what, Simeon?" Beatrice prayed for patience. She had no desire to emulate her mother, who played the saint rather too well. But, she did envy Eleanor's enormous tolerance, forced to endure a philandering alcoholic husband, two sons bent the way of their father, and the burden of caring for a tormented brother. Indiscretions, anxiety, death. It was no surprise that Eleanor had spent hours praying the rosary in that old damp church.

Simeon chewed his cookie and tapped his nails on the wooden table. He tended to fidget when forced to reveal anything disagreeable, as if his body wanted to wriggle out words his brain preferred to hide. "It wasn't very nice, Beatrice."

"Simeon, you can tell me." Beatrice ate a cookie, too. It would take the edge off until lunch. What had he heard? Their neighbor, Mrs. Mackie, had attended the Ferris funeral. The whole town had been there. Simeon had heard the shrews gossiping.

"You won't like it." Simeon tried to look obstinate by crinkling his face, but he only looked silly.

Beatrice laughed. "Nothing bothers me, Simeon. I have the hide of a rhino." Simeon grinned a little. Beatrice was aware of her reputation as a rich eccentric. 'Tis better to be a trifle odd than too normal, her father used to say. And, Percy was an expert. She was assuming someone had insulted her at the funeral.

"It was about Roger Ferris."

"I see." Her uncle was trying to be tactful. "And who said what about poor Mr. Ferris?"

"Mrs. Mackie told another lady in a green hat that one of the Wrenns murdered Roger Ferris." Simeon began jiggling his legs up and down in spasms of nervous energy. "And, most likely Marjorie Verdun too."

It was like talking to a five-year-old, Beatrice reminded herself. What would they do when they were very old? She placed her hands on top of Simeon's and he grew calmer instantly.

"She didn't mean you, Simeon." An innocent trapped among the sinners. Life was such a struggle for Simeon. "People get funny ideas. They say mean things. What else?"

"She said only a fruitcake like Beatrice would stab a man in his bed and put a mask on his head." He paused and added, "She said you were a spook."

He was like a child tattling on a sibling. But, a reliable child who never lied. "A spook and a fruitcake?" Beatrice grasped the old man's hands and laughed as if he'd told a very good joke. "You and I know I'm no spook; and I promise you, I didn't kill Roger or Mrs. Verdun." Her reputation was intact. Good. Who would pay to visit a psychic who wasn't a bit peculiar? It was just good business. "I just look like a fruitcake, Simeon." Beatrice deliberately cackled and ruffled up her nest of curly hair. This usually made Simeon snicker.

Simeon smiled broadly this time and then consumed another cookie. His earlier distress had been relieved by her words of explanation…the catharsis of dialogue and peanut butter cookies. He had returned to his state of detachment, a simple world of books and music and the Lincoln.

Beatrice poured them each a glass of milk. "Roger came to me for help, like all the others. Some of the Wrenns and the Ferrises may not like each other, but that shouldn't worry you."

"You told the policeman that Roger didn't come here."

Such honesty….no wonder he'd withdrawn from the world. Beatrice said, "Roger didn't want anyone to know about the cards. I told a little white lie to Inspector Poole."

With Beatrice's assurance of her innocence and therefore his, Simeon finished his milk and returned to the back yard. "Life should be that simple for all of us," she muttered to the walls.

Returning to the dishes, Beatrice found comfort in watching Simeon bathe the car. The dear old thing. As she scoured cookie pans, her thoughts returned to the night Roger Ferris did indeed stop to see her. He was horridly frightened. Had Annette finally taken her revenge? Slipped into town, accomplished her deed and then disappeared again? Beatrice ran her hands beneath a stream of warm water. Possible. Had she run Marjorie off the road? Beatrice could feel disaster in her bones. Instinct had warned her about Annette years ago, and Beatrice could feel her presence again. She was close by. Beatrice shivered in spite of the warmth of the morning. Sometimes it was difficult being a Wrenn.

Beatrice began drying her pans. Oliver Poole was back too, no doubt sent by the gods. The man was quick to pick up nuances ignored by others; he was a well-trained hound. Beatrice pushed the cookie pans into the cupboard and put away the bowls. How much could he find out? Wrenn secrets were numerous and well-kept, but there were people in these parts with good memories. And, Poole was a charming, savvy cop, and, therefore, a dangerous one. What were her responsibilities here? How far would all this go? A kind of heaviness pressed down on Beatrice's firm, square shoulders. The burden was still there. Perhaps Poole deserved to know that Roger came for advice. Perhaps he deserved a call.

Outside in the yard, Beatrice could see Simeon picking up the garden hose. He directed the polished brass nozzle at the Lincoln and released a spray of water that sheeted the windshield and spread over the gleaming green hood like a shimmering curtain of mercury unrolling in the sun. It was hypnotic. There was purity in what the old man did which allowed her to forget for a moment some of the things she knew.

Donovan pushed open Poole's office door that afternoon and exclaimed softly, "I had a dream!" The Irishman leaned against the door jamb, neither in the room nor out of it, rather like the man himself, Poole thought. "About the gold charm!"

Poole thought Freddy's eagerness might swallow him up. "What about the charm?" Poole motioned for Freddy to come in and close the door. Too many Pfeiffers at lunch again.

"I fell asleep in my chair and saw that damned gold charm swinging in the air like an ornament." Donovan interrupted his story long enough to take a swig from Poole's Dr. Pepper. "A choir of children were singing 'Joy to the World' with an accordion player. It was awful." Freddy made a face and then hurried on. "The charm suddenly turned into a real house with candles in the windows and a tiny lighted Christmas tree in the cupola." The lieutenant was grinning inside his whiskers now.

Poole said that was very nice and circled the air with his hand. "Get on with it."

"Nice? The house, Oliver. The charm! It's Wrenn House!" Donovan patted his stomach as if rewarding a portion of his body for doing good work. "Every Christmas Eleanor and now Beatrice put a lighted fir in that cupola." Donovan was beaming like a school boy, and then, he sprang into a kind of lopsided Irish jig which left him panting.

Poole jumped to his feet and banged his stick against the edge of the desk. "Remind me, you big Irishman, to fill you up with Pfeiffers every noon." He giggled; they both did. "I knew it! The Wrenns and the Ferrises. I knew it!"

"The missing link is solid gold and right under our noses." Donovan skipped around the room. "You were right; there is a connection. But, what? Is it Beatrice, Annette? Kenny? Reggie?"

"Take another nap, Freddy. Figure out what that damned mask means. Figure out who was driving the black SUV that killed Marjorie. We have to figure out why."

Donovan scowled. "I'm not too partial to masks, Poole." He'd seen Beatrice Wrenn's tarot cards....like a deck of macabre masks.

"Do you think the spirits are talking to us, Freddy?" Poole eyed Donovan, a man visibly uncomfortable with any spirit other than the Irish Catholic kind. "The killer's telling us what to look for."

Donovan headed for the door; the bounce had gone out of his step. At the door he said, "Now that I'm awake, I don't even want to think about it."

Looking cool and elegant in a pale blue shirt and a long white skirt, Ingrid Ferris greeted Poole at the door and suggested they sit on the porch. It was Tuesday afternoon about three, just two hours after Beatrice Wrenn's call. Beatrice had admitted to Poole that she had lied about Roger Ferris. He had stopped by to see her, seeking her counsel. She read the cards for him. Ferris told the psychic that a woman was trying to kill him. Poole thanked Beatrice for clearing things up. Beatrice insisted she did not know who was threatening Ferris, but she was sure Roger knew.

Ingrid Ferris poured two glasses of lemonade. "How can I help, Inspector?"

"I need to know more about Annette Wrenn. We're stuck in neutral on where to find her." He would keep the Wrenn House charm a secret for now.

"Odd, isn't it? In a little town like this where everybody knows your business. It's the one thing I dislike and can't get used to." Ingrid smiled. "I'm originally from San Francisco."

"I agree." Poole rocked gently in a wicker rocker painted pale pink. "Annette's whereabouts have been hidden by a complex set of legal arrangements."

"That kind of maneuvering is usually accomplished through attorneys on behalf of wealthy clients," Ingrid astutely pointed out.

Poole was now under the impression that Ingrid might know more about this sort of thing than her husband. Ingrid Ferris, too, was a wealthy woman.

"I haven't heard a thing about her since she left twenty years ago. First Roger and then Annette. I'm ashamed to say that Reggie was pleased to see them both leave."

Poole leaned forward. It was this kind of casual chat that often bore fruit. "Why was that?"

"Reggie was annoyed that Roger preferred the theatre to medicine. And he didn't much care for Roger's romance with Annette, for obvious reasons, the old feud and his humiliating union with Beatrice Wrenn, Annette's aunt." The afternoon light striking Ingrid's fair hair created a halo around her head. Poole found her enormously attractive.

"The feud? Why should your husband care?"

"This old animosity seems to demand loyalty from both sides, Inspector Poole. It's ridiculous but real." Ingrid laughed.

Poole smiled. "Remnants of the old days. But, wasn't Annette removed from all that?"

"Not really. She reminded Reggie of his public embarrassment. Add to that the usual suspicions and rivalries piled on top of prejudice and envy." She wrinkled her nose at the idea.

"Describe Annette again."

"Shy, quiet, studious. She loved horses. She and Roger were friends because they both liked to ride at Trotter Stables."

"Do you think Roger and Annette agreed to leave separately and then meet again in New York?"

"I don't think so. Their break-up was unfortunate."

"How was that?"

"Annette was pregnant, and Reggie threatened to disown Roger if he married the girl. Not very likely, since Roger was determined to have a career, not a family." Ingrid looked troubled. "The circumstances were cruelly managed, and I'll never forgive Roger or my husband for simply dismissing the girl with an envelope of money."

"Money? You mean Reggie paid her off?" Medieval, even for Reggie Ferris. Poole was stunned, but he liked the tight connection between Annette and Roger.

"No, the money was for an abortion. Reggie arranged it."

"Did she have the abortion?"

"Yes; she told Roger. And then she moved away."

The two sat for a moment without speaking. Poole felt as if he'd crossed a threshold, but the room beyond was still dark as pitch. He said, "Did you know that Roger consulted Beatrice a few nights before his death?"

"Did Beatrice tell you that?" Ingrid's eyes widened.

"Yes. She read the cards for him. He told her someone was going to kill him."

Ingrid gasped and put her hand to her mouth. "Beatrice never said a word. And, we're such good friends." She was obviously upset.

"She didn't want to alarm you. Roger said a friend sent him to her for advice."

"Good grief. Roger wasn't particularly superstitious, unless he picked it up working in the theatre. Actors often attach themselves to charms and omens." Ingrid paused and said, "Do you think Beatrice knows something about his murder?" Poole watched Ingrid stiffen. It was the first time she had looked guarded.

Poole said he doubted it. "I do think she knows more about Annette than she's telling."

"Yes, Beatrice can be secretive when she wants. She figures things out in her head and then holds back to see what happens."

Poole nodded. "One or two more questions. How did your husband and your son get along when Roger returned last winter?"

"It was strained, unfortunately."

"Why do you think the killer threatened Roger with limericks?"

"Reggie remembers Roger and his friends making up silly limericks about teachers and kids they didn't like. Harmless and rather funny."

"You mean Marjorie and Froggy, Annette and Meredith?"

"Yes. They were close."

Ingrid Ferris was missing the important connection between the past and the present. Could it be deliberate? Poole was uncertain.

"Do you think the same person killed Roger and Marjorie?" Ingrid asked, looking puzzled. "Frankly, I was beginning to think Marjorie killed Roger and Froggy got rid of Marjorie. Heaven knows he had motive."

Poole wasn't surprised by Ingrid's conclusion. Marjorie had been trouble coming from two directions. He said, "We're not sure."

The two talked a bit more and then Poole departed. The inspector was certain he was making progress but remained fuzzy on just where he was going.

The following afternoon Iris accepted a ride with Oliver on the way back from Marjorie Verdun's funeral at the Unitarian Church. It had been a simple ceremony with every seat taken and a handful of mourners left to stand outside. Froggy and the two children remained dry-eyed and outwardly unemotional throughout. A young minister with little aptitude for sermonizing had summed up Marjorie's life in ten minutes of considerate remarks about her role as wife, mother, and selfless community volunteer. He noted the senselessness of her unfortunate death and announced that the burial would be private. Marjorie's parents seemed to be in charge, while Froggy moved through the throng like a sleep-walker. No social gathering or luncheon followed the bare-bones service, which Iris found unfortunate and curious for the socially prominent Verduns. Marjorie would have loved an elaborate send-off; she would have demanded it.

Oliver offered no commentary on the funeral or Marjorie's demise. The coroner had ruled the death an unfortunate accident, since there appeared to be no proof or any witness to confirm that another car forced Mrs. Verdun from the road. The deceased's hospital bed account of the incident apparently had fallen on deaf ears. The D.A. believed the victim simply missed the sharp turn and crashed. Hikers who saved Marjorie from the explosion never saw another vehicle.

At the moment, Oliver preferred to talk about Annette Wrenn. "The woman might think she's been given a legal burial, entombed as she is in a ton of corporate papers, but we're gaining on her." He grinned and circled the block again, looking for a parking place. They were meeting Freddy and his wife for a late lunch.

"You're still going on about this Annette?" Iris asked. "My God, Oliver, it's been twenty years. What possible reason would she have to kill Roger?"

"We have a solid link between the Wrenns and the Ferrises."

He told her about Freddy's dream and the mystery of the gold charm. "The charm is a perfect replica of Wrenn House. Wrenn House!" Oliver couldn't stop grinning.

"Psychic forces and beer at work." Iris laughed. "Why don't you have Beatrice contact Roger at her Friday séance?"

"It might save time. Trouble is Freddy is not comfortable with the spirit world."

"Odd for an Irishman," Iris quipped. "But, seriously, which Wrenn could have dropped a charm at the murder scene...next to the body, for heaven's sake?"

"I know. I know. I'm thinking Annette made an unnoticed comeback."

"Very iffy. Is this the way the F.B.I. operates? This is a small town. Beatrice would have spotted her by now, don't you think?"

"The younger Miss Wrenn might move under cover of darkness." Oliver was deliberately dramatic.

"Spooky," Iris replied, and then, her mind immediately seized on a strange experience she'd had just recently. She was revisited by a peculiar image, a disjointed picture which had stayed in her mind, an image that irritated like a sliver. "Oliver," she finally said, "I've just remembered something odd; it's related to this cover of darkness thing! I saw a tall person…in a long dark coat...kind of loping through Charlotte's yard. It was right after Roger's murder. Under cover of darkness." She grinned.

"Loping?"

"Yes, loping. Well, let's say, a half-hearted lope. The person was trying but needed more practice." Iris laughed. "A clumsy person loping."

"Good grief, my girl. Is this the way you write books? A half-hearted lope. Freddy will love that." Poole laughed and began circling the neighboring block. Belmont's downtown was crammed with visitors and regulars today.

"Let's not get too critical here, darling." The 'darling' had slipped out unintentionally and nearly automatically. It was hard to shake off the old Oliver. "I couldn't imagine who would be sniffing around Charlotte's back garden after sunset."

"Maybe it was Charlotte."

"No, she was gone. She told me she was going out."

Oliver shrugged and then swore when a nice parking space was grabbed by a sports car. "Maybe it was a dream. Any break-ins in the neighborhood?"

"No. Oh, well, I suppose it was kids playing after-dark games."

Oliver nodded in agreement. "I spoke again with Ingrid. She said Roger and the old gang…that would be Froggy and Marjorie and Annette and cousin Meredith... used to make up nasty limericks about people they didn't like." Oliver pulled right and headed around another block, still looking.

"So, the limerick form had meaning. Nice clue, Oliver. That would link Froggy and Marjorie to the crime." Iris hurriedly pointed out a spot right in front of the restaurant and Oliver pulled in sharply. "We live right."

"At this moment we do. Getting back to Ferris. We have no prints or forensic evidence to show that either Verdun had been in Ferris's condo. Freddy and I think the writer of the limericks was definitely identifying himself, or herself." Poole turned off the engine, and the two waited to spot the Donovans. They were early.

"Find anything else?"

"A blockbuster. I've been saving it, like dessert." Oliver grinned and turned in his seat to see her face. "Annette and Roger were pregnant at graduation, and Reggie paid for an abortion."

"You are kidding!" Iris gave Oliver's arm a solid punch. "Reggie did that?"

"According to Ingrid, who is still upset about it."

"In other words, Annette was paid to leave Roger alone? Could be she wanted the baby."

"We may never know."

"So, any which way you look at it, Annette's motive for murder is a trifle old, but you think it's still viable."

"Righto."

"There they are." Iris pointed out Joanne Donovan walking toward them. Her big hat was flopping in the breeze. Freddy gave them a salute and loosened his tie. Iris waved back.

"No need to tell you to keep this under your hat."

"No need."

Music usually helped, but not tonight. Poole listened to the Beethoven Emperor, the Schubert Impromptus, five Paul Desmond tracks and remained suspended in a vacuum. A nameless, faceless image niggled at him. He had traced the undercurrent to Iris's party, where it lay like crumbs under a rug. The alley fight seemed to be a part of it, but there was something else.

Poole lay stretched out on the couch with Ferris's photo albums and yearbooks on the floor next to him. The ceiling needed paint. Maybe he should quit thinking and unpack a few more moving cartons. He had taken off a few hours to get settled in his new digs, a roomy condo carved out of a restored turn-of-the-century office building on Capitol Square. He now had five good-sized rooms and a perfect view of the statehouse across the park, a reminder of the nation's capitol, complete with classic dome, porticos, and Doric columns. He could almost hear flags flapping in the wind.

Poole's furnishings were well-chosen and expensive; his tastes ran to contemporary and Bauhaus when he could afford it. His library was extensive with the weight on American history and twentieth century plays and novels and biographies. Recordings, tapes, and CDs covered music from the baroque to Brubeck, which explained his favorite possession, a rebuilt Steinway grand which occupied one corner of the living room. Freddy said the piano looked like a fat lady on a settee. Poole fantasized that he played like Teddy Wilson and painted like Winslow Homer, but hell, everybody had delusions of grandeur once in a while. He fully understood that he was part Renaissance man and part cop. Not bad, considering he'd never been in analysis...apart from a handful of post-trauma sessions with a shrink in Washington. The hospital psychiatrist had suggested extensive therapy. Poole argued that he only needed work. His interrupted sleep often prompted him to think the docs might have a secret formula, but he wasn't going to give in just yet. He liked playing the tough guy part.

While sorting his thoughts, Poole thumbed the *Belmont High Bugle* with its rows of faces grown all too familiar. He flipped over the slick pages and munched potato chips, the bag open on his chest. Marjorie Drummond Verdun smirked at him with sweetly frosted lips and black penciled Bambi eyes. Poor thing. A very short life. Arthur 'Froggy' Verdun posed stiff and uncomfortable in a suit and turtleneck, powerful even without his football pads. Poole studied the quite ordinary features of Annette Wrenn, decidedly mousy compared to the others. No make-up, no fancy hairdo. She looked like a girl who preferred horses to people. Her eyes were pretty but the chin was weak and her nose a trifle long. What would she look like now? Twenty years might have turned her into a plump matron. The silly aphorism beneath her photograph read 'Still waters run deep.' Plain kids always got that one. Why was Roger attracted to her? Was she easy? Or was it just the horses?

Roger's beach boy-rock star face grinned at him with a mouthful of perfectly straightened teeth and a long haircut. Definitely charming and naughty, like an adorable two-year-old intent on shoving his fork into a light socket. Roger's caption read 'I want to be bashful, but the girls won't let me.' Cute. Did anyone's basic personality change much after adolescence? Or was the die cast at birth? Poole's old Dad used to say, 'Once a bastard, always a bastard.' And that son-of-a-bitch ought to know.

"I must be getting old, quoting my wayward father," Poole muttered to himself. "And talking to myself. Jesus."

Poole groaned, sat up and moved to a comfortable lounge chair near the window. A call to one of his lady friends might be in order. Charlotte had offered to help initiate the new apartment, but he was finding her more demanding than he needed right now. Sharon from the Repertory theatre was more fun and didn't like strings.

His mind returned to Iris's party right before Ferris's murder. The old gang had been there, balder, fatter, one or two thinner, and not necessarily wiser. By midnight, it had turned into the same old bullshit. Iris had been prickly and full of fire that night, obviously still uneasy having her former husband back in Belmont.

Ferris had wandered among his adoring fans, a lean, hollow-cheeked stud, who had probably had his back molars removed just to improve the camera angles. The actor's smile was cocky, the eyes cool gray granite and as warm as a tombstone. His boyish haircut made him look like a maliciously handsome kid who might deliver the paper, if the price was right. It was a spellbinding combination; he must have made a terrific TV villain.

Guests jabbered about television and Broadway shows as if they knew what they were talking about. Ferris was a trifle unsteady on his pegs and spilled his drink at one point. Perhaps he hated the spotlight when off-camera. Now that Poole thought about it again, he wondered if Ferris wasn't more preoccupied and nervous than drunk. Booze jitters. Poole had dismissed him as a bore. Not these days.

Drinking problem or nerves? Or both. Poole's recollections merely confirmed what they had learned so far. Froggy Verdun was in the same shape, behavior easily attributed to male territorial syndrome...the battle for a female. Both men desired Marjorie, a lusty fact difficult for Poole to comprehend but nevertheless true. But, there had been something else going on too. What the hell was it? And, where had Ferris come up with all that cash for his art gallery? Blackmail and cash. Transactions between two people who knew how the cash system worked. No checks. And, oddly enough, no stocks and bonds. Poole found it hard to believe that Ferris had never invested in the market. But, so far, no stock records had turned up. No bank box keys either. Ferris was hiding something. Why and where?

Disappointed with his lack of progress and disgusted by the curled up remains of a bad microwave dinner, Poole grabbed the plastic plate and took it to the kitchen where he tossed it into the garbage container under the sink. Another day without dishes, about the only good thing he could say about it. He ordered himself to finish unpacking and hang his paintings. Propped against the wall were three large watercolors executed almost a year ago during a solitary holiday on the eastern shore of Maryland. The coastline and boats, the sky and the sea were broadly and gently stroked with fragile color like the diffused light near the sea. His technique, he'd been told, was reminiscent of John Marin's stream of consciousness style. The trio of watercolors were Poole's favorites.

He decided without much hesitation where he wanted the paintings and put them up. The watercolors and the Steinway meant he was home. And, his one good Persian rug. A dog might be nice. Well-behaved animals were welcome in the building. A dog might be more challenging than homicide. He would think it over.

Thinking about dogs reminded Poole of Iris. He howled at this, because she would not find the connection all that amusing, even though she loved dogs. At any rate, Iris was able to sort through details with a kind of marvelous precision, much like a large dog neatly circles his bed before dropping down to sleep. Her instincts about people were astute and often right on the money, like Ambrose Feather's. Poole poured two fingers of Famous Grouse scotch and tapped out Iris's number.

It was nearly ten, and Iris was settling into the four poster with a novel recommended by Dolly, probably a mistake. Dolly's taste ran to steamy best-sellers with lots of run-on sentences and run-on sex. A quick skim ought to take care of it. Cecil sprang from nowhere and snuggled near her hip with his engine running. "Spoiled rotten cat, that's what you are," Iris told him while rubbing his nose. Cecil blinked knowingly. When the phone rang, he jumped as if it were a new sound. Cecil was a great actor.

"It's me. Do you keep that thing under your pillow?"

"Just about." She was cordial but hardly effusive. Never let Oliver get the wrong idea. Regulation number one in her revised edition on how to get along with the opposite sex. "It generally rings when I'm in the shower. The work of the fairies," Iris reminded him.

Poole laughed appreciatively.

Poole knew all about the fairies, her tiny enchanted folk. When they were first married she believed fairies occupied their house and played havoc with everything. Two lived behind the shower stall, mischievously turning the cold tap to hot and the hot tap to cold. Another rearranged the refrigerator; another lost library books at an alarming rate. And, a young one, in training, Iris insisted, stole the belts to her dresses and just one earring at a time. She still believed they lived in Woolsey House. Just last week a pot of geraniums moved from one side of the patio to the other. Fairies.

"I'm hoping your fairies can help me out before I lose another night's sleep."

"My fairies aren't very helpful, Oliver. They're generally pretty naughty. What do you mean?" What did he have up his sleeve?

"Your party. Didn't you get a feeling that something was going on that night?"

"Lots of things were going on." Iris allowed her voice to drop to an impudent, low register, as she remembered Oliver escorting her very friendly, long-legged neighbor out the door. She said, "How about the lusty rendezvous between Marjorie and Roger in my office upstairs? Or, Froggy getting blotto and throwing Ferris into the trash barrels? Or, Ferris acting like a nitwit and dribbling his drinks on my favorite Turkey carpet? Lots of libidos out of control that night." Iris pushed her glasses to the top of her head.

"I remember. But, what about the subtle details? Innuendo, subtle body language, the off-hand remark, a sexy touch that nobody's supposed to see."

"What good are my impressions?" Iris was suspicious. "You need hard evidence. I write thrillers, Oliver, I don't try to live them."

Poole groaned audibly. "You have good instincts. Was Ferris into something nasty? Did he say or do anything that might indicate another life?"

"He said he liked his new life here. Said he was tired of daytime soaps. That was his story." Iris stroked the cat's thick apricot fur.

"He ran out of New York like a dog with his tail on fire."

"Maybe somebody wicked lit the match. Roger was pure animal magnetism, but only a fool would have trusted him completely. He gave himself away when you watched him closely."

"What does that mean?"

"Most people only saw the Roger Ferris package....the clothes, the face, the sex appeal, the voice, the star-power."

"Ferris had layers and a nice wardrobe. So?"

"A complex man. Shrewd gray eyes. Roger watched out for Roger every second."

"I noticed the eyes. Did he always drink that much?"

"Could be he was mightily bored with us all, Oliver. Belmont has its limitations."

"True. Females were pushing his buttons."

"Marjorie wanted him for dessert. How are you doing these days.... sitting out there on the singles branch."

"No woman can resist a lame detective driving an old Porsche."

"I can think of one."

"Ouch." Poole paused. "What did Dolly have to say about Ferris? She never misses a trick. One of the Marx brothers in drag."

"Oliver Poole asking for gossip and female intuition?" Iris slid further under the light blanket and scratched the cat's head. This was one time she was glad Poole was lying in his own bed.

"A weak moment. Forgive me. Mea Culpa, mea culpa."

"I'm immune." Where was this sexy banter leading?

"Why don't I drive over?"

Iris yelped with a combination of perverse delight and real indignation. "Try a sleeping pill, my sweet, or a boring book." And she rang off before Poole could make a counter offer.

"Does he really think I still need him?" Iris exclaimed to the cat, who had slunk to the foot of the bed at the yelp. Cecil glared at her as only a cat can and refused comment. "The only thing bigger than Poole's nerve is his ego." Cecil wasn't going to argue with that either and closed his eyes.

Iris pulled her glasses down from the top of her head and picked up Dolly's must-read novel, so far, two hundred pages of nonsense. Did real men and women natter on like this? Did the characters have to be so nauseatingly sweet? Egads, she longed to find six who were absolutely beastly. Where were those delicious characters you love to hate? She always created at least three or four, and her fans adored them.

The cat soon crawled back to her hip and Iris gave him a snuggle. While the animal dozed, she waded through another chapter. Two minutes later, she tossed the paperback across the room and rather wished Poole still lived in Washington. Damn it. He was getting to her again. Better he was out of sight and out of mind. She supposed.

11

WHEN ROCKS WERE FORMED

The following morning Iris called Dolly before getting out of bed. Dolly heard about the bad paperback and Oliver's generous offer to make life more interesting.

"Be grateful, sweetie," Dolly said, "our darling Oliver is back to normal!"

"That's what makes me nervous. A normal Oliver and a normal Max Tarry going head to head, as if life is the same as it was. Nothing is the same, Dolly."

"That's what makes it all so marvelous; I'm waiting for Act Two."

The dialogue soon ended leaving Iris more annoyed than was necessary and Dolly amused. Some divorced couples stay married for life, Dolly had reminded her, a brutal fact Iris would deny under torture. Dolly was simply delighted the Pooles were back in business, even if they were operating from two separate establishments.

Iris pulled on shorts and a knit top and trotted downstairs. It was a gorgeous morning. Cecil pranced along behind, eager for Frisky Cat. While Iris scooped, the cat danced on his hind legs. It was his only trick. With that chore out of the way, Iris poured out a bowl of Cheerios...

no sugar…and a large orange juice, and made coffee. She would drink it black out of respect for her thighs, but it would never taste as good without cream and sugar. Cursing calories and cholesterol, she turned for consolation to the very fat and nearly a week old Sunday *New York Times*. She plucked out the Book Review section first. It was always wise to keep your eye on the competition. A review of her latest novel was coming up in another week, according to her agent.

Sunday or not, her own work soon beckoned, and she reluctantly stacked the dishes in the dishwasher and left her cat to sit in a pool of sunshine where he began his elaborate toilette. The sun was rising higher and hotter in a pure cerulean sky, straight from the tube. She reminded herself to refill the birdbath.

Upstairs again, she admired the view from her study window, not quite a Constable landscape but close. Bucolic without the sheep, pastoral, if nobody noticed the Alfa Romeo tucked into the driveway. The peace was abruptly broken by a breakfast club of crows seizing control of the hickories across the street, their noisy scolding and gossiping hard to ignore as the wind chimes hanging in the trees next door. Iris prayed the crows were plotting an attack on the bells. Her kids called the incessant noise Japanese tinkle torture.

A soft breeze ruffled the papers on her desk, and Iris set to work slitting mail addressed to Aunty Em. It was a name out of Oz, she'd remarked to Bombay when she took the job years ago. Bombay said Ambrose Feather had probably been to Oz. The editor's only advice had been simple: 'Rely on your good instincts; keep your ears cocked for phony stories; and enjoy everybody's secret desire…to practice psychiatry without a license.' And she had done just that with great success. Several dailies around the country tried regularly to lure her away, but she would remain loyal to Bombay. Her mother still suggested she find a real job. Writing thrillers was too tawdry, Catherine insisted, for a Woolsey. An embarrassment for the family, she would say. Iris ignored the insult, but found it amusing that dear Catherine always wanted an advance copy of the latest book.

As she sorted and read the letters and complaints, most from husbands and wives who never would understand each other, Iris thought again about Oliver. Why did it bother her that he might find her neighbor, Charlotte, or any other woman charming enough to take out to dinner? Or to bed, for that matter?

"I don't like what he is doing simply because he does like it." Iris remarked to Cecil, who always kept her company. Poole was out of her life, right? He might be the father of her children and a familiar soul, but that was it. Knowing this did nothing to assuage the pangs of disappointment. People. Men. Oliver. Hell and damnation!

Going over the mail, Bombay's advice about phony stories kept running around her brain. What wasn't ringing true? As she glanced out the window, the fleeting memory of the dark figure, the half-hearted loper returned. Was this important? A spook in the garden? Sounded like a good book title. Iris scratched it down on a note pad. And, who among them managed to drive Marjorie off the road? Iris believed Marjorie's death bed story...she wasn't the kind of woman who made up such stuff. Someone murdered Marjorie Verdun. And, it wasn't Froggy.

"Who knows more about everybody around here than anybody else?" Oliver asked.

"My mother, hands down," Iris replied.

"Going back how many years?"

"To the time when rocks were formed."

Iris skinned leaves from a handful of snapdragon stalks and plunged them into a vase of water. "She's the best gossip collector I know. Started young, like a ballet dancer. It was called listening in." Iris grinned a little. Oliver, the ultimate professional, sniffing out local lore. He called early that morning to apologize for getting pushy on the phone. Right now, he was playing the patient ex-spouse trying very hard to like her awful coffee and acting sweet about it.

"And?"

"When Catherine was five she overheard the word *pregnant*, whispered in those mysterious, hushed tones ladies used those days. Little Catherine knew she was onto something, because the ladies changed the subject the minute she stepped into the room."

Iris rearranged the blooms while Oliver poured more coffee. They were in her big kitchen that faced the back garden. It was sunny and warm and redolent with the scent of zinnias and roses. The table was strewn with limp leaves, vases, a water jug, and glass frogs.

"When I was little," Iris was saying, snipping stems as she talked, "there were lots of words that commanded hushed tones...*cancer, divorce, mistress, sex*, and all parts of the body normally covered with clothing." They both laughed. "What a generation. Mother wasn't any more liberal-minded than her grandmother."

Oliver daringly said, "She taught you everything you don't know."

Iris crossed her eyes and replied, "Watch it, fella."

Oliver waved a white paper napkin. "Who said Queen Victoria was dead? Your mother got the part."

"Let's not get started on my mother. What do you want her to remember? Something about the Ferrises? Marjorie's family?"

"Believe me, I hope I'm not going to regret dragging the Woolsey women and their computer-like memories into this." Oliver laughed and helped himself to an Oreo. "I could use some inside history on the Wrenns and the Ferrises. Simeon Dorsett claims Judge Percy Wrenn was killed by somebody, and that his wife paid off the killer." Oliver raised both eyebrows. "Of course, we all know Simeon isn't always playing with all the cards."

"In other words, a Wrenn might still have a score to settle with a Ferris?" Iris put down her scissors.

"A long shot. I'm thinking that if Annette and Roger ...somewhere, sometime...picked up where they left off twenty years ago, a Wrenn or a Ferris might have taken great exception to the whole thing. Members of each family, it would seem, shall never cross wires, exchange fluids, procreate, or dine together."

"Pretty Gothic," Iris said thoughtfully. "You're saying that Roger was murdered out of revenge. But, what about Marjorie? A separate issue altogether?"

"I'm just pitting members of the opposing feud teams against one another. Annette's a Wrenn; Roger is a Ferris. She is unaccounted for. And, the limericks threats do include blackmail and a fair young woman."

"Pretty imaginative stuff, my sweet. It makes more sense to believe that Marjorie killed Roger. But, then, we're left with who had a motive for pushing Marjorie off the road? Froggy is the most obvious suspect.

And, I cannot see Froggy killing anything. Half the female population of Belmont had the hots for Roger."

"I know, I know," Oliver allowed, rising briefly to snatch Cecil for a bit of comfort. "But, Marjorie's fall in the bluffs has a familiar ring. Very stagy ...like the rest of this case. Masks, actors, a car chase, bloody kitchen knives. Soap opera stuff." Oliver absentmindedly stroked the cat. "We're missing something BIG."

"I'll pick mother's brain," Iris said. She filled a vase with water and set it on the counter. "It'll cost you though."

Iris playfully brandished her shears close to Oliver's chin; she said she would extract a fair payment sometime in the near future but refused to say what it might be. Earlier, they'd agreed to a truce. No prying into each other's personal business. No questions about Max Tarry; no comments about Oliver's lady friends. He promised to avoid Iris's close acquaintances and pals, although he did think Mrs. Liebermann down the street was pretty damned cute. Iris warned him off the wife of a psychiatrist who collected working antique firearms.

"How's Froggy doing?" Oliver asked.

"He's angry. The children are numb. Froggy's mother is staying with them for a while." Iris stopped a moment and then said, "Maybe Marjorie knew who killed Roger."

Oliver nodded. "Exactly. Murdered to keep her mouth shut. I still think the two homicides are connected, but executed by two killers." Oliver put down the cat and carried his coffee mug to the sink. "Time to shove off. While you're talking to Catherine, find out why Roger and his father hated each other. I have Ingrid's notion, but often an outsider's take on it is more accurate."

Iris gave Oliver the evil eye (one eye open and the other closed) and said, "Another subject for hushed tones." And she tucked a pink rose in among the snowy white ones.

Later, around midnight, as Poole dozed on the sofa, the phone rang. It was Iris sounding cheery. He had forgotten how cheery she could be in the dead of night.

"Up, up, up," her voice sang. "Mother's memory has been jogged." Iris sounded triumphant.

"Be a darling and wait while I fix a drink." Poole quickly poured scotch into a coffee cup and returned to the phone. "Ready."

"Lovable Percy Wrenn, who fancied gin and ladies and usually in that order, died one night about twenty-five years ago after misjudging the height of a curbstone. He hit his head on a lamp post, or so the story goes. There was a half-baked inquest and the death was ruled an accident. You could recheck that, I suppose."

"I will."

"Catherine says a woman was involved but can't recall her name. She was Percy's mistress for years; they even had a child. She was an exotic dancer in a club down river." Iris made it sound racy, and it probably was, and she began singing a few bars from 'Gypsy.' Poole listened and savored the scotch. Iris was a runaway train past midnight. "Catherine will check with Sybil and call me back."

"Sybil Crowley? Damn it, Iris! Sybil and Catherine sniffing the ground! Jesus, what a combination. What about the woman who was paid off?"

"A blank, so far. Could be the dancing mistress."

Poole groaned. "And the Ferris boys?"

"Reggie is of the mind that actors aren't real men. He was plainly embarrassed that his son was a soap opera star. And, Roger was taller than his father…always a sore point with Reggie. Odd, he is married to a statuesque female."

"My God, you and your mother have a remarkable grasp of detail. I take it she doesn't buy Simeon's story about the Wrenns paying off a witness to Percy's murder?"

"Simeon may not be the most stable Wrenn, but he doesn't lie, she said. Of course, he's not on the planet most days either."

Confused or not, Poole remained tantalized. "I await the next installment. Tell those two dolls that this is confidential police business. My regards to the Dowager."

The phone jingled again at six the following morning.

"Poole here." Actually, he wasn't quite sure who he was.

"Sorry to wake you, Oliver, but Mother and Sybil have solved the riddle. Judge Wrenn's mistress was Veronica Trotter. Her son was

Leonard Trotter. Remember? He was killed years ago in a riding accident in the bluffs."

Poole was now fully awake and rigid with attention. Trotter. The Leonard Trotter case. He had meant to look it up days ago. Abner's Coulee. He and Freddy had guarded the corpse. It was ruled a riding accident. "I don't suppose the Dowager knows where I can find Veronica Trotter?"

"Sandy Hook. She's lived there since her son's death."

"Why was Leonard Trotter in the horse business?" Poole asked, as he thumbed through the old police file on Trotter's death.

"He sure had a great name for it," quipped Freddy. "A bit of levity, my son. Lowers the blood pressure."

Poole laughed. He had just relayed Iris's scoop on the Trotter family. "If memory serves," Poole went on, "Leonard Trotter was not a lover of animals. Says here that Maybelle told police she was shocked her husband had ridden up to the quarry. Trotter, she said, rarely sat on a horse and especially if he'd been drinking."

"A set of circumstances that should have been looked into twenty years ago," Freddy replied in all seriousness. "It was Maybelle who had the horse-sense...to hit you twice with a play on words," he added with a grin. "According to Sergeant Freelander, whose family's been in the horse business for decades, Maybelle was a sweet girl from Kentucky horse country who knew what she was doing. She ran the show at Trotter Stables."

"I've forgotten so much of this," Poole confessed. "I can't believe we didn't check this angle sooner." He paused and added, "Where did a shiftless drunk like Trotter get money to buy the stables in the first place?"

"My notes tell me that Maybelle came into family money. A large inheritance."

"Why come back to Belmont? Says here Trotter lived out of state for years."

"Less competition? Nice scenery."

"Again, the question is why was a man who hated horses riding in the bluffs? The autopsy report puts him in the pickled range."

"Maybe he was with somebody else. Could be Leonard was out collecting his fees. There were rumors at the time about Trotter's knack for putting the screws to folks who might be willing to pay him off."

"Ah, extortion. Easy work for those who don't like to."

"What if his latest pigeon wanted Trotter to squirm for his money. Made him climb or ride to the top of the bluff for his money. Trotter gets there, drunk and pissed off; the two adversaries quarrel and our mystery man pushes Trotter over the edge. Perfect. An inexperienced rider falls to his death in the hills. Front page news. No suspects."

Poole nodded. "The circumstances might be tied to those damned limericks.

"So, who's our pigeon?"

"Look who was at the stables that day. Annette, Meredith, Roger, Marjorie, and Froggy. Rich kids. One might have had a secret Trotter was using to fatten his bank account."

"Factor in the limericks. If Ferris was blackmailing a woman about something that happened years ago when Leonard Trotter was around, this is a very old grudge. Now, two of the old gang have been killed, three if you count Trotter." Freddy rocked back and forth in his chair; the squeaky springs added an even tempo to the dialogue.

"Of the six of them, three are dead." Poole was pacing now. "Nobody saw Trotter leave the stable yard, and he didn't tell a soul what he was doing. He took Maybelle's mare." Poole was reading from his notes as he paced.

"He got himself up there and took the shortest way down. Roger and Annette found the body at the bottom of the pit and called the police. Pretty straightforward. No other witnesses."

"So they say. What if Trotter found out about Roger and Annette and the fact that she was pregnant. Nice foundation for blackmail, I'd say. Annette tosses him over the side and Roger backs her up. Or, Roger did it and Annette backs him up." Poole looked over the tops of his glasses at Freddy.

"Very nice. Or, it could have been Froggy and Trotter up there. Maybe Trotter was making a move on Marjorie. Froggy's the kind of guy who wouldn't take any crap from a loser like Trotter. Roger would have backed up his best friend. So would Annette. Who would question Roger and Annette if they simply claim to find a body?"

"Years later, Roger decides to blackmail Marjorie about it? She's rich and Froggy doesn't want his empire to crumble." Poole liked that theory too.

"That leaves Froggy as Roger's killer, which doesn't hold up and doesn't feel right."

Poole stared out the west window. The River Queen was pulling away from the dock for the afternoon cruise up the river. Poole felt a rush of envy. "Trotter's the link in this mess. I can feel it in my bones."

"Maybelle had the best motive to kill him. Trotter regularly beat her up, according to police reports...the typical Saturday night binge and abuse syndrome. But, Maybelle had a solid alibi for that afternoon."

Poole took a doughnut from the pink box. "Where's Maybelle these days?"

Freddy said, "Freelander told me she went back to Kentucky after Trotter's death. Didn't have any great love for the Mississippi valley."

Poole returned to his chair and continued to leaf through photographs of the crime scene and the victim. "These pictures bring a lot back. I'd never seen a dead body before. Broken neck. Jesus."

"You know, Oliver, I still remember what you said about those kids who found the body... 'as cool as the other side of the pillow.' Damned near literary, you old Protestant."

"Cool because they sounded prepared. Completely unemotional. I still think they knew more than we ever found out. I mentioned it to Holmgren at the time, and he told me not to mess with a simple accident case." Poole shrugged. "We were too young to be good cops." He finished his doughnut. "So, Uncle Simeon knows about an old murder. Maybe Trotter was blackmailing the Wrenn family, and Annette was the go-between."

Freddy lighted up a stogie. "My mother says trouble followed Judge Percy like a bad smell. She used to pray for the Judge because his wife was one of her best friends. When are you going to see Veronica Trotter?"

"Tomorrow morning, your grace."

Freddy picked up the folder of crime photos and leafed through them. "Did you see this one of Trotter's face? Pretty deep tear along the cheek." He handed the glossy print to Poole, who looked up the coroner's report. "Says here the cut was sustained earlier than his other injuries. It was a clean slash with very little dirt in it. The blood had already clotted over the wound. In other words, Trotter hurt himself maybe a good hour before he died. A question never addressed. Maybe our cowboy got into a fight with somebody at the stables that morning and rode up the bluff to escape further punishment."

"More sloppy police work."

Freddy was tapping a pencil against the edge of the desk. "Trotter would have made a vicious villain. Something craftier than a horse was chasing that bad boy that Saturday afternoon."

Late Tuesday morning Poole set out for Sandy Hook and figured he'd be there before noon. Donovan said he and the boys would follow up a lead on the Verdun accident…even though the D.A. wasn't too fascinated. Donovan was hoping to change a few minds.

A fresh coat of asphalt had given a soft voice to the highway which followed the broad contours of the river just as willingly as the railroad tracks one level down the slope and closer to its banks. Since there was little traffic on the road or on the water, Poole found it easy to concentrate on the scenery. Little had changed since the days when he made this drive as a young man; he used to see a girl in Sandy Hook. The valley was holding tight to its primeval aura, as if the great glacier had backed off only yesterday leaving behind this spectacular water-filled gorge.

Rising above the river were the familiar biscuit colored bluffs, sitting there like choirs of old bald men, their sloping shoulders robed in black spruce and oak, their homely muffin faces wrinkled and squinty in the sun. An occasional steel bridge, silvery and knobby with rivets spanned the fast current and reminded Poole that man did indeed inhabit this wilderness. But for the most part, geography obscured signs of humanity. The land and the water had been left to their own devices. The shoreline was a wild and shadowy place that often extended into soupy marshes choked with lily pads and reeds. For long stretches the brown water flowed unobstructed by the drab concrete dams that controlled it or the bridges that clasped its sides together. And then, unexpectedly, the channel would be clogged and diverted by a treacherous maze of wooded islands, just as if nature had changed her mind and decided to let the land have its way.

Another thirty minutes later, Poole spotted Sandy Hook squatting at the Mississippi's edge, half the town on one side of the road, the other half cozying up to the stone ridge on the other, just like every other village up and down the highway. For the most part these were all obscure, isolated pockets of late 19th century brick storefronts and a few dozen clapboard houses that stared dumbly at the water. All of it seemed unaffected by time. Many of these small river towns were undistinguished perches where people caught fish and got by, satisfied to do little more than keep company with the river. An occasional entrepreneur tried to lure tourists with an art gallery or pottery shop, but Poole doubted anybody would get rich.

He slowed at the city limits and pulled into a two-pump Mobil station with a Coke machine holding up the hut. The owner directed him to Delacourt Street down the main drag and one level up the side of the steep hill. Main was what he expected, a double row of modest enterprises, a pizza joint, a home cooking café, one barber shop, a beauty shop (spelled 'shoppe'), three taverns, a cut-rate gas station, and the Whiting Hotel with peeling paint. The thoroughfare reminded him of a necklace of cheap beads.

Poole found Delacourt and pulled in behind a rusted out Fairlane with a ticket on the windshield. He strolled up the cracked sidewalk to number four forty-five. The houses had given in to age and poverty. Their scruffy front yards of packed earth and weeds teamed with bands of sweaty kids screeching and brawling, banging in and out of porch doors with punched out screens whining for things their mothers didn't want to give them.

The heat was oppressive and a boulevard of thick maples, far grander than the houses had ever been, offered little relief. Veronica Trotter's address turned out to be a run-down Queen Anne with fake brick siding and a sulfurous yellow trim. Loud rock music spilled from an open, screenless second story window. Poole climbed the sagging steps to a porch outfitted with a broken charcoal grill and two aluminum lawn chairs. He pushed the bell under Mrs. Trotter's name and waited. The sun-baked paint smelled chalky.

The woman who opened the door had never been beautiful, sultry maybe, when she could fulfill the promises in her dark eyes. Today, she leaned heavily against the door jamb and blinked into the midday light. She shielded her worn face with an ill-kept hand, first to form a visor and then to push back damp strands of dyed black hair.

"What'd you want?" the woman asked hoarsely. She wasn't accustomed to visitors anymore.

"Are you Veronica Trotter?" asked Poole politely, fearing she might dart back inside.

"Who wants to know?" Her raspy voice was that of a used-up prostitute in a B movie.

"My name is Oliver Poole and I'd like to ask you a few questions." He flashed his lady-killer smile.

"About what?" the woman demanded suspiciously, so far, unaffected by charm.

He wouldn't mention the police at this point. He said, "I'm looking into the death of an actor named Roger Ferris." No reaction. "I believe you may know some of his friends and relatives. The Wrenn family?"

Bull's eye. Mrs. Trotter's bloodshot eyes widened, and she took a step back into the security of the dim hall, leaving the door ajar. Poole quickly pushed through and found the vestibule as hot as the porch. The woman had retreated to her own doorway and stood guard like an aged raven with her barrel torso and stick legs. Her dark hair rose like storm clouds around her puffy face.

"I don't know nothin' about nobody. You'd better get outta here." The threat was shaky. "Are you a cop?" She continued to barricade the partially open doors, sliding oak panels with lizard skin varnish.

Poole ignored the question. "I don't want to worry you, Mrs. Trotter, I just need your help." He moved closer up the dingy hallway, its walls covered with peeling wallpaper and grime rounding out the corners. The stale odors of a thousand suppers seeped from the dirty carpet.

Mrs. Trotter pulled nervously at her dress with an unsteady hand while Poole took another step forward. The distinctive smell of gin escaped her apartment like a precocious child eager to tell a secret.

"May I come in?" More charm, which didn't come easily.

"I don't suppose you have anything to drink on you?" Mrs. Trotter's train of thought had strayed.

"Let's talk a bit. Then, we'll have a drink and a bottle down at Louie's." He'd seen a tavern on the corner.

For Mrs. Trotter a deal had been struck. She shoved the doors into their pockets and directed Poole inside. "Yeah, Ok. Excuse the place; I'm a little under the weather today. The heat."

Poole doubted if health or heat had anything to do with Mrs. Trotter's housekeeping. The high ceilinged room had once been a grand Victorian parlor; it now resembled a Salvation Army store. It was so packed with furniture and clutter that Poole could barely see the walls. A generous bay window faced the street out front and accommodated a daybed with rumpled, gray sheets. The windows stood open to any breeze, the top halves concealed by yellowed shades, crisp and brown spotted like the skin on an old woman.

Mrs. Trotter sank wearily into a flowered couch with lumpy cushions. She kicked off grimy terry slippers and tucked her legs beneath her in a grotesque display of coquetry. Poole imagined old habits died hard for everyone.

The only chair held a pile of magazines and newspapers, which Poole scooped up and set on the floor before sitting down. Mrs. Trotter didn't seem to notice.

"Do you remember Judge Percy Wrenn, Mrs. Trotter?" The blunt question jolted the woman to attention. She narrowed her eyes, as if realizing that the interview might be more than she'd bargained for. Before answering, she grabbed a glass from a table at the end of the couch and gulped the clear liquid. Gin protection against the world, Poole figured.

"Wrenn? Wrenn." She acted coy. "Yeah, I think I knew some Wrenns once down in Belmont. You gotta cigarette?" She would make him pay a fee.

Poole fished a Winston from his pack and Mrs. Trotter grabbed it, ready with her Bic. Poole said, "How about Percy Wrenn? Wasn't he a good friend?"

Sucking in the smoke, Mrs. Trotter released a hoarse chortle. "I don't know what you mean by friend." The gin and the cigarette had perked her up. "Nah, I'm kidding. The judge and I were friends when we weren't fightin'." She cackled. "Of course, all this friendship stuff was very hush, hush in those days. The Wrenns didn't like ladies like me. The Lady Wrenns, that is," she smiled at Poole, who was having a hard time imagining what the bloated face and body had looked like thirty years ago. "The gentlemen Wrenns thought we was just fine." She winked. "I was a pretty good dancer in my day."

Poole smiled agreeably. "How long did you know Percy Wrenn?"

"Good question, Mr. Poole. Off and on for ten years or so, I guess." Poole was surprised at the duration of the affair. "There were times when he'd get an attack of the guilts or he'd be up for re-election and have to disappear for a few months. But he always came back." She sat quietly a while, smoking, daydreaming. "He's dead, you know." Mrs. Trotter managed to look sad, either for Poole's benefit or for her own; he couldn't tell.

"How did he die?"

Again she squinted, screwing up her face, as if tightening the cortex might squeeze out a better memory. "It was an accident. A terrible accident." This time it was she who watched for his reaction. Poole showed none. "You know, I could use another drink. The heat." She pushed herself out of the sofa, her dress riding up thin bare legs, and began wandering about the room, opening drawers and cupboards, occasionally disappearing entirely behind a stack of newspapers. As Poole waited he spotted an electric fan on a nearby dresser; the small motor was humming against terrible odds. He pulled it closer.

Mrs. Trotter soon returned, a glass of gin in hand. "Can I gettcha anything?" Properly fortified, she would play the grand hostess.

"No, thank you." Poole couldn't imagine drinking from anything in that room. "We'll go down to Louie's on the corner, in a minute or two." The carrot would keep her alert. "Tell me again how the Judge died. Were you there?"

"Sure I was there. Hell, we was all there." She took another drink.

"You and who else? Leonard maybe?"

"Sure. Acourse, Lenny was just a little kid." She stopped abruptly, not sure how the conversation was turning. "Wait a minute. How do you know about Lenny?" She leaned toward him smelling of age and bad habits.

"Lenny's your son, right? Who else was there? The judge's friends?"

"Nah, Percy never brought his friends over." She managed to fold her arms across a pendulous bosom, still holding the glass. "We had a fight. Percy was drunk as hell. He always pushed me around when he was tanked up. He could get real mean. I screamed for Lenny to call Kenny and Rick. Those are Percy's boys; they always came to get their old man when he got bad." Mrs. Trotter moved a hand over her face as if remembering one of the blows.

"Did they come?"

"Sure, they showed up. Old Percy put up a helluva fight. Thought he was a tough guy." She paused and then said quite matter-of-factly, "Kenny didn't mean to hurt him bad. It was just a terrible accident." The woman's dark eyes moved to some distant place and then she aimed them at Poole and said, "I threw away that damned Eiffel Tower."

Poole was lost. "What Eiffel Tower?"

Mrs. Trotter was annoyed. "You know, that damned, cheap statue he gave me. That fake gold souvenir from Paris, France. Percy's hotsy-totsy wife got the trip and I got the stupid statue." She fell silent again. "Kenny hit him with it. Went down like a dead tree." She peered at the floor as if old Percy might still be lying there.

"Then what happened?"

"The boys drove him to the hospital, but he was dead already. We all knew that."

"Then what?"

"They fixed it so it looked like the judge hit his head on the lamp post. Got a doctor friend to fix things up. They told me about it. 'Course, I had to keep quiet." Participation in a conspiracy appealed to her even now.

"And did you?"

"Why not? The Wrenns sent me a bundle of money to keep my mouth shut." She was close to the bottom of the gin glass. "Orders from headquarters!" Mrs. Trotter cackled again.

"What did you do then?" Poole produced his handkerchief and wiped his forehead.

"Lenny and me went back to Kentucky. To my folks. Stayed there for a long time. When Lenny got married, he and his wife moved to Belmont. Started a stable. Dumb idea. Lenny didn't know nothin' about horses. 'Course Maybelle did. I came along to help out."

Veronica Trotter didn't need any encouragement to tell her story anymore. "Belmont was bad luck," she continued. "My Lenny fell off a cliff and broke his neck. Terrible accident." Again, sadness shadowed her eyes, and Mrs. Trotter held up her glass to see where all the gin had gone.

Poole suddenly found the room insufferable. The sourness, the heat boiling behind the shades, the pathetic hum of the fan, and this pitiful woman. He held back a strong desire to run. His pulse was racing and his mind was hiding something bad again. The hospital psychiatrist had told him this would happen. He took a couple of deep breaths and urged himself to hang on a few more minutes.

"Who was Lenny's father?"

Mrs. Trotter looked surprised. "The judge, acourse! Lenny looked just like him. Handsome as hell. Big guy." She sank back against the faded roses and sighed. "Everybody's dead now. Half the people I ever knew are dead." Her features sagged with melancholy.

Poole pushed on. "Do you remember the name of the doctor who helped Kenny and Rick with the Judge the night he died?"

"Jesus, you do ask a lotta questions." And then Mrs. Trotter hooted, as if a good laugh might drive away the memories. "What the hell! Old Percy wouldn't care. It was one of those damned Ferrises. Always a lot of doctors with that name around Belmont. One of them lah-de-dah families. Jesus." She pinched her nose with her thumb and finger and made a snooty face. "What a town! I moved here to Sandy Hook after Lenny's funeral. Couldn't stand Belmont anymore. Lah-de-dah."

Mrs. Trotter leaned across the space between them and boldly snatched a cigarette from Poole's pocket. He recoiled, but she didn't seem to care.

"Which Doctor Ferris helped? Was it Reginald, Roger's father?"

Veronica Trotter sat and smoked, and Poole was afraid he had lost her. "John." she finally said. "It was John Ferris. The only nice one in the bunch. Took care of Lenny's broken arm once. Never charged me a nickel. The doc had a crippled leg, like you. Maybe that made him nicer." She smiled at Poole almost tenderly.

Alcoholic wisdom. Maybe it had. So John Ferris played Good Samaritan for the Wrenns. Interesting. The feud had not enveloped them all. "You're sure it wasn't Reginald," he insisted.

"Nah. I met Reggie a few times. He wouldn't have helped his own mother get into a cab." Percy's old mistress shook her head with great assurance.

"Why did John Ferris come to the rescue? I thought the two families hated each other."

"Couldn't say for sure. Maybe John was doing it as a favor to Beatrice. He was always sweet on Beatrice." Mrs. Trotter kept track of local lore almost as well as Catherine and Iris.

"Where did your son get enough money to start the stables? From Maybelle's family?"

"Nah. No money there. It was from Eleanor, Percy's widow. Guilty conscience money." Veronica Trotter looked a trifle smug. "The old lady got sentimental after Percy died."

Poole thought extortion might be the word. "Did Leonard have any enemies?"

"He hated the Wrenns, that's a fact. What do you mean?" Mrs. Trotter was paying close attention now.

"Did Lenny know Roger Ferris back then? Or Annette Wrenn and Marjorie Drummond?"

Mrs. Trotter looked confused. "Nah, he never mentioned any of 'em."

"Did you ever think your son might have been deliberately killed?"

"Murdered?" Mrs. Trotter was shocked at the suggestion. "Jesus, Poole, what gave you that idea? My kid fell into the damned quarry. One too many that day, I suppose. Took after his old man." She tried to sit up straight and focused all of her attention on Poole's face. "Who'd want Lenny dead?"

"Think hard."

"Lenny made people sore sometimes, but nobody kills for that. Maybe his wife. But, nah." Mrs. Trotter shook her head. "The police never said nothin' about murder." She remained skeptical.

Poole was certain they hadn't. Homicide was never seriously considered. Small town cops didn't think that way about rich people. "Have you heard about Roger Ferris's murder? Or Marjorie Verdun's car accident?"

"I read the papers. I don't live underground, Mr. Poole. He was a big TV star. I seen him on the box." Mrs. Trotter waved at her portable with its bent rabbit ears. "And, who doesn't know the name Verdun around here. Jesus, poor thing could have been fried to a crisp in that fire, huh?"

"Any idea who might have killed either one of them?"

"Who knows? You're barkin' up the wrong tree here."

Mrs. Trotter seemed uninterested and unconcerned. She leaned her head against the back of the sofa. The heat, the liquor, and the questions had made her drowsy. Just as Poole was contemplating a quick get-away, the old woman bounced back. She said, "How about that drink, soldier?" And with that, she pushed off and headed for a closet on the other side of the room where she dug out a pair of plastic sandals. "Let's see what's cookin' down at the corner?"

His escape foiled, Poole watched solemnly as Leonard's mother wriggled her dirty feet into the shoes and then stand in front of a streaky mirror. She inspected her reflection and gave the frizzy hair a quick pat.

"Ah, what the hell?" she chirped brightly. "It's dark as a tomb down at Louie's."

12

PREDICTIONS FROM THE DEVIL

"Would you like to see the cards as they were that night?" Beatrice asked. Without waiting for Poole's response, she moved to a cabinet beneath the front windows and removed an old leather bound box. From it she withdrew a black felt cloth and a stack of thick pasteboard cards, larger than the normal playing card. She cleared a space on a gate-legged table and drew up a chair. The lamplight was soft, and the room was silent. It was a gloomy, dark Wednesday afternoon.

Poole drew up a bench and sat down beside her. When he returned from his interview with Veronica Trotter the previous day, he called Miss Wrenn to suggest they meet a second time. Mrs. Trotter, he explained to Beatrice, was one of the links in their case. Doctor John Ferris had lied for the Wrenn family years ago. Another link. Annette might be their best connection in the Ferris murder. Beatrice said she would expect him.

"He told me that night that someone was going to kill him."

"Did he know who it was?"

"I think he did, Inspector. That made it all the more terrifying for him."

"Was it Annette?" Poole would be relentless.

"I couldn't say, Inspector."

After spreading the cloth, Beatrice chose nine brilliantly painted trump cards, the images in vivid primary colors with gold and silver leaf highlighting the figures.

"I used a simple cross pattern for Roger's reading. Easier for him to understand. He sat across from me, shaking as if he were cold." The psychic's bony fingers, the nails cut short and unpolished, placed the cards in order. Four cards were reversed or upside down. "Are you familiar with the trumps, Inspector Poole?"

"No. Please explain as you go."

"The simple cross pattern has five parts. The center card is the heart of the problem, you might say. I chose the Lovers from what Ferris told me before we started. The two cards to the right represent events leading up to the significant central card. The two cards on the left indicate the future without change. The two cards below give us the adverse influences and the final two cards above symbolize the action that might be taken." She let Poole absorb the spread of bright figures on the black cloth, a collage of ancient knowledge going back six centuries.

Poole saw the nine picture cards as a spooky game that might frighten most adults. He was reminded of cruel fairy tales read to him by his father; he hated fairy tales and decided that he probably wouldn't like the tarot predictions any better. Most of the images had the smell of doom about them.....that dark treachery and vague mysticism often seen in Ingmar Bergman films. The hunchback fool, the terrifying horned devil, the falling black tower. He would never want the cards read on his behalf.

"After I selected the Lovers," Beatrice was saying, "the remaining eight cards were randomly picked. There are no tricks in the tarot unless the cards wish to trick you." Her laugh was pleasant and not particularly frightening, so far. On the night Ferris came to call, the room had probably looked much like it looked now, Poole thought. Lighted candles, the gaunt psychic dressed in an exotic orchid robe. Poole noticed that Beatrice glanced from time to time at Simeon reading nearby; his bridge lamp cast morbid shadows. The old man seemed not to hear them.

"Please go on, Miss Wrenn."

"The Lovers signify choice. As you can see there is a man standing between two women, one beautiful and one plain. The card represents decision. Not necessarily sexual even though the imagery is."

"The card is reversed. What does this mean?"

"Roger chose between vice and virtue sometime ago. And the reversed position of the card tells me that he may have chosen unwisely."

Poole said nothing, automatically making mental notes, as if these were important clues and hard facts that he could check later. It didn't matter how foolish all this was; but he knew he would stay until the story was played out.

"The two cards to the right of the Lovers are the Chariot, reversed, and the Devil rightside up."

Poole observed the figure of Mars, the warrior god, driving a red and gold chariot pulled by two powerful white horses. Was it possible that Ferris saw himself as a kind of god? Had he recognized the symbolism of the horse?

"The Chariot signifies success and triumph. But the reversed position tells me that the driver might overturn his cart, turning success into defeat." Beatrice touched the heavy cards with great care. Poole knew that their age and value meant a great deal to her. "The Devil is a frightening image," Beatrice explained patiently. "He symbolizes the adversary and its power. He is the dark side of human nature." Poole saw an ugly, bearded creature with a tail and short horns. A serpent was twisted around his naked body.

"I'm glad these aren't my cards," Poole said lightly. He found the tarot ritual oddly disturbing and disquieting. He could only imagine how Ferris must have felt that night.

"Roger found the pictures horrifying, but then, his life was filled with terror." The psychic was stating a fact.

"What about the rest of the cards?"

"The two cards below are first the Hermit, reversed, and then Fortitude, the second of the classical virtues. As you can see, Inspector, the tarot trumps encompass mythology, Christianity, and wisdom, things that educated men were supposed to know in the fourteenth century. The cards were probably the remnant of some medieval instructive game, a kind of memory system based on images that people understood. The saints, gods and goddesses, and symbols of the cardinal virtues. The invention of printing put an end to this kind of instruction." She told him this matter-of-factly, like a school teacher might instruct a class of students. Her speech, he noticed, grew less abrupt when she spoke about the cards; she was clearly in her element with the tarot.

"I can see that. We're living in the past right now. But, was this really Roger's past, his story? Did he believe any of this?" Poole remained fascinated as well as skeptical.

"Roger came to me on someone's advice, he said. His friend told him he might find answers here." Beatrice didn't know who the friend was.

"He wasn't particularly superstitious then?"

"I don't think so. Roger Ferris was desperate."

Poole believed that. He switched his attention to the Hermit, robed in a hooded cloak and carrying an hourglass. This card, too, was reversed.

"This image is sometimes called the Traitor card. The Hermit is concerned with time in all its aspects, time that can be reversed at any second. He spends his time alone doing nothing, protected from the real world. And this exploitation is like a wise man who can exploit and misapply his wisdom. Ferris understood this message. I could tell."

Poole said nothing. He was consuming the images on the card of Fortitude.....a powerful woman in a broadbrimmed hat was holding the snarling jaws of a lion. My God. He was stunned. Was this a coincidence, or was Roger's lady friend in the big hats into tarot as well? Beatrice said she had warned Ferris that he would require strength in the face of coming danger. Poole had no doubt about this message; it nearly made a believer out of him.

"The two cards on the left were the Tower, the symbol of punishment, and the Fool, known as Fate. The black, castellated tower tilts beneath bolts of lightening. Two male figures tumble to the ground. "Clearly Ferris was to be punished for his past transgressions."

"And the Fool?" This exercise in the esoteric was more chilling than a horror movie, Poole thought. He wondered how much of this Beatrice actually believed. It was certainly grand entertainment.

"The Fool here is a giant in a gaudy fool's cap with bells. A dog is snapping at his heels. He is the joker in today's playing cards. He is the end of things and warns us that he may escape the dog, but will we?" Beatrice laughed.

"And the final two cards at the top?"

"Ah, the Woman Pope, simply robed, wearing the triple crown of the papacy. She represents knowledge, secret knowledge and strong feminine principles of intuition and prophecy. But she is reversed, and by this I see she is more subversive than divine. She may signify emotional instability."

Poole didn't like the sound of that. "And the Moon card?"

"Here we see Diana holding the crescent moon with two hounds baying at her side. This is an intensely feminine symbol. The moon has traditionally represented all that is changeable in women, thus Diana, who turned on those who loved her. This card can warn us of madness, nightmares. To beware of trusting in appearances."

"What was Ferris's response?"

"Nothing very overt. But I could tell that the cards were playing out a kind of drama. They had meaning for him."

"What advice did you give him? Considering the fact that he thought he was going to die."

"The advice anyone would give. The cards may seem mysterious to you, but common sense and experience still dictate how I interpret what I see. I told him to be careful of those close to him. I told him that he might be killed by a very unstable woman. You would have told him the same thing, Inspector."

Yes, Poole thought. But, which woman? He couldn't help wondering why Beatrice, so basically logical and sensible, had chosen to cavort with the occult? Her famous eccentricities were probably more hype than anything else, part of smart packaging. But, hype aside, Beatrice Wrenn clearly believed that Ferris was a sinner who would be punished. How much else did she know?

"Why did John Ferris cover up Percy's death?"

Beatrice remained unruffled, as if she knew he would ask. "He did it for me, Inspector. Not all the Ferrises are bad." She smiled, almost shyly.

"And, Veronica?"

"How is Veronica these days?"

"Shop worn. But, her memory's pretty good. She claims Kenny killed your father and the circumstances were altered to make it seem like an accident. Says she was paid to keep quiet about it."

"Could be some money changed hands. I wouldn't know. My father and Veronica had a long-standing arrangement that defies explanation." Beatrice put away the cards and the cloth and poured them each a sherry.

"And Leonard?"

"Leonard was their son. He was killed in a fall when he was about twenty-five." Beatrice would speculate no further.

"I think he was blackmailing your mother about the judge's murder."

"Anything's possible.

"I'm placing Annette in the middle of this mess. I think she may have given Leonard a shove from the top of that quarry....to shut him up about Kenny killing your father."

"Gracious, Inspector, that's a pretty big leap. Annette didn't pay much attention to family matters. She kept to herself."

Did she? Poole wasn't so sure.

"Did you know Annette was pregnant at that time?"

Beatrice looked startled and shifted in her chair. Before replying she drank more sherry. "Who told you that, Inspector?"

"Ingrid Ferris. Apparently Reggie paid for an abortion. Neither Reggie nor Roger wanted any marriage to Annette Wrenn. Perhaps Annette killed Trotter because he knew about the baby."

Beatrice listened to this and took a long minute to answer. "A very disagreeable time for us, Inspector, and very sad. I had little control over Annette those days or ever. She went about her business and soon left us." Beatrice's tone was so matter-of-fact that Poole felt a chill. But, when he looked closely into the woman's eyes again, he could see that the psychic was covering up pain that had lived with her a very long time.

"I'm sorry, Miss Wrenn." Poole paused and then went on, "Where does Marjorie Verdun fit into this puzzle?"

"She was infatuated with Roger, according to all the talk around town. I suspect it got her killed."

"How's that?"

"She may have known who killed poor Roger. Or, pretended to. Or, she could have been an innocent victim. There are innocent victims, you know. Killed because they're here, alive, in the way, or disagreeable."

"A necessary murder. Like cleaning house."

"It's possible. Maybe Marjorie was disloyal in some way and the killer got even." Beatrice refilled their glasses.

"Anyone in mind?" Poole was enjoying this.

"No."

Poole doubted her answer. And, he knew he wouldn't get much more out of Beatrice today or perhaps ever. She was still lying. He had to admit the allegorical story of the tarot seemed to tell some of the Ferris story, the bits he knew. Could he believe Beatrice's claim that she picked the cards at random, that she hardly knew him? Or did she make the cards and story fit what she already knew, what she believed was true, what she believed was going to happen?

"What did Ferris say he would do?"

"He said he felt relieved. The cards seemed to confirm something for him. He stopped shaking. Roger was prepared, Inspector." Beatrice swallowed the contents of her glass and stood; her long silk gown swept the carpet.

Poole felt drained, as if he'd just gone through another awful medical procedure. Why would anyone consult a seeress? The cards stood for good and evil, success and failure, but why take a chance on seeing such a graphic depiction of something bad?

Poor Ferris. Poole pitied him. He had been handed nine predictions from the devil.

"When all is said and done, Oliver, what have you got? The meanderings of an old woman who sips gin all day and used to sit side by side on the sofa with the Judge." Freddy whizzed by a Toyota truck in his new SUV, gift from the police department. Pressure had been applied; he was forced to update his wheels and the city would pick up the tab.

"Maybe."

The detectives were returning from the capital and a meeting with the D.A., an officious little man in a black suit who walked like a bird with big feet. He was called 'the penguin' behind his back. A disturbing lack of solid evidence in the Ferris case had his feathers ruffled. Belmont's mayor (connected by marriage to the police chief) had suggested in an interview in Bombay's weekly that the police department paddle a lot faster. Donovan told the chief where the mayor might store his paddle. Small town politics, Poole was thinking, wasn't any different than politics in big cities.

"How's your mother, Freddy?" Donovan's mother had taken ill the day before while Poole was talking with Beatrice.

"Out of the woods. Dicky ticker, as the Brits would say. Busy praying to all the saints now, bless her heart."

An Irishman's devotion to his mother, Poole thought, was a spectacle to behold. His own mother lived in Los Angeles with a step-daughter still trying to break into the movie business at the age of 45. He rarely saw either one of them. Poole said, "Tell her I'll pray to the leprechauns, if she thinks it'll help." Poole liked Donovan's mother. She was the worst cook on the planet, next to Iris, but bad cooks were so often such very nice people.

"Let me know when you do, you old sinner, I'd be first in line to see you on your knees." Freddy chuckled. "My sainted mother will sell tickets. She's your greatest fan."

"I'm lucky to have one. Where were we?"

"The Wrenns and the Ferrises, all tied up in hate with a dash of manslaughter and obstruction of justice. Funny how a few of them tried to defy the law of the feud. Roger and Annette, Reggie and Beatrice and Dr. John."

"I like the rope that ties Annette to Trotter. Trotter returns to Belmont. He's no longer a kid with a secret. He knows Kenny conked the judge with the Eiffel tower. So, he puts the screws to Eleanor Wrenn, the rich widow, for more money. Lady Eleanor sends Annette to pay him off, only Annette gives the brute a shove over the edge instead."

"Annette was seventeen, for God's sake. Do you honestly believe that kid could have killed Trotter?" Freddy fished out his sunglasses and slid them on a severely sun-burned nose. He had managed a round of golf after leaving his mother's bedside. "Trotter was a big man."

"It fits those damned poems, and it might explain the girl's disappearance."

In trying to locate Annette, they had learned that Wrenn house was owned by a Chicago real estate company and the company was owned by another company and so forth. Annette Wrenn had buried herself within a mountain of dummy corporations. "Hell, she's probably in the Peace Corps. But, she did find Trotter's body with Roger, and Trotter was her grandfather's bastard." Freddy stepped on the gas and they flew toward the exit. He braked a little, as if frightened by his own power.

"Veronica's a drunk. Simeon's been off plumb for years. The Judge, Leonard, and Ricky Wrenn are all dead. That leaves Kenneth and Dr. John Ferris, and Beatrice, Queen of the Schwinn Bicycle Club. Quite a group." Poole laughed. "Beatrice was pretty evasive. She did suggest Marjorie may have been an innocent victim simply because she was infatuated with Roger Ferris."

"We have old crimes committed by rich folks who didn't want to face the music then or now. They got away with it because of who they were. Enough to piss you off." Donovan grunted and lit a cigar. "Maybe we should talk to Ingrid again. She's outside the feud loop. In-laws are like outlaws."

Donovan liked being an outlaw in his wife's clannish French family. He felt protected by standing beyond the grip of ancestral genes, he liked to tell Poole.

"Freddy, you could wring secrets out of a Norwegian."

"Ah, hell, I don't scare anybody."

Donovan, Poole knew, was grateful for his easy-going, whimsical Irish relatives, neither complicated nor bitter, a trifle devious but never dangerous.

"I didn't make a single soul twitch at Roger's funeral. An Irish cop at a wake just isn't going to make a killer fall to his knees and confess."

Poole chuckled. "Roger was like Ben Quick's pappy in these parts. Wandered into town, started a few barn fires and then scrammed." Poole rested his arm on the open window and admired the rolling hills, sun-baked but still green, acres of God's country where the land hid the people in smoky hollows. "We're heavy on volatile, impulsive types, like Fitzhugh and Froggy. Marjorie's out of the running, thanks to somebody who thinks we're going to get all confused."

They were rolling down Main, very smart these days with designer awnings on the store fronts and baskets of purple petunias swinging from lamp posts. Donovan stopped for a red light by Budreau's Bakery. He said, "Remind me to buy a rhubarb pie at the bakery on my way home. And, how about a beer and a brat at Billy's? No murder talk for an hour."

Poole agreed without argument. He, too, was weary of Ben Quick and all the fires.

The next morning Poole took a call from an attorney in the capital named Gerald Kinney. He had just returned from his honeymoon in Italy and heard about the Ferris murder. Ferris, Kinney informed Poole, hired him two weeks before his death to add a codicil to his will.

"What codicil?" Poole asked. The will found among Ferris's papers indicated no modifications. Ferris had left everything to his mother.

"Mr. Ferris," Kinney said, "decided to leave his art collection to a young drama student at Ashbury College. A young man named Evan O'Neill, who doesn't know about the will yet. I'll be calling him today. You must understand, Inspector, that I'm giving you this information because my client has been murdered. I'm hoping this will help your investigation. Normally, I wouldn't divulge the contents of a will in this way."

Poole thanked the man and asked if Kinney knew anything about the beneficiary, Mr. O'Neill.

"He is the son of a Mrs. Charlotte Dolbere. They reside at 310 Two Tree Lane in Belmont."

Charlotte's name shot along the line like an electric current and yanked Poole from his chair.

"Are you certain of that?" Poole barked. Poole wasn't sure he was breathing and sat down again.

Kinney calmly reassured Poole of the facts. Mr. Ferris had informed Kinney that since his mother didn't much care for modern art, he would help a promising young actor in an uncertain business. Ferris had told Kinney that he did not anticipate having children of his own, and this bequest would fill a void. End of explanation.

Poole informed Kinney that he and Lieutenant Donovan would be dropping by within the hour.

"Charlotte's son is a beneficiary?" Donovan's voice squeaked a little when he asked this. What the hell gives, Oliver?" Donovan was not only perplexed but concerned. Poole was up to his neck in this damned case. Circumstances tying a police detective personally to a homicide investigation required a full explanation.

"Don't back me into a corner, Freddy. I don't know anymore than you do." Poole suddenly looked haggard. "The case is growing like a cancer."

"Yeah, soaked with bad Miracle-Gro. So, what's with Charlotte? What kind of game is she playing with you?" Donovan could feel suspicion in his bones this time. And, he knew Poole was living his own kind of horror.

Poole was pacing the perimeter of Donovan's office, taking a therapeutic whack at the three-legged sofa with his stick, a few cracks at the scarred window sills. When he placed a gentle tap to the signed Packer football on the bookcase, Donovan warned him off touching the mighty treasures in his collection.

"What's the connection?" Poole's mind was racing. "Just who the hell is this kid? He doesn't share his mother's name."

"Don't get hysterical on me. Maybe Charlotte was married before. The kid has his father's name; she has her own or another husband's name. Jesus, Poole, don't you converse with this woman?" Donovan couldn't believe Poole's lack of information about Charlotte. Poole and his women. "Has she ever indicated that she knew Ferris?"

Poole frowned at the insinuation and kept moving. "No, she has not."

"Shit, Poole, don't get short with me about this. The chief'll fry you up for supper when he hears about it."

"Yes, yes. The woman's a friend, not a murder suspect."

"That could change." Donovan wanted to deck Poole about now.

"I saw Ferris and Charlotte together at Iris's party. They acted like strangers. She seemed bored to death by him." Poole kept moving.

"What facts do you have on this gal?"

"She is Iris's new neighbor. She has acted available and eager; we've been out a few times. She has a son…never met him. She said they were from the coast. She has money. Her jewelry is real; the house is a modest palace."

"Something stinks, Oliver," Donovan said plainly enough. "And, whoever he is, young Mr. O'Neill is going to need a big flat for his new toys."

"Men Ferris's age rarely fool with their wills, if they even have one. And men like Ferris are rarely philanthropic." Poole stopped by the window. "Why leave an expensive art collection to a strange kid who already has a pile of money?" Poole lit a cigarette. "This is tied to those damned limericks, Freddy. The son-of-a-bitch knew he was going to die and never did a thing to prevent it. All he managed to do was buy a gun that we can't find and change his will. Brilliant." Poole pounded the desk with his fist.

Donovan wasn't quite as worked up. "With his assets you would think the man could have hired a body guard. Our young Roger had a powerful death wish."

"The will immediately points a finger at this O'Neill kid. And, if the lad killed his benefactor and gets caught, Ferris has the last laugh... from the grave. A morbid move. Maybe Ferris was the nut in this case." Poole moved over to Freddy's office blackboard and wrote O'Neill and Charlotte in the suspects column. The chart was crowded.

"What about the gay angle?" Donovan asked with little enthusiasm. The D.A. had thrown this at them, laboring under the impression that men in the arts are rarely straight. "Maybe Evan and Roger were lovers."

"I don't buy Ferris painting with all the colors," said Poole firmly. "We'll know soon enough, when we talk to kid. Right now, we're going to see Kinney."

"I'll bring the assault vehicle around to the front."

The drive to the capital, the interview with Kinney, who ran a small, respectable firm on Capitol Square, and the return trip were accomplished by noon. Kinney didn't have much to add, except that Ferris had been impressed with Evan, whom he described as an exceptional talent. Ferris offered no explanation other than a desire to give O'Neill a boost, in the event Ferris, his mentor, died prematurely. Ferris told Kinney that the young man had lost his father, and he wanted to make sure the budding actor would be financially secure. He added that Ferris had asked for the name of a financial adviser in Augusta and the name of another good bank. For some reason, Ferris wanted his safe deposit box at another location. Kinney mentioned that Ferris had remarked about a splendid, secret place in his library where he could hide the keys. Kinney found Ferris's remark strange and hoped the man wasn't a bit off his tracks. Donovan found it odd that he and his men had not located this secret spot and found the keys. Another search lay ahead. Kinney reminded the detectives that a court order would be required to open the strong box at Farmers and Merchants Bank.

Back at the station house, Donovan was dividing a pizza and trying hard to understand just how needy Evan O'Neill might be. First, he managed to test-taste lunch. Not bad. He said, "He and his mother live in a castle; the kid drives an expensive Italian sports car…I heard Iris talking about it. My gut tells me this guy is not hurting for cash and never will. Ferris had to know this." Donovan may have been troubled by the logic, but the pizza was good. Nourishment had a way of smoothing the rough spots.

"The coroner's report mentioned no terminal illness that could have prompted this codicil business. It's either a legitimate impulse or Roger Ferris was trying to tell somebody something." Poole neatly rolled a slice of pizza into a kind of burrito. "We're going to find out about this kid and his mama."

"You're completely in the dark on this?"

"Yes, Freddy. I'm bumping into the furniture. Charlotte was reluctant to talk about herself. She and her son moved to Belmont because of Ashbury College and its drama school. It's highly regarded. And, the lad wanted a small school. She came along for the change of scene. I didn't press for details."

"Where did they live before?"

"The coast, she said. I figured L.A. The boy is a budding actor. The coast usually means California…Hollywood. Find out what you can."

"After this splendid repast, we question, Mr. Lucky." Donovan flipped open two Dr. Peppers. A break in the case and a chink in Poole's armor. Not bad for a weekday morning. "And, then his pretty mama."

Evan O'Neill met them at the station an hour later, joined by Attorney Kinney. It was decided to leave Charlotte and the Ferrises out of it for now.

The young man was poised and cordial, a handsome kid of six feet or more, anointed with the blond good looks any leading man might need and want. The meeting was anti-climatic. O'Neill was astonished by Ferris's gift and could offer no good reason why Ferris had left him a fortune in art. He admitted he and Ferris got along well at the college, but he had never met with the professor outside of class. And, he had never met Ferris before coming to Ashbury. He only knew the name from television credits and the occasional mention in the media. He said he would not have called Ferris his mentor. He found that overstated.

On the surface there appeared to be no link between the two, other than the college and the summer theatre workshop. O'Neill had an alibi of sorts for the night Ferris was murdered. He had gone home directly after the cast party. He said good night to his mother who was reading in bed and then retired to his own room. O'Neill could have slipped out during the night, of course, but denied leaving the house and denied having anything to do with Ferris's death.

When shown the gold charm, O'Neill claimed ignorance. He didn't know anyone in the Wrenn family. Most of his acquaintances were at the college. Poole tended to believe him. So did Freddy.

Their surprise visit to Charlotte an hour later was unrewarding and uncomfortable. Poole sensed she was blaming him personally for any suggestion that her son might be involved in the homicide. Roger Ferris had been her son's drama coach, his teacher, nothing more. She found it absurd that Ferris had left part of his fortune to a stranger who would never need it. Poole had the undeniable sensation of being dumped into some ignominious hole filled with others who had failed or disappointed her. Poole was sorry they had ever met. On another level, he knew she was not above suspicion.

As they were ready to leave, Charlotte gave Poole a cold stare and said, "Have you considered the possibility that Mr. Ferris may have wanted to offer monetary support when and if he could no longer give instruction and moral support?"

A possibility, Poole admitted to her, but a weak one. Ferris was too selfish. He found it hard to picture the television star as Evan's mentor. And he was surprised by Charlotte's conclusion. He was certain the woman was cynical about most things.

After several hours of work, the new wrinkle remained wrinkled. It would seem that Roger Ferris had managed to complicate his own murder very nicely.

Tuesday morning a yellow cab with no springs took Poole directly to Seaboard Investments, a firm which occupyied offices on the eighty-fifth floor of a newish skyscraper in Manhattan. Charlotte's late husband, Alfred O'Neill, ran the business with a partner, Theodore Cookson. Charlotte and her son were New Yorkers. And, Poole was feeling like a damned fool.

Low-key lighting washed chocolate walls in the corporate lobby and softly illuminated six fine contemporary oil paintings, expensive visual interest if clients ever tired of looking at Miss Doversmith. The striking, conservatively dressed beauty greeted Poole from behind a sleek desk that reminded him of a block of bow rosin. When she asked if she could help, Poole invested a few extra minutes with her, his brand of insurance, having learned years ago to never underestimate the importance of secretaries and receptionists.

Cookson came out to greet him and ushered him into a grand corner office with a view of the New World. He seated himself behind a swept-clean executive desk equipped with a space-age telephone, a laptop computer, and an expensive ink pen. Poole presumed the gentlemen had been and were highly successful at whatever they did. And, why didn't these desks have drawers?

Poole took a contoured guest chair and reviewed the case quickly, showing Cookson a photograph of Ferris and asking if Alfred and Charlotte knew the actor or conducted business with him. Cookson didn't think so. He said he and O'Neill had been personal friends as well as business partners, and he couldn't recall ever meeting Ferris; he had never heard of the actor.

Poole asked if either Alfred or Charlotte might have invested in Ferris's two television production companies. Another negative. When Poole asked about Charlotte, Cookson told him she had been a highly paid fashion model for over fifteen years, working for the very prestigious Edwinna Simms Agency. He suggested Poole talk to Edwinna, who was one of Charlotte's oldest friends. Cookson said Charlotte had been on magazine covers for years and was surprised that Poole didn't know who she was. Poole, too, found it odd that no one in Belmont had made the connection or bothered to mention the fact that he was dating a fashion model of some fame. Or, had Charlotte denied her identity to maintain her privacy? On the other hand, the majority of small town Midwesterners did not think in terms of east coast celebrity.

When asked if he knew of a connection between the O'Neill family and Ferris or any reason why Evan would be chosen beneficiary in such a large estate, Cookson admitted he had no idea. He tended to believe that Ferris merely wished to help a fellow Thespian. "I've heard of stranger bequests and reasons for legacies, Inspector Poole," declared Cookson, who did not sound like a suspicious man.

Poole thanked Cookson, left the office, and stopped again at Miss Doversmith's post. He showed her the photograph of Ferris and asked if she'd ever seen him.

"Certainly, Inspector. That's Roger Ferris. He was a big soap star here in New York…before he was murdered." Miss Doversmith's beautiful hazel eyes saddened. Poole thought she looked good enough to be a TV star herself. "I recognized him right away," the secretary said.

"You mean here, in these offices?"

"Yes. It was snowing that day and he had snow in his hair and on his coat. He was so handsome." Miss Doversmith blushed. "It must have been early December, because we had just ordered the holiday greens." The young woman paid attention to details; Poole liked that.

"Did he have an appointment?"

"With Mr. O'Neill, if I'm not mistaken. I can check our appointment book, if you like." Her desk had a drawer, and the young woman pulled out a large leather bound business diary for the previous year and paged through it. "Here it is. December 7 at 1:30. Roger Ferris to see Mr. O'Neill." She paged ahead and said, "He returned two weeks later for another appointment. Oh, dear. That was just two days before poor Mr. O'Neill died." Again, she looked grieved.

"Do you know the reason for the meetings?"

"I couldn't say, but Mr. O'Neill's secretary, Mrs. Webster, would know. She knows everything that goes on around here." The receptionist's tone indicated a slight professional jealousy. Poole doubted it would take long before Miss Doversmith moved from reception to an inner office.

"Do you think you could find out? I'll call back later." Poole slathered on the charm.

"I'll see what I can find out, Inspector." Miss Doversmith was the picture of cooperation.

"By the way, how did Mr. O'Neill die?"

"He fell from the balcony at his home. I believe he died of head injuries." Miss Doversmith closed her eyes for a moment, either out of respect or against the horrible image.

"Too bad. Was he alone?"

"Yes. His wife found him. Isn't that awful? Poor Mrs. O'Neill." Again, she closed her eyes, thick black lashes resting against flawless skin.

"Yes, indeed. Tragic. I'll ring later this afternoon. Thanks for your help, Miss Doversmith." Poole gave her his best smile.

On his way to the elevator Poole was seized by an uncontrollable desire to whistle.

A second kidney-jolting ride in another cab built in hell transported Poole to the Edwinna Simms Agency in yet another swanky suite of offices. These were presided over by a very contemporary young woman with moussed hair, mini skirt and dagger nails painted dark blue. Cookson had suggested he see Edwinna or Fernando, Charlotte's favorite photographer and one of her oldest friends.

Miss Mousse explained that Ms Simms was out of the country and that Fernando was at home recuperating from dental surgery. A call to his apartment found him there. He agreed to see Poole later in the afternoon.

After killing two hours at the Guggenheim, Poole arrived at Fernando's apartment in SoHo about four o'clock. If fashion photography had benefited from Fernando's artistic eye, then Fernando (first name only) had made sure he shared in the rewards. A barren, high-ceilinged loft had been converted into a gallery-apartment with immaculate white walls lined with moody black and white shots and intriguing color stills for advertising and fashion layouts. Charlotte's exotic face appeared in dozens. It was obvious that Charlotte had been his favorite.

Fernando was about fifty, small boned, and olive skinned, his lean face decorated with a perfect Vandyke. Poole guessed he was as unique as his work, the old-fashioned preening artiste. His Spanish flavored English moved as rapidly and dynamically as his engaging jet eyes. Poole had to pay close attention to every word. He asked the man how he came to be a photographer.

"I wanted to be an artist, like Picasso, when I was young." Fernando was firmly guiding his guest by the elbow along the entrance corridor and into an enormous sun washed room with pale wood floors and bare-bones architecture. "Such arrogance! Inspector Poole. As if there could be another Picasso, eh?" The photographer laughed heartily at this confession and in spite of a swollen jaw that looked painful.

"We will sit here," Fernando directed. The space was divided by simple walls and cabinetry of various heights. The furnishings were expensive contemporary and vintage Bauhaus school pieces, which Poole immediately noticed and envied. The sleekness of the place reminded him of Ferris's penthouse in Belmont.

"I was going to fix myself a gin and tonic; would you care to join me, Inspector Poole?" Poole said he would have the same, and Fernando presided over the table of liquor bottles with great flair, cutting limes with precision. The photographer loved an audience and was accustomed to people watching him work. Poole liked him.

"Since I could not be a painter of great talent," Fernando continued his autobiography, "I decided to become an artist with my camera. And I have made my fame and fortune surrounded by fascinating objects, breathtaking scenery, and beautiful women." He turned from his limes and winked at Poole. "I have always dreamed very large dreams and they have never disappointed me." They laughed together and sat down in two classic van der Rohes.

"I can see that your life has proved equal to an artist's dream, sir. I admire your work." Poole saluted him with his drink and took a long swallow. It was just what he needed.

"Thank you, Inspector." The photographer inclined his handsome head slightly; his manner pleasantly Continental. Dolly Bishop would have swooned and called Fernando a Spanish masterpiece.

"Now, how can I help you? Anything for my Charlotte." He raised the glass to his absent friend. "This is far better than pain pills."

Poole reviewed the case and the circumstances of the new will, explaining that it was customary police business to check out beneficiaries in a murder case. And since Ferris had been a well-known actor in New York, Poole asked if he had ever met Ferris? The artist-theatre community is often thrown together, the inspector suggested, and produced the photograph of Ferris. He did not, however, reveal the fact that Charlotte claimed she did not know the actor.

"I never forget a face, Inspector. But, this one? No. I have never seen him. Good teeth."

Poole wanted to laugh out loud. The vain actor would have been chagrined to hear that the great Fernando could only compliment his teeth.

"Do you think Charlotte or her husband knew Ferris?" Again, Poole did not mention Ferris's visits to O'Neill's office.

"I can't be certain, of course, but I do not recall them talking about him. I never saw him at their parties." Fernando smiled pleasantly. The gin must have been taking the edge from his discomfort.

"Tell me about Charlotte and her son, Evan."

Fernando hesitated, gently massaging his puffy cheek, and then sipping on his drink. "I do not know how to proceed. I wish to help and I wish to preserve Charlotte's privacy. Her friendship means a great deal to me. We made our fortunes together, Charlotte and I. Her face and my camera." His sensuous mouth curved slowly into a grin; the black patent leather eyes fixed themselves on Poole's face.

"When it comes to a homicide, sir, there is little privacy left for anyone close to the victim. I am sorry. But, we do need to find the connection between Ferris and her son. Was her husband's family related to Ferris?"

"I understand, Inspector. But, facts about Charlotte are few. She married Alfred about twelve years ago; they were relatively happy. Alfred was much older, of course, and very wealthy. A terrible snob." Fernando wrinkled his long elegant nose and added, "Alfred was not my first choice for my Carlotta. Too intense. Too conservative." He sighed dramatically. "But, he was her choice."

"They were married only twelve years?" Poole was confused.

"Yes. A beautiful wedding. But could it have been anything else with Charlotte as the bride?" Fernando was clearly infatuated.

"I thought Evan was their son? He is twenty."

"My dear fellow, Evan is Charlotte's child. He was adopted by Alfred, who I must say, treated the boy like his own son. Alfred was a proud and generous father. Such a pity he is dead."

New information was swamping him, and Poole could smell the unmistakable stink of old fish. Fernando returned to his drinks table. "A refill? My jaw is insisting upon another." Poole joined him at the table and handed over the slender frosted glass.

"First things first. Who was Charlotte's first husband?"

Fernando performed his lime ritual once again. "The very point of my complication. This is where my conscience must guide me, my good man. This must be confidential. I cannot harm my Carlotta." The photographer handed Poole his drink and they sat down again.

Poole leaned forward, elbows on his knees, and said, "In a homicide investigation, we cannot guarantee confidentiality." The solemn warning produced a dramatic frown on the photographer's face. He adjusted the black silk handkerchief tied around his neck and looked clearly uncomfortable in the role of informer.

"Very well. I do not know who Evan's father was. No one knows. When I first met Charlotte, she was a poor waitress living with her cousin here in New York. We were all poor those days. Charlotte was pregnant. Her cousin and the husband, Peter Knox, both worked at Edwinna's agency. We all became friends." Fernando took several sips of his tonic.

"The baby arrived, and we adored him. Then..." Here, Fernando paused and winced with pain at what he was about to say, "the auto accident." He rose abruptly from his chair and strolled to the broad, steel-cased windows that overlooked his neighborhood. "Peter was killed. The two girls were in hospital. Broken and hurt. Edwinna found a plastic surgeon who was a genius!" Fernando interrupted his tale to lower wide canvas blinds against a late afternoon sun.

"What happened?"

"It was a miracle. The surgeon gave Charlotte a new face. It was as if the gods had decreed she have a different life. To make a long story short, my dear fellow, Charlotte's new face was more beautiful than the old one. And with time, she became an entirely changed person. A little magic, a little help from Fernando and voila! We had a new model for the agency, a beauty for my camera, for the world to see. I even convinced her to change her name." The photographer was enjoying the story as much as Poole. "She became Charlotte Dolbere....an old family name." Fernando swept both arms through the air as if ending a brilliant soliloquy on stage. "Dolbere was my mother's maiden name," Fernando explained.

"Charlotte is Cinderella," replied Poole with a grin. "It's an amazing story. What was her real name?" Poole was pretty sure he knew.

"Anna Taylor. Too plain for someone so exotic, don't you agree?" Fernando strutted about now, baggy white cotton trousers rolled up around his ankles and flouncing as he moved, leather sandals snapping on the floor. He looked like a cocky shore bird wading in the surf, proud of his part in the girl's transformation.

"Anna Taylor?" Poole was surprised by the double deception from the start. "What happened to her cousin?" Poole knew exactly what happened to her.

"Merry never completely recovered. Only enough to help Charlotte with Evan. She cared for the boy while Charlotte took assignments. Dear, sweet Merry Knox. It sounds like an old English ballad."

"Was that spelled M-e-r-r-y?"

"Yes, like Christmas. Why do you ask?"

"Just a hunch. Where was the family during this ordeal?"

"Family?" Fernando snorted. "The girls refused to talk about family. Taboo. No one dared ask. The cousins only liked each other." The man shook his head, as if still perplexed.

"Do you think Charlotte was ever married?"

"She told Alfred her husband was dead, and Alfred never asked any more questions. The man hated scandal, but he wanted Charlotte more. And he did want a son very badly." Fernando sipped the last of his tonic.

"And the taboo family?"

"She told him her parents were dead and she didn't wish to talk about it. I do miss her so. And I cannot persuade her to return to New York. I am desolated, Inspector." Fernando looked lost.

"Why did she give up her career?"

"She was tired of working and wanted to be with Evan." Fernando snickered. "You, sir, live at the ends of the earth."

"And where is Merry Knox?"

"She followed along to your part of the world." Fernando made it sound as if Belmont might be a trading post where riders changed horses.

"Tell me how O'Neill died?" Poole was doing mental arithmetic and didn't like the total.

"He fell from the balcony in his townhouse and broke his neck. Just before Christmas. I am grateful Charlotte did not see it happen, poor darling. She and Merry returned from shopping and found him dead. He'd been drinking."

"Was he alone in the house?"

"Yes, the housekeeper had the day off. Alfred could be charming, when he tried." Fernando put his hand to his face once more, and Poole realized that the man wasn't feeling well.

Setting down his glass, Poole immediately extended his hand and prepared to leave. "I appreciate your help, sir." He gathered up his cane and briefcase. "My thanks and my apologies for staying so long."

"I am pleased to help, Inspector. Charlotte and Evan are mere innocents in this case. Like Mr. Ferris told his attorney, he wanted only to help a bright boy with a promising future. Evan may be standing under a lucky star like his mother twenty years ago. Luck sometimes runs in families, you know. Why would either one be involved in violence?"

"Why indeed, sir?" replied Poole, as he left Fernando at his studio door.

Poole walked to the corner and hailed a taxi. On the drive to the hotel he decided that Charlotte and Evan had indeed been living a charmed life after an unfortunate beginning. And luck does run in families. Good luck and bad luck. Poole reminded himself that some people have a knack for creating their own.

"Ducky? Oliver Poole here."

"Poole. I take it you are in the Big Apple."

"Manhattan. Thought I'd drop by your office, or better yet, how about a few beers and a steak?"

They worked out the longitude and latitude and agreed to meet at Sylvester's at seven.

Poole arrived early, ordered a martini with extra olives and took a table by the window. The green checked curtains were pushed aside for a view of pedestrian life in New York, pretty much the same as always...a lot of serious faces and tired feet intent on going somewhere in a hurry.

Bliss showed up shortly after, tucked himself into the tight space, and ordered a Beck's. Bliss was a character out of Damon Runyon, a warm-hearted pretend gangster who might break into a tune from 'Guys and Dolls' any minute. Tall, pole-thin, lantern-jawed, Bliss favored black pin-striped suits, dark shirts, and wild wide ties. He could have driven the get-away car.

In the big world, Poole and Ducky Bliss had been thrown together at the F.B.I. in Washington. Bliss had abandoned the bureau a few years ago to open his own P.I. agency. He had acquired his nickname on assignment a long time ago...by slamming his head on a low door frame just as Poole yelled, 'Duck!' His given name was Lester.

"A cafe without ferns, Poole. We need not worry that tropical snakes will crawl from the ivy." Bliss's laugh rose like an echo from the bottom of an empty rain barrel. His peculiar speech with its precise cadence of uncontracted verbs was pure theatre to Poole's ear. The Runyonesque dialect was generally sprinkled with forties' gangland slang.

Poole laughed. Sylvester's was Billy's with class. A tavern of the old school with an oak bar, polished brass rails, and waitresses in black uniforms that covered their knees.

Bliss got his beer and they both ordered steaks and the works from Agnes, a pleasant, middle-aged woman who had been a waitress for a century or more.

"How's business, Ducky?"

"I do not complain. The same old racket, Poole. Ducky Bliss, finder of lost loves and stray husbands, or is it the other way around? You should try it."

"It's under consideration. Ever think of moving west? I could use an old bloodhound like you if I go it alone."

"The Midwest, Poole? Suburbs, I presume. I would have to peruse the terrain. You do have delis and cabs and race tracks?" Bliss swigged his beer while training a skeptical eye on his old colleague. "I have never resided in a small town."

"There are racetracks around Chicago, not too far away." Poole lit a cigarette. "Before we get you packed, I'd like your help on a case." Poole gave Bliss the facts, including the gist of the limericks and Fernando's story about Anna Taylor turning into a famous model with a new name and face. "Our victim changed his will shortly before he was murdered," Poole said. "Left an expensive art collection to one of his college students. The kid and his mother deny knowing the guy."

Poole stabbed an olive with the toothpick and swirled it through the ice before eating it. He explained about the missing link, Annette Wrenn, and his contention that she was Charlotte Dolbere, the rich socialite widow, whose son was Ferris's beneficiary.

"Ever hear of Alfred O'Neill? Philanthropist, Mayflower family. Recently deceased?" Poole asked.

Bliss screwed up his lean face. "In the papers around Christmas, if I recall correctly." He tapped long fingers against the beer glass. "Why toss the loot in the kid's direction?"

"The attorney who drew up the codicil said Ferris wanted to give the young man financial security because he has a bright future as an actor." Poole looked skeptical. "My guess is the kid is his son. My second guess is he took one look at the kid and put two and two together."

"I sense there is more." Bliss washed down salted nuts with beer. "Why the masquerade by this Charlotte in her old home town?"

"The kid obviously doesn't know his mother's background. And, Miss Wrenn apparently wants to be known only as Charlotte Dolbere. No other ideas."

"Pure Hitchcock, Poole."

"On the big screen. Annette fled to New York where the boy was born. Cousin Meredith knows the story and has lied about it. So has Charlotte." With a martini inside Poole was beginning to feel human again.

"Why all the monikers?"

"We think pregnant Annette pushed a certain Leonard Trotter off a cliff twenty years ago; he was probably blackmailing her family. Ferris was the only witness but promised to keep his mouth shut if she left him alone. Meaning, get rid of the unborn kid. Ferris's father paid her off. She lied about the abortion, had the child and started a new life.The new face and the new identity were a lucky fluke after the car accident. Annette Wrenn never set out to get rich or famous."

"Or notorious," put in Bliss. "Do not jump the gun, Poole, the dame is not behind bars yet." A chortle rumbled in the detective's skinny chest.

Before they could go on, Agnes delivered their dinners and whisked away the empties. Steaks sizzled in steel platters; the cottage fries were home-made.

Poole described his visit to O'Neill's office, about the man's unfortunate fall from a balcony."

"Aspects of this case stimulate my interest. Did O'Neill conduct business with Ferris?"

"Maybe. O'Neill died two days after seeing Ferris the second time." Poole motioned to Agnes for coffee. "What if Ferris ratted to King Alfred about the evil queen?"

"And the Queen requires her pound of flesh from the king and the jack." Bliss liked it. "A pal of my acquaintance who operates his own establishment often brags about his up-scale clientele. He is heavy into background checks. O'Neill may have used his services." Bliss carefully cut his steak into small square pieces and doused it all with A.1.

"I'd appreciate it, Ducky." Poole dug into the salad. "Who do you know in the NYPD these days?"

"You are suspicious about O'Neill's accident."

"See if any of the detectives smelled foul play. Maybe Roger gave the old boy a shove. We know Annette likes high places." A flash of Beatrice's tarot cards flickered behind Poole's eyes. The black tower, tumbling bricks, and two bodies falling to earth. Damned creepy stuff.

"Ferris ran out of New York like a man who's just seen the devil. Either he's guilty of killing O'Neill or the lovely Charlotte has something on him. But, which and what?"

"The limericks must give you clues."

"This case started decades ago when Kenny Wrenn brained his father with the Eiffel Tower." Poole related Veronica's bizarre tale of the family feud. Bliss said he was enchanted.

"We need the legal papers on Charlotte's name change and any birth and adoption records on Evan."

Ducky Bliss inclined his large head toward Poole and said, "I am at your disposal. Nobody could figure this caper without a dance card." Bliss's thin-lipped grin cut a wide slit in his cadaverous face, a face only a mother or Charles Addams could love.

"And, you are familiar with dance cards?" Poole grinned.

Bliss laughed and waved his fork at Poole.

Agnes swept over with coffee and the two men ordered apple pie with ice cream.

"Give me your best scenario, Poole."

"Ferris blackmailed Charlotte here in New York…for some reason we don't understand. Probably about killing Leonard Trotter. She daringly called his bluff. Then, she had the unbelievable nerve to follow him to Belmont. She taunted him with the three limerick letters and then stabbed him to death. After that, we think she got rid of a rival by forcing her off the road and over a cliff…more high places. That woman died of her injuries. Charlotte knew nobody would recognize her as Annette, nobody except Ferris. And that's what she wanted. What I can't understand is Ferris's reaction to all this."

"Instead of having her iced, he altered his will and gave his kid some nice statues. Perhaps your Mr. Ferris was a few acting lessons short."

"Or, did somebody else tell Ferris about the kid?"

"The cousin?" Bliss suggested.

"She says she knows nothing, but she tends to drink a bit."

The pie arrived, huge juicy wedges with scoops of cinnamon ice cream on top like party hats.

"What do Ferris's bank statements tell you?" asked Bliss.

"Not much. His receipts for the artwork indicate that he used cash for all the transactions. Another mystery. No purchases were made after he moved to Belmont."

"Sex and money, the cornerstones of our business."

Agnes dropped off the check and moved on.

After finishing their meal the two divided the next day's work and agreed to meet the following afternoon. Poole clasped Bliss's hand, the thin fingers like claws. He was reminded of Digger O'Dell, the friendly undertaker, of radio days.

Overtones of theatre continued to crop up. Coincidental? Or, were these melodramatic clues leading him to the truth? Poole thought again about Beatrice.

13

NEW TWISTS

"Our evil queen legally changed her name from Annette Wrenn to Charlotte Dolbere eighteen years ago. O'Neill's adoption papers list the boy as Evan Knox. The birth father is listed as Peter Knox. He would be Meredith's husband, killed in the accident that battered Charlotte's face and crippled her cousin." Bliss and Poole were going over the data at Joe's Broadway Deli not far from Bliss's office. "Cousin Meredith is a generous woman."

"An astounding amount of deception. She claims to know nothing about Annette."

"My distinguished colleague, Sam Orbach, states that he is cooperating only because the two gentlemen who hired him, Roger Ferris and Alfred O'Neill, are both deceased." Bliss winked broadly and took a long swallow of beer.

"Ferris hired Orbach?" Poole was astonished by the coincidence.

"Alfred O'Neill was inquiring about his wife's past and about a fatal accident in Belmont many years ago. During the course of his investigation, Orbach discovered certain interesting facts, which I have just divulged. Likewise, yourself."

"O'Neill learned that Roger and Annette discovered Trotter's body in the quarry. Not illegal, but it puts the two together a long time ago."

"I would make a small wager than Mr. Ferris suggested to Mr. O'Neill that Annette did indeed shove the bad seed over the cliff."

"Did Charlotte and Roger have an affair here in New York?"

"Ferris was seen at one of the O'Neill swanky gatherings on Long Island last June. Otherwise, nothing."

"The timing is right. His diary lists appointments with someone with her old initials from June to December. When did O'Neill hire Orbach?"

"December nine. Two days after Ferris paid him a call."

"How did Roger find Annette in New York? He couldn't have recognized her."

"Perhaps the cousin is the link. How about a pastrami on rye? Coleslaw and pickles?" Bliss didn't look as if he ate that much in a week.

"Fine, I'm starved." Poole hailed an angel-faced young thing, probably waiting for a big part on Broadway, and they ordered.

"Why Meredith?"

"The doll has a weakness for vodka. Orbach says she spilled her sad tale after a few drinks. Sam has a nice way with ladies. The cousin cared for the kid while Charlotte smiled for the cameras. She coughed up the fact that Charlotte is really Annette Wrenn and married O'Neill for his bank balance, in the billions, and the O'Neill jewels...a collection of stones worth millions, I am told."

"The benefits of booze." Poole shook his head. "How about Ferris hiring Orbach?" A bizarre coincidence or what?

"Orbach figures Ferris noticed the Orbach firm name on a report on O'Neill's office desk. Ferris hired Orbach to find out if Evan was his kid."

"He didn't know in December?" Poole thumped his fist on the table. "Annette kept him in the dark. She never got the abortion and used the money to go to New York."

"Orbach says Ferris did not appear surprised."

"I have to hand it to the ladies. They've kept their secrets like pros. Even Fernando didn't know the best details. She's been under my nose for weeks, Ducky." Poole didn't tell Bliss just how close to his nose. Had Charlotte's pursuit of him been a dangerous game, a little private flirtation with the law? This woman was frightening, and Poole felt a trifle sick.

"O'Neill was informed about the Wrenn family, as well. The Wrenns are an old American family, but not old enough and rich enough for O'Neill." Bliss made a snotty face which made Poole laugh. "They missed the *Mayflower*. Forced to take a later boat, poor wretches."

"And how did O'Neill handle this?" Poole liked to see the big guys get a little dirty.

"He paid Orbach's bill, but, Sam said, he was not happy."

"And, we can only wonder what he did about it."

"He did lose his balance three days before Christmas." Bliss grinned wickedly.

The pretty waitress brought their sandwiches and hustled off to the next table. Joe's was filling up fast.

"Your source at NYPD said the case is closed," said Poole. "The final report concluded that O'Neill accidentally fell from the balcony in his New York townhouse and died of various internal injuries, a fractured skull and a broken neck. He was intoxicated. His wife and her cousin reported finding the body upon their arrival home. Mrs. O'Neill, by the way, inherited a fortune. O'Neill did not have time to change his will, if that was his intention." Poole's sandwich was five inches thick and dribbled with pickle juice. Life didn't get much better.

"Did any detective on the case question the conclusions?" Bliss carefully tucked a napkin into his dark blue shirt collar. His tie was a marvelous creation of orange and green triangles. Poole's former life came flashing back.

"One investigating officer named Quinn thought it odd that O'Neill would be leaning over the third floor railing if he was alone. Could he have been talking to someone in the entrance hall? O'Neill's bedroom was on the second floor and his wife's on third. If she was out, why was he up on her floor?"

"Why are they sure he was on three?"

"Booze was soaked into the third floor landing carpet. The coroner believes O'Neill fell from that height. Our Detective Quinn was told to keep his mouth shut. Big money, old family, no flies. Case closed."

"The queen and her lady-in-waiting alibi each other. And now they reside ten minutes from each other?" commented Bliss around his pastrami. "Familiarity often breeds contempt."

Poole nodded. "And secrets don't always stay that way."

"I am thinking about Mr. Ferris's use of pure cash, Poole. Perhaps the evil Queen paid her blackmail bill in large stones from the King's collection. A person can make deals in the New York diamond trade if that person knows the right dealers."

"You may have figured out the riddle, my friend." Poole asked Ducky to check further and Ducky said he knew who to talk to.

"Catch the early bird back home, Poole. And to shift gears, I think we could use more slaw."

It all fit together, like the solid red puzzle the kids gave him for Christmas years ago. Only this made more sense. Poole reviewed his findings as the plane soared over Lake Michigan, the sky a celestial pink streaked with gold. He could almost see angels snuggled among the clouds rehearsing a Bach chorale.

Early complications were not complicated anymore. The puzzle had taken shape and the limericks were the picture on the box cover. Poole attached real names and faces to the cut up pieces. The fair maiden of the limericks wasn't fair at all. Charlotte Dolbere had discovered hair coloring in a bottle. Jet black. She had paid her blackmail bill with prized jewels, then wielded a wicked pair of shears and concocted a series of poetic threats before wielding a knife. And, he figured she had sacrificed Marjorie as a lamb to be tossed from a bony precipice. Marjorie needed to go because she irritated the hell out of Charlotte. Poole doubted this woman required any other excuse. The Verdun case could very well lie stagnant until they solved the Ferris job.

The tricky lines in the limericks were embarrassingly simple now. 'Sky diving,' indeed. It was horses and Trotter taking a dive off the ledge! Poole felt stupid and amateurish over this particular gaffe.

He could clearly see the scene in the bluffs that afternoon twenty years ago. Trotter and Annette had struggled on the edge of the abandoned quarry. They had fought over money he was squeezing from her grandmother. Poole had to admire the young girl's nerve, but that was where the admiration stopped. He was now close to terrified of the woman's capabilities. So far, this beautiful female very likely had killed Leonard Trotter, the rich New York husband, Marjorie Verdun and Roger Ferris. The total was chilling. Proving it would be daunting, maybe impossible. Poole had to wonder if Charlotte's list of victims might be longer than anyone knew.

Patches of bluish water blinked at him through the clouds and reminded him of evidence still hidden, facts still murky, like the gritty, foaming waves that pounded the beaches thousands of feet below. A school girl's nerve two decades ago. How had it grown into something this deadly?

"Meredith Wrenn phoned this morning," Donovan said. "Said she couldn't keep the secret anymore, under the circumstances. Then she said, 'Charlotte Dolbere is Annette Wrenn' and hung up."

Poole wanted to hear the story one more time. He and Donovan had been hit with the same information at the same time. How often would that happen? Donovan had picked him up at the airport and suggested a late breakfast at the Half Moon.

"The drought's over," Poole remarked as they settled into their favorite back booth. "I just hope we're not going to drown in a flood of good luck."

The two sat quietly for a moment, to let the new developments sink in slowly, like the thick syrup they'd soon be pouring over their waffles. The diner was still crowded and smelled of frying bacon and strong coffee.

"Merry Knox or Meredith Wrenn, whichever you prefer, has developed an amazing sense of civic duty all of a sudden," Poole said, breaking the silence. "One minute she remembers nothing and the next she's revealing the private secret of a lifetime." He sipped the delicious coffee.

"But, why spill the beans now?" Donovan's mind was weary of suspects and victims and motives.

"Collateral. Wants to stay in our good graces, considering Belmont's in the middle of two violent death cases." Poole put his napkin in his lap.

"Add to that another death from a high place... Charlotte's unfortunate husband in New York."

Donovan screwed up his face and swallowed the hot coffee with his eyes shut. "Don't we have enough on our plates without dragging the NYPD into our little party?" He tucked a large white napkin into the neck of his green knit shirt. Two buttons were missing.

"We may not have much choice, Freddy. Ducky Bliss is still sniffing around."

Betty swung by with two big plates of waffles and thick bacon and went back for more coffee. Donovan pushed back the curtains to see how Ching was doing. The dog was hitched to the awning pole and sniffing the air for food.

Poole said, "I'll save him a few bites, too." He poured on the maple syrup and got busy.

"Your pal Charlotte's been around a lot of dead bodies in one lifetime." The Irishman was carefully balancing pats of butter and dollops of strawberry jam between each waffle. "Roger's her only witness to Trotter's death and he's dead. Evan's her alibi for Roger's murder, and he's her beloved son. And the up-until-now-loyal Meredith is her alibi for Alfred's accident."

"Proof or not, we've found the hard kernel of this sorry business. Trace the gold charm and nail her. That bit of jewelry was commissioned somewhere."

"The D.A.'s going to want more than a handful of old maids, Oliver."

Old maids, Poole thought. Yes, maybe not a handful but definitely one old maid. And he wanted to see her after their chat with the beautiful Charlotte.

Charlotte was accustomed to the eyes of strangers after spending years in front of a camera lens. She simply ignored the intrusion and thought of all the money she was making.

As she sat in Lieutenant Donovan's military drab office in the Belmont police station, she noticed that Oliver's gaze had an inscrutable quality today; the Irish cop was openly curious. She would face them with her usual composure. But, what were they up to?

"Tell us again what you know about Roger Ferris, Miss Dolbere." Oliver was going to go formal.

"I've told you, Inspector." She would repay him in kind. "Ferris was my son's teacher. Apart from that, I know nothing about the man." She smoothed her hair, severely arranged like a ballet dancer's.

Poole asked, "What did you and Ferris talk about at Iris Woolsey's party?"

Charlotte smiled brightly and replied, "The weather, Evan, Ashbury college, New York theatre...the usual small talk."

"Ferris acted a trifle uneasy. Spilled his drink on the carpet at one point... a clumsy move for an actor, wouldn't you say?" Poole smiled back.

"Did he? Perhaps he didn't like parties. Some actors are quite shy, I'm told."

"Point taken, Miss Dolbere. Did you ever meet him in New York? Folks in the arts...fashion, theatre, television...are so often thrown together, socially."

"I wouldn't have believed you knew much about the art world, Inspector Poole." Charlotte could see Donovan cringe at that one. "Besides, I would have remembered Roger Ferris. A handsome man." She opened her handbag and pulled out a filtered cigarette. Donovan offered a light and then sat back, as if eager to let his partner do all the work. What were they after? She rested an elbow on the chair arm and watched the cigarette smoke curl into the air, like a cobra wiggling from its basket.

Poole paused to light his own and then said, "Apart from the new will, we have new information. From New York."

"Really?" Charlotte re-crossed her legs. So, he'd been to New York.

"And, Lieutenant Donovan talked with a nice lady named Meredith Wrenn, right in Augusta. Not all that far away." He paused and then added, "We've been trying to locate her cousin, Annette Wrenn. Miss Meredith told us where to find her." Poole paused, took a drag on his cigarette, blew the smoke to the side and added, "She claims *you* are Annette Wrenn."

The only sound in the room was the dog's soft snore from beneath Donovan's desk.

Donovan asked, "Is this true, Miss Dolbere?"

"I'm amazed," Charlotte replied with a little laugh. "What can I say? Your Miss Wrenn is mistaken." She twisted an amber ring, heavy on her finger.

"Why is that?" asked Donovan.

"Perhaps, she's crazy." Charlotte felt as if she were whirling in space, clearly in danger of spinning across the room. Her head was screaming, Meredith, Meredith! What have you done?

"She didn't sound crazy, just a little tight."

Poole leaned toward Charlotte and said, "When you left Belmont, after high school, you moved in with her in New York. She told us about the accident that disfigured you."

Charlotte suddenly felt like a little girl longing to escape punishment from a stern father. She'd been brutally betrayed by the only person in the world she trusted. Meredith and her damned liquor!

"Do I look like a disfigured woman? Perhaps you should be checking out this Miss Wrenn." Charlotte shifted in her chair.

"We have no wish to harass you," Donovan interjected kindly, "but, homicide forces us to check every lead."

Poole went on. "We know about the plastic surgery and about your new name. We know about your career as a model. Why the secrecy at this point?"

"There is no law against changing one's name. My identity is my business. Your Miss Wrenn is as mad as a hatter!" Charlotte ground her cigarette into the ashtray. "My identification is all in order."

"We have no doubt that your name is Charlotte Dolbere and that you have the proper papers." Poole had risen and was making his way around the room as he talked. "We've seen the originals."

"What originals?"

"These. Photocopies." Poole dropped a file into her lap and limped to the windows.

Charlotte sat without moving for a minute or more. She did not speak. She did not blink. She did not breathe. Poole and Donovan waited without twitching a muscle.

"All right." Charlotte finally responded quietly. "You win." She placed the file on the desk and stood, hugging her arms after putting out her cigarette. She would concede this point, but nothing else.

Poole turned to look at her, leaning heavily on his cane. "Why this charade?"

"Many years ago, gentlemen, I had the misfortune to lose some of my face and then the incredible good fortune to acquire a much prettier one. With it came a new life and a new name. I wasn't Annette any more. I became Charlotte Dolbere. I want only privacy for myself and my son." Her explanation was unemotional.

"Why come back here? Didn't you run some risk of recognition?" asked Donovan.

"Not really. I was more likely to be recognized as an anonymous but familiar model in the big fashion magazines. Quite a few people have, you know. Evan wanted to attend Ashbury and I wanted to retire and leave New York. It was quite simple. My appearance is vastly different. Most people are not very observant or clever, and my relatives are reclusive."

"Why would your cousin reveal your secret now?"

"Meredith drinks. She's confused and misguided." Charlotte would be loyal.

"You and Roger never met in New York?" Poole wouldn't let go yet. What else did he know? His reel was spinning out plenty of line; he wanted to get her.

"I saw Roger for the first time at Iris's little party. Pure coincidence. He must have felt the need to return home….just like me." She tried a smile, but it felt false. "Why did you come back to Belmont?" Charlotte looked directly at Poole this time.

Poole didn't answer.

"Did Ferris recognize you?" asked Donovan.

"No. He said nothing to indicate it. He would have called if he had. We knew each other in high school."

"Does your son know your real identity? Does he know about your past here in Belmont?"

"Evan knows nothing. And I want it kept that way." Charlotte narrowed her eyes at Poole; she wanted to frighten him somehow.

"That may be impossible under the circumstances. You and Evan are part of a murder investigation. Perhaps this would be a good time to tell him the truth," Donovan advised her with some care. "Was Roger Ferris the boy's father? He sure looks like Ferris."

"I will not answer that," Charlotte replied as fiercely as she dared. Donovan, she noticed, flinched. "It is none of your business."

"In light of the new will, we might assume that Mr. Ferris may have thought he was Evan's father," replied Donovan, having regained his composure.

"I have no interest in what Roger was thinking."

"Are you and your cousin still friends?" Poole asked.

"Yes. Evan adores Meredith. He would do anything for her."

"She doesn't live with you?"

"Meredith prefers to live alone."

"Where were you the night Roger Ferris was murdered?" Poole moved to the door behind her as he spoke. Charlotte felt immediately disadvantaged.

"Home. Alone. Evan came in to say good night after the cast party, about midnight, I think."

Donovan pulled out the plastic bags containing the charm and the cigarette case. "Recognize either one of these?"

Charlotte examined the pieces and smiled when she read the inscription on the case. "I suppose you think I'm the gift giver. Sorry gentlemen."

"Do you own a gold charm bracelet?" Poole asked.

"I own a lot of jewelry, Inspector. I may have one. I can't recall."

"We'll be examining your bank records. And we'll be searching your property. Do you own property other than the house on Two Tree Lane?" Poole asked.

"I have a summer place called Rumsford Farm, near Howard's Grove. Search it all. I have nothing to hide." She waved her arm through the air.

"Thank you, we will." Poole remained business-like. And, he stayed behind her. "Do you recall the day you and Roger found a body in the old quarry? The body of...Leonard Trotter?"

Charlotte felt herself spin around almost involuntarily…as a dog might turn upon hearing its name. She laughed lightly and said, "I'd forgotten." She turned back to face Donovan, a safer and kinder inquisitor.

"Odd that you and Roger found the dead body together."

"Odd? Someone would have found him. It just happened that we did." Poole was facing her again.

"Trotter was your grandfather's bastard son. And not a very princely fellow." Donovan grinned at her through the dense whiskers. "He was extorting money from your grandmother. Why?"

"That's ridiculous. My grandmother never paid Leonard Trotter a dime. Trotter was a lazy drunk who beat his wife, if I remember it all correctly. And, you are mistaken about his lineage." She laughed at the absurdity of it.

Poole sat on the edge of the desk now, nice and close. He said quietly, "We don't think so." He said nothing more. So, the inspector wanted their questions to start growing a culture in her brain. He was trying to break her down. He told her she would be fingerprinted.

She nodded and wanted to slap the superior look off his face.

"You can go now, but not too far."

Charlotte her face expressionless picked up her handbag and walked out, leaving the door open.

Poole's parting shots had failed to ruffle the plumage, Donovan noticed. They were quite a pair. Now that Poole had finally found his mystery woman, his Annette, what was he going to do with her? The elusive Miss Wrenn was locked up in the very remarkable body and face of Charlotte Dolbere. Knowing Poole as well as he did, Donovan hoped Charlotte would hire herself a good lawyer.

"I've just come from the police. You called them?"

Meredith faced her cousin across a small table in the small kitchen. The day was overcast and humid, the kind of day that breeds storms.

Meredith didn't answer. She was more than a little drunk and craved oblivion. Charlotte's remarkable eyes were watching her, waiting for her to fall apart. Meredith rose from the table and stood near the cabinets.

"How could you betray me?" Charlotte's voice sounded queer and dreamy to Meredith, as if they were chatting about what to have for dinner. She had just been instructed that Charlotte was the name they would use from now one. No more Annette.

Meredith also knew better than to trust those controlled, soft-spoken questions. Her cousin staged things like a Broadway theatre director. Her stomach gave a lurch. She knew that Annette would pop out again, sometime. Annette was the bad girl. She had always been bad and would always be bad.

"The police would have found out," Meredith answered, levelly. "Poole's no fool." She giggled at the unplanned rhyme. "Neither is the Irishman." Christ, Meredith thought, look at her. Charlotte was getting more like Grandmother Eleanor every day. That phony tinge of piety, that mask of self-sacrifice, like a new shade of make-up. What would Grandmama think?

In a spurt of confidence, Meredith poured herself a drink and dug ice cubes from the freezer tray. In honor of the Queen. Normally, she drank her courage undiluted and at any temperature it wanted to be. "Want one?" She gestured with the glass.

"Isn't it a bit early? You have turned into a lush! A traitorous lush." Disgust curled Charlotte's cover girl lips.

Figuring a lecture might be in the works, Meredith said, "Don't blame this on me. Roger knew what he was doing when he wrote that will. The police investigate any beneficiary in a murder case." She leaned comfortably against the counter and swallowed the vodka. At that moment, Meredith felt if not superior to her famous cousin at least her equal.

"What do you mean by that?"Charlotte stood and began roaming the room, looking out of place in a kitchen. She straightened a calendar hanging from a nail and readjusted the dusty blinds. She was skirting the real question. She circled closer to Meredith, who was near the sink now.

"Just what I said. Roger believed you were sending the limericks to scare him." Meredith chanced a smug smile and another swig. "The will was his way of getting in the last swipe." A tiny sensation of victory spun over her. "He was sure you planned to kill him."

"Roger had enemies. He was stupid. My big question is this... how the hell did he find out about Evan? He never knew about Evan." Charlotte ended up screaming this time and banged her fists on the counter. “Did you tell him? Did you?” She grabbed Meredith’s shoulders and shook her so violently that liquor erupted from the glass and splashed down the front of her shirt. Meredith clung fiercely to the nearly empty glass and squirmed free. She backed into a corner and stood there like a naughty child.

“Tell me what you did. I don’t like talking to the police, and I don’t need their noses in my business. And you, dear Meredith, were supposed to keep your mouth shut. To the grave.” Charlotte’s perfect face was so close the stink of gardenias made Meredith dizzy. “How much did you and your liquor bottle talk?” And, as if to punish the vodka too, Charlotte snatched up the bottle and poured the remaining contents down the drain. Meredith watched silently and hoped she had another stashed in the cupboard.

What was happening? Meredith thought. For years their lives had been so tranquil, so private. They had never needed anyone. It was frightening to witness the collapse of your universe. Charlotte could feel it too; Meredith could tell. Charlotte had to be afraid, on some deep interior level. Surely, the core of a human being wasn’t bone? Even the center of the earth held heat.

Meredith blamed Alfred, the poor dumb bastard. He’d never been a match for Charlotte. She had fleeced him out of a fortune in exquisite diamonds…sold them to Manny Weinstock. The old man never knew.

“Roger just knew about Evan,” Meredith explained as she edged around the corner and moved off into the living room. “Don’t ask me how he found out.” She chose the couch for protection and sank into a corner of it. “Probably figured it out just looking at his face. They were twins, for God’s sake! “ Meredith grinned a little.

“Come back here! I’m talking to you.”

Meredith ignored the order. A familiar buzzing filled her head, and the room took on softly torn edges.

Charlotte followed and sat tentatively in an arm chair a few feet away. “Tell me how you met Roger.”

“By accident...in a bar. I knew who he was, but he didn’t recognize me right off. We got to talking, had a few drinks. Then, it dawned on him. I was Annette’s cousin. Couldn’t even remember my name. Jesus, what a jerk. Full of himself to the end.”

"What did you talk about?"

"He was surprised to see me. Must have thought I stayed here all these years. Then, all of a sudden, he gets jumpy, like some mobster is going to bust in and shoot him. His eyes swept the crowd and the door every few seconds. Real nervous." Meredith grinned like a cat. "He must have thought *you* were going to show up next." She laughed. Booze power. "I played dumb. Told him I hadn't seen you since high school."

Charlotte smiled a little. "Yes, I thought he'd collapse when he saw me at that party." Charlotte's good humor was short-lived, and she turned cold, unforgiving eyes on Meredith and asked, "How about Evan?"

"I called Roger the next day, said I hoped I hadn't said something to bother him. Offered to buy him a drink, for old time's sake. He agreed, and we met at the same bar and he got pretty stinko. Out of the blue, he tells me he's a father. Never knew it until this summer. Said the kid's one of his students."

"What did you say? Or were you too drunk to remember?"

"Watch it! I don't have to tell you any of this." Meredith pushed herself from the couch and ambled off in search of the emergency bottle. She fished clumsily through the shelves of a French armoire on the other side of the room.

"Answer me. What are you doing?"

"Not all of us have your control." Meredith slowly rose to her feet, triumphantly brandishing a quart of Gordon's. "My liquid lunch." Tossing Charlotte a crooked grin, Meredith disappeared into the kitchen.

"God, this wretched family is buried in drunks."

Meredith returned carrying a glass with great care and walking in that measured gait drinkers use when they want to appear sober. "Our Roger hired a private detective." Meredith pointed a finger at her cousin and lowered herself to the floor where she rested her back against the front of a lounge chair.

"Who gave him the idea that Evan might be his son? He must have had some clue before he hired an investigator." Charlotte sounded skeptical. "Just seeing me didn't necessarily mean my child was his child. He thought I had an abortion twenty years ago." She lit a cigarette.

"He said it came to him in a flash...like a vision! Maybe he went to see Auntie Beatrice and she saw Evan in her crystal ball." Meredith found this funny and giggled until vodka dribbled down her chin. Her speech was slurring into long phrases. "Up to this point, he never let on that he knew you were Charlotte. He never divulged a thing." Meredith narrowed her eyes in mock seriousness.

"What did this brilliant detective tell him? He could hardly prove paternity without involving Evan."

"He said you were Charlotte Dolbere, rich widow and hot shot model. That you lived in Belmont and your son, Evan O'Neill, was his child. I played ignorant. But, we did have a good laugh over it. The coincidence and all." Meredith traced a pattern in the carpet with her finger and didn't look up. "'He didn't say you were trying to scare him to death with crazy poems." That was the truth. Although, Meredith was certain Roger would have confided all of it to her if he had lived another week. "The man needed a friend. He was near the breaking point." Meredith knew all about breaking points.

"When were you going to tell me this?" Charlotte ground out the cigarette and moved to the picture window.

"My view isn't quite as swanky as yours." Meredith snickered. Her neighborhood was homely and common compared to Two Tree Lane. "Hey, I kept quiet because I knew how mad you'd get. Look, Roger's dead. Let it be. Who cares? When Evan finds out, he'll handle it. He's bright and stable. Not like you and me." The last words slipped out and Meredith held her breath.

Charlotte whirled from the window. "Are you saying I'm unstable? This from a woman who drinks her breakfast?" The shrieked accusations bounced off the walls. Meredith watched Charlotte pick up a book. It flew through the air, missed her, and crashed into a table. Before Meredith could blink, Charlotte had grabbed her and dragged her to her feet. She was shaking her now. The two women were exactly the same height and each met the other's eyes with a dangerous mix of fury and fear.

"You have become my Judas!" Charlotte whispered hoarsely and let her arms drop.

Meredith stood her ground and took the punishment without a word. Fighting back was never wise.

Then, Charlotte reached out and took hold of Meredith's long hair. "Was it you? Did you kill Roger?" She gave the hair a sharp tug. Meredith winced. "Are you setting me up?"

Meredith wiggled free. "Are you nuts? It was that bitch, Marjorie."

Charlotte stepped back and clasped her thin arms across her chest. "Was it really Marjorie? Did you help? Somebody gave her the gold charm." She took hold of Meredith's arm and squeezed.

"Don't touch me!" Meredith wrenched away again. "I hardly knew Roger. Why would I get involved in his murder?" She took a swallow of her drink and heard the glass clink against her teeth. "It had to be Marjorie!"

Meredith watched her cousin collect her handbag and slip her model's mask into place. The anger was gone now; the revulsion had vanished. Bad Annette was tucked away for the time being. Meredith didn't move a muscle. She said quite confidently, "Roger was going to kiss her off again. Hell, Froggy couldn't stand her either...probably the reason he ran her off the road."

Charlotte listened to this and replied, "I wonder," and stepped into the corridor.

Her words hung in the air like a curse.

Ferris's Augusta attorney called again that afternoon. His client, Roger Ferris, had rented a safety deposit box at Augusta First Bank. According to state law, the box could be opened with a court order or with Ferris's key and an attorney present. Poole said they'd be over in an hour... without a key. None had turned up. Donovan knew a judge who issued the court order.

An hour later Ferris's secret bank box life was spread out in front of Poole, Donovan and Kinney in the nearly soundless bank examination room. A black velvet bag contained what looked like ten beautifully cut large diamonds lay on top of several stock transaction sheets for November and December of last year and January of this year, a fascinating mix of assets to be tucked away in a steel box. Poole figured Ducky Bliss's theory that Annette had paid off Ferris in O'Neill family diamonds might have been right on the money...so to speak. Stones for cash, if you knew the right chap on the streets of New York. And, it looked like Ferris might have saved a few sparklers for a rainy day.

That evening Poole and Donovan went over the new evidence at Poole's condo.

"Between October eighth and December second, Roger Ferris purchased thirty-five pieces of art…paintings and sculpture… estimated value placed at about three million…all paid for in cash, according to dealer receipts," Donovan recited calmly.

He lay sprawled on Poole's living room floor with the pertinent papers in front of him. "This was in addition to his normal bank deposits…residuals from three commercials, his earnings from Eagle Eye and Vista Productions, other investments, and his TV salary." He took a long swig of beer and continued. "Three days after he saw O'Neill for the second time, his stock market account shows a transfer of airline and railroad securities valued at two million. These were not purchased but transferred."

"I'm sure Mr. O'Neill's stock market records will indicate such a transfer," Poole answered. Benny Goodman and the sextet were playing something smooth; a good steak dinner was out of the way; and crickets were buzz-sawing outside the open windows. It was a very pleasant night.

"According to his appointment book, Ferris's last meeting with 'A' was December fourth, five days before he made his final purchase from the Rothman Galleries. The big kiss-off payment from Charlotte?" Poole wiggled his bare feet, his one concession to the season, besides white tennis shorts.

Donovan could see several incision scars around Poole's bad knee. Several other spots on his skinny legs appeared to be burn scars, which sent a chill up the Irishman's spine. Poole said nothing about any of it.

Donovan said, "We could easily assume three things. One, Roger and 'A' were having an affair until something made him decide that blackmail was more fun. Two, she agreed to pay until she decided that paying wasn't any fun. And three, the lady told him the party was over, and he called her bluff by running to Alfred with enough bait to make the old coot bite. More fun."

"Don't forget number four," Poole put in. "O'Neill falls over his balcony and breaks his neck two days after he pays off Ferris. Who pushed him and why?"

"Ferris got a nice batch of securities. You think he expected more and when he didn't get it, he got rid of O'Neill?"

"A possibility. O'Neill could have died accidentally; he was drunk. But, my gut tells me O'Neill was given a helping hand over the edge. Just like Trotter and Marjorie Verdun. And, who knows who else." Poole blew a series of perfect smoke rings, attracting Ching's attention for a few seconds. The dog soon thought better of smoke and returned to gnawing steak bones. "I like the similarities. The old push and shove routine. Skydiving. And, Annette's in the right neighborhood for Alfred's plunge."

Donovan was calling Annette by her new name. Poole insisted on using Annette, a little game, Donovan assumed, which provided Poole with the psychological distance he needed.

"What did Bliss find out in New York?"

"Ferris has an alibi of sorts for the night O'Neill died. He showed up at a Christmas party thrown by some TV pals...a quick cab ride from the O'Neill townhouse...and, it was a big bash. He could have left and returned without anybody missing him. Annette, of course, has Meredith as her alibi...which means nothing." Poole reached for a carafe of coffee and poured himself a cup.

"Ferris gets richer by confessing to O'Neill that he's banging his wife and that she's a murderer to boot."

"Rather like Leonard and Veronica Trotter witnessing the death of Judge Wrenn. Witnesses get pay-offs and rich folks get cover-ups. I wonder what Annette promised Meredith for her silence and loyalty all these years?"

"Free rent and retirement benefits." Donovan poked a fork into the defrosting cheese cake sitting on the coffee table. "Ready," he announced.

"Meredith's still here. Could be Annette has a soft spot in her heart for her cousin." Poole put out his cigarette. "We're getting down to the wire, Freddy. I don't want to see anybody else fall from a high place." He was jiggling his legs up and down in a habit as old as they were.

"We've no proof against Charlotte." He cut two fat wedges of cheesecake and plopped them on paper plates. "Is this the kind of woman who cuts up decorating magazines and pastes together nasty poems before she stabs her lover? Did she move across the country just to taunt him? Did she tie tin cans to his tail for fun or did she really mean business?"

"Yes, to all of the above, Freddy. I don't think Annette had anything on Ferris except pure fear. He knew she'd killed Trotter and when he read O'Neill's obituary, he broke out in hives and packed his bags. He flew out of New York because he knew he'd be next. Bombay will be proud of us. I think we know now why Ferris refused to read obits." Poole laughed.

"So, why did Alfred get the heave-ho?" Donovan savored his dessert; the Irishman loved anything on a plate with a fork next to it.

"O'Neill's horror of scandal made him pay off Ferris. Could be his puritanical streak forced him to threaten his pretty bride with divorce. She didn't like that." Poole licked his fork.

"Jesus, Oliver, you've been keeping company with a mighty treacherous female."

"Not lately." Poole's face was grim.

"You're lucky you're alive."

Poole grunted. "I'd like to know what she's up to right now."

"Maybe she likes to flirt with danger."

"You could be right. This is one babe who possesses more than her share of brass." Poole poured a cup of coffee for Freddy. "The gold charm is our only real link to her. If her son ever saw it, he's covering like a pro."

"College boys don't pay much attention to their mother's jewelry."

"Ducky's working on the New York angle. If she had the charm made there, he'll find out where. And, he's checking his diamond trade sources. They carry stones around in their pockets, you know."

"I prefer Hershey bars." Donovan smiled. "Our Charlotte's been batting a thousand, Oliver, and she's going to get real mad if we spoil her fun."

"Getting away with murder can be tough."

The two sat quietly awhile, finishing the cheesecake and listening to the music. Poole was trying to act cool, but inside, he felt a jolt of fear, the kind that's been seared into the nervous system. He automatically drew a curtain over the sensation, this nearly anonymous emotion that brought up no images, except bloody steel. He instinctively tightened every muscle in his body, as if to ward off the blows, and then he reached down to stroke Ching's thick coat. He needed to touch something warm and friendly.

"Ducky found the jeweler!" It was the following morning, and Donovan was standing in Poole's office doorway, nearly exploding with boyish excitement. "Line two!"

Poole picked up the phone and talked to Bliss for five minutes. Charlotte Dolbere, the jeweler said, commissioned the gold charm and ten others five years ago. She had supplied the goldsmith with a photograph of Wrenn house, explaining that it had been her childhood home. The jeweler will send the photo and all records. And, Bliss informed Poole he was considering a move to the heartland but had definite reservations about burgs that went to bed at midnight. Poole suggested a trial run. Bliss said he would take it under advisement, and he was going to talk to a diamond dealer he knew later that day.

"Charlotte's up to her pretty neck in it." Donovan sounded eager.

"She is indeed." Poole believed Ducky's information but doubted its potency. "Don't you still get the feeling we're being led down the garden path? It's like Marjorie's murder. The message is there, but I can't read it."

Donovan came all the way inside the office and closed the door. "We're making progress, Oliver. We don't need to read all the messages, do we? Maybe just one will lead us to the killer." He sat down across from Poole.

"Iris called again about her 'interloper,' the limping spook who was prowling around Charlotte's back yard a day or so after Ferris's murder. She's pretty sure this person drove off down the alley in a big car. She's certain it was an adult, walking unsteadily, and not the neighbor kids playing games." Poole raised an eyebrow and waited for Donovan to fill in the blank.

"Not Miss Sprain again?"

Poole smiled. "The limping spook."

"We can ask Charlotte about it." Donovan laughed. "That's what I love about this case, new twists every minute. It's hard to take naps around here anymore." He rose slowly and shuffled back to his office, softly whistling a nameless tune.

Meredith Wrenn arrived at the police station the following morning at nine. Poole said he had just a few routine questions.

Poole's initial chat with Meredith had been early on and unproductive. He had found her to be a once pretty woman in her early forties, who looked as if she no longer cared. That particular day, she had confined herself to the couch. This morning she walked carefully into Donovan's office, tall and slender like her cousin...a tall woman… with a noticeable limp.

Neither Donovan nor Poole missed the obvious. Was this Miss Sprain, Ferris's mysterious companion? Had a crippled leg been Meredith's legacy from the horrific car crash that killed her husband and savaged Annette's face? A bum limb, Poole decided cynically, was hardly as glamorous or useful as a pretty, new face. The case was getting Biblical.

Meredith settled herself nervously, showing signs of fright and confusion. She was dressed in a good quality pink linen dress that needed ironing. Poole wondered if it might be a cousin's cast-off. The woman's long hair was as dull as bark and carelessly secured in back with a barrette. Rose lipstick had been unsteadily traced on her lips and a bit of rouge tinted her hollow cheeks. The effect was not as good as it could have been. Poole immediately noticed a distinct resemblance between the cousins in the eyes, unusual and unforgettable, blue-green pools flecked with gold. Unlike Annette, Meredith showed signs of age and alcohol and deep disappointment.

Poole eased gently into the questions, asking Meredith about her life in New York with Evan and Annette. How long had they been together? Forever, she replied. He asked about the accident that had killed her young husband, and then about Annette's marriage to Alfred O'Neill. Had Meredith liked O'Neill? Had she lived with the couple?

Meredith said her leg was injured in the car crash; O'Neill was old and prissy and rich. She lived with them only a short time before taking an apartment several blocks away. She now resided in Augusta, but had to be reasonably close to her cousin and Evan. She said Evan still needed her.

Meredith felt mixed up. Sometimes she had difficulty remembering what she said to people. She recalled a conversation a few months ago with a private detective. In New York. Long before Roger's murder. She remembered Inspector Poole coming to her flat in Augusta to ask about Annette, but that was weeks ago, wasn't it? What had she told him? She couldn't keep things straight. These two detectives knew about the accident, about Annette's surgery. Had she told them this? They asked where she was the night Ferris was killed. She said the late show at the Orpheum Theatre, a few blocks from her apartment.

When they showed her the limericks, she pretended she had never seen them. They showed her the gold charm, the tiny Wrenn House. It was Charlotte's; it was found next to Ferris's body. Had Charlotte told her the charm bracelet was missing or stolen? Meredith admitted the bracelet belonged to her cousin but admitted nothing else. She was having a hard time keeping track of the truth and the lies.

Poole asked, "Where do you work, Miss Wrenn?"

"I'm still looking. Charlotte helps me out. Of course, I've always looked after Evan." Meredith tried smoothing the wrinkles in her skirt. "I was his nanny."

"Why did you wait to tell us about Charlotte's real identity?" Poole asked.

Meredith's heart thudded faster; she needed a drink. To calm herself she concentrated on the small flask in her purse and wondered if she could get a short recess to go to the ladies room. A second look at Poole made her doubt it. He was a determined cop.

"I figured you should know. You would have found out, once the will became public."

"Who told you about the will?" Donovan asked.

Charlotte, she said.

"Was Roger Ferris Evan's father?" Poole asked.

"Oh, yes." Should she have said that? Oh, who cared? If they couldn't figure it out now, they were pretty stupid.

"Were you and Ferris friends, Miss Wrenn?" Poole was relentless.

"No, we weren't friends." The answer came too quickly.

"Did you see him after you all came back here?"

"Here? No, no, Inspector. I never saw Roger." Meredith's nerves twitched beneath her skin. Poole would know a liar when he saw one.

"You and Roger Ferris were never in the Superchief Bar?"

"No, I don't like bars." Meredith wanted to scream.

"Do you recall the night Alfred O'Neill died?" Donovan was back in. "What was Charlotte's reaction to finding her husband lying dead in the hall, his skull crushed and his neck broken?"

Meredith cringed at the graphic description and looked down at her hands; the blue veins bulged like worms. Her short, chipped nails looked terrible. How much longer would this go on? What was the question? Oh, yes, Alfred. "He fell from the balcony," she answered matter-of-factly, not looking at either of the detectives. "We couldn't believe it. He was so....dead." She wanted to tell them how treacherous it was to know too much about Queenie.

"Was Mr. O'Neill in the habit of drinking alone?" asked Poole.

"How do I know? I didn't live there."

Meredith accepted M&Ms from Donovan who must have sensed her nervousness. Then, he asked if she still saw Evan, now that he was in college. She said he visited often; he was a wonderful boy. Dear Evan. She told them how much she loved him. He was like her own son.

"Did you visit Charlotte and Evan in Belmont?" Donovan asked. "You know, Sunday dinners?" He smiled at her.

"Sure. Evan comes to get me. Sometimes I drive over when I have a rental car. I'm going to get my own car next month. I rented a nice Toyota this morning." Why did she tell them that?

"Did you stop by Charlotte's house one evening shortly after Ferris was murdered, when she and Evan were out?"

Meredith scowled. Had she stopped that day? "I might have done. I don't remember. Sometimes I go over to watch movies on the VCR. Mine's broken."

"Do you like big hats, Miss Wrenn?" Donovan asked.

"Big hats?" What was he driving at? Meredith didn't understand. "Yes, I do. They keep the sun out of my eyes."

Before she was allowed to leave, another officer took her fingerprints. Just routine, Donovan told her, nicely. Soon after, Inspector Poole escorted her downstairs to the street where her car was parked. He was very gentlemanly and helped her into the driver's seat. Meredith wanted only one thing…to go home and find the gin bottle. She knew how to do that.

14

IMPRESSIONS

Meredith Wrenn made a big impression. Poole was getting his old closing-in-on-the prey feeling.

"So," Donovan said, "we found Miss Sprain, complete with big hats and black hair. And, a genuine limp." He bit into a chocolate doughnut.

Poole was savoring their small victory by playing with Ching. He tossed a chewed tennis ball, looping it into the air in the direction of a wastebasket on the other end of the room. The dog made a classy leap and caught it at the rim. The detectives applauded the dog's office Olympics.

"But, why the disguise with Roger? The ace bandage, the hats." Poole heaved another tennis ball against the wall, and the dog snapped it up on the first bounce.

"Could be Meredith was doing detective work for Charlotte," Donovan said. "She is one spooked lady for an innocent bystander. She's either scared of Charlotte...with good reason. Or, she's scared because she'd done something bad."

Poole tried to tease Ching into giving up the toy, but the dog played it cute and hid under the desk where he gnawed on the ball, making ownership noises. "Good point."

"Somehow, I can't see that poor woman stabbing Roger. Maybe she was a decoy, to catch Roger off-guard." Donovan sighed and rocked in his chair.

"We'll check the movie theatre, see if Meredith bought a ticket. Ask if anybody saw her leave. Search her apartment. Look for that damned gold bracelet and the blood stained clothes. We'll need a warrant." Poole took Ching's leash from a hook on the wall. "Let's take the pooch for a walk in the park. I need fresh air to think."

"Good idea." Donovan led the procession down the stairs and outside where Ching took charge in the park.

"My guess is," began Poole, "Meredith had grown disenchanted. Look at life from her perspective. She devotes herself to Charlotte and the boy. Then, Charlotte goes back into the murder business. This terrifies Meredith, and her terror turns to fury and hate. She knows Charlotte's secrets and doesn't want to go to prison as an accomplice. But, the new Charlotte is as cocky as ever. She flips Alfred over the balcony and decides to get even with Ferris because it's all been so damned easy. Charlotte glues together the limericks, hoping to scare the shit out of Roger before she gets him." Poole untangled the dog's leash from a bush and handed him back to Freddy. "But, Charlotte hit a snag."

"What do you mean?"

"Charlotte may have planned this little caper, but I'm beginning to wonder if it might have been Meredith who did the deed. All the clues point to Charlotte...the limericks, the wads of money for art, her husband's diamond collection, the gold charm, and the mask, as a clue to Charlotte's new face. Meredith sees this and moves in before her cousin gets there. She stabs Ferris and runs for cover." It dawned on Poole that he was now using the name Charlotte, as if there were two people.

"But, why? Charlotte is Meredith's meal ticket, her buddy, probably her only friend. I don't get the motive." Donovan stopped and bought everybody ice cream from a vendor.

"My guess is that the motive is love, a bit misdirected, but love, nonetheless. Did you listen to the way Meredith talked about Evan? The woman thinks the kid is her own golden boy. If Charlotte's convicted of murder, she goes to prison, and Meredith will have Evan all to herself.

What else does the poor woman have? What has she ever had? Charlotte got the gorgeous face, the money, the kid, the good life." Poole licked his butter pecan.

"Hey, I like this, Poole. The unfortunate house-bound, lame cousin. No glamour job. But does she have the guts to kill this guy? It took some planning to pull this off. She's a big drinker who probably has trouble remembering the day of the week." Donovan ran his tongue around the cone; a few drips clung to his beard. Ching was sitting on the pavement with his cone.

"Drunks aren't drunk all the time, Freddy. She had many chances to pick up the charm bracelet at Charlotte's place. She fits Iris's spook loping in the yard. A long coat would disguise her bad leg. When she went out with Roger, she wore the wig, the hat, the sunglasses, the bandage. She was protecting her identity and, at the same time, making herself look as much like Charlotte as possible."

"Then what?"

"So, she makes a date with Ferris for after the cast party…his midnight call from a phone box in Augusta. Miss Southern Belle. She made her up just for fun. She kills Ferris, plants the charm, believing the police will tie the replica of Wrenn house to the family name faster than we did. She slips the mask on his face, an obvious reference to Charlotte's new identity. She believed we would figure out the Charlotte-Annette angle in time. Didn't think we'd be this slow." Freddy scowled.

"In other words, she knew about Ferris's new will and figured we'd be on to Charlotte in a flash? She never counted on the long delay or the complication of other suspects."

"Ferris took her into his confidence. They were drinking buddies, and Ferris was very vulnerable. He needed a friend more than anything. He was going nuts and Meredith probably offered him a sympathetic ear. Maybe more. She probably told him she and Charlotte were estranged. She tells him about Charlotte's big chill plan, her move from New York, the limericks. Remember, Meredith squealed to us...an alcoholic's lapse of loyalty that was probably calculated."

They started a second turn around the small park. Ching was very interested in a French poodle with a rhinestone collar.

"What about Marjorie?" Donovan asked.

"Let's get Meredith squared away first. I have a feeling all else will fall into place after that."

"How about car rental stores within an easy walk of Meredith's apartment. She needed her own car that night."

"Sounds good." Poole headed for the parking lot. "We'll take Ching with us."

Ching barked twice as if he understood every word.

"Somebody is trying to frame me, Oliver. It's so obvious. Why can't you see it?"

Charlotte chose to use his given name again, a phony familiarity. Poole presumed it was meant to keep him off-guard. Close by, notebook in hand, Donovan said he'd let the senior inspector handle this interview.

Poole and Donovan sat in two antique French chairs in a room nearly as lovely as the murder suspect. Poole felt modestly disadvantaged on this woman's turf. He would have preferred the police station but had bowed to her request. He found it odd that she refused to have an attorney with her. She still felt safe, even at this stage of the investigation. It was a good indicator of her colossal nerve.

He would be courteous and use her new name. "Charlotte, you lied about the charm. You have a solid motive, and your alibi is weak." Poole watched her more closely than any suspect he'd ever questioned.

"My son will testify that I was home in bed the night Roger was killed. Somebody stole that bracelet and planted the charm just to incriminate me. My God!" Charlotte sat in a corner of the sofa, thinner than ever, he thought, that anorexic, ballerina-fashion model skinny that made him wonder how these women stayed alive. "Why in the world would I want to kill Roger after all these years? My anger disappeared a long time ago." She sounded convincing.

"He was blackmailing you. We've seen the O'Neill family stash of diamonds. Many are missing, according to Alfred's financial advisor. We spoke with him this morning. And, Ferris left a few diamonds behind in his safe deposit box. Insurance for the future, I would imagine. The D.A. is intrigued. You and your son benefit from Ferris's death. The will is clear. And, there are the limericks."

Poole stood again to stretch his leg, preferring the advantage of height but a trifle hesitant to pace around a room that looked this perfect. He walked carefully across the nearly colorless Oushak, as faded and mysterious as a rare map of the ancient world. English and French antiques had been arranged on it and around it by an expert. Paintings in gilded frames warmed the walls with subtle colors. Yards of rose silk fell on each side of the French windows, effusing the room with a flattering glow. Would she really have given up all that this room represented, just to be rid of a man like Ferris?

"That's all circumstantial and you know it. I admit I met Roger again in New York, but it was just business. He came to see me, recognized something familiar in a magazine photo. His curiosity got the best of him. He could see I had plenty of money to invest and he didn't mind asking for some." She sounded confident. Her beautiful teal eyes held Poole's without wavering.

"So, you invested in his companies. How do you explain his appointments with Alfred, Orbach's Detective Agency, your husband's generous stock contribution to Roger's account at a brokerage firm. We checked with Alfred's attorney. Come, come, Charlotte, don't take us for fools." Poole picked up a small bronze bust of a boy. The young Evan. The artistic advantages of wealth.

"Alfred was incredibly jealous. He found out about my association with Roger and I'm sure Roger never hesitated to taunt him about it. He probably made it sound as if we were lovers. Roger could be vicious." This time Charlotte didn't look at Poole or Donovan but concentrated on twisting a heavy gold bracelet around and around on her thin wrist.

Donovan concentrated on his notes and occasionally checked a small tape recorder humming on the table next to him.

"Why didn't you tell Roger about Evan?"

"It wasn't his business, or anybody else's. He must have figured it out on his own. The resemblance was uncanny. Roger wasn't stupid, simply vain." A slight smile curved the suspect's pretty mouth.

"He must have taken the limericks quite seriously to change his will at age thirty-eight."

"I don't know anything about those silly poems or the will. He was probably just clearing his conscience, if he actually had one."

A weak possibility, Poole thought. "Who would want to frame you? Nobody in Belmont knows you're Annette Wrenn? What connection could there be? Unless it was Evan or Meredith? Do Beatrice and Uncle Simeon know? Or someone else from your past? How about Marjorie and Froggy? Strange isn't it, how Marjorie died? But, who hates you enough to murder the father of your son and then place the blame at your feet?"

The questions were disturbing her; Poole could tell. She frowned while Poole continued his tour of the room, picking up and putting down expensive treasures.

"How do I know? Evan and Meredith are family. Beatrice and Simeon are innocent and too old to care. Someone else must have recognized me, put it all together, and decided I'd be the perfect target, once the police found out who I was. It was probably Marjorie. She never liked me. Couldn't stand the fact that Roger preferred me to her. Years ago, of course. You must know by now that she was having an affair with Roger and his father, and my guess is they both dumped her. Maybe Reggie ran her off the road or Froggy." Charlotte could still smile at the sexual machinations in Belmont. "Reggie Ferris would rather kill someone than lose Ingrid and her money."

Poole couldn't buy this, but, at times he had to agree with the conspiracy theory. And so did Freddy. The evidence against Charlotte was pretty pat. He was surprised she knew about Ingrid's fortune. Village gossip, no doubt.

Donovan spoke now. "Iris Woolsey saw a tall person in your back garden at twilight, around the time Ferris was killed, when you and your son were gone. Do you know who that was? Was someone staying at your place?"

"Certainly nobody broke in. We have an alarm system. The person would have needed a key, and it wasn't me." She spoke distractedly for the first time, as if she were thinking intensely about something else.

"Who else has a key?" asked Poole.

"Just Evan, Meredith, and my housekeeper."

"A short list. Is the maid trustworthy? Or could she hold a grudge? Or could she have been helping someone else in the family? The old family feud thing." He was giving her the benefit of the doubt now.

"There are dozens of second cousins and shirt-tail relatives in both families around here, if you have the time to find them."

"What about Meredith? She's tall."

"My cousin, Lieutenant, stays at her flat unless Evan or I pick her up. On rare occasions, she rents a car or takes a taxi over here. Certainly Meredith wouldn't wander around the back garden in the evening; she hates bugs and the out-of-doors." Charlotte allowed herself a small laugh, at her cousin's expense.

Poole returned to his chair still holding a glass paperweight, the interior like a dense forest of flowers growing beneath the sea. "That still leaves the limericks, and they do test you. We can't ignore the story they tell. It's easy to believe that Roger saw you with Trotter at the quarry site. You were arguing with Trotter about the blackmail money. A fight started, got out of hand, and Trotter went over the side…a bit of sky-diving."

"You can't prove any of this. It's pure fiction."

Poole went on, undeterred. "So last fall you decide you've invested enough money in Roger's ventures and refuse to give him another dollar. Roger doesn't appreciate his well running dry and threatens you, as punishment. He blackmails you, figuring your very proper husband won't like to know you'd been seeing an actor, making secret investments, lying about your past. You pay him off a few times with the family diamonds or cash from the sale of the stones and then you call his bluff. And, to your surprise, he calls yours. Roger runs to Alfred." Poole waited for her to react.

"Your imagination is astounding." Charlotte tried another laugh but it caught in her throat. She looked to Donovan for comfort and found him scratching his beard.

Charlotte's eyes showed fear. Poole went on. "Roger gets his big pay-off from Alfred, who hates anything messy, and Roger runs home to Belmont, where he thinks he'll be safe. Now, why would he do that? That's always been at the heart of this whole case." Poole put down the paperweight and got to his feet again, allowing his height to dominate, allowing the break in his accusation to lend a kind of power to his argument. "We know why, don't we?" He smiled.

"And what is that?" asked Charlotte.

Poole thought the widow sounded pretty smug for a woman accused of so much conspiracy.

"Roger Ferris had you figured for one very dangerous lady, and he didn't want to stay around for the third act. He knew you killed Trotter. He was damned sure you murdered your husband and who knows who else. And, he was convinced you would get him too. Just to get even."

It was Charlotte's turn to stand. She looked dumbfounded at Poole's grasp of it all, but refused to sit like a frightened rabbit. "I'm not answering any more questions without my attorney. I did not murder Roger Ferris, gentlemen. You can be sure of that. If you had proof, I'd be sitting in your pitiful police station."

Poole headed for the door. Donovan rose.

"I'll hire that private detective, Orbach, to get to the bottom of this. Heaven knows he's familiar with the case. If he won't take it, I'll find out by myself."

"Don't get cute. Playing detective is more complicated than smiling for Fernando. Murder is easier. My guess is you rented a black SUV to run Marjorie off the road."

"You think you're the only person capable of reason and deduction."

Charlotte's lovely features turned more imperial than ever. Poole was almost afraid of her himself. He knew Freddy was.

"I'm just warning you," Poole said and opened the heavy door. "Orbach's good, but, if I were you, I'd spend my money on a good lawyer. Burton Dance is the guy you want."

And with that, he and Donovan made their exit.

As they drove off, Poole glanced over his shoulder. Charlotte was standing in the doorway like a fierce and determined guard dog. If they were wrong and she was innocent, she would find a way to prove it. If guilty, she might very well find a way out again.

Charlotte slouched low in the Mercedes a half block away and watched Evan help Meredith into his car. He had volunteered to drive Meredith on errands that afternoon. Charlotte waited until the little car disappeared around a corner and then hurried toward the entrance of the apartment house.

Once a gleaming art deco masterpiece with terrazzo floors and marble columns, the cavernous lobby now lay fallow and dim. Charlotte imagined it in its heyday with soft velour couches and deep club chairs where elderly gentlemen read the afternoon newspapers and drank sherry within the shelter of potted palms. Today, her footsteps echoed hollowly as if she were tapping on a scooped out pumpkin.

She walked up the three flights to avoid meeting any of Meredith's neighbors in the elevator. Once inside the flat, she felt safe but rushed. The rooms were fairly tidy for a change, empty gin bottles out of sight. The housekeeper must have been there that morning. A closet in the foyer held two cotton jackets, a long plastic raincoat, three suitcases, and two handbags on a hook and a big hat on the shelf. Nothing looked out of the ordinary. She opened the cases and purses and found them empty. She wasn't sure what she was looking for, besides the charm bracelet.

Moving to the kitchen she checked the pantry and broom closet. Nothing. The cabinets were nearly empty, just a few dishes and pans, very little food. Meredith was either eating out these days or just drinking her meals. The armoire in the living room was a jumble of tapes and records, extra bottles of liquor, and boxes of cards, letters, and photographs from the early days in New York. How sentimental.

By the time she started searching the bedroom, the afternoon sun was pouring through the windows. Rather than risk a neighbor seeing inside, Charlotte pulled the curtains and turned on the lights. The closet held the usual collection of clothes. Most were hand-me-downs from her own wardrobe in need of laundering or dry cleaning. Meredith no longer cared how she looked. She pulled out dresser drawers, messy nests of old cosmetics, pill bottles, underwear, and bad paperback books. And, surprisingly enough, the bottom dresser drawer held a pistol wrapped in a towel. Charlotte had no idea her cousin owned a gun. Frustration was beginning to take hold. There had to be something somewhere. Where was the bracelet?

Charlotte returned to the closet; she'd forgotten the boxes on the shelf. She took down box after box, more old clothes and shoes, Evan's school papers and drawings. The last carton had been shoved into a corner near the back. It was quite heavy. Carrying it to the bed, she opened the carton and discovered the one thing she never expected.

Diaries. A couple dozen, going back many years. She sat down on the bed; her knees were weak.

Last year's diary lay on top, most of it long, rambling accounts of how Meredith occupied her days and nights. Skimming quickly Charlotte stopped at December and found what she needed to know. The sneaky bitch! The journals were a remarkable secret; one they had not shared. Charlotte wondered how many others there were.

The drawer in the bedside table held the current diary; the handwriting was noticeably deteriorated. Meredith's drinking had become worse since New York. It didn't take long to locate the horrid and incriminating details of her cousin's betrayal. Reluctantly, her hands trembling, Charlotte returned the book to the drawer. Put together, the journals were evidence that could either save or destroy either one of them, depending upon which installment you read. And there wasn't time to read it all now. She must hurry. If she took the old books, Meredith would never miss them. They could be destroyed. Paging through this year's journal once more, Charlotte decided to leave it behind as insurance. It was a chance she would take. The cops could be tempted to search these rooms. Let Meredith hang on her own words. The remaining diaries would make a lovely fire.

Charlotte closed the carton, left it on the bed, and then carefully rearranged the remaining cartons on the shelf to hide the space where the diary box had been. Then she turned out the lights, opened the curtains, picked up the box, smoothed the bedspread and exited the room. Her head was spinning and she felt disconnected from the floor. Why had Meredith done this? Why had her dearest friend recorded everything they'd ever done? Their private lives lay exposed by pen to paper. Charlotte Dolbere had been defiled. The old Annette Wrenn was exposed. Either way, she was meant to play the fool's part.

As Charlotte walked through the living room, she heard footsteps in the corridor and a fumbling of keys. Was Meredith back already? Or was it the maid?

Quickly detouring to the kitchen, Charlotte carefully turned the lock on the back door and waited. She could hear the front door slam shut. A woman was humming. Was it Meredith? She couldn't tell. She turned the knob and the kitchen door opened without a sound. Her arm ached from the weight of the heavy box and an edge was cutting into her ribs. The passage was deserted and quiet. She slipped out; the door closed with a soft, precise click.

Once downstairs again, Charlotte trotted to the car. Her chest ached with the exertion; her head was pounding. She was stunned by Meredith's acts of treason. Her cousin had betrayed her over and over again, year after year. Inside the car, she lighted a cigarette and sat quietly for several minutes, thinking and smoking. When she was calmer, she put out the cigarette and started the engine. With a few expert swings of the wheel, she turned the car in the middle of the block and headed for River Road, all the while talking to herself in a low soothing voice, telling herself to stay calm, ordering her heart to slow.

But, as she sped toward Belmont, another shriller voice kept interrupting, asking the usual questions…what if something went wrong, what if Meredith had struck a bargain with the police, what if they had concocted a trap? Charlotte gripped the wheel more tightly; she could feel the muscles in her arms pinch and pull. The nagging voice inside her head was insistent, demanding solutions. She had listened to the hypnotic voice many times and knew the advice by heart. 'Steps will have to be taken,' it always said. 'Steps. They must be taken.'

Yes, yes, Charlotte agreed. She always agreed.

The girl at the Orpheum Theatre remembered Meredith buying a ticket for the late show at eleven on the night Ferris was murdered. It was Hitchcock week, she told the detectives. *Rear Window* was playing. Miss Wrenn, she said, was an avid fan of old films; she had seen each one. The theatre manager told Poole and Donovan that he noticed a woman who looked like Miss Wrenn slip out the side door about a half hour into the movie. He thought she might have been ill.

Mac's Rent-a-Ride, two blocks from Meredith's apartment and just around the corner from the Orpheum, rented a 1998 Honda Accord Saturday, the third of July at six-forty-five in the evening to M. Wrenn. She had a valid state driver's license. His description of the woman fit Meredith Wrenn. Her limp certainly gave her away. She returned the car the following Monday morning at eleven.

The detectives asked for records of the transaction, and then they all moved out to the lot for a look at the car. After noting dark smudges on the back seat, Poole informed the manager that the car would be impounded for examination by the state crime lab. The manager said it wasn't going anywhere because the automobile needed a new air conditioner. The car, he said, had not been driven since Meredith returned it. Business, he added, was slow. Ching, who sniffed all the tires, was finding the car more interesting than the police station.

Donovan asked if the same woman rented an automobile on the dates surrounding Marjorie's fatal accident. After examining his records, the manager said no. Only male customers rented SUVs on those days.

A call to the district attorney kept them on the trail. The district attorney agreed that all leads should be pursued. Pressure to solve the case was sky high. He would secure the necessary search warrants immediately. Could the suspect have killed Mrs. Verdun as well, he wanted to know. Poole said they didn't know.

Search warrants in hand, Poole and Donovan arrived at Meredith's apartment later that day, after first dropping Ching at home. The gloomy green lobby was empty and cool, and Donovan remarked to Poole that this wasn't exactly the Beacon Street Arms. Poole pointed out that it wasn't Charlotte's fortress on Two Tree Lane either.

Upstairs, nobody answered the bell, and they asked the building manager to let them in. He said Miss Wrenn had just left in a taxi for St. Paul's chapel. A cab, he said, picked her up each afternoon at the same time. It was her habit to visit the chapel every day. There was a standing order with the cab company.

A search of the apartment turned up a journal in a bedside table drawer and a pair of red espadrilles with dark stains on the hemp covered heels. Donovan threw the canvas shoes into a plastic bag and marked it for the lab. Sitting on Meredith's bed, Poole paged through the diary. A half-finished glass of vodka sat next to the lamp. The room was stuffy and untidy. Meredith must have dressed and left hurriedly.

"Here it is," Poole announced. Speed reading had its advantages. Donovan was going through dresser drawers. "I think we can give ourselves an A-plus for figuring out this one."

"Read me the story. Make it better than the Brothers Grimm."

Poole read whole passages out loud and paraphrased the rest. "She met Ferris at his apartment after the guests left. They had a few drinks. He told her he was terrified of Charlotte and was planning to run again. She agreed that Charlotte was dangerous; that maybe he should get her first. She doesn't tell us his reaction to this. In the end, she stabbed him after he dozed off. She removed her bloody coat, put it into a large tote bag and cleaned up in the bathroom. Before leaving she stuck the mask on his face and dropped the charm near his foot. Not a hitch. Where in the hell is the coat?" Poole looked up, as if expecting Donovan to produce it like magic. Donovan shrugged and thought about running away himself.

The Irishman went through the closets a second time. Nothing. "Keep reading," he said, "maybe she'll tell us where she put it."

"She killed him to get Evan. Blaming Charlotte for the murder was the easy part." Poole paused. "Lots of hate and fear here. The limericks were meant to terrify him before the murder. She doesn't say who sent them. I would almost bet it was Meredith who wrote them."

"Where's the bracelet?" Donovan found the small bedroom stifling and frightening. "Jesus, Poole, let's get out here. I can just see this woman jumping out from behind the curtains with a steak knife. Why can't you read that damned thing in the car?"

"We'll leave in a minute. No wonder she drinks. Sworn to secrecy and dependent on a vain nut. Odd, there's nothing particularly incriminating about Charlotte. Just vague references to threats and revenge."

"Human nature. Go figure. After a few years, it probably didn't matter which one committed the crime. They're both guilty." Donovan stooped to look under the bed. Nothing.

"Let's go. This can't be the only journal. She makes references to earlier entries." Poole grabbed his walking stick and got up from the bed.

"This place is clean; no murder costume here, except the shoes." Donovan headed for the door. "Maybe she's wearing the damned bracelet."

"She's either hid them in her storage locker or..." Poole didn't finish but followed Freddy. "We'll need another search warrant. I would bet my old Porsche the stuff's planted like roses bushes in a flower bed."

"In Charlotte's back yard." Donovan held the door for Poole, and they set off down the corridor like hounds on the trail.

Poole called the D.A. and arranged for another warrant. He notified the lab and then swung into the one-way lanes that funneled traffic around Capitol Square, a park shaded by oaks and watched over by statues of Civil War heroes. The capitol rose from the center like the one in Washington, its dome crowned by the gilded Lady of Progress. Poole's condo was tucked behind the bank building on one corner. He took West Washington off the square and headed for the outskirts of town.

"Do you think Ferris changed his will so somebody would eventually find out about Charlotte?" Donovan tried to get comfortable in the small seat. "What a fatalist. Must have believed he would never escape the woman."

"A gruesome plan with an obscure clue dreamed up by a man who wasn't thinking too clearly. Ferris wanted her caught and was as eaten with revenge as Charlotte or Meredith. Jesus, what a group." Poole passed a concrete truck, its revolving cylinder cranking like a turbine. It reminded him of time clicking away. Time was important now.

"Damned fool put suspicion on his own son first. But, I suppose he was counting on Meredith to tell the truth. Ferris must have thought she was his only ally." Donovan sighed and rolled down the window. The afternoon clouds were clearing away and shafts of blinding sun struck the windshield. He pulled his canvas hat closer to his eyes, dug out a cheroot, and set it afire.

Poole nodded and drove in silence.

"How about a plate of catfish and a couple of beers before we dive into Charlotte's treasures? We need to keep up our strength." Donovan grinned broadly.

They were about a half mile up River Road when Donovan pointed his cigar toward a weathered clapboard diner on the river side of the highway. A bright blue neon sign flashed, The Blue Heron Cafe.

"A class joint, Freddy." Case or no case, Freddy was right; they deserved to eat just like anybody else. Poole pulled into the gravel parking lot. It was crowded with old pick-ups and beat-up gas-guzzlers;

respectable patches of rust decorated most of the fenders. Donovan whistled and peeled off his jacket.

The husky voice of Waylon Jennings and the sweet, greasy smell of pan-fried fish floated through the screen door. As Poole entered, he felt a little more at home. Billy's Bar and Grille had started him off that first day. He wasn't all the way back, but he was closing in.

Poole dropped the car keys into his pocket and took a stool at the counter. Maybe this new life wouldn't be so bad. Catfish and beer, river towns and playing detective. Old friends, new enemies. New rules, old nightmares.

A year ago, the food alone would have turned him off. Now he wasn't so sure. The appetites of middle age and the convolutions of homicide still mystified and tempted him.

15

OUT OF TIME

By four-forty-five Poole and Donovan were pulling into Charlotte's drive on Two Tree Lane. A grumpy housekeeper warned them about disturbing Miss Dolbere's private world. Poole smiled and waved to the driver of the lab van making its way toward the house. He was certain Iris and her neighbors were watching from their windows. It wouldn't be long before Nathan Bombay showed up with his pad and pencil and every TV reporter within fifty miles.

A thorough search progressed quickly, and the crew soon realized that Charlotte had inadvertently made it all quite simple. A carton of Meredith's journals had been shoved into a bedroom closet. Ironically, pertinent passages, passages that condemned Charlotte, were marked. A cursory glance confirmed Poole's suspicions. He hoped other entries would solve the Verdun homicide case as well.

"I'm surprised she didn't burn these immediately. Must have run out of time. My God, if she stole them from Meredith, and I'm sure she did, these diaries are deadly." Poole settled on a small sofa in the bedroom with several journals in his lap.

"She must think she has all the time in the world."

The detectives reviewed the accounts quickly, choosing specific dates near the various homicides. They would read the rest later. "Young

Annette pushed Trotter into the quarry after a quarrel. He had been blackmailing her grandmother. And, he'd tried to molest Annette at the stables. Charming fellow. Roger witnessed the murder and agreed to keep quiet if Annette would have an abortion and set him free. She took the money and fled to New York to live with Meredith and her husband."

"My God, Oliver, says here our young Annette poisoned a friend named Suzannah when they were eleven. The girl had been disloyal." Donovan was amazed.

They stayed to read entries another ten minutes and found more than they ever imagined. "Charlotte got rid of a rival French model about fifteen years ago….by pushing her from a roof garden in Paris. Sketchy on details. But, holy Toledo! How many bodies were there?"

"Belmont has just inherited its first serial killer."

"What's Meredith doing in the middle? No conscience? No backbone?"

"Plenty of fear, Freddy. Meredith subjugated herself in that household. She was crippled and willing. She took the back seat. She had the love of the boy and Charlotte's appreciation. My version of pop psychology, but it seems fairly reasonable. Charlotte simply eliminates anyone who isn't true to her." Poole shuddered. "I wonder how close I came to getting shoved down a flight of stairs?" He didn't laugh.

The stories went on. Marriage to Alfred was a financial move. Her affair with Roger in New York was her biggest mistake. He made great demands and one was marriage. When she turned down his proposal, he got mightily pissed off and blackmailed her. He threatened to tell Alfred everything and when she quit paying, he did.

"Judas Priest! The treachery is awesome. Evil treachery! Year after year that woman recorded the life of the friend who trusted her. The diaries are an ignoble act."

"Fortunately for us, Meredith liked to take notes." Poole kept reading. "Annette pushed Alfred over the balcony after he threatened to divorce her and take away Evan."

"Charlotte doesn't believe in debate."

Another finger of ice crawled up Poole's spine. "Freddy, find out from the housekeeper where we can find Charlotte."

As Donovan turned to leave, a lab technician poked his head around the corner and said they'd found an interesting bag in the garage. Everybody moved downstairs and outside.

A canvas tote had been wedged behind the storm windows in the back of the garage. Inside was the missing murder costume...a black wig, a pair of bloodied plastic gloves, a big straw hat, and a trench coat, badly stained. Still wearing his plastic gloves, Poole turned over the coat; the right cuff was stitched with Charlotte's monogram. He told Sergeant Shipstead to look for anything else that might relate to Marjorie Verdun's death, like credit card receipts from car rental shops, gas receipts. "And, don't forget the kitchen knife used on Ferris." They were dealing with two killers.

Donovan trotted off to find the maid and soon returned saying that Charlotte had taken Meredith shopping.

"Find out where we can find Evan, and I'll finish up here," Poole said anxiously.

He gave instructions to his officers and hauled the box of diaries out to the car. Donovan jumped in and announced that Evan was at the Beaumont Theatre, painting scenery backstage. Donovan said he left a message with the drama department office for the young man to call the station as soon as possible. "I have a bad feeling about this."

"So do I, Freddy."

Evan O'Neill called Donovan's office ten minutes later. He said his mother and Auntie Meredith were on their way to the summer house in Howard's Grove a few miles north of Belmont. He planned to join them there about seven. He gave Poole the number of Rumsford Farm, its location, and asked what was wrong. The lieutenant said they had a few more questions.

Nobody answered at the country house. Poole and Donovan decided to leave immediately and set out in a police cruiser.

After speaking with Donovan, Evan experienced a queer premonition. He and a friend had taken a break from painting and were having a Coke and a sandwich at the Student Union. Evan couldn't get Donovan out of his mind. What questions? What did his mother and Meredith have to do police investigations at this point? Or, was the cop talking about Marjorie Verdun's death?

Two days ago his mother confessed to him that Roger Ferris was his real father, a fact that nearly blew him away. Years ago, he was told that his father died in a car accident before he was born. Knowing the truth about Professor Ferris made the actor's generous bequest understandable. But, knowing the truth had hardly set him free. Adjusting to the information was more difficult than Evan imagined. Adjusting to the professor's murder was almost terrifying. He was still trying to take it all in. He was still trying to absorb the death of Alfred, the only father he'd ever known.

When Charlotte went on to divulge the truth about her own life, the jarring, bizarre story of her transformation from Annette Wrenn to Charlotte Dolbere, Evan felt as if he had just jumped into somebody else's skin. His mother had been born and raised in Belmont. Her parents died in a plane crash right here in the bluffs. Nobody in town recognized her because of her surgeries. Why the damned mystery? Why not come home and tell people the truth? Evan was confused and angry. He must have aunts and uncles and cousins everywhere, people he never knew existed. Why had Charlotte and Meredith kept this from him? The long-standing cover-up bothered him more and more. Evan had grown angry about it. In the last two days he found himself looking at Charlotte and Meredith with new eyes. He was suspicious of them for the first time. The truth, as they told it now, was too strange to be completely believed; their secrecy was unsettling. His anxiety about these two women had grown overpowering. He wasn't sleeping. Were the police right to ask more questions about Roger Ferris? While he was afraid for his mother and Meredith, Evan found he was afraid for himself, as well.

Sitting on the Union terrace with his friend, his hands spattered with paint and the sun warming his back, Evan wondered what else his mother had failed to tell him? What had Meredith kept from him? And, more unnerving, why were the police so eager to talk today and this late in the day? Couldn't a few questions wait until tomorrow? Surely, neither one had killed Ferris or Mrs. Verdun? Was something terribly wrong? He had to find out for himself.

Evan made up an excuse to leave and raced from the Union terrace to the parking lot behind the theatre. He knew a shortcut to Howard's Grove.

Charlotte had bought her a bathing suit, a lovely linen dress, and a DVD player for a big TV. The two women had shopped, stopped for lunch, and then started out for the Rumsford Farm. Some farm. More like a country estate with its pool, a stable, and acres of grounds tended by gardeners. It took a dozen employees to take care of Charlotte's new world.

"Where's Evan?" Meredith asked.

"Painting scenery for the next production. He's coming out later with his friends for a pool party and a barbeque." Charlotte sounded happy and pulled into the passing lane. She drove aggressively and skillfully.

Meredith wished Evan were there right now. His mother sounded too cheerful. The shopping spree this morning was a peace offering for her brutal behavior the day the police made their accusations. The day Charlotte called her a 'Judas.'

"Why do you want this country place anyway?" The old love of horses had come back to haunt them again.

"Country air, long walks, riding. It's good for us." The string of reasons reminded Meredith of Charlotte's excuses for marrying Alfred. That, too, was to be good for them. Good girl Charlotte, always thinking of others.

Meredith stared glumly out the window and feared a fresh lecture on the evils of alcohol. Her cousin could be evangelistic. "I don't like the country," Meredith said, obstinately. "If I want to see trees, I look out the window at the park."

"That pathetic neighborhood. Really, Meredith. I don't understand why you want to live in Augusta." Charlotte fished a cigarette from her handbag and carefully touched the end with the dash lighter. "What did the police want yesterday?" She slipped in the question like a card shark pulling an ace from her sleeve.

How did she find out? Meredith responded a bit too brightly, "They wanted to know where I was the night Roger died. How about that? Maybe I'm a suspect too."

"So, where were you?" Charlotte passed several cars going well over the speed limit, then exited the freeway and headed for Howard's Grove on Highway K.

"It's Hitchcock Week at the Orpheum."

"What else did they ask you?"

"Not much. I told them I didn't know Roger too well, which is pretty much the truth. He was your pal, not mine. They're checking the whole family because of his will." Meredith wanted the conversation to end.

"Did they ask about that gold charm?" The question owned a sharp edge, and Meredith could see Charlotte's hands tighten on the wheel.

Gathering courage, Meredith replied, "I said you probably lost it at Iris's party. Somebody found it and took advantage." Meredith was close to giddy. "I think Marjorie's still at the top of their list," she hurried on. Was Charlotte buying this crap? Poor old Marjorie. Dead as a flounder.

"That society whore. Poole thinks I killed her too."

"Where's his proof?"

They drove in silence until Meredith began to feel lost. They were somewhere between Belmont and Lynton Station, but who would know? One farm looked pretty much like another. The landscape cranked by as if a stagehand were winding scenery on a roller. Fat sheep and Holstein cows foraged in steep pastures, nearly vertical in places. The grazing land alternated in wide ribbons with fields of corn and grain. In another month or so fields and pastures would turn into a patchwork of black earth, pale stubble, and lettuce green blocks of new winter wheat. Meredith preferred autumn; it wasn't so damned green.

"Is this the same route we took last time?" Was the vodka turning her crazy or did she have reason to feel afraid today?

"This is a short-cut. It won't be long now." Charlotte threw her a glance and smiled. "We'll cook steaks on the grill, have a swim before dinner, a few drinks. It'll be fun. Evan's friends are so cute." She turned on the radio and soon violins and sweet soprano voices filled the space. Meredith found the music and the ride as soothing as electric shock.

A short-cut? God, she hated the country. The highway stretched on with more red barns and white houses nestled in the hollows. They looked so damned isolated. People with cows for company. Meredith could relate to this remote life on some level and it scared her. The car engine hummed like a church organ and Charlotte seemed light years away. I need a drink, Meredith thought nervously.

The road carried them across a narrow bridge that spanned a young river. Silky branches of willow bowed like plumes over the olive water. The dark side of Meredith's mind suggested that the branches were being pulled into the water by a wicked troll, Charlotte, no doubt. And like a fairy tale coming to life, she suddenly had a clear picture of what her cousin was up to.

Meredith said boldly, "We're not going to the farm, are we?" Panic had loosed her tongue and turned her brave.

Charlotte frowned and clicked off the radio. "Of course we are. What's the matter with you, Meredith?"

"You're going to have me locked up in a sanitarium, aren't you?" Meredith felt sick. "I've heard about those places buried in the country, miles from civilization." She put her hand to her mouth, nearly afraid to breathe, wondering what life would be like without booze.

"Don't be silly! Listen to yourself. Alcoholic paranoia." Eleanor's holier-than-thou voice slid from Charlotte's lips.

"I want to go home! I'm not going to any hospital!" Meredith's head felt oddly detached from the rest of her body.

"You're acting like a child." Charlotte laughed and kept driving. "It's not a bad idea though; you do need help."

A fragile wisp of dignity still lingered within Meredith and on some days it allowed her to talk back. "My drinking is none of your damned business. You can't tell me what to do." She wanted to jump out the window.

"Where do you get these insane ideas? Evan is counting on you. Do you really want to disappoint him?"

Meredith began to feel helpless again and slightly embarrassed. Was Charlotte innocent of treachery this time? Maybe this was nothing more than a day in the country. Dear Charlotte knew which buttons to push. Meredith wasn't sure who she could trust anymore. She couldn't even trust her own instincts half the time. Her real fear lay in the fact that Charlotte was still free. Why hadn't the cops hauled her in? What were they waiting for? This ordeal should have been over by now. What about the evidence planted in Charlotte's garage? Maybe the cops were really as stupid as Charlotte always said they were.

The narrow blacktopped road began a steep, winding course through dense, dark bluffs. Few people lived up here in this wild tangle of trees. Just rattlesnakes and eagles. The car cornered sharp bends with ease, passing a series of old painted posts that marked dangerous drops near the edge of the road. Meredith tried not to look down. Her nerves were shot to hell today...with good reason. She would always associate high places with Charlotte. Both were lethal. Poor Marjorie.

The ride was taking too long. Had Charlotte figured out the frame-up? What if Charlotte was planning to dump her from a very high place....like Trotter and that silly ass, Alfred, or Marjorie? Punishment for betrayal. Meredith chewed on a nail and prayed.

"I hope you weren't this edgy at the police station. Poole notices things." Charlotte looked over at her. "Evan will swear I was home in bed the night Roger died." She turned her perfect profile and produced that odd secret smile, as if she were giving Meredith a gift.

Meredith didn't answer. Should she kill Charlotte, too? It had been surprisingly easy to kill Roger. He had dozed off, and she pushed the knife into him, several times, just to make sure. His struggle had been short and feeble. She and Charlotte were too much alike. Neither one had the proper moral code for this world.

Why not grab the steering wheel, Meredith thought, and plow the car into the headwall? Or turn the wheel the other way and tip over the side? Meredith could hear the screams and feel the drop as the car plunged, diving like a wingless plane, crashing clumsily through trees, rolling and careening off rocks until it hit bottom. She imagined the car lying on its side as quiet as a dead animal. And then without another sound, it would explode into an enormous fireball of orange flames and black smoke. Like Marjorie's accident. Like the accident that killed Charlotte's mother and father, right in these hills. Had he crashed the plane on purpose? Meredith always believed he had. The man was never been right in the head. Were any of the Wrenns?

But, none of this happened. The horrible images faded as they wound their way down the road and into the valley on the other side.

Charlotte didn't ask any more questions. She seemed uninterested. If she suspected Meredith's betrayal, she gave no indication. As they turned into the drive at Rumsford Farm, Meredith felt oddly relieved and thirsty for a drink.

Maybe, she was safe after all.

For the next hour Charlotte and Meredith sunned on two yellow cushioned lounges next to the swimming pool, an irregularly shaped chunk of turquoise that could have been plucked from a desert oasis. The water shimmered like tinsel beneath a cloudless sky. The warm late afternoon air barely stirred itself, and Meredith could see a faint burn on her arms and legs.

The concrete patio that surrounded the pool was arranged with white mesh chairs and three round tables shaded by daisy yellow umbrellas. Huge Italian clay pots spilled over with pink petunias and long green vines. The colors were as cheerful and pure as Hockney's palette. The main house stood behind them, creating a shadow near one end of the man-made pond where the sun was sinking behind the peaked roof.

Charlotte fixed them each another gin and tonic. They'd had several and both were getting giddy. It was almost like the old days, before Alfred and Roger and the others. Charlotte handed Meredith the glass and announced that she was going to swim before the light was lost to them completely. Through half-closed eyes Meredith watched her cousin slip into the blue-green water.

Charlotte dove deep and then slithered underneath like a long, dark fish. When she came up for air, she swam the length of the pool in neat, powerful strokes and then stood in the shallow end. She playfully splashed in Meredith's direction and shook water from her ears.

"Come on in! The water's fabulous. It's like a warm bath." Charlotte scooped handfuls of water over the hot concrete apron.

"All right. All right. I'll come in." Meredith took one long swallow of her drink, left her sunglasses on the table and limped to the end of the pool. Even in front of Charlotte, she was still self-conscious about her legs, one good and one bad. Charlotte never commented. The disability was accepted and had gone almost unnoticed through the years, unlike her drinking.

Four broad tiled steps eased themselves into the shallow end of the pool, and as Meredith lowered herself in the water, the liquid felt like a lovely smooth salve on her burned shoulders. "Ah, chlorine and gin, two of my all-time favorites," she said, giggling and relaxing against the weight of the water.

Charlotte smiled and dropped back to float with her face turned up to the sky, her arms and legs limp and passive in the shadowy water. The two floated and paddled like children for several minutes. Meredith found her lame leg less awkward and useless in the water. Her arms and shoulders were strong enough to compensate.

Meredith side-stroked the width of the pool and squinted into the electric brilliance on the surface. She was enjoying herself when she hadn't meant to. She watched Charlotte toss a flat round stone into the deep end and then execute a perfect dive from the edge of the pool, disappearing into layers of color and light. Meredith knew the game; they had played it as kids….groping along the bottom for the gray rock, the water pressure pinging in your ears, your lungs aching for air. But not today. Meredith just lay back and floated aimlessly; her legs dangled slightly below the rest of her body.

Suddenly, Meredith felt a tug on her foot. It was followed by a powerful pull on her bad leg. Her first thoughts were of sharks. How ridiculous! She giggled. Charlotte was playing shark, another old game. But, this time, the pull yanked Meredith beneath the surface where she found herself in Charlotte's powerful grip. They began to wrestle, face to face, Charlotte's image distorted and pinched in the green water, her long black hair suspended in a devil's halo around her head. This was no game.

Charlotte slid her arms around Meredith's waist and forced her deeper into the water. Meredith twisted and clawed and got hold of her cousin's hair, but the water was turning her efforts into slow-motion ballet. Her arms and legs were leaden and clumsy. But, one last violent twist freed her and Meredith wriggled to the top where she gulped great lungfuls of air and swallowed as much water. She coughed and choked and tried to get her bearings through the veil of water and glare blinding her.

Charlotte, too, bobbed to the top, gasping. The expression on her face meant only one thing. Meredith tried to swim away, but Charlotte was quicker and stronger. She grabbed Meredith's shoulders from behind and pushed her head under water. Meredith scratched Charlotte's arms and shoulders; the scraped skin stuck beneath her fingernails. And then, miraculously, they both broke through to the surface again, choking and spitting.

Meredith let out a shrill scream, but Charlotte's powerful arms were around her chest again, dragging her down. This time Charlotte wrapped her legs around Meredith's, like a python coiling around its victim, holding on until she thought her lungs would burst. Charlotte's grasp weakened as her need for air increased, and soon the two women were rising to the top once more.

Meredith managed another gurgling cry, the chlorinated water flooding her mouth, burning her throat. It seemed as if the water alone was the enemy, sucking her under, gorging her stomach, stinging her eyes. This time a sharp yank on her hair drew her into the iridescent green, and her thrashing grew weak and aimless. A sickening fatigue overtook her limbs. For an instant, Meredith thought she might go to sleep. Fighting exhaustion and Charlotte seemed futile. Sensing Meredith's weakness, Charlotte let her go and swam to the top for air. By giving in, Meredith found that her body refused to rise and instead sank slowly toward the bottom.

As she drifted down, her body weightless and unnecessary, she became acutely aware of the intense light from above and the deep quiet slowly swallowing her. Shafts of sunshine penetrated the water at long angles like polished steel blades, as close to anything ethereal she'd ever experienced. The hypnotic spell broke the instant her feet touched the rough concrete floor of the pool...she was making contact with what was really happening. With pain crushing her chest, Meredith allowed herself a moment to rest on the bottom, and then she pushed against the floor with all her strength. As she began to rise, she fluttered weakly toward the layer of light overhead.

Charlotte was waiting. And, Meredith knew she had lost. A brutal shove sent her beneath the surface again; her mouth and nose filled with water. This would be the last time.

As she dropped again through the sun-sparkled water, too tired to fight, Meredith saw the faces of her mother and father. And then Evan. And finally, she saw herself, as a little girl riding a bicycle. Then, she simply lay down on the hard floor of the pool, like one of Charlotte's smooth stones.

Evan turned sharply into the drive at Rumsford Farm and parked behind his mother's Mercedes. He figured he had beat the police by about ten minutes. He had his own questions to ask.

As he hurried up the bricked walk with arcs of zinnias and daisies brushing against his legs, he knew he was home. This proud old farm house, like a handsome aging gentleman with fine lines around his eyes, was honest and comfortable, the way he liked things. He wasn't at ease on English estates and in New York townhouses.

The young man let himself in the front door. Music was coming from upstairs. He figured his mother and Meredith were unpacking. Taking the steps two at a time, he called out, but nobody answered. His mother's bedroom was cluttered with packages and boxes; the canopied bed was strewn with colored tissue and new clothes. He called again as he moved down the hall to the guest room. Still no response. Meredith's bedroom resembled his mother's. Another shopping haul. He'd seen it before.

Before leaving the room, Evan turned off a radio sitting next to the windows. He pushed aside the curtains and looked down on the great curved terrace and its surrounding gardens and the big pool. He could just make out two shadowy shapes moving under water in the deep end. He laughed, finding it funny that his mother and Meredith still liked diving for stones. It was such a silly game for women their age. Just as he was about to turn away, he saw Meredith's head break the surface of the water; she was gasping for air and splashing wildly. In the next moment Charlotte's sleek dark head bobbed up behind Meredith's, and she too gulped the air as if she'd been under too long. At first glance Evan thought they were horsing around, but it became apparent in the next few seconds that this was not the case.

What was his mother doing? Evan pressed his hands against the glass panes of the window and watched Charlotte grab Meredith by the hair and then viciously push her head under water. Meredith thrashed violently and disappeared, like a big fish fighting the sting of the hook. It looked like Charlotte was dragging Meredith deeper into the water.

These unimaginable acts were happening so quickly that Evan found himself transfixed and unable to move. He couldn't comprehend what was going on. Was his mother trying to drown Meredith? Was this a nightmare? Before he could move, Evan saw his mother's head clear the silvery skin of the water. Instinctively holding his own breath, Evan waited for Meredith to reappear. She did not.

Evan raced from the room, tore down the stairs, through the hall, and out the French doors in the back of the house, peeling off his shirt as he ran. He kicked free of his loafers and dove into the pool. He could see Meredith lying in a huddle on the bottom, as if she were asleep. When he reached her, he clasped his arms beneath hers and tried to lift her, but her body was heavy and awkward. His chest ached to breathe.

Swimming straight to the surface again, Evan took three great breaths. He could see his mother clinging to the edge of the pool. He screamed for her help and dove again to the bottom. This time his grip on Meredith was stronger, but he sensed despair and frenzy in every muscle. As he struggled, a large dark shape loomed above him in the water. It drew closer. It was the bearded face of Donovan, the cop.

With an unspoken coordination as beautifully choreographed as dance, Donovan seized Meredith by one arm and Evan took hold of the other, and the three rose to the surface as one.

As they broke free of the deep water Evan could see Charlotte climbing out of the pool. Inspector Poole was standing in the shallow end, the water lapping around his trouser legs, his shirt sleeves pushed to his elbows. He called to them, saying the paramedics were on their way. Soon, Donovan and Evan were placing Meredith very gently on the warm concrete apron, and the policeman hunched over her, breathing into her mouth and forcing water from her lungs.

In all his years dealing with death and violence, Poole had never witnessed a drowning this close to the fact. He kept expecting big results from such valiant efforts. He wanted to see the woman move a foot or turn her head, at least open her eyes. But Meredith lay still on the gray hard surface. Evan held her hand and spoke to her as if she might hear him. Charlotte stood nearby, silent and rigid, a yellow towel draped around her shoulders. More minutes went by, and soon it became clear that all the efforts had been too late. Meredith Wrenn was dead.

Days later, when he thought about that early evening at Rumsford Farm, Poole decided that the scenario had taken on another dimension, both macabre and believable, the moment they knew Meredith Wrenn was dead. They became privy to a tragedy begun years ago when a young woman took it upon herself to solve her problems, to seek retribution for all perceived wrongs in the most vicious way open to her. Annette Wrenn had learned to kill. And, the horror of it was that she had done it again and again, without mercy and, apparently, without conscience. The bigger tragedy, Poole came to believe, was that they had discovered everything too late. They'd been running several days and several clues behind from the beginning, and he blamed himself for his failure to fully anticipate Charlotte's behavior. He blamed himself for not understanding earlier on that two murderers were on a tear. Charlotte and Meredith. And now, he had contributed to the death of Meredith Wrenn.

With remarkable poise and an eerie lack of emotion, Evan stood before Donovan and Poole, chilled and shocked, his face drawn with grief. He calmly and precisely accused his mother of murder. With astounding composure, so like his mother's, Evan related with great clarity exactly what he had witnessed from the second story window. How he had watched helplessly as his mother pushed Meredith beneath the water. How Charlotte held her cousin's head below the surface until the thrashing stopped, until Meredith finally drifted and dropped to the bottom. Evan insisted that Charlotte had done nothing to save her cousin.

Poole had expected something evil in the end, but he had never figured the boy would be a witness to his mother's crime. Donovan was stunned into silence. Charlotte began by denying it all, saying Meredith had been quite drunk; she had slipped and fallen into the pool and, unable to swim well, had simply panicked. White-faced, Charlotte denied her son's accusation, explaining that she was trying desperately to save her cousin, but Meredith had fought against it and eventually dropped to the bottom. Traces of their struggle were visible in long, deep scratches crisscrossing Charlotte's thin arms and shoulders.

Whether suffered during some heroic effort to save a life or to take it, Poole could not be sure.

Evan boldly accused his mother a second time. He called her a liar and a murderer. Poole and Donovan watched as mother and son locked eyes in a horrifying recognition of what and who they were.

Charlotte began to pace, moving among the chairs and tables in nervous, jerky strides, as if her long, graceful legs had suddenly become unreliable. She began repeating her story, nearly word for word. The detectives and Evan watched and listened as she sat stiffly in one of the chairs, looking at no one, her voice spitting out the tale in a mechanized cant, in an odd staccato rhythm that didn't sound natural. Poole couldn't be sure if she was breaking down or simply play-acting to save herself.

Donovan quickly suggested she rest and say nothing more. Her rights had been read to her. Evan said his mother would need an attorney. Then, wrapped in a towel, the young man knelt beside Meredith's body, shrouded now in a long white terry robe. The sun had slipped behind the gable of the house, leaving the terrace in shadow. The air had grown chilly.

The paramedics and then the medical examiner's arrivals seemed unnecessary and disruptive. Doctor Sutter pronounced Meredith dead, and he and his technicians went about their business as they had before. Poole was always struck by the efficiency of it all. It took so few people to take care of a homicide...one demented soul to kill another, two men to try to save a life, one to pronounce her dead, and, another two to cart away the remains. Society, it would seem, did not deem it necessary or civilized for a corpse to insinuate itself into life's routine for any lengthy period of time.

Charlotte remained silent, as if she'd gone away somewhere, out of reach. When Evan, crouched only a few feet away began to cry, she took no notice. From now on, they would be dealing with Charlotte's attorneys and then her doctors. Her beautiful face, washed clean of makeup, was just as stunning without it. Her long black hair lay in thick, wet ribbons around her shoulders. When it was clear that she would not or could not speak, Poole took her arm and guided her to the house. As they walked through the door, she looked up at him. He could see that all had gone very wrong; her beautiful eyes were quite dead.

Charlotte and Evan changed into dry clothes; both obeyed the detectives' suggestions like automatons. Donovan waited, wearing his big towel like a cloak, standing barefoot in the grass. Poole was thinking he would never again relish this lovely countryside the way he used to. Evan closed up the house and got into his car, while Poole settled the handcuffed Charlotte into the back seat of the car. He sat next to Donovan in the front. Then, the caravan of official vehicles drove up the road.

Poole remembered the night he and Charlotte drove to the Flying Dutchman, the night he had sat in with the jazz quartet. He had wanted her to see the other side of him, his swing piano side. She had stayed with him that night, hungry for him. What game had she been playing? Let's see how far we can take the dumb cop? He had never discussed business with her; he knew better. Had she hoped he would give away police secrets? Did she think he was weak and vulnerable because of his injuries? They were strangers to each other again. He didn't flinch when he was obliged to touch her, but he had no desire to feel her skin beneath his fingers. For some odd reason, he had been her reluctant lover. It had been Charlotte's pursuit of Poole and not the other way around. Or was he making excuses? What had she hoped to gain or to learn from entering his life? And, had he instinctively known there was a flaw? Had one precinct in his brain figured her out long before the others? Was his judgment below standard these days? He would never know. He did wonder how the story would play out in a court of law. A slick, smart attorney could set Charlotte free. And, she had the money to buy such a wizard.

Without further delay the last two cars headed for Belmont, down the narrow rural road with its shoulders fringed in tall, parched meadow grass. The faint trill of birds drifted through open windows, breaking the solemn quiet inside. For a few miles the warm sun glinted off the windshield and reminded Poole of light shafts transfusing turquoise pool water, an image he was sure Evan and Donovan would never forget.

Within the next few wheel revolutions, the sun's red-orange fireball slipped behind the low hills, leaving them in the cool shadows of early evening.

EPILOGUE

Twelmeyer helped himself to white wine and asked his wife if she would like a glass. She nodded demurely, demurely for Valerie was Fitzhugh's conclusion as he watched them. The Twelmeyers were trying to patch things up. Again. Tiresome for the audience, Fitzhugh supposed, but an admirable effort. What the hell? Why should he give a fig about Gilbert's love life? Valerie made Gilbert miserably happy.

Fitzhugh polished off a plastic cup of so-so merlot and took another. It was a clear and cool September night, a good night for celebrating, a time for patching. God knows they all deserved a break from suspicion and accusation and guilt. Annette Wrenn, or Charlotte Dolbere, as she preferred, had been arraigned for the murder of her cousin, Meredith. At this moment, the infamous Charlotte was confined to the state mental hospital for a lengthy psychiatric examination. Personally, Fitzhugh believed Charlotte was too shrewd to be insane. She had murdered a good many people, according to her cousin's diaries, even bumped off Marjorie Verdun out of spite, thinking the woman had stabbed Roger Ferris in his bed. Heaven help them all, he thought. Actually, it was Meredith Wrenn who had done the deed, hoping to frame Charlotte for it. Classic drama. Fitzhugh couldn't believe it was happening in Belmont, land of the righteous, small pond of artistic geniuses. Fitzhugh smiled to himself. How fortunate for him that he didn't fancy women. He laughed lightly to himself and considered the advisability of getting drunk.

"Justin, you darlin' man," the reinstated Mrs. Twelmeyer was saying, glass raised. "We are so very delighted at your appointment. Aren't we, Gilbert?" Valerie spun gracefully on her toes and reached possessively for her husband's arm. Gilbert took her hand; his brown eyes behind the horn rims grew liquid with affection. Christ, Fitzhugh muttered under his breath. Would he ever learn?

The Twelmeyers and the other guests toasted Fitzhugh and his new position. Twelmeyer called Fitzhugh's promotion 'the grand elevation.' Justin Fitzhugh was now Dean of Theatre Arts. Fifty friends and colleagues were gathered in the faculty lounge at Daly Hall, where a modest spread of domestic cheeses, crackers, and inexpensive wine weighed down a lopsidedly draped table. Twelmeyer had arranged the tribute.

"And another toast," Twelmeyer quickly added, raising his glass again, "to the stunning, and I use the word advisedly," his resonant stage voice played with the words, "the infamous..." Another dramatic pause. "...Charlotte Dolbere, Belmont's first serial killer." Fitzhugh figured Twelmeyer must be completely stoned to have come up with this one.

The guests weren't sure if they should laugh or not. Valerie and Justin tittered; they could easily be amused now that they were off the suspect hook. Several others joined in nervously. Was Professor Twelmeyer drunk? asked Mrs. Lippencott's husband. The department secretary suggested her boss might be acting silly because he was free at last.

"Has there ever been a resident of our fair city with such a daring taste for retribution? And such nerve?" Twelmeyer's eyes twinkled naughtily. Fitzhugh knew full well that Twelmeyer was conscious of what he was saying. After all, he was simply stating what every one in town was thinking. Fitzhugh understood Gilbert's brand of humor.

Those who were listening snickered self-consciously. Belmont had been thrust into the national spotlight by its beautiful, notorious lady serial killer. Charlotte had gone from the cover of *Vogue* to the front page of the New York papers, and many others, including the *Bee.* She could very well become a folk heroine, some observers predicted. She and her cousin. The Wrenn family was adding to its already overflowing list of illustrious relatives. Keepers of village lore would automatically include the Wrenn women, wicked or not, in its modest assemblage of immortals. Legends would spring up around their memory. No doubt, horror stories would circulate about Charlotte's house on Two Tree Lane and about Rumsford Farm. The woman's son, Evan, who had quietly gone off to live with Beatrice and Uncle Simeon at Wrenn House, was well aware of the gossip and speculation. The handsome young drama student, who looked so much like his famous father, rarely appeared in public, except to attend classes at Ashbury.

"They say this Annette person poisoned a friend at thirteen and pushed Leonard Trotter into the quarry at seventeen," exclaimed Valerie, in awe of the girl's boldness.

"And, forced Marjorie Verdun off the bluff road," put in the old professor of stage management."

"Don't forget her rich, Mayflower husband who was tossed over a balcony," put in Fitzhugh. "And the French fashion model, who flew off a roof garden with some help, of course." He had a fear of heights and shuddered at the thought. "Little Annette must have been a charming child." He rolled his eyes comically. "Evil women are so delicious, don't you think?" Some in the congregation of guests didn't agree and grimaced at Fitzhugh's comment. One or two female professors from the English department muttered that Fitzhugh and Twelmeyer had gone too far this time.

"Her attorney, Burton Dance, claims she's as mad as a hatter," remarked Dean Whitehead rather matter-of-factly. "Her cousin was too, I suppose. Out of her misery now, that is sure." The absentminded old dean was a bit drunk and turned to ogle the bosomy wife of the assistant Chancellor.

The story telling of the town's stunning series of murders had become so common place and yet so intriguing that Twelmeyer told Fitzhugh he was thinking of turning it into a play, with prudent alterations. One or two characters, he promised, would be changed a little to protect their innocence. Fitzhugh said it was a fabulous idea.

"I feel terrible about Marjorie Verdun," said Professor Applegate, a soft-hearted woman who taught acting. "Caught in the cross fire, it would seem. We sat together on one or two college committees."

Twelmeyer sighed sympathetically, recalling how close he had come to wanting Ferris dead and to the terrifying power of the law. And, he understood Meredith Wrenn's desperation.

Fitzhugh could have wept under the weight of such pathos. "Absolutely Shakespearean!" he pronounced loudly and ambled off in search of more wine.

"Don't you just love all this notoriety? All this media attention? It's so...so..." Valerie's exclamation drifted off into the surrounding babble.

"Pathetic?" came a deep voice behind them, near the lounge door. No one had noticed the arrival of Froggy Verdun. No one expected him to come. The professors and their spouses were immediately silenced.

"Mr. Verdun," Fitzhugh exclaimed, a trifle too heartily. He came forward to greet the man and shake his hand. "So good of you to stop by." Verdun clasped Fitzhugh's hands and wished him well in his new position. Verdun served on the Ashbury College Board of Regents, and Fitzhugh appreciated the man's effort to congratulate him. Verdun's gesture had a grander meaning too, as one murder suspect might regard another after the real killer has been flushed out of the weeds, as one man who despised Roger Ferris might feel for another whose loathing ran just as deep. Or course,Verdun's loss was far worse.

"I can see that homicide continues to thrill," Verdun commented without apology, openly mocking the assembled well-wishers. Coughs and throat-clearings shot through the lounge.

"So sorry about that," Twelmeyer said quietly, offering an apology for his wife's imprudent remarks. "Please, have a glass of wine."

Verdun accepted and chatted with Twelmeyer and Fitzhugh privately, unwilling or unable to chastise anyone further.

"Annette's last stand," Verdun declared wearily. "That's what we could call this. She never liked any of us twenty years ago, you know. Had a genuine vendetta against Belmont and the Ferris family. Humanity in general, now that I think about it and see her handiwork." He sounded as if he were still trying to make sense of it. "Meredith was just as peculiar."

Fitzhugh could see Valerie, standing apart from them. She was saying in that Blanche Du Bois accent of hers, "I wonder who Charlotte would have killed next?"

"What a horrid thought!" cried the dour wife of the college bursar. "It might very well have been you, Mrs. Twelmeyer," the woman shot back with deadly accuracy. The retort caught the guests up short, and the bursar pulled his wife away by the arm. Valerie looked more amused than alarmed.

"I've heard that Charlotte will end up in the state mental hospital. She'll never go to prison," remarked Fitzhugh. The trial was due to start in another week, and the outcome was on everyone's mind. There were murmurs of agreement.

Valerie ran a pretty finger around the rim of her glass and drawled with obvious pleasure, "Wherever Charlotte is sent, prison or institution, I would bet the fine reputation of this old college..." and she paused here for effect, "...that she escapes!"

THE END.